D1020259

DOUBLE STITCH

ALSO BY JOHN ROLFE GARDINER

In the Heart of the Whole World
Great Dream from Heaven
Unknown Soldiers
Going On Like This
The Incubator Ballroom
Somewhere in France

DOUBLE STITCH

A Novel

JOHN ROLFE GARDINER

COUNTERPOINT
A Member of the Perseus Books Group
New York

Copyright © 2003 by John Rolfe Gardiner

Published by Counterpoint
A Member of the Perseus Books Group

All rights reserved. Printed in the United States of America. No part of this book may be reproduced in any manner whatsoever without written permission except in the case of brief quotations embodied in critical articles and reviews. For information, address Counterpoint, 387 Park Avenue South, New York, NY 10016.

Counterpoint books are available at special discounts for bulk purchases in the United States by corporations, institutions, and other organizations. For more information, please contact the Special Markets Department at the Perseus Books Group, 11 Cambridge Center, Cambridge, MA 12142, or call (617) 252-5298, (800) 255-1514, or e-mail j.mccrary@perseusbooks.com.

Interior design by Lisa Kreinbrink
Set in 11-point Galliard

Library of Congress Cataloging-in-Publication Data

Gardiner, John Rolfe.
    Double stitch : a novel / by John Rolfe Gardiner.
      p. cm.
    ISBN 1-58243-231-7
    1. Twins—Fiction.   2. Orphans—Fiction.   3. Sisters—Fiction.   4. Identity (Psychology)—Fiction.   5. Infants switched at birth—Fiction.   I. Title.
PS3557.A7113D68 2003
813'.54—dc22

                                                                    2003015129

03   04   05 / 10   9   8   7   6   5   4   3   2   1

In memory of
Christo Bentley
and
Edward Cohen
and their haunting second selves

Contents

Any of us could be the man who encounters his double.

DÜRRENMATT

Part 1

Arrival

Sometimes I can't remember which one of us is me.

LINDA OR REBECCA CAREY

Arrival

"You see the way they cling? How could they know what's best for them?"

"What's your interest here, Dr. Westin?"

"Their welfare. They're identical twins."

"You hold a brief?"

"Friend of the court."

"What kind of friend? What kind of doctor are you?"

"Two kinds actually. A doctor of psychology and a doctor of sociology."

"Refresh my memory. What are identical twins?"

"Your honor, identical twins occur when an embryo splits in two after fertilization, and two babies develop in the same amniotic sac."

"The spermatic arrow knocks the egg in half?"

"Well . . . "

"So the sisters can kick around in the same bath? And now you want to break up the party?"

"That's very colorful, your honor."

"Indulge me, doctor. These sisters carry the same genetic information?"

"We have to presume so."

"Isn't this your real interest in them? Aren't identical twins the capital laboratory of sociology? I don't see you here when other siblings are brought before us for placement."

"When there's an opportunity to study comparative development, it's foolish not to take advantage."

"Isn't this why you'd like one of them placed at the Drayton Orphanage, and one in foster care?"

"Miss Croft favors Drayton. My suggestion is a compromise."

"You'd accept the judgment of Solomon. Let them be cut in half?"

"I think you know that isn't fair."

"And you have research going on. Orphanages versus foster care."

"I'm pleased you're familiar with my work."

"I'm not. And I don't think you've ever spoken to these children."

The twins' heads, in perfect synchrony, moved side to side in agreement with the judge.

"I'm ruling against your petition, Dr. Westin. Miss Croft, come forward. You're not getting off scot-free. I'll have a go at you now."

He hardly gave her time to reach the bench.

"How many orphanages? Eight hundred? Nine hundred? With a bad odor coming from almost all of them. Why do the newspapers dislike them so, Miss Croft? And what makes this Drayton place any different from the rest?"

She could have told him, but he didn't want to hear it.

"Oh, I know," he said. "All your progressive guff. So what will these girls be over there in Flourtown? Just two more lumps in the family porridge? All very normal?"

Normal? Not the girls themselves. This was a pair who took their time, even for a judge. They were in no rush to leave the courtroom if it meant getting on with the next phase of life, another submission to adult whim, unprotected by family love, or any interest of common blood. Approached by the matron wearing a sidearm, the same who delivered convicted women to their cells, they did a little sit-down at the back of the room, pointed at the gun on her hip, ignored her command to follow, and turned to each other for private conversation.

It was a kind of twin talk, unintelligible unless you knew the keys. One key: one spoke for two. That is, when Becca said, "I'm not going anywhere," she meant, "we're not going anywhere," and when Linny answered, "Yes, I am," she meant, "Yes, we are."

The matron was asking, "Will we have to carry you out?"

Again they ignored her. Linny asked Becca the questions. The answers came back in gibberish.

"In the highchair?"

"Guster."

"The doctor?"

"Goosh, groose goosh."

"The lady?"

"Grint lossy."

"Why didn't you say anything?"

"You didn't want me to."

"I wanted you to want to. If you wanted to, you would have. Then they'd know you weren't going."

"But you are."

"I don't like it when you contradict us."

"Me either."

Their arms were around each other again.

"Maybe we'll have the same bed," Linny said. "Soft jums."

"I'm not going."

"Yes I am."

When the matron left to get help, they shuffled out of the courthouse. They were two blocks away, talking in their fugitive tongue, when she caught up with them.

"Which one are you?"

"Either one."

"We're not sure."

"It changes."

"What do you mean? One of you is Linda and the other Rebecca. It won't do you any good to act smart."

"Linda means pretty."

"Rebecca means servant of god."

"So you share names? Just to be fair?" The matron, still out of breath from her pursuit of them played along for a moment, a signal for both girls to begin talking at once; one, "I think she was Rebecca first," and the other, "She was Rebecca first." Then echoes, "Aunt Gwen Gwen said said they they . . ." until the two of them came into synchrony: "got the birthmark mixed up. It was on Linda first. Not anymore."

"Where's your Aunt Gwen?

"She's dead."

"Yes, she's dead. Weren't you listening in the court?"

∞

Tessie Croft wrote to Eula Kieland in April of 1926:

I've had a session with the Carey twins I mentioned at the luncheon in the city. They are mesmerizing and much in need. Both puckish and prickly with a defensive self-assurance that I figure might soften under your Drayton roof. The court has put me in charge of them in the interim with the understanding they'll be coming to you when the papers are ready. It was presumptuous of me to follow through on this without your consent, but of course you can refuse them. I doubt you will. When you see them you'll melt.

The judge is a testy old bird and nobody's fool. He'll have his eye on us.

He skewered Westin, and then came after me with a lecture. He doesn't trust anyone in this. He wanted to know if Drayton would put the twins under a microscope, or over one. How do you like that? Here's one man I believe is pleased we got the vote. As for the Careys, there is one catch for you, a Negro grandmother on the father's side. Very light, I'd imagine, but I'm aware of the restrictions in your charter. To the more vigilant gatekeepers on your board the twins will be colored. I assure you they can pass in our white world. In fact, their hair is blond as a corn tassel. This may be the foot in the door of reform you've been hoping for. If someone gets into the

twins' records and squeals, perhaps it's time for you to make your stand. Easy for me to say.

That Mr. Johnson you brought to the luncheon seemed very attentive.

I don't quite understand his part. Just another one of your trustees? Or. . . .

Tess

Typical, the way she changed the subject and put Eula on the defensive, as if the first matter had already been settled. Just as she would in conversation. As Director of the orphanage, Eula was amenable to the advice of her distinguished friend, but sometimes Tess pushed too hard. Who but Tess would be pressing her to talk to one of the new-fangled therapists from Vienna? As for Mr. Johnson, she knew full well Eula was not in the mood for a suitor. Cyril Johnson was on her board, and related to the Drayton family by his father's marriage. She had to indulge some of his meddling. If he had notions beyond a professional cordiality, it was all his fantasy.

∞

That was the start of it. Drayton had been up and running for six years, had its feet firmly on the ground with a staff of housemothers, all single women, though some had been married, and widowed or divorced, all chosen for their commitment to the happiness of vulnerable children. There were unsolicited gifts. The Singer Company sent seven sewing machines, and a representative to instruct a teacher in their use. From a cotton company in North Carolina came a hundred fitted sheets, high-count percale, and another hundred of flannel. And bicycles from Schwinn, top-of-the-line with three gears and headlamps powered by dynamos on the wheels. The girls, thrilled to have them, rode up and down the long, curving driveway, and around the service road.

There were also the donors Eula suffered for their purse, as Tess put it. A woman, for example, who came to ask if she might attach a string to her contribution to a teacher's fund.

"No R.C.'s."

No, she could keep her money.

The woman winked, as if Eula would oblige her in her own way, and asked, "What can you do for them, anyway? The children."

"Humanities and Printing are taught in the same three-hour period. The girls move back and forth from shop to classroom, publishing their own compositions."

"But what do they look like?"

Eula showed her the last group photograph and gave her a magnifying glass for a better look at the faces.

"Oh my, but that one's homely. Aren't they a little closely bred?"

"No."

That was that. When the woman was gone Eula examined the picture again with a heavy heart. You could see this was a group with a common misfortune. You didn't have to know the photo was from the Drayton album. So many stolid faces, and plain, it was true; more than a fair share. And she knew the bitter reason. The handsome and beautiful were first to be snatched away for adoption. The leftovers were for the institutions, for Drayton. But the two just on their way to her orphanage were lovely to look at, even stunning.

There were forty-three children, all settled comfortably into the four campus houses, and here came the identical little beauties, the Carey twins, taking them all into a realm where innocence and deceit were going to be made of the same tricky stuff, something concocted by these two fallen angels. Eight years had passed since the death of Eula's adopted boy Tony, and while all her energies still went to the welfare of children, she was aware of her heart's distance from them, a distance the twins would travel across in spite of her, and in spite of themselves.

With their worn cases hanging at their sides, Mother Crane said they looked like a matched pair of immigrants frightened by their journey abroad. They'd never been in a motorcar before. On their arrival they took the first opportunity to disappear. While the grounds were searched Eula went through their papers again, wondering if she'd missed some telltale item that might have alerted her to trouble.

There was something she hadn't noticed before: "At several months of age the twins, when in distress, offered their thumbs to one another for sucking." No mention of when the practice had stopped.

Mother Crane, amazed as the rest, said, "They could have been stolen from each other's mirrors."

It didn't occur to Eula that their remarkable likeness could already have turned them into actresses who could slip into each other's name and person without a second thought, that sometimes they might forget which part they were playing, confusing even themselves. Or that it might take an intellect beyond hers, someone outside the Drayton walls, to explain their tangled heads, and hearts.

On that first day, the two of them, equally clever and moving with a single purpose, had not run away from the country campus, but into the very heart of the orphanage. They were found hiding in the fireplace of the Schoolhouse building, their fingers playing over painted relief tiles that told the Cinderella story. It was too much for them to believe they could have landed in a world made for children. They couldn't know the tiles were from the famous Enfield factory, and part of an architect's vision in keeping with the founder's will, that they had fallen into a community of family-style cottages, surroundings intended only for their delight and nurture.

They were ten years old when they arrived in that Spring of 1926. Off on the wrong foot with their surrogate mother, Julia Crane, who had given them only a gentle scolding for their game of hide-and-seek. They were adorable to look at, just as promised, but hell to manage. Tess didn't warn Eula about that, and she'd exaggerated about the hair as well. It was actually a dark straw blond. Rebecca and Linda, Linny and Becca. They were indistinguishable. Their skin was a lovely rust hue, a Gypsy copper. They took themselves for white children, and so did Eula. Most anyone would have.

They didn't realize they were part of a new idea. There would be no long rows of beds, or fevers sweeping the length of a dormitory where the night terror of one was the lot of all. In the new age a measure of privacy was affordable and desirable for the healthy maturation of a young woman. From the start Drayton had to be different.

It was clear the conventional orphanage would soon be a thing of the past. Adoptions had come into favor and were preferable in every way.

The trustees were well aware they were dragging some of the past along with them. Eula had a majority behind her as she pushed against the restrictions of her charter with some guile and a little common sense. Matriculation was supposed to be limited to healthy white girls between six and ten, both of whose parents must be deceased. But what about girls with deceased mothers, and fathers whose whereabouts were unknown, or whose identities had never been known? And the abuse cases? She'd taken her share of such children already, and wards of the court, who'd been removed from their negligent parents' care.

Eula *was* a little reckless taking on the twins. The will establishing the orphanage had been contested by a number of the Drayton heirs, who took their case all the way to Pennsylvania's high court. There were two family trustees, one of them Cyril Johnson and the other Renee Drayton, a niece of the founder and the one who made so much of the New Year's Eve sherry and cigarette scandal, that "bohemian revel."

Yes, one night of the year when all of the children were away on holiday visits, Kerstin Lambert and Eula had served sherry at the house they shared, a Drayton College house, and all the staff were invited. And, yes, there was smoking, and they all got tipsy. This made fine gossip about Kerstin and the Director, just as people liked to talk about Tess, who ran the School of Social Work and the city's Child Guidance Center, and her housemate Celly Harrison, colleagues and neighbors down Bethlehem Pike, two proud professional women, whose names were run together like salt and pepper for the naughty flavor they gave a conversation.

Drayton was a college only in the European sense of any educational institution. Eula hoped the name might give her girls that degree of self-confidence they'd lost when sent to an "orphanage." The twins were sure there had been a mistake. The bolder of the two (Becca?) said, "We haven't even been to high school yet."

They were sullen with their burdens. Their parents, like Eula's adopted son Tony, had been taken by the flu in 1918, and the girls

were sent to live with their Aunt Gwen, south of the tracks, in Ardmore. Tess Croft's files showed that Aunt Gwen had given them eight grudging, dotty years under the influence of a contemporary messiah whose church was an apartment further out the Main Line in St. David's. They had recently seen Gwen carried off in her coffin. The two of them had the same nightmare, their aunt's handkerchief stained crimson over her mouth with the blood of tuberculosis.

It was Eula's style to keep a distance from her girls. With experience she'd learned the controlling authority and disciplinarian of the academy could not also be a chummy pal to the residents. The loss of her little Tony before she came to Drayton had done its part to leave a chilly chamber in her heart. The Carey girls drew her in willy-nilly. She noticed in a letter to her mother of November 1923 a confession that, at the time, she thought a failing, a sudden revelation:

> I realize I don't really know the children of Drayton College. I talk to them. I know their names, but my devotion has been to my orphanage and its progressive reputation. You know my message: "Home is school is community; all subjects are one subject." And no one in America has a better progressive laboratory than I do—an orphanage—to prove it. So what's missing?

At that writing, it seemed selfish that her passion for a progressive revolution in America, for a seamless connection between school and life, could be so divorced from an emotional connection with any of the children in her care. Her conceit had been that Drayton was a model for the nation, and her time too short to wipe a runny nose. Then the Careys turned her head. Her closest friend, her housemate Kerstin, watching over this evolution stopped calling her "Mummy Superior," as the authoritarian instinct softened into affection for the troubled sisters. In fact she started calling her "Mummy," this too enclosed in audible quotation marks.

Found and brought to the Director's office on that first day, the twins made it clear they expected a punishment beyond which they would feel no regret and find no redemption. They were dressed

identically in brown corduroy jumpers and white blouses, but one had black-and-white saddle shoes, the other brown-and-white, and the one who first called herself Becca had a red scarf around her neck. Eula leaned down behind her desk to gather a notebook and some papers, and when she looked up again it seemed to her the other, Linny, wore the red scarf. Had they simply changed places?

"How will we tell you apart?" she asked them.

They smirked in unison. This was a game they had played all their lives. Looking deep into their slate-gray eyes where the real secrets would be kept, Eula was aware she was nowhere near bottom.

But it was part of her job to read children's minds. The twins were circumspect and distrustful in this too-perfect village. Their doubting expression accused her of nurturing false hope as they walked out, and through the little community of mixed stone and Tudor-framed cottages. She might as well have been leading them past gingerbread houses. There were children of mixed age and motley dress, sitting dangle-legged on a courtyard wall, in Sunday freetime, chattering, teasing, shoving. They calmed to dumbstruck silence as this double image came forward beside their Director. Would the twins be expected to sit like these, who stared at their approach, and who might have seemed to them like ignorant Humpty Dumptys waiting for a fall into the real world?

They were a fine sampling of Eula's little demons; she had an affection and a fear for the future of all of them. There was Erica Cochran, ten, from Thatch Cottage, full of devilishness herself, a black-eyed imp, equally unafraid of punishment, jumping down and running up behind the newcomers, singing in their ears, "You'll hate it here, what's your names anyway?"

"Erica!"

"Yes, Miss Kieland."

"What's the idea? Go wash your face and clean your room."

"Yes, Miss Kieland."

The girl trotted off to Thatch, ahead of them, looking back over her shoulder every few steps to make sure they were following.

Someone behind the wall was shouting, "The milk tastes like onions!" The others were squirming again, arranged in their row, lit-

tle to large. The youngest, Jodie Shiflett, last month's arrival, who came with scabies on her hands and an open heart on her sleeve, grateful for her rescue from abuse, and already assimilated as baby sister of Stork Cottage, was struggling now with Emily Berry, shy bed-wetter, for a more secure perch. Eula wondered if the itchy red plague on Jodie's hands had been completely cured. Or was it being passed down the line as Emily pushed into Jennie Alexie, trying to maintain her balance.

Jennie Alexie, a year older than the Careys, given up for adoption at birth, called out, "She didn't mean it. Don't worry. She didn't mean it." Jennie, the pianist manqué, who dreamed of singing for her supper and playing Chopin. When she sat down to the piano in Schoolhouse basement, she stretched her arms with a flourish and . . . out came "Chopsticks," over and over again, "Chopsticks" at its most insistent, "Chopsticks" without the frills. Miss Rankin, brought in from the village to teach piano, confided it was a hopeless case. Jennie would never play a nocturne.

"Jennie."

"Yes, ma'am."

"Take your finger out of your nose."

"Yes, ma'am."

Eula knew their names, knew their pathologies, but still feared she didn't know them. Normally she left orientation to the several housemothers. This time, giving the campus tour and inspirational message herself, she had a first inkling that looking at the twins could become an addiction, a fascination with their near-perfect symmetry, and a search for some difference between them.

"Whose is that?" one of them asked, pointing at one of the bicycles, fallen from its kickstand, and lying in the driveway.

"No one's," she said. "Everyone's."

Girls shared the bikes, but were not allowed to take them onto any public road. They were left here and there on the campus for anyone's use, and were supposed to be parked under the portico at Schoolhouse overnight. Names were painted on them, horses' names—Sirocco, Whirlwind, Ahab, Echo, and the like—so the girls could imagine themselves equestriennes.

The twins shuffled along. Eula stifled a command to "pick up your feet." There was cockiness in their indifference to all she was showing them. Why should they be impressed with a charity so offensively on display? They must have known they were exciting to look at together. They tilted their smudged round faces to one side and then the other as they moved, like birds shifting on the wing by a flock telepathy. And the straw-colored hair fell back and forth in unison across their identically dimpled cheeks.

Eula knew they were doing what all children did on arrival at the orphanage, appraising their chances of survival. It occurred to her how convenient in their case that there was no uniform at Drayton—to avoid the appearance of charity—since she would soon be able to distinguish the twins by their separate wardrobes. In a forgiving humor she begged them to take pity on the staff, and let some item of clothing, or some pin perhaps, be a constant of differentiation. They made no promise.

Eula suspected they might be as offended by ignorance of their well-disguised singularities as by attempts to separate them. She offered these two the same Drayton credo she'd give any of her girls. As orphans they'd suffered a handicap of missing love; the loss was immeasurable. Their compensation for this loss was a freedom to invent themselves. Here they'd have every chance to prosper, not through charity, but their will to succeed.

They were only ten, but sophisticated enough, she thought, to receive the same message she passed along to her older girls: "This place was born out of a man's head." She made it clear this was not always a good thing. The messages carved into the walls betrayed the underlying prejudice of men. Of course it was a novelty to Linny and Becca that the views of architects and their masters could be seen as a danger to a girl's life.

"Look at her. No example for you. She was a brainless sap."

Eula was pointing up at the terra-cotta casting of Snow White and several of her dwarfs framed by the half-timbers in the gable end of Stork Cottage. As they passed the other end of the building, they puzzled over the words carved into a wooden plaque that was set into the stucco.

"That's a lot of silliness, too. *Une Femme Doit Plaire; C'est Son Bonheur;* a woman should please; that is her happiness. Just as well you won't study French here with that as a primer."

She'd caught them off guard, trumping their doubts about the place with a complaint of her own.

"Now, tell me again, which one are you?" she asked the one in the black-and-white saddles.

"Becca."

The girl pronounced it very slowly, very carefully, as if obliging a simpleton. They had both noticed Eula looking at their feet, and at least for the moment, she had them split and named. But was it really Becca in the black-and-white shoes? Thinking back, she wasn't sure.

She told them how sorry she was for the loss of their aunt, and that she hoped they would work hard and make the staff and girls of Drayton their new family. It wouldn't be just schoolwork here. But keeping a garden, and community programs, dances, field trips, and picnics at the swimming hole. And of course the same kind of house chores they'd do at home, along with care of the farm animals.

"Not everyone is interested in cooking and sewing."

They stopped mid-step and looked up at her as if she were totally untrustworthy, as if she were offering a bribe for their submission.

She thought it was Linny who pushed Becca to the front to speak for both of them.

"Maybe," she said, again, very slowly. "Maybe we'll get used to it here, if you don't call us cheaters first thing."

"Why would we do that?"

"The others did."

"The others did," Linny repeated. "We both have the same bathing frock."

As if this followed without need of explanation.

"I'd love to see them on you."

"Yes," Becca said, "but Linny's came from Carson's and I got mine at Kinney Square. They're red plaid with a sea horse on the side."

"I suppose it bothers you when people try to dress you in the same clothes."

"No!" Becca said. "Linny went with Aunt Gwen, and Mr. Bing took me. So's we'd get something different. We came home with the same suits."

She noticed for the first time how close in timbre and inflection their voices were.

They came at last to their cottage, Thatch, which was not really thatched at all, but roofed in a steep pitch of blue, red, and ochre tiles. They were introduced to Julia, Mother Crane, who hurried back into the house to tell her other girls what had just arrived on their doorstep, calling, "You may come down now, Erica. Your new sisters are here."

"They're not my sisters," she called back, but came quickly to the top of the staircase, not to miss anything.

Eula chose Thatch for the twins for the simplest reason; that's where the free room was.

"So this is your Mother Crane," she said.

"More like a butterball than a crane," Becca said, hardly under her breath.

Julia Crane, a short stout woman with a soft full face to match, broke into delighted laughter, and began to introduce her household. The twins seemed used to the fuss being made over them, but did not care to be taken for a curiosity. Their responses were mumbled and diffident. Erica came down step-by-step as the introductions progressed, and eventually came forward to shake their hands, which they immediately put behind their backs.

Eula joined the small party led by Julia as they were taken up to their second-floor bedroom. She watched Erica, following behind the twins, telling their backs, "We're never whipped. Mother Greene slapped one of her girls yesterday," and she saw Erica thumb her nose at her antidemon, the weak-chinned Susan Bailey, little goody two-shoes of the cottage, Mother Crane's constant tattler, difficult to love. But this behavior, too, was understood by Eula, as just another technique of survival.

The room was a generous space, up to the standard of any child over on the Main Line. There were twin beds with carved headboards and down comforters. Casement windows gave onto the rolling meadows of the old Drayton estate, now the spacious acres of the orphanage. Eula tried to take in the view from the girls' perspective. In the distance, beyond aged elms, a hedge of forsythia, but no walls to hold them in or protect the outside world from this oddly rich display of their misfortune. They were meant to feel privileged here.

She could see the twins were hiding their satisfaction with the room. Becca, or the one with the black-and-white shoes, was holding her sister back from jumping on the bed, not to seem too pleased. Their troubles had trained them to a privilege of bad manners, and this was strengthened by their mutual appreciation. They were rude, allowing Mother Crane to overhear their disrespect. They complained to her about having to share a bathroom with girls who could not keep the seat clean. And one of them said, "We don't like girls with dirty habits."

Eula was about to step in, but Mother Crane was up to the moment.

"Then I advise both of you to go right back to the lavatory and wash your hands and faces. The two of you look a sight."

Erica giggled.

"If this is our room," Becca asked, "what's she doing here?"

"What are any of them doing?" Linny followed.

As Eula walked away she could hear Julia shooing the other children off: "Give our new girls a chance to get settled in."

And to the twins: "Wash up, unpack, and join us downstairs for the wildflower walk."

Mother Crane came to Eula later that day a little shaken by her first afternoon with the Careys. They did not come downstairs as asked. Eventually she went up to get them. Opening the door she found them lying on one of the beds. Arms and legs all tangled together, moving in the slow rhythm of a cradle rocking.

Startled, they pulled apart and sat up staring at her like wild animals.

"I'm sorry," she said, quickly shutting the door, wondering if she should have scolded them.

"Please come down," she called through the door. "We can't wait any longer."

The twins would not come down. They stayed in the room all afternoon, until suppertime, when hunger finally moved them.

"What should I have done?" Mother Crane asked.

Eula confessed she wasn't sure.

Tess Croft and her pals at the Child Guidance Center must have had an inkling of the problem they'd sent her. Eula spoke to her a few days after the twins' arrival.

"You might have told me a little more about them."

And the chastened Tess put herself back on the case. She was thorough. In fact she followed them all the way back to their records at the city hospital where they were born, and from these details, behind birth, and into the womb.

"Did you know," she wrote to Eula, "there are several ways identical twins may develop? The doctors think your Careys shared everything nature would allow them through gestation. Not just the same egg, sperm, and placenta, but the same chorionic and amniotic sacs. They must have waited till the last possible moment to separate. Fortunately not any longer than they did, I'm told, or they might have been joined at the hip, or worse. There was no membrane between them at any time. They were in each others' arms from the start."

Still apologetic, Tess followed her letter with a visit. She was more eager than ever to introduce Eula to her friend from Vienna because he had a special interest in twins. He was one of the wise men who were traveling two continents, treating troubled psyches with a deep review of the patients' sexual abuse and anxious dreams. Tess anticipated Eula's protest: "Yes, yes, he started out with the Freud bunch. But he's not one of them anymore. Not at all. I know how little patience you have with all that."

Eula listened politely, then ignored the advice. She was trusting her own devices to lure the twins out of their private world.

When she'd taken the Careys through the chapel she explained that all the girls chose their own faith. In the twins' file it said, "Religious refusal," and mentioned their brief affiliation with the "Assem-

bly of Love," their Aunt Gwen's church, and a Reverend Light in St. David's, who had tried for the girls' religious commitment after the aunt's death, but without success.

"That's a cross, isn't it?" Becca went to the heart of the matter.

"There are lots of religious opinions here," Eula assured her. She thought of her staff, so motley in creed, all chosen by her for the generosity of their love for children; yet all of them full of their own quirks and neuroses. A Lutheran; two Catholics, one totally lapsed, the other an irregular communicant; the nominal Protestant, Julia Crane, godmother to six though a stranger to all but a few of the words in Drayton's ecumenical hymnal; and Mother Greene, the only Jewish member, whose faith was silent, unknown, and of no interest to the children, the one who labored against the grain, arguing for memory work and traditional academic discipline.

Mother Greene's skepticism kept Eula's progressive team on its toes, but the crankiest of all the staff was Beverly Rice, the math teacher. She had warned Eula of her agnosticism in her hiring interview. Ellen Reilly, the lapsed Catholic, was Eula's favorite. The children in Stork loved her without reserve. Jolly and lovely to look at, whatever dogma she'd forsaken was more than balanced by a spiritual glow.

Not for Eula—raised to a loose Unitarian observance, and trained to follow conscience before doctrine—not for her to fault any of them. The trustees assumed her chapel would embrace the Christian message in all its catholicity, as handsomely liberal as they could afford to be. There was a wooden cross behind the little altar; no other icon. The chapel windows were diamond- and square-shaped stained glass, without figure or story.

The groundskeeper and gardener, Henry Davidson, known to all as Mr. Henry, who drove the orphanage station wagon, was a light-skinned Negro, the grandson of slaves. Hardworking and religious, Mr. Henry went about, sickle in hand, muttering skeptically about all of the "nondescripts." Without a formal faith to label the ladies, how could an ordinary upright man get a useful grip on any of them?

The twins, exposed to the loopy catechism of the Assembly of Love, had long ago lost any faith in an errorless god. Experienced in

one litany of paradoxes—full of words like *eucharist* and *epiphany* which they were expected to repeat without comprehension, indeed, had been punished if they asked for explanations—they were not ready to accept another.

"If you take all religions, why is Jesus' cross there?"

"All religions within the Christian family," Eula explained, putting the best face she could on the favoritism.

The visiting physician examined the girls, and gave positive identification of the twins at last. Nurse Jean, guardian of an infirmary that comforted the heartsick perhaps more often than the truly ill, watched as a birthmark was discovered on the one calling herself Becca. And from that day forward she would be Becca whatever her name might have been before.

"Beautiful!" the doctor said, "a cherry with a stem!" reaching out to touch the stain on her chest.

Becca knocked the stethoscope aside, grabbed for her undershirt, and let Nurse Jean know she could make trouble for this man. The doctor had never seen such an aggressive modesty in one so young. He thought it suggested a troubling knowledge. The physical exams were over; the girls were pronounced free of lice. Measles done with, mumps to come. The one without the birthmark was prone to tonsil inflammation. They were cleared for admission, though they'd already been there for several days. The staff learned of the hidden cherry, but what use to them through the day? They could not undress one of the sisters each time identity was in question.

∞

Eula lived uncomfortably with her mission statement. It had been written by the benefactor, Estin Drayton himself, and a committee of his friends. The merits were debated through the courts by family opponents of the college and by defenders of the orphanage. It was far from an ideal blueprint, but the details had been closely examined, and one could not jigger with impunity.

Preparation for marriage was stressed, along with motherhood and the distaff: the domestic arts of laundering and sewing, and

something called domestic sciences. By this the founders had cooking in mind, though woodworking was also mentioned in the same category.

The manual said, "If the girls can grasp the elements of algebra these should not be denied to them. The same with as much applied physics, chemistry, and natural history as they may be able to comprehend."

Eula had an answer for the skeptical largesse. She pursued the very best math and chemistry teachers she could find, offering them half as much again as they were making at their secondary schools. When Renee Drayton attacked this "misguided emphasis" at a trustee meeting, Eula was ready: "Is the capacity of their brains in question? Is math reasoning impaired by the loss of parents? Are these girls less deserving than children being prepared for college?"

Eula was well aware Renee was passing along board-meeting strife to disgruntled family members who had lost their suit. They wanted nothing so much as to bring the institution down and recover the Drayton assets for themselves. It gave Eula no pang of conscience to remove mention of the twins' colored grandparent from their files. But Renee was an adder in waiting. If she ever struck, the fangs would hold fast and the venom would be plentiful.

"Pay no attention to the harpie, Eula."

Kerstin's advice was at once comforting and useless. In Eula's worst despair it was her housemate and dearest friend Kerstin who offered the soft shoulder with wry wit. Kerstin had the mobile face of an actress, comely or plain, at her command. There were moments when Eula could have reached out and touched it, not in intimacy, but out of curiosity with its plastic variety.

It was Tessie Croft who introduced them. They had moved into the little house on Bethlehem Pike in the same year. Kerstin was head of nurses at the public health clinic on the city line, a woman like Eula, whose energy and ambition could be confused with each other. She was pleased to feel part of Drayton College by Eula's proxy. On weekends the two often made the rounds of the cottages and Schoolhouse together, sharing news.

This weekend they were discussing Beverly Rice.

"I never should have hired her."

"The one with the aggressive eyebrows?"

And here she was coming out of Schoolhouse, down the walk toward them. With so much invested in her, it was perhaps too important to Eula that the math teacher should succeed. She was tall and wispy, but sharp spoken. Her eyebrows were indeed imposing. Run together, they cut a single stroke across her forehead, a black line that rose and fell with her mood. She was the one teacher at Drayton whom the Director permitted to intimidate the girls, and whom most of them feared. She had allowed Miss Rice her severe method because the woman ceded nothing to the patronizing charter, and right away her severity brought results in the girls' computation skills.

Though not the skills of the twins, who would not be intimidated, and had lessons of their own to teach, not just in arithmetic, but a foreign language, too. The staff at first thought they might be a little soft in the head, the way they mumbled to each other and sometimes burst out in the classrooms with unintelligible noises.

"Groose goosh," Miss Rice reported. "Can you make anything of that? A lot of gibberish, I expect. One of them speaks, the other laughs. The Cochran girl makes fun of them. It's a terrible disruption. They don't care."

"Groose goosh." Eula made a note of it in their file, along with "speech instruction?"

Beverly Rice had little patience for underachievers and none at all for deceit. She was alert to backsliding, and quick to anger at disrespect. It was her pride to keep her students ahead of their counterparts in the public schools. Where else but here would ten-year-old girls be subjected to the phantom zeroes of square root calculation, or asked to find the volume of the cone-shaped dunce cap that sat on Beverly's desk.

They were two weeks into the Fall session in 1926, when Beverly approached Eula again, this time to say she was expelling the twins from the math room.

"Never," she was told.

"Yes," she insisted. "Their game of switch is a constant distraction. They prevent the others from learning. I won't have it."

She said they were changing seats to confuse her, and stared defiantly when challenged.

"They stay," she was told. "They stay and they learn."

It was only a week later that she came back yet again. This time in triumph. She had caught the twins in a steel trap. The only question now, she said, was how they'd be disciplined. Beverly wanted their pelts on display as a warning to others. She held them in front of her, hands clamped on their shoulders. They wriggled to be free of her grasp, and defied her:

"Get off me, goosh."

Eula's recording calendar for September 23, 1926, gives this account of the incident:

This evening came Beverly Rice with our matched pair. In front of me, to their faces, she called them liars and cheaters. When the twins were gone, I reprimanded Beverly for the summary judgment. What did she expect, putting me on the spot that way? And what now? Their response was "Grint lossy." Whatever that means.

"I told you," they said. "Didn't we tell you?"

Not a bit contrite. Pleased with themselves, as if they'd proven a point, and were waiting for my apology. Beverly was confused by my hesitation. The twins wouldn't speak to her. I sent them to their rooms to hear the teacher's side of it without them. I then went to Thatch for the girls' version. Their satchels were stuffed with all they could hold. The rest of their things were scattered around the room. They were holding hands, waiting to be sent away.

The twins had looked cornered, as frightened as they were defiant, and Eula forgot, for the moment, she was their Director. She sat on one of the beds and asked Becca what had happened.

"No, I'm Becca. I don't know."

". . . not Becca," Linny two beats behind. "I don't know."

"You're not going anywhere."

"We are sometime."

". . . . sometime."

"Well, not today," Eula said, reaching for one of the bags, turning it over on the bed. Out came underwear, lots of it, two toothbrushes, and a single saddle shoe.

"You wouldn't get far on this, Becca." She was holding up the shoe.

Saddened by the fear, the haste, the pathetic omissions, Eula reached for the other satchel.

"I can do it for myself," Linny said, pulling the bag away. "Mother Crane lets us do for ourselves."

"Yes."

"Well."

"Well, what, dear?"

"Do you have to watch us?"

"No, of course not, I'll give you some privacy."

Regretting her intrusion, she left and never saw the contents of the second bag. There was no underwear in it, but two jumpers, two dresses, toothpaste, and three shoes. In sum, one correct answer to the packing problem.

It had started with a math exam, which they both failed. The day after the test Beverly called Becca to the blackboard, but thought it was Linny who came forward.

"Have it your way," she said. "You too, then Linny. We'll have both of you together."

She gave them their test papers and told them to copy their calculations on the board. They refused and started in with the gibberish again: "Lossy," and "Lossy groose goosh."

Warned to stop and get on with it, they followed orders, but with utter disrespect.

One said, "No rabum for you, bad girl," and the other's cheeks puffed out till her mouth could no longer contain her laughter. During the course of their ordeal they asked several times to be excused to the bathroom, and each time Beverly denied permission.

The first problem, long division, required a decimal solution. The two of them moved the chalk slowly and in identical steps, and the

same mistake appeared simultaneously in their answers. The error led to the same repeating figure in their common quotients. They ignored the dilemma, and kept on writing as if the endless repetition was a joke that could save them.

The other children began to giggle.

Beverly ordered the twins to copy the second problem.

They produced another faulty answer in tandem, number by identical number. And gradually the room went silent in shame for the twins. They'd been allowed to sit side by side in the class, and were now on display as patent cheaters. They were forced through two more examples of duplicate mistakes before being sent back to their seats.

Later that week Eula wrote, "Beverly Rice too practical to sense a phenomenon here. Let it cool for a few days. But will she stay at Drayton? Should she?"

Beverly expected her to accuse them, point-blank, of cheating. Eula wouldn't do it. She let their mischief ride. If they switched identities to avoid blame where it was deserved or to take credit where it was not, she hid her doubts. She allowed them the magic of telepathy. It was obvious they believed in some degree of unspoken communication between themselves, and were even a little frightened by it. As if they sensed that higher crimes and dangers lay ahead of them, the result of a duplicity beyond their control. Their profound likeness, she believed, was not an affect, but resided in their natures, their voices of identical timbre, their identical handwriting, and their frequent synchronous thinking.

Erica Cochran's tactic of attack and retreat had gotten nowhere with the Careys. All efforts at friendship after insult were rebuffed and doubled back on her. She called into the lavatory while they were on the toilets, "You smell twiced." Afterward, she invited them into her room to sniff a vial of perfume stolen from the staff room in Schoolhouse. They told her, "Pig smells her own hole," and "Why don't you pour it on yourself?" Later, still trying to appease, she told Mother Crane, "The twins smell just alike. It's not a bad smell," knowing they could hear everything she was saying. They snubbed Erica, and with good enough reason, Eula supposed.

The confrontation with Beverly festered. The twins withdrew further into their own society, hardly speaking to their housemates, doing only what was required of them. They would no longer meet the Director's gaze, placing her, she supposed, with the rest of the adult world born to betray them.

Eula called them into her office and treated them to a story she'd never shared with her other orphans: "The flu that took your parents also took my son Tony."

As if she could pass over this without a crack in her voice. It was no way to reassure children.

"At nine he could throw a baseball right over our house."

Memory of the feat, and the pride she had taken in his precocious athleticism, restored her balance. She turned back to her own childhood.

"I had very understanding parents," she said. "They let me be who I would."

She'd been the second of six children, raised in a large country house above a lake several miles outside Minneapolis. In the upper hallway, she explained, was a long blackboard. Her mother used it to introduce the alphabet and numerals before Eula was sent off to primary school. For the older children, she sometimes left quotations to be copied, or problems for those who needed extra help with grammar or computation. And little notes like "Eula, do you want to try this one? Hint, the answer is a whole number. Garrison, copy this word seven times and you will never misspell it again."

Eula said they would come in from outdoors and find these little exercises, as if a phantom teacher had paid a house call while they played. With no pressure on her, Eula explained, she could respond or not, as she chose.

The twins rolled their eyes.

"I wasn't always honest," she said, and they began to listen more closely.

"I had no excuse," she told them. "My parents loved me and let me be a tomboy. I could play in the mud and show my dirty shorts to the world just like any boy."

Their eyes grew large, and one of them started laughing.

"Is that you, Becca?"

"Yes."

"What happened?" Linny asked.

"Happened?"

"When you showed your dirty shorts to the world?"

Becca, thinking her sister might have gone too far, reached over to cover her mouth.

"It's all right; that's not the point. You see, I had my parents' trust. They knew I never lied to them."

They were paying full attention now.

"My older sister Clara was only twelve but she had an excellent cursive hand. I was very jealous. She could make beautiful letters on the blackboard. I used to watch her move the chalk in perfect loops as the letters flowed out. When I tried to copy her, my line was all angles and jagged shapes. I couldn't bear the comparison.

"One afternoon she put her alphabet on the board, and left the house to spend an overnight with a neighbor. I erased her name, and put mine in its place. My mother was amazed."

When she asked if it was my work, I said yes.

"Wonderful," she said, "you've been practicing. We'll show it to your father when he comes home."

And something in her, Eula told the twins, had refused to confess. Her mother knew, but she was the smart one. It was her father who said, "Eula, I believe you're lying. You've taken your sister's work for your own."

Before Clara came home the next day, Eula erased the whole thing, leaving only the memory of her lie.

"And you see, it's a lifelong memory, not much fun to live with. But I always resented my father's accusation."

Linny asked, "How could you do it?" but Becca said, "So?" as if the story was nothing out of the way.

Eula supposed she had split them into their two personalities, at least for the moment. They looked reproachfully at each other, mutually betrayed and a little panicky. She stepped out of the office

briefly to answer a question in the hall. When she returned they had switched chairs, or hair ribbons, or perhaps both. Or had not.

Without saying so exactly, Eula was trying to tell the twins her father had been wrong, just as Beverly Rice had. She felt this strongly: If children are aware that you can't be sure of their guilt or cannot prove it, they have every right to resent the presumption, even if they're guilty. And even if they're guilty, they'll lose trust in you.

Eula preferred to answer Linny.

"I did it because I wanted to be somebody else, because I wasn't satisfied with the person I was."

"You *were* somebody else," Becca said, almost to herself, and then, "It was the other one that did it."

This was their confusion, the same these two lived with every day. Tess said they were atoms of the same element, identical nuclei with common electrons orbiting, ineluctably binding them together. The elegant comparison held no hope of a separation, explosive or controlled. It was too pessimistic.

To be consistent Eula could only go on as if nothing had happened, as if there had been no switch of identities in the room, no changing of places. And perhaps there hadn't been.

The one who was Becca for the moment said, "Why don't we have one here?"

"A blackboard? There's one in every classroom."

"No," she said. "I mean one that we could write on anytime."

"Anyone?"

Linny finished the idea: "You, or any of the housemothers or any of the children. Or Miss Rice," she said.

"Yes," Becca said. "Or Mr. Henry."

This was so promising that Eula agreed without hesitation, though she was as familiar as any educator in America with the opportunities for abuse in the combination of blackboard, chalk, and children.

Two weeks later it was done. Right in the basement of Schoolhouse, the heart of the community, where the children gathered for assemblies and lectures, or games on rainy days. If they had a free hour they could pass it there, visiting with girls from other houses, or sit in front of the fireplace with the Cinderella tiles for storytelling. There was a long bare wall opposite the hearth, perfectly suited.

A triple blackboard was fastened to the wall, and under this single surface, a thirty-foot trough for chalk and erasers. There was room for a dozen or more people to be writing, posing or answering problems, at the same time. The girls began to write things before the men were even finished, before Eula had a chance to call a meeting and explain the rules.

It was not a bulletin board, she said; it was a community wall for learning and expression, for asking and answering, for poems and narrative, equations, mathematical posers. Observations, queries, and answers. And not to be used for thoughtless expression, but after a time of contemplation and preparation. As the twins had suggested, it would be open to all, staff and girls alike. It might provide uplift or practical advice, maybe conundrums that stretched the mind. But the first and abiding rule was everything written there must be signed. All must take responsibility for their contributions. It was up to the writer to erase her own words after a week.

The idea first struck the other girls as just another chore. Eula didn't want them rushing up to write trivia—the time for all good men . . . the quick brown fox . . . and that sort of thing. And it was not to be used like the piano in the far corner of the same room for hammering out a string of mindless notes, or for any meanness.

Eula went straight to the board with an example, something her father had said:

Never make a display of newly acquired knowledge.

Miss Kieland

Too preachy. She began again:

> *Oh, give us pleasure in the flowers today;*
> *And give us not to think so far away*
> *As the uncertain harvest; keep us here*
> *All simply in the spring of the year.*

The giant board hung with nothing more offered for several days. The children had been scared away until one afternoon a little pattern of stars appeared.

> Last night on our star walk in the meadow I found a new consolation. It is named for me, Mary Walker, your sister in Thistle Cottage. You can see it is a sailboat. You won't see it if you don't look at the same stars.
>
> *Mary Walker*

No one dared suggest she might have misspelled a word. Her work inspired a half dozen other constellations, each named for the young astronomer who'd discovered it. One day these were all wiped clear, and replaced with soulful verses a composition teacher had coaxed her girls into sharing. Dust storms, cactus, and tragic prairie life appeared from somewhere in the collective consciousness. These disappeared and the long board was covered with Miss Rice's rate, time, and distance problems, trains pulling out of stations in opposite directions. And the children's calculations were a maze of figures tumbling into one another. Here and there a "very good" was written in pedagogic cursive beside an answer.

Within a few months most of the children had signed their names to some contribution, and Mother Crane called the board "The Drayton Enquirer" after the city's newspaper, but the twins came up with "The Drayton Slate," and that was the name that stuck. It was carved on a wooden sign and fixed to the wall above the board.

If the poetry was doggerel, the spelling spotty, or the computations off by a decimal point or more, the failures, like the triumphs, were instructive. A weekly copy of all its contents would show the generally warmhearted nature of their village. And some division in the ranks, as well. There were several times Eula copied everything on the board into her notebook. Of course there was the occasional abuse. The unsigned insult, or insinuation, quickly erased by the alert staff.

Miss Kieland, Queen of Fairyland

What was that child thinking? Was it a child? And much later:

Mother Crane is a squash.

There were weeks when the board was little more than a suggestion box, weeks when Eula had to encourage staff members to turn it
again in a more thoughtful direction.

∞

By the end of the twins' first year, their impact on Drayton was a regular subject for staff discussion. They were only eleven, yet some of
the oldest children of Drayton were ambling around the campus with
the Careys' odd gait, part shuffle, part swagger, a walk that suggested
private knowledge and indifference to community. Unacceptable;
there were assemblies given to mood, deportment, uplift. "Pick up
your feet, girls!" wasn't getting the job done.

Like the Director, the children had been moved by the strength
of the Careys' twinned personality, their will to be who they were and
nothing more. Erica Cochran, working vainly to ingratiate herself,
was the obvious one to begin mimicking their style, and the shambling pose of sophisticated distance, heard in their voices as well,
spread through the rest of Thatch, even to the docile Susan Bailey,
and eventually into the other cottages. Yet the twins offered no en-
couragement for the imitative flattery.

They were far too young to hold sway over the orphanage. It
wasn't something they worked at or deserved. The enchantment,
Eula saw, came from their striking appearance, their unique double
image in combination with the indifference. And how could she fault
her children when she recognized the truth of Kerstin's judgment;
the same narcotic had a grip on their "Mummy," the name Kerstin
was still using for her with a teasing and flattering affection.

Walking out of her office Eula heard a child calling down the service road, "Groose goosh," and an answering "Grint lossy," yelled
back from someone hidden in the branches of an apple tree. The

children had no idea what they were saying. It was only a sign of admiration for the source of the nonsense.

Julia Crane strolled into Eula's office one morning in the twentieth month of the twins' residence, pleased with herself, holding a sheet of paper by its corner between thumb and forefinger, as if to keep a distance from germs.

"Do you know what groose goosh means?"

"Do you?"

"It means a wet movement."

Julia was holding the rosetta stone of the Careys' private language, a list they had written down themselves, maybe against the chance they'd forget it, the first words of their crib, translated. Julia's little informer Susan had taken it from their room. Instead of atrophy after infancy the fugitive tongue had survived and was perhaps still growing, a vocabulary of a hundred words or more.

Whoever had taken it might be their enemy forever. So why was Eula pouring over it so carefully? *Rabum,* maybe from pabulum, for "food"; *guster* for "like," and thus *guster rabum* for "I'm hungry"; *jums* for "sheets"; *groose* for "wet"; *lum* for "mother"; *lub* for "milk"; *mung* for "teddy"; *grint* for "don't like"; *lossy* for their Aunt Gwen, or any person that was not their mother or father; *goosh* for "movement in the diaper."

This wasn't normal. Eula had heard of twins developing their own language in the crib, but she knew the practice always ended with the overpowering influence of the language spoken around them. These two had called Beverly Rice groose goosh, and now children were calling the same words back and forth to each other across the campus. Halfway down the list Eula stopped herself.

"Take it back," she told Julia. "Have Susan put it back where she found it. No need to talk about it." The staff might believe her now when she said the Careys had no need of speech therapy. She advised the teachers and housemothers not to squelch the invented language. It would only provoke them, she said, and prolong its use.

Eula's recording calendar, which doubled as daybook and journal, the daily record of her tenure at the orphanage, shows that 1928 was a peaceful year for Becca and Linny, if not-on-the-calendar can be equated with not-in-trouble.

Their names appear only twice that year, and both times in connection with a drama written and performed by the girls of Thatch. The entries show, first, the Director's pleasure that the twins were taking the lead parts in the production, and that the play might have a therapeutic value for them. The protagonists of the piece, twin sisters, were in a competition for the hand of a confused boy who didn't know which one he was asking to a dance.

Eula welcomed their involvement as a healthy sign. Her concern, recorded in the same week, was for the drama instructor, who was complaining that unless both sisters were onstage at once, she was never sure which one of them was.

∞

Eula was dealing that season with the attentions of Cyril Johnson, who invited her to a series of dinner meetings, supposedly to discuss the building program and the designs of the architect for completion of the Drayton campus—specifically an elegant, towered administration building, which would be more a monument to the designer than a practical addition to the orphanage.

This is why she spent so many Wednesday evenings with Cyril. The time should properly have been shared with all the trustees around a conference table, but with Cyril there was always some business that kept him in the city and busy through the day, so that a rendezvous for dinner at his club held the advantage of respectable necessity.

The building plans led the trustees' agenda that year, and Cyril was chairman of the building committee. The little community of stone and Tudor-framed cottages was already the Ruskinian dream planned by its architect, the walls chiseled with the spirit of the place, a wonderland intended for the inspiration and development of girls into young women, though as Eula explained to the twins and all her girls, the expectations for their femininity needed an overhaul.

Ruskin's belief that a woman "grows as a flower does" was branded on the four cottages—Narcissus, Cornflower, Primrose, and Thistle. Thistle was the only one of these tough enough for the generation Eula meant to loose on the world. With the exception of

Thistle, she would have preferred Kerstin's subversive names for the others—Bakery, Borstal, and Bedlam, but she had changed them to Greystone, Stork, and Thatch.

Their doorways were already surrounded by relief tiles of the blossoming flowers of the structures' maiden names. Really, the steep-pitched roofs of colored tile that fell to low-slung eaves, and the Mother Goose fantasies modeled into the gabled ends, were so friendly and amusing that no one could object to their influence. No, Snow White had to be stopped, and her pathetic dependence ridiculed.

The romantic notions of the architect now threatened to run wild. His Gothic ambulatory was already decorated with a sculptor's bas-relief Sun Baby, an infant born out of a blazing sun whose rays were interwoven with butterflies and hobbles, representing the pleasures, troubles, and restraints that lay ahead for all women.

Now this man proposed to add four more allegories to stone walls not yet laid—Childhood and Play, Girlhood and Study, Maidenhood and the Melody of Life, and the Glory of Motherhood in the Mystery of Time and Space. Over the new structure he meant to raise a central Gothic tower, decorated with a terra cotta molding of a young mother holding her baby aloft with four supporting maidens, caryatids bound together by a chain of flowers—the Dawn Maiden, the Zenith Maiden, the Eventide Maiden, and the Maiden of the Night.

Please!

The romantic allusions rankled, but not so much as the misallocation of large sums to buildings unsuited to family living. The money should be spent, not to complete an architect's misty-eyed vision, but on houses of the real world. Eula would prefer they'd build a village of wooden bungalows rather than go on with this miniature university of Gothic stone that would only glorify a feminine ideal and the architects.

There she sat at dinner, obliged to gratitude because this could only happen on ladies' night at Cyril Johnson's club. He was trying to change her mind, and she was trying to change his. He was an earnest man whose longish hair suggested a nice indifference to fashion. He was phlegmatic, but not overbearing, in fact prone, she

thought, to too easy a brimming eye at some nicety of expression, a line of poetry perhaps, or even some *mot* of his own invention.

They were sitting there under the flickering light of a gas sconce. A soft glow suffused the paneled room, burnishing the high-polished veneer of an English sideboard. Quiet conversations at a dozen tables around them suggested the earnest concerns of a dozen proper marriages. Just as Cyril's busy schedule gave cover to the dinner meetings, so the orphanage agenda could be used to disguise the little probes and embarrassments of his infatuation. She never conceded it was more than that. Why should her acceptance of dinner invitations in the city be understood as acceptance of his courtship? The excuses for these rendezvous were all Cyril's inventions, not hers. Their evening meetings were no secret from the Drayton community. Against the troublesome chatter that carried Kerstin and her beyond professional admiration and deep friendship, there was the convenience and the inconvenience of Cyril's attention.

He jumped ahead in their conversation to the very reasonable price of the locally quarried stone that was being used at Drayton, stone that tied their buildings nicely into the tradition of the finest estates in the nearby countryside. It was Chestnut Hill stone, which the geologists called Wissahickon schist, a handsome alternation of blues, grays, and browns, all flecked with mica that made the buildings sparkle in sunlight.

"If you don't mind, Eula, the very same coloring as your eyes."

An awkward excess. If she wanted to put an immediate end to this, she could have asked which of the three colors. But he had already embarrassed himself. After reaching across the table to touch her arm, he quickly withdrew his hand to wipe the corner of his eye.

He gathered himself, strengthened his voice, and said, "Renee Drayton has raised questions about the admissions policy."

Could Eula reassure him about the twin sisters who were causing such a commotion? Was it true, as Renee had told a few of the trustees, that information was missing from the girls' files?

"You know she doesn't really trust you, or Tess Croft," he said.

"How would she know anything about the files?"

He was apologetic. He couldn't say how, but Renee had told him that Tess could no longer be trusted as a referral agent, and that Drayton had the two girls to prove it, girls whose racial identities were uncertain, whose behavior was stained. "Off-white," she called it.

"Mr. Johnson, you tell her and the others I won't accept interference in the selection of my girls. If the board wants my resignation they may have it."

"Oh no! We're not there at all! Really, you're the institution, Eula! Without you, what would we have? And please, I hoped you felt free to call me Cyril."

Such a kind man, she thought, silly man, useful man!

He went back to a discussion of the Drayton plant, as he called it.

He reminded her that she'd known from the beginning what the architect's full vision had been. And wouldn't their completed village of allegory in stone be a beacon to all the educators of the world? Once cast, the lesson would be immutable. Against the tide of machines and institutional thinking, their example would be the paradigm, not just for orphan girls, but all womankind, eternal truths for healing and restoration of the spirit.

He had to turn away, as if something behind him demanded his attention. She gave him another moment to recompose himself, and clear his throat. What part of this did she want to argue with? None of it, really. The human scale of the place could not be faulted. Most of the girls did love it, even some who were pretending indifference. They were comforted by it. But she was thinking of something the twins had said—"These are like gingerbread houses"—and their tacit objection to the sweetness of the place. In this matter they, not the trustees, were her kindred. With them, she was turned in a direction quite blind to stone laid on stone, and its architectural decoration.

As happy a village as they were building, she was as aware as the twins that there was something artificial about it. The gentle lie in the false half-timbering of the gable ends, the fables in the pargeting, the feminine as a ubiquitous, cloying ideal. All she needed to say in the end was "Cyril, this isn't what we need."

He nodded slowly, pushing out a deliberative lower lip.

"No," he said, "I suppose it isn't. But you know, I think these meetings of ours are very useful. Don't you?"

As easily as that he was converted. The dinners in the city continued as Wednesday night habit.

∞

"You mean we've got four of them now?"

Laura Baker, housemother of Greystone Cottage, the house Kerstin called the Bakery, where the children were often white with flour and zinging dough across the kitchen, was half serious in her question. It amused the others; the notion of the Careys as four indistinguishable sisters was bizarre.

"Actually, the opposite," Eula explained to her gathered housemothers. "Mr. Rank thinks Linny and Becca have the instinct to reduce themselves to one. But this requires each to imagine herself as the other. Only in that sense is each of them two people."

"There you are," Mother Laura said. "We do have four of them."

They buzzed together over their conundrum. Eula slapped the conference table and declared, "It's our job to split them into the two selves who were born into this world."

"Tell us then," Beverly, said, "are we to think of them as one person, when they wish it? Or four? Or what?"

"Two, two, two."

"Well that makes six." Laura up to tricks. More laughter, and chatter. It had seemed so simple when Mr. Rank explained it to Eula, but now it flew apart again, multiplying into hopeless complexity. Twins doubled? Could they split again into multiples that would never be gathered into a manageable model? If she couldn't explain it to her own satisfaction, what could she expect from her housemothers and teachers?

They had something else on their minds, an article from that weekend's Sunday supplement. What kind of sand had their Director thrown in the eyes of the city journalist who described her as "a tall, fine-looking woman of Norwegian and Colonial blood, with steady, blue eyes; and hair trained gently back into a rounded light-brown

crown. Her features are soft, but her mouth is firm, and she speaks at once with conviction and humility, a combination disarming to any who might attempt to draw her into argument."

Who in the world had he been talking to? Eula knew he had interviewed Tessie Croft about her. And there was more, far too generous, as if a publicity man had written the thing:

> It's said she rules her domain with a bold and clear-eyed love. She was chosen by the Drayton trustees for her experience in the progressive schooling project in Gary, Indiana, and her work in a New York settlement house. She is the daughter of a businessman and a suffragette. Trained in the liberal tradition, Eula Kieland has sometimes been at odds with the Drayton College charter over a restrictive enrollment policy.
>
> Preoccupied with her work, she remains single, though not militantly so. Her friends say she has had many suitors, but none able to turn her head from her devotion to the cause of progressive education.

And who but Tess would have told him something like that? The nerve of her! The nerve of him!

Eula had just returned from her first session in the city with Otto Rank to find her housemothers gathered in the anteroom of her office, their cottages unattended. They were all atwitter over this admiring column, which made them all weekend celebrities and invited the irritation of the trustees. Eula had come back with new hope, and as something of a convert, after this first session with the Vienna therapist. As Tess explained, he'd been cast out by the Freudians, and was presenting a new and abbreviated sort of analysis to his American patients. Most successfully in New York and Philadelphia, where Tess was acting as his champion. A known end date for each therapy was part of the cure, an anticipated separation that would encourage a willed improvement.

He was a thoroughly generous spirit, a joy in conversation. The established psychoanalytical societies were stung. Not just by his reproach to all the father-and-mother business and their meandering method, but by the challenge to their indefinite tenure as well-paid

listeners. He spoke a cultured English, with a grand vocabulary, and endearing European leftovers—*terapy* for therapy. But how could he help the orphanage if he refused to admit children for treatment?

Since Tess had encouraged Eula to take the Careys, Eula assumed she had also prevailed on the busy man to give Eula an audience, hoping to mend some of the trouble she herself had caused. Actually it was to push Eula into her own treatment, though all in the name of her problems with the twins. Tess had warned Eula not to over-indulge her anxieties. And Tess belonged to that growing number who thought everyone should submit to modern analysis.

At first, Eula had refused to see him. For this he was completely forgiving.

"You are terrified of terapy, I tink."

How could she harden her heart against this?

He let her go on about the Careys. She'd expected long silences, the excused rudeness of modern treatment. Instead he kindly filled each pause in her presentation with a gentle speculation.

"We all make doubles of ourselves," Rank told her. "To carry the baggage. In the case of your twins, perhaps this is unnecessary, yes? Nature has provided the double, and no need for the subconscious to produce another."

It took him only a moment to break down her defense. His voice was carefully measured, and his demurs so gentle. He had a wide general knowledge. Layered with subtle caveats, his explanations made a balm of logic. Of course he could not offer a solid professional opinion of the twins, having never met the girls. Yet with each detail of their story, his face signaled a wider comprehension of their pathology. She should not, he said, take his reactions as any more than speculation, though he'd gone right to the heart of the girls' gaming, the strategy they used. It was not just a counter to their misfortune; it was innate, as a cat was destined to stalk a bird, as exciting as it was inevitable.

He knew before she told him what had happened when they tried a separation, putting Linny and Becca in different rooms in the same house.

"Yes," he said, "each sat in a corner, eh? And would not move or speak. They'd as soon shrivel and starve."

"I suppose they would have," she agreed. "We didn't push it that far."

"You should understand," he warned. "The distance they keep from you is as valid as the distance you keep from them. For them also, too close is dangerous. Though as doubles, you see, their armor is twice as thick. An utter ting. You should not concern yourself too much with this cheatink. In their subconscious they are so much one person, and if one person, how can cheatink exist?"

She hadn't thought of it that way, and now it seemed so obvious.

"Don't forget," he went on, "the most common uses of the alter ego. The double accommodates all manner of self-infatuation."

She thought of the twins tangled on the bed, but he had something else in mind. Without realizing it, she'd already revealed a good deal of her own life and doubts, even her ambiguous sessions with Cyril Johnson.

"Who is it that keeps our little egg nest?" he asked. "Is it the prudent us, or the greedy us?"

"Egg nest?"

"Oh dear, is it turned around?"

He laughed with her, and went on: "When you last looked in the mirror, Miss Kieland, perhaps this morning, did you see the educator, or the temptress?"

"What?"

"The one who might lead a gentleman to pursue the unattainable? I ask only teoretically."

"But the children are too young for this."

"Please. Forget the children for a moment. Is it possible that the guardian of a young community's welfare is sometimes possessed by a voice not her own?"

She couldn't answer him.

"We must all recognize the double who stalks us."

She was irritated. Not by Rank so much as by Tess and her meddling. Only her parents had ever dared such a blunt approach. Even they wouldn't have gone this far. But the man's questions were so sincere, and his eyes wide with honesty. She couldn't dislike him. Too tactful to demand answers by waiting for them, he turned without

pause to the general: "Guilt is shifted to the shoulders of the double. Fear, too. In the end there may be paranoia, extreme mistrust of the other. And if the other haunts relentlessly it must of course, in the end, be destroyed. When this happens, one hopes there is no longer confusion of the imagined intruder with the corporeal self."

She sat straighter.

"We leave such extremes, the suicides, to literature and myth," he said. "The stories of such tortured lives we can't bear in the flesh. Do you know *The Student of Prague?*"

He hardly gave her time to say no.

"He was tormented by an alter ego taken from his mirror. This second self always returned in a crisis, always anticipated, always interfered. When the young man looked in the glass, he had no reflection. His shadow was busy elsewhere."

She inferred a duty to train the Careys into separate wardrobes, rooms, minds, and lives, before one did harm to the other. She was grateful for the warning, though not sure of her obligation to him.

"Oh, he said, "You're not to worry about the expense. Miss Croft has taken care of that. Yes, I tink we should talk again. Next week maybe? I've put aside a regular hour for you on Wednesdays."

Convenient. Before her Wednesday dinners. She supposed it was Tess again, the informer, the facilitator. Should she protest? It wasn't clear to her that Mr. Rank already considered her the patient, that the Carey twins would be a fascinating study, but only in support of her own treatment.

Before she left his office he said, "Next time you will lie over there, facing the window." He was pointing to a small couch.

It was more an order than a prediction. It presumed her submission; it was exciting, familiar and businesslike, sexual, confusing. Avoiding his gaze, she was staring at his hand. And as if to hold her attention there, he began to drum a finger on the arm of his chair. Up and down went a clear red stone set in gold.

"That's an unusual ring," she said.

"Carnelian," he told her. "Intaglio."

He settled his hand beside him in the chair, out of sight.

"It's elegant. Where did it come from?"

"A gift," he said.

"I'm sure it makes a striking seal." She gathered her things, thinking she'd made a thorough fool of herself.

∞

Explaining the man to her staff, she found herself using the same description Tess had: "A nondoctrinaire therapist." Was this a contradiction in itself? From Vienna, he had broken with the Freudian circle, and was vilified by them for this treachery, but refused to answer their attacks in kind. She found him gentle and provocative. Tess said he was one of the few geniuses she'd ever met. His publications, tripping off her tongue, meant nothing to Eula. Tess wanted her to know he'd written this and that, and such and such. The titles relentlessly impressive, but of little moment to Eula until she heard *The Double*. Published first in German as *Doppelgänger,* Rank's analysis of the twin in myth and literature.

All of a sudden, a place for him in Eula's Wednesday schedule seemed useful. She was relieved to hear that his treatment relied on no firm dogma other than the will of the patient to pull anchor and sail into new seas. No promise of a final halcyon port, only of eventual contentment with a healthy voyage.

"Where was I?" she'd asked her people.

Mother Reilly rescued her: "First you said that we all have alter egos, we all split ourselves into distinct halves, hoping for a higher existence, leaving the dirty work to the devilish other."

The summary was succinct if oversimplified; Ellen was leading the others in the right direction.

∞

In order to observe the Careys more closely Eula had their community chore moved to her office. The whole college had housekeeping duties for one hour after lunch. Dusting, carpet sweeping, emptying the wastebaskets, and tidying up in her anteroom could not really keep two of them busy for the whole period. Beyond the notice of the staff or the other children she could sit them down for a chat most any day. With glasses of lemonade they mixed in her office pantry they could talk of anything they pleased.

Eula began to flatter herself that she could at last tell them apart, not because she'd found a physical difference, but because she thought they were beginning to trust her, were willing to deal honestly with her, and would only answer to their real names. When Julia Crane told her they sometimes called themselves "Miss Kieland's slaves," she was forced to a reappraisal.

∞

On March 4 of 1929, seven months before the crash and long before the country's deprivation and hunger threatened her own kitchens, Eula copied the contents of "The Drayton Slate" into her daybook. A historian of the orphanage calls this entry the most significant in all her years of record keeping. It was the first time she transcribed the whole "Slate," before the words flew off into chalk dust and oblivion.

The better part of the material on the board at the start of that dismal economic era was the work of the teachers and housemothers. In fact, this entry revealed a testy debate going on between Ellen Reilly and Mother Greene. Eula wrote, "They bore down in bold capitals and swept double and triple lines under their conclusions." It was a philosophical tug of war with only adults pulling on a rope that stretched far over the children's heads.

Eula chose a moment in the evening when the meeting room was empty to make her copy, but Mother Crane came in looking for Erica, in trouble again, wandering the campus after "doors closed," and caught Eula, writing in her notebook. Not a crime, really, especially since a part of the display was her own, but she did feel like a spy. After all, this was not supposed to be part of anyone's permanent record. Her own contribution came first:

"The Drayton Slate," copied March 4, 1929:

To my Staff:

A young life is not a piece of clay to be molded, that we might turn it according to our desires into a model citizen, a model housewife, a model teacher, a model nurse, or whatever conventional shape. The developing child should surprise us as a plant, watered and offered nutrient to prove, in its own time, what its blossom or fruit will be.

We should harden the stock, expose it to the cold before transplanting in the outside world. Like the strawberry. The strawberry child grows tough, even a little callous, while another one I call the celery child is shut away from the elements. And what happens when we turn this celery thing into the stormy world? It withers and asks to be taken again into the greenhouse.

Free the child. Allow her to take some risks. Be a little daring. There comes a time when a girl must be encouraged to swim across the lake by herself, even to walk into the forest on the other side. Why else do we teach the skills of independence and survival?

Miss Kieland

Someone had followed this with:

Miss Kieland, Queen of Drayton, and her hardy mums.

Then:

Please! No more drawers left to soak in the sink in Thistle's upstairs bathroom. Are you so proud of your monthly?

This she erased before continuing to copy.

> *Oh for a friend*
> *To lay his head*
> *On the counterpane*
> *Of my small bed.*

Below this Mother Greene had gone on another rampage:

Have any of our children heard of Mr. John Dewey? Girls, you must ask about him. I think your leaders have fallen into step behind a Pied Piper, and he's not leading you just to the river. No, rather into a quicksand of self-indulgence and self-esteem where you will wallow until you're swallowed up in your own ignorance.

Do you feel the ground under you getting mushier as you are promoted, grade by grade? You wander back and forth from one classroom to another, but do you stop to ask what you have accomplished with all this shuffling to and fro, or what you have learned at the end of your day?

You've been told to let your thoughts spill into your composition books. Should it surprise you that they are filled with misspelled, flabby thought and poor grammar?

She'd gone too far this time. There would have to be apology, maybe a firing. The next section in her bold capitals was underlined, too, as if it were time to yell:

WE ARE WEAK! LOOKING FOR EASY SOLUTIONS! WE SEEK THE EASE AND APPROVAL OF OUR STUDENTS WHEN WE SHOULD DEMAND THEIR HARD WORK AND RESPECT. CONSIDER THIS; NOT ONE OF OUR GIRLS HAS BEEN ASKED TO MEMORIZE A PASSAGE FROM SHAKESPEARE, OR ANY OTHER POET. IT MIGHT AS WELL BE AGAINST THE RULES. NO MEMORY WORK! ROTE IS NOW A FILTHY WORD!

Perhaps her hand had grown tired, slipping into a hurried cursive:

Wake up, teachers. Wake up, girls. Learning isn't always fun.

As she finished copying this, Eula was more discouraged than angry. Of course she wasn't going to fire Mother Greene, only ask her if she wanted to stay. Because the curriculum wasn't going to change for her. The mood of the "Slate" turned again:

TWINS

A chipmunk scurried up and found her lap;
She didn't care, she moved and let it fall.

> *If scared, the thing refused to let her know,*
> *But climbed back up to settle for a nap;*
> *Trained or wild, not inclined to grieve,*
> *A bit of brown fur nesting in a sleeve.*
> *Remarkable to any watching there,*
> *The way she turned aside a wild heart.*
> *For chipmunk, she was life, and warm to touch,*
> *Turned unwilling platform for its play;*
> *Here was proof of her dominion,*
> *The proof that she could whistle it away,*
> *And have it back, if whistled back or nay.*
> *Was there a like to such a frigid thing?*
> *Could this be twin to one with softer heart?*
> *Who'd take a special gift of grace like that,*
> *And treat it as a motor-driven toy?*
> *Who'd brook such a twin, day after day,*
> *Without, as well, the daily urge—destroy?*

She read this in disbelief. No one in Drayton was given to this sort of modern musing. It seemed to have arrived from a long distance. As prophecy, it was dire as Otto Rank's worst forecast for the Careys. All of Drayton knew of the chipmunks living under the stone wall, opposite Stork Cottage. And they knew the Carey girls took part in taming them, offering food and affection until several of the creatures had become bold enough to climb up any child's leggings and eat from her hand. One had been found dead on the service road. Susan Bailey, always the child of equity, even on behalf of the difficult Carey girls, wrote under the poem:

> This isn't fair. Linny and Becca didn't kill the chipmunk. It was
> Mother Crane's cat. All cats at Drayton should wear bells.
>
> *Susan B.*

Her complaint missed the point. The twins were a danger to themselves according to the anonymous poet: One stewing over the other's

heartlessness while their natures chained them together? Which was which? Otto had told Eula of identical twins he'd treated in Vienna. One had asked him, "Why does she want to tear me from myself?" This one, he said, had committed suicide. And the sister was still in a mental hospital at Salzburg, where her daily conversations with her missing half were indulged as inevitable, that is to say, incurable.

Eula read on and copied the next piece, signed by Ellen Reilly. There were X's and O's around her name, signs of the children's affection. Eula was happy for her, such a favorite. Ellen didn't condescend, or dispense soft soap. She knew better than to curry favor with young people; they liked her because she expected so much of them. And she didn't tolerate lolling about. If the thoughts of youth were long, long thoughts, what use if the thoughts did not lead to action and change? She had written:

Vicarious adventure is no adventure at all. Don't live in your dreams. Will you grow old never crossing the ocean, the country, the state, or even your street? There is too much living in books and dreams here. If the imagined thing is enough to conquer, you might as well stay in bed.

Work hard. Play hard. Enjoy the dance. Stand up when the music starts. Dance with a girlfriend if you must. But dance!

Mother Reilly

Thank God for Ellen, though she could be salty, too, even shocking: "Out of bed, you lazy sluts, and get your naughty fingers busy on the loom." Mother Laura heard her say that on the way into her cottage one morning. There were no looms here, but it made a nice figure.

"Did the girls hear her?" Eula wondered.

"No," Laura said, "but I did. And well she knew it."

There was more:

Dear Miss Kieland,

You say you'd let us swim across a lake. You won't even let us ride our bicycles into the village.

Sally Kesterson

Sally? Knees and elbows constant scabs. The last one Eula would want riding down the Bethlehem Pike.

∞

At thirteen the Careys were wiser than many of the older orphans. Reaching onset less than a week apart, they didn't rush to the infirmary in ignorant panic as some of the girls, but were aware of what was going on and how to deal with it. Given the appropriate supplies, they did not want Nurse Jean's assistance.

And the twins, who had been so wary of a Drayton sisterhood, began to take an interest in the boys they met in the village, especially those who came to the dances. One evening they attached themselves to a young man with a warmth that required a chaperone's interference. They were using their twin beauty in a game of now-you-see-me-now-you-see-her. It was a little cruel, and worrisome to Eula in its carnal provocation. She knew they saw her watching them, and it didn't slow them down a bit. The boy turned away for a moment, and Eula watched the Careys change places as in a magic act: same face, different costume. The boy's pleasure turned to bewilderment, then distress, and, as the game continued, to disgust.

Kerstin chafed Eula for spending so much attention on the twins and their influence on her campus to the neglect of other matters like the general economic collapse. And the neglect of Kerstin herself, Eula supposed.

"You're letting them talk back, Mummy."

Your double demons, she called them.

"Mummy, you're letting them frighten you. They take liberties as your own children would.

"What about your little Bakers and Borstal gals, Mummy, and the children of Bedlam?"

"If the twins are on a self-destructive path and a danger to each other, shouldn't you be a therapist before a mummy, Mummy?"

Eula might have said, "Stop the mummy business, Kerstin, it's tiresome," but there was a strain of affection in the teasing name that Eula didn't really want to squelch. And there was something else

Kerstin had said, "a danger to each other." She had given herself away. Who else could have put the verse on the "Slate"? True to principle, Eula wouldn't confront just on the strength of suspicion. She'd wait for Kerstin's confession.

The financial disruption in that first year of the Depression seemed like very distant trouble. Eula believed the orphanage investments were in well-positioned real estate, and they could go on with the redefined building program. She'd been myopic. Her recording calendar for the months before the crash is filled with the details of another gambit to conquer the twins. Their behavior was a regular topic at staff meetings. It wasn't so much what they did as what they didn't do. They didn't mingle. They weren't as rude as in their first months, but they still held something back from their peers and guardians.

At one of these meetings Julia Crane proposed animal care as therapy, a dog for the Careys. The orphanage had chickens and a few sheep in the meadow, but this would be different, a pet living in Thatch with the twins, and for which they'd take full responsibility. Eula thought it was a grand idea. She relaxed the no-house-pets rule. A mutt would be brought out from the city pound to live in the twins' room. They'd been chosen by lottery (fixed), and the two of them could share responsibility for the dog. Eula's guile was a match for the twins' suspicions, and the plan moved forward with their approval. They were excited.

In the week set to collect the dog, Linny came down with a horrid sore throat. Her temperature spiked, and she was taken into the city in the station wagon, and sent directly from a doctor's office to the hospital for a tonsillectomy. After ether, she reported a dream in which she said a drum throbbed while a moon and stars circled her head. She was kept an extra several days in recovery, until the doctors declared her in her right mind again.

The dog arrived in Linny's absence, and Becca named it Tonsils. If the name was meant to honor loss, it might also have been called Adenoids. A spayed mongrel, it was what the shelter called a "Philadelphian," because there were so many others that looked just

like it in the city's streets, with medium hair, tawny and black. It had a quick affection, though a tendency to cower, an animal that had likely suffered serial masters and abuse. But Tonsils jumped, licked, and stuck to Becca's side in a heartwarming introduction.

Beverly Rice's attitude was not softened by Tonsils's arrival. She referred to Becca as "our formerly identical twin, the one who has both her tonsils." Seeing her walking in the meadow with her new pet, Beverly asked Mother Crane, "Can you tell which one is the bitch?"

But Eula was pleased with the way Becca attached herself to the dog, taking it everywhere with her. She saw the girl's pleasure in the nuzzling offered in return. Tonsils was even allowed into classrooms, and sat at Becca's feet at the dining table in Thatch. She let no one else feed the dog. Table scraps could only be offered from her own hand.

It was judged a success. There was a thaw in Becca, and gushy mother talk. "Tonyonyonyonsilitis." Dog and mistress squealed with devotion. She brought Tonsils right into the Director's office at chore time; the dog's tail going ninety to the minute, so excited she forgot herself, dropped into a squat, and did a quick, nervous squirt on the floor. Becca rushed through her duties, promising Eula the rug would dry, but now she had to get back to Thatch because her sister was coming home any moment, and she and Tonsils must be there in the room to greet her.

Julia Crane watched it all. So did Erica, who pushed through the door of the twins' room following Linny. Becca was on her bunk, cuddling with the surprise for her sister. Tonsils jumped down and started eagerly across the floor as if she'd forgotten whom she'd been next to on the bed, tail beating again with happiness at a sudden reunion.

Julia said the dog stopped in its tracks as if someone had jerked back on her collar. Her hair stood up on her neck. She began to whine, and the whining rose to a painful pitch as she turned and started back toward the bunk. "Here," Linny coaxed, holding out her hand. Tonsils turned again, lowered her head, and began to growl at the newcomer. Then whirled back again in doubt, and snarled at Becca on the bed. She, too, called softly to the dog, and held out her hand. Tonsils lunged at her and bit hard.

Becca stood up, trying to escape, but Tonsils lunged again and bit her leg, breaking the skin, then snapped higher and closed her jaws on Becca's arm. Here Julia's account differed slightly from Erica's. Each reported a different sister kicking at the dog, trying to force it toward the door and into the hall. At this point Linny, too, was bitten. Tonsils had hold of her arm, and as she shook herself free the teeth left a cut from forearm to wrist.

The four of them were finally able to push the dog into the hall. Julia's thought was to protect the rest of her children, to get Tonsils downstairs and outside the cottage. She went for Mr. Henry's help, but couldn't find him. Returning a few minutes later with Nurse Jean to treat the girls' wounds, she found them lying together on the bed soaked with blood. They were moaning softly, sucking each others' thumbs.

Nurse Jean poured most of a bottle of iodine on the wounds, wrapping them with gauze and adhesive. There were punctures and long lines of broken skin with several places that would need stitching. The girls fought like little tigers against tetanus inoculations. Meanwhile Tonsils was splayed in the hallway outside the twins' door, whimpering in shame. After wandering the campus, she had found her way back into the cottage, back to the scene of her confusion.

Mr. Henry took the dog back to the city pound in the station wagon and the twins took refuge in their room. They pasted a sign to their door: "Do Not Enter. This Means You." More worrisome than this childish regression, they had found the forbidden room keys in the bureau in the front hall, and locked their door from the inside. Pleas to come out were met with silence. Eula was sent for, but was smart enough not to risk her authority in a confrontation she was likely to lose. She left the problem to Mother Crane and the children of Thatch.

When sweet talk failed, Mother Crane thought of moving them with music, then prose. There were eager volunteers: by turns, Jennie Alexie pounding away on the piano in the parlor beneath their room, Susan Bailey reading earnestly from *The Pilgrim's Progress* outside their door, and Erica Cochran beating a tattoo on their wall from her

adjacent quarters. Far from soothing, it was a triple torture, and they screamed once for silence, but still wouldn't show their faces.

Suppertime passed. Mother Crane shooed the curious children from the hall and stood outside the twins' door herself, waiting silently for some sign of activity. She could make out whispering and then they were talking as if they didn't care who might hear.

"They took your dog away."

"My dog?"

"You had all the time with it."

"It liked me."

"It didn't like us."

"Nothing likes us. They only like one of us. And they don't know which, because it doesn't matter."

"Maybe if Tonsils had met us both at the same time."

"No, Miss Rice met us both at the same time. All of them did."

"We have to go somewhere."

"Miss Kieland believes us. She says she does."

"Do you believe her?"

"No."

"Why should they believe us anyway?"

One of them went into a fit of giggles, then the other, and both together, until they lost control, and reached such a pitch that Mother Crane could not be sure whether she was hearing a shriek of joy or scream of distress. It was enough to bring the other children back into the hall. The twins unlocked their door, and Mother Crane had to step back and pretend she was just arriving on the scene.

∽

That week Beverly Rice chalked on her blackboard, "IF WE TEASE ANIMALS IN JEST, THEY MAY REPAY US IN TEMPER."

There were frightened discussions among the girls about an overheard edict: "The animal will be destroyed." The scar on Linny's arm could be useful in identification, but only in the hottest days of summer as it turned out. For the rest of the year the twins had matching long-sleeved jerseys.

Eula told the assembled children that Tonsils had been taken to the pound. They knew what would be done to her there. The twins didn't want to see the dog again, and they didn't want another. Once Tonsils was turned over to the Animal Control with the report of the attack, her fate was out of their hands. The twins hadn't really recovered from their shock, only ignored it long enough to get to sleep that first night. For the first time they cried in front of Eula. What was going to happen to them if not even a dog could tell them apart?

"Aren't there times when you try to be exactly alike?" she asked.

"No!" they moaned together.

Eula was still learning just how tangled they were, though they might imagine themselves as different as circle and square. It took a few weeks before they stopped having dreams of dogs coming after them. They were frightened now, and trying to break the habit of imitation. There were times when they just couldn't help it. One of them told her, "Sometimes I can't remember which one of us is me."

∞

In 1930, the Drayton girls were still sheltered from the worst of the country's economic trouble. The twins were only fourteen but as socially sophisticated and physically mature as some of the departing seniors. Four more years with them stretched ahead, daunting. As they cleaned her office one afternoon, Eula heard Linny warn Becca against one of the boys coming to the Winter Dance.

"I don't want you pushing up against him."

Linny looked to see if the Director was listening.

Becca asked, "What about your . . . "

"Shut up!" Linny said.

". . . about your Grayson?"

This was a young man who had caught their attention in the village, and had since begun to hang around the edges of the Drayton estate, keeping an eye on the orphanage, and on the twins. There were others like him, young men fascinated by the elegant village of unfortunates. Men who had fallen out of work, and saw the Drayton girls and their chaperones prospering with full kitchens out of their

reach in the fine stone cottages. Orphans living better than they were. Girls, some of them reaching womanhood, with consciences to be pricked for favors from their pantries. Young men with fantasies, pure or unbecoming, sitting in the Drayton woods, playing cards on blankets, and maybe thinking of the young ladies who might bring apples, oranges, or sympathy. A reciprocity for the reversal of fortunes.

The girls referred to these men who crept around the edges of their campus as newts. Not parlor lizards as they might have been known in better economic times, but "wood newts," as easy to spot in their fraying suits as the orange lizards on the forest floor. In fact, Becca called this boy Grayson "a newt."

Eula made it clear that such a man would not be welcome at the dance. Anyway, he'd be too old for them. He'd be turned away at the door, she said. When the special evening arrived the Careys were up to their old mischief, appearing and disappearing from the hungry hold of the confused young men. One or the other. With all their trading of shawls and hairpieces, and retreats into the ladies' room, neither let the other overplay a flirtation.

The week after the dance, Beverly Rice was teaching her class about equations with two unknowns. Linny leaned over to Becca, and whispered, "She means us."

Her sister's answering giggle turned heads, and set Beverly off: "Go to the board, Becca . . . no, you!"

Miss Rice came down the aisle, eyes boring in on the other, on Linny.

"Yes, you!"

And Linny rose to follow the order.

"Now you can share with us what you were saying to your sister . . . go ahead, write it on the blackboard . . . well, go ahead."

Linny picked up the chalk and slashed at the slate, all in straight lines, the first thing that came to mind: I HATE IODYNE.

"Yes, I should think you would after your experience. But it's D I N E."

On the way back to her seat, Linny called back over her shoulder, "You spell it your way if you like."

Miss Rice came rushing across the room, grabbed the girl's arm, and pulled her into the hall. Linny let loose a long stream of strange words as the teacher slammed the door behind them. The children could hear her yelling in the hallway:

"Drop your tunic!

"Unbutton your blouse!

"Take it off, I said."

A moment later they heard her say, "It's you, is it? I should have known!"

She had forgotten which name went with the cherry, and which without. By that time Becca had joined them in the hall, and was helping her sister into her shirtwaist. Beverly ordered them straight to their room in Thatch. Too angry to see what trouble she had made for herself, she shut her classroom door in their faces.

Instead of reporting to Mother Crane in Thatch, the twins went straight to Eula. Linny was in tears again. She said Miss Rice had made her get naked in Schoolhouse. Becca was crying too. She said they wanted to be sent somewhere else; they didn't care where. That wasn't going to happen. Becca dried her eyes, and looked right past the Director with a bitter promise: "We're going as far from here as a dollar sends a postcard!"

A week later they were picked up carrying their satchels down Bethlehem Pike after dark. And it wasn't too long after that they took a cross-county bus and a hike of several miles to St. David's, familiar to them as the scene of their aunt's religious ecstasies, and from there, the local train into the Thirtieth Street Station, where they were intercepted, ticketless, boarding a parlor car destined for Washington, D.C. They'd been approached by a man who said he'd give them work at a house in Philadelphia; they could even live there.

The second escape began with the theft of several dollars from Eula's office. They confessed before she knew the money was missing, hoping the crime would be enough to have them sent away. Again, they were disappointed. If they were going somewhere better, they had no idea where it might be. She thought they were surprisingly willing to toy with the heartlessness of the world beyond their campus.

In the Fall of 1930 Tess Croft arranged for Eula to address an annual symposium of social workers in Philadelphia. Eula knew the Careys, in their office chores, had once again been looking at the mail on her desk because they accused her though it exposed them as office spies: "You're going to talk about us."

It was true. Tess expected her to speak about her experience with the twins. And Otto Rank, too, wanting to hear more about alter egos and doubles, hoped she would describe the Careys' case. Caught off guard, Eula momentarily lost her temper. If the twins ever read her mail again, she said, they'd be removed from their office duty to less pleasant chores.

They gave her a couple of smirking "yes ma'ams," and a quick exit. Admiring their courage, she said no more about it. They pushed to the edge of her tolerance. But their fine features, their confidence, even their erect carriage when they weren't putting on the slouch, were like her own. She knew these had contributed to her successful and independent way in the world, and why shouldn't they be an equal advantage to the gifted twins?

Let vanity take its honest place here, she thought. Kerstin would sometimes do a mock swoon when she caught Eula uncovered in the cottage they shared, but the Director didn't look in mirrors. And she didn't brush her hair with a hundred strokes as Mother Crane taught her girls. She *was* aware of the sturdy and well-chiseled figure she made for any audience.

Recalling Eula's childhood, her sister drew a different picture than the city journalist had. She told a later biographer, "Eula was a like a boy angel, tall and athletic with bright blue eyes and golden curls." The curls were gone, and the gold. Now she was more a template for St. Gaudens than for Gibson, more monument than fashion plate, but for her purposes looks were only another kind of rhetoric, useful aesthetic trim to help carry a worthy argument. She imagined herself more cunning than vain in front of the audience Tess was gathering for her.

When the night came she had nothing to say about twins. Her people were in the front row—Tess, Kerstin, and a few of her teach-

ers. Cyril Johnson placed himself discreetly several rows back. He made a little wave as he sat down, a gesture that it seemed awkward to return. The rest of the crowd, she assumed, were also disposed to like her. There was a delegation from the Bank Street School in Manhattan with no leader, but a dozen questions. They had been asked to probe Eula on the advisability of psychoanalysis for everyone.

She had a fame in this audience as the outspoken woman who ran the Philadelphia area's most progressive orphanage. They didn't know she was in a trough of self-doubt that month, thinking of retreat, almost ready to concede that America did not want a progressive educator, or any kind of holistic wisdom. What use was her local model if she couldn't even convince the Flourtown schools to cross her threshold? She had offered to share her classrooms and teachers with them. In return, she proposed they share theirs with Drayton, and at a good saving to the public. But no, they would allow the orphans into their schools only at a price per pupil. And they balked at the Drayton doorstep. All right for the community's young boys to be sent to Drayton's dances, or for their slower children to take part informally in the orphanage summer school. But come Fall, they would not enter the Schoolhouse. No "college" to them, but a home of unfortunates, children of awkward provenance.

Otto Rank, sitting beside Eula on the dais, made the introduction. As he spoke the reading lamp had caught the red and crystalline translucence of the mysterious ring that rose and fell as his finger tapped the podium in a slow and calming rhythm, a pulse, it seemed, for Eula. He began with a line of his favorite American, Samuel Clemens, about a boy who returned home from college to discover how much his father had learned in the last four years. She laughed with the rest, grateful that Rank wasted little time on her résumé. He had told her to think of public speaking as an offering, a gift, not as a badge of wisdom or a sleeve of rank. If the subject was not herself, but her warm message, she'd have no cause to flutter or stumble, anticipating someone's poor opinion. She rose in perfect composure and began: "Progressivism in America is all but dead."

Even, she said, at its paradigm institution, Drayton College. She destroyed the Gothic monument that was Drayton, knocked it all the way back into its birthing quarry of Wissahickon schist. Then, slowly, she began to rebuild it into a village of frame houses for children who would be taught what lay behind the walls that sheltered them, the framing, pipes, and wiring that supported, cleansed, and lit their lives; and a schoolhouse where the community was not ashamed to enter or learn the trades that went back and back as far as the mythologies that informed their manners and morals. An educational system in which no doors were closed.

"Until one day everyone understands that school is life."

She repeated the lesson she'd written on the "Slate" in Schoolhouse: Children are not bits of clay to be molded into shape, but plants that must be allowed to blossom in their own symmetry.

There was clapping, even a voice calling, "Well done!" Behind her, Mr. Rank smiled in admiration. She turned back to the room and the applause seemed to swell. Cyril seized the moment to rise and continue clapping, until he was standing and applauding alone.

The Bank Street group had questions with little or nothing to do with her talk. She brushed them aside as politely as she could, and was stepping down from the dais when a lady in the back of the room called to her—someone in a dark suit and one of those inverted-bowl hats, with a feather on each side, and a veil. Eula could imagine the woman walking a poodle in Rittenhouse Square, though the twin feathers were something like a beetle's antennae.

"I don't understand," the woman said. "If one doesn't believe in the institution she directs, isn't it her duty to resign?"

The reedy voice of Renee Drayton.

"I believe especially in our potential, Miss Drayton," she replied, identifying Renee for the group as one of the trustees. "That's not to say we're useless as an orphanage. Rather that we're in danger of being a very ordinary one."

A man next to Renee, someone she must have primed, stood and asked if the Director realized the one who introduced her had writ-

ten his own ten commandments. And did she know that the first of these was "Thou shall have no God"?

"Sir," she answered, "if Mr. Rank wrote that, I'm sure he was writing symbolically. He believes that we should all be less dogmatic in our ideologies, a good deal less sure of our own inventions . . . "

Not mollified, the man would not sit: "Miss Kieland, aren't you taking therapy, or instruction, if you prefer, from this man yourself?"

People began to shout at him. Someone told him to sit down. Rank, distressed by the embarrassment he had caused her, was trying to get Eula's attention.

Neither her endorsement of him nor his apology could be heard in the room because the man was on the attack again, with no regard for the pain he might be causing.

"Miss Kieland, do you believe in mixing of the races?"

"I believe . . . "

"Because you have two colored children in your care right now."

He set his jaw at a challenging upward tilt.

"Sir," she said, "is your argument with atheism or racial integration? What is your point? Why are you here?"

The hall was alive with indignation. Tess Croft didn't want this going any further. She turned on the man and called him a provocateur, which only made him bolder: "I think you've known it for a long time, Miss Kieland. Didn't you know it when you accepted your twin Negroes?"

They discovered later this was an attorney Renee had hired to discredit Eula, as a first step to shutting the orphanage down. His performance was all in support of a motion he was preparing for the board, and papers he was presenting to the court. He was calling for an investigation of the whole operation.

"Do these people know," he asked, "that your orphanage punishes the colored children by having them undress in the halls?"

And he had the last word: "You're in violation of your charter, Miss Kieland, and you know it very well."

His charges were reported in two city papers. Never mind what happened to the Careys, Renee meant to have the world know they were colored, by whatever fraction of blood.

"Why did you let Miss Rice leave?" Linny asked, passing a dust rag over Eula's desk, while her sister ran the carpet sweeper back and forth over the same strip of floor, making her work last longer, not wanting to miss Eula's answer.

"What do you mean? Watch what you're doing, Linny. You're not paying attention."

"I mustn't look at your papers. We heard Mother Crane say you let her go."

"If you're finished, Becca, why don't you run on back to Thatch? See if Miss Crane would like you to help her with anything. I'd like to talk to Linny alone for a while."

Becca went out, and Eula had Linny sit down in front of her.

"Becca," Eula called. "You're still outside the door."

A moment later, they heard Becca shuffle away down the hall.

The other children had no idea the informality the Director allowed from these two. Nor did her staff. And the twins were clever enough not to show off the familiarity in front of others. They took secret pride in the attention she paid them when they were in her office, however much they complained about it. In front of her they might behave like birthright children, sometimes sassy, sometimes obedient. When questioned boldly, they answered boldly. Eula wasn't used to children who could stare her down, and they'd do it, too, if she gave them a chance.

"Linny," she said, "what did your Aunt Gwen tell you about your family?"

Linny set one arm akimbo, and thrust her hip like an insulted barmaid.

"She said we made our mother and daddy sick, and they died and we didn't, and too bad it wasn't the other way around."

"But you know that's not true, don't you?"

"It might be true if we got sick first and it made them sick."

"What about your grandparents?"

"They came to see us Christmastime. All but the one who shamed the family. She wasn't allowed in Aunt Gwen's house. And she didn't care to come in anyway. She always stayed home. You fired Miss Rice, didn't you?"

"I don't think Miss Rice was happy here."

"I think she was angry."

"Why, do you suppose?"

"Because we're always fooling?"

"Is that what it is?"

"That's what it is."

"Why do you like to fool?"

"I *don't* like to."

"Does your sister make you do it?"

"She doesn't like to either. We don't decide. It just happens."

"You can't stop it?"

"I guess not," she said.

"Do you want to stop?"

"I think so."

"Well, that's something."

Linny finished her work and went back to join her sister in Thatch.

∞

Eula's meetings with Cyril Johnson continued that winter. She wasn't sure why, except that her thought was to be considerate of his feelings, and do nothing to jeopardize his supporting vote on the board. At dinner, the standard steamship round was usually her choice, rather than some sort of curried delicacy. This always seemed to please him.

"I like a hearty appetite," he'd say with a wink, as if her secret was safe with him, and maybe wondering if she wasn't a woman who was going to spread a little before her time. He ordered the meal for them, then asked what wine she'd like. There was a choice of three at

his club, each known not by its vineyard but its color—red, white, or pink—though he made a regular continental fuss over the choice. There was just no denying he was a bit of an ass.

The wine would come. Her glass would be filled, and as the meal progressed she'd drink maybe half of that while Cyril slowly inebriated himself on the rest of the bottle. Appetizer, entree, desert, coffee, course by course his hand came creeping across the table until at last, fortified by a final gulp of wine, it made the fearful little leap onto hers. There was a tilt of his head as his eyes searched for a sign of communion. Besotted, you might say, though not really with her. More the wine and his loopy euphoria with the world as it was. She was a little cruel in the way she broke the spell.

"It's late, Cyril. We haven't talked about the severance we're giving Beverly Rice, or Renee's proposal for board oversight of admissions, or the Flourtown student fees, or the investments."

"Well, Eula, someday we'll have to turn these little business dinners of ours into a picnic lunch by the river," a hope lurching out of nowhere toward a romance that he didn't dare suggest.

She did her best to describe these sessions to Otto Rank. She was calling him Otto by then. She was hoping he'd see practicality and sensitivity; that is to say, maybe he'd find her blameless in her behavior with Cyril. He didn't. He made it clear that her request for approval was proof enough that something was out of balance.

A critical Mr. Henry would sit waiting for her in the station wagon outside, and she'd make an excuse to Cyril about not wanting to keep her driver out too late. Cyril had a house on Garden Street, in walking distance of his club. He was forever reminding Eula of its convenience, and at last gathered courage to suggest that they take coffee there after a meal.

"That wouldn't be appropriate," she told him.

When Otto called that "prissy," she was puzzled.

"You mean I should have accepted?"

"There'd be nothing inappropriate about it. You could have just said what you meant. Perhaps you'd miss his flattery if it suddenly disappeared?"

An odious presumption, but why was she being so coy with Cyril? The next week she told him there could be no more dinners at his club; she felt guilty about the money and attention he'd already spent on her. After a moment of embarrassment, Cyril became quite spirited, actually relieved. It became clear that for several months he'd been carrying on this halfhearted suit as a gentlemanly obligation, a gallantry. Eula nursed her vanity as he blossomed, in one evening, into an interesting companion, joking and laughing away the hour, and revealing himself a scholar of Mr. Wilde's tragicomic life and wit, a risky passion for a man in Cyril's society.

Motoring back along the Schuylkill she fell into a depression, a reckoning with the vanity of the sister Otto had already identified as her sorry, second self, her double, and with the problem facing Drayton—the economic tragedy of the nation now settling over her once secure village of stone. She was repeating "the price of everything and the value of nothing," to herself, transferring its burden of shame back and forth between her own shoulders and Renee Drayton's. Renee was the one who quibbled over Beverly's hiring and now over her severance. The one who, behind the scene, and in her cousins' names, filed to have the orphanage charter revoked for violating the admissions policy and, by her sly rectitude, changed the beautiful gypsy copper of Eula's twins to a despised and legally certain black.

"The price of everything, the value of nothing." She must have said it out loud because Mr. Henry looked back, over his shoulder, and said, "It's the truth, Miss Kieland, the prices are beyond all common sense."

In 1929 the financial collapse had only been a cautionary tale for the orphanage girls—a story of greed and its consequence in a distant city, where men had fallen to the pavement from tall buildings. It had to be explained to the younger ones, that *crash* did not mean worlds had collided. Behind the shame of it all, the housemothers taught there was a certain justice, though now it came clear that the shame was also their own. Till then Drayton had held steady and was poised to grow. The girls ate heartily, gardened, gathered eggs, swam, skated, studied, sewed, wove, cooked, and ran the press.

In 1930 their first graduating class of eighteen-year-olds was sent—far too young Eula thought—into the world. There was precious little opportunity for them, and too many, she saw, were taken into domestic service as nannies, maids, and cooks by families still wealthy after the crash. She despised the line she'd first heard in Flourtown and now heard repeated in Chestnut Hill: "Oh, their girls are very clean." She took heart from the two guided by Kerstin into nursing school in the city, and one who was sent to a new teachers' college in Georgia.

There was bad news, late arriving. The Drayton income fell sharply. The building program stopped. The enrollment dwindled with the attrition of the graduates. Eula closed the upper classrooms and sent the older girls to the Flourtown High School. For a time, no one could explain what had happened to all the secure investments. Cyril was confused by the Drayton portfolio, and not the best one to challenge the financial counselor. The trustees had deferred to the broker's experience, all except Renee Drayton, who had manipulated the man.

By then Eula's alarmist talk was no exaggeration. They *were* in danger of becoming a very ordinary orphanage. And she was falling into despair. She could call Mr. Rank, Otto now, but her therapy with him was finished. Instead of liberation, her alleged recovery seemed to chain her to loss. She wasn't thinking of the several men she had thrown over since her university years while she pursued this ideal that now looked so vain, but the loss of Otto as her weekly confidant and counselor. First she'd been addicted to his counseling; now she was devoted to *him*. Though there'd been only a series of hour sessions, he was a preoccupation almost as constant as the twins. She missed him as much as she'd miss Kerstin if her housemate were to pack up and leave.

Eula wanted to make another confession, to tell Otto she'd been no more honest with Kerstin than with Cyril. Kerstin, who deserved complete candor; Kerstin, who was coming up in the world in spite of herself, and her rustic imperative that required a vegetable garden and the time to tend it. And even now, in winter, a daily retreat from

the city, where she had just been made the director of a national nursing organization, and a retreat each night to stars, and country silence. Not exactly silence; there was the occasional engine of a jitney plying Bethlehem Pike, reminding Eula that their diminished haven was bound to the city and the anxious dreams of a larger economic despair.

The two of them were still aware of a nosy scrutiny of their lives. They were annoyed by speculation about what happened after dark in the household of two professional women. Bothered by the curiosity itself, and the attendant innuendo, even that of the well-meaning. There was that edge of ambiguity in a voice that pronounced their two names in a single breath.

Though her "terapy" sessions were over, Otto still warned her against wasteful worrying, sensing her shame in sensuality, and giving license to the possibilities in her singularity. She knew a closer friendship with the provocative Otto might be a liability, but if a woman of Tess Croft's reputation could endorse him and thrive in his company, who was Eula to deny support? It wasn't true that he believed in free love as his enemies charged.

"Free love leads to syphilis," he told Eula. His own marriage was full of tensions, he confessed to her. One of his woman patients told him that sexual experimenting generally leads back to monogamy. "Yes," he mused, "but unfortunately most of us do our experimenting after marriage."

My God! Eula thought, he's confessing his adulteries to me! Not as a provocation, but out of plain honesty. And with risk to his professional standing, which was already under attack by the school of psychoanalyst sharks circling Manhattan, and patrolling the lines of communication across the Atlantic against his return to Europe.

In private Eula was affectionate with Kerstin. If one of them was exhausted with work and worry or down with a cold, the other might come to give comfort before sleep, to bring hot lemon water to the bedside, and hold a hand, or rub a back, or read a few lines from the

teacher-poet from New Hampshire who had caught Kerstin's attention with the iambic heartbeat of his verse, linking natural phenomena to human truths, the poet she'd tried to imitate on the "Drayton Slate."

If there was ever an inclination on Kerstin's part to leave off with a back rub and climb into bed beside Eula, she never offered the first squeak of longing. They had never pledged themselves to this companionship, though Eula thought Kerstin might have begun to take it for granted, that after five years of sharing quarters they would always live together.

Was it only humility, she wanted to ask Otto, a reasonable humility that kept her silent in her belief that she was still intended for a conventional marriage? Approaching forty, she still believed she could accept the proper man, though she'd been off the romantic field for years. She wanted Otto to affirm that the delay was admirable, if not the silence about her prospects. Kerstin was anxious about Eula's growing reliance on his judgment and even more with their shared preoccupation with the twins, but still able to cloak her anxiety in humor.

"You're one of his terrapins, aren't you, Mummy?"

If the world could see all the way into her heart, if it knew the names of the three people whose trust and admiration Eula most desired, and what she might have done to ensure their regard, she might have been out of a job. Two of them were immature children, and the third, a married man who had once professed that the trauma of birth was the controlling event in a human life. Linda Carey, Rebecca Carey, and Otto Rank, those three. They were the family she coveted. An impossible confession for the Director of an orphanage.

Otto she could trust completely, and beyond, to the nth degree of awkward honesty. With the twins, her trust had never been totally free of doubt. She was never sure of their sincerity, not even when they looked her in the eye, and spoke with all the guileless timbre their voices could convey. Perhaps that's why she lingered under her open window at midday while they were at their chores in her office, listening:

"You shouldn't be reading that, Becca. What does it say?"

"None of our business. It's about the milk orders."

"What about them?"

"Never mind. They're sorry about the noise in the morning. The horses will be replaced with motor vans later this year, and that should make the delivery quieter."

"So? What else?"

Becca began to read: "We regret the girls are complaining of the flavor. This is the season for onion grass, which cannot be eradicated without general damage to the pastures. The slight taint will soon be past."

"No. What other letters?"

"They're not open. One's from Miss Croft."

"Lossy."

If they were snooping again, so was Eula, bending down to examine the snowdrops of a false Spring, pretending absorption with the flowers, pulling a weed or two, very pleased to hear her name and "guster" uttered in the same breath. They were moving around her office again, and Eula stayed put, waiting for more. They didn't name each other, and she couldn't be sure which of them was speaking:

"If she dripped on the seat again, I'll clean the bathroom. If she didn't, you clean it."

Eula could hear them fussing with each other, opening the door to the little washroom connected to her office.

"You clean it!"

"No, there's nothing there."

"Yes, look."

"Just a drop. It's not even pee."

"Yes, it is. A drop counts."

"I'm not mopping the floor."

"Yes you are, that's part of it."

"Do you like Grayson?"

"He's much too old."

"But you like him."

They were coming out of the bathroom, into the office again.

"Do you think she's read all these?"

"No. People like her have a lot of books. They don't read all of them.

"It's creeps when Miss Lambert calls her 'Mummy.'"

"She doesn't mean her Mummy. She means our Mummy."

"But sometimes you can't tell, can you?"

"That's why they talk to Mr. Rank. That's what he's a doctor for."

"Guster."

"Yeah."

Later that Spring the twins in their daily visits to her office were aware of something wrong with Miss Kieland. Their eyes flicked suspiciously here and there. They heard a slight hesitancy in her voice. If she lost control, who would brake their own descent, their further fall into double mischief? Julia Crane was really no match for them. They didn't intend meanness. They couldn't help themselves: "It must have been my sister."

Maybe encouraged by Tess Croft, Otto sent Eula a note. She turned the envelope at several angles, looking for a design in the sealing. There was nothing but a careless splash of blue wax. Inside:

> Since you ask, by now your twins should have developed their own hairstyles, clothes, etc. By normal pattern they should be highly critical of each other's choice of friends, most especially friends of opposite sex. They should be doing things to test the limit of your patience.

The letter reestablished that her therapy had been mainly successful. He would help her with whatever children's cases might need outside perspective, no therapy, just advice. She was not to worry about the cost. If a fee should be necessary, again Tess wished to provide it as part of the retainer he received for counseling the adult students in Tessie's School of Social Work. He was still fascinated by her twins and wanted regular reports on their development.

The race story spread from the back pages of the city paper into their little conference room. It was not on any staff-meeting agenda, but Mother Crane got to the point, innocently enough, at the first opportunity.

"What is this about the twins? Is it true? What am I supposed to say if they ask me about it?"

Suddenly the room was full of experts on color.

"You tell them to look in the mirror," Mother Laura said, "and ask themselves what they see." For her, this was a rhetorical question whose only answer could be "white."

Mother Greene offered, "They have such lovely skin, don't they? Surely it's not colored."

Eula looked around her, dismayed.

"What is it then?"

"But, I mean, it's not quite white, is it? I couldn't honestly say . . . "

"I live with them," Julia interrupted, "I see them every day, dressed and undressed, and I can assure you they're no darker than a healthy tan." As if this testimonial—motherly largesse for two prodigals—was all the protective cover they should need.

Ellen Reilly, more thoughtful, and perhaps the most cheerfully honest of the housemothers, and so outspoken against her children's indulgence in vicarious satisfactions, raised both of her hands, and her voice: "Ladies! We're not in a paint store! We're not looking at a color chart. We're not matching tints to please us just so."

She was saving Eula from saying, "Of course this is a community of Caucasian children. It is by charter. The question is not the perceived hue of the Carey girls. The question is whether we can or should protect them from this labeling of their skin, from some mindless legal settlement on their bloodline."

"Can or *should*?" Mother Crane asked. "I would say surely we should."

Eula, too, thought this was a foregone conclusion, their clear duty to save the twins from the prejudice of the world beyond their campus.

Mother Reilly was the one troubled by the coming consequences of the denial.

∞

The Drayton income fell from a hundred and eighty-five thousand to thirty-five thousand. Too late they were learning that Renee Drayton had directed their funds into bad mortgages in which she had a personal interest. Liquidation and partial restitution brought only thirty cents on the dollar. Eula's hopes for a twelve-year community school had evaporated. Her juniors and seniors had already been sent into the public system, and now the next two grades were going as well.

The only benefit of their financial decline was Renee's resignation from the board. Forced to stop her legal action against the orphanage, her retreat seemed to promise a silence about the Careys' color as well. Erica Cochran, who with so many others had ceded the twins an unrequited respect, may have sensed the issue fading away. She was as close to them as any in the orphanage, though seldom allowed in their room. She couldn't resist the temptation to stir the pot.

There had been conversations among girls in all the cottages about the Negroes in their midst and their telepathic witchery too fascinating to go away. One morning at the breakfast table Erica asked the twins point-blank in front of all their housemates, "Are you colored?"

Linny answered, "You're blind, aren't you? If you weren't a blind fool you could see for yourself."

"Erica!" Mother Crane stopped them. "What a question! Why would you ask such a thing?"

But Erica went on with it: "I didn't think you were, Linny, because colored aren't allowed here."

"So why ask us?"

"That's enough," they were told. "Get ready for your classes."

Erica kept on: "Well I'm sorry, but I heard Miss Greene say a woman was trying to prove it, and you could be sent off somewhere else."

"Well, good," Becca told her.

"No," Erica said. "If you go, I want to go, too."

"Well you can't."

"I told them, 'You know the house rule about unkind gossip,'" Mother Crane explained to Eula. There were two days of extra duty in the kitchen for Erica. She didn't whine about it. She wanted the punishment, wanted to be seen by the twins paying for what she'd done.

∞

"Wait long enough," Otto assured Eula, "and it will happen. All the trickery will be finished. And they'll never be the same."

She was soon marveling at his prescience. First, there was Becca's brand, the cherry-shaped and cherry-colored birthmark, whose stem rose from the little fruit on her left breast, up to her clavicle. To show it or hide it was simply a matter of the cut or styling of a blouse. With reasonable modesty she could display the stem of the mark and be once and forever Becca. In the past she had chosen to hide this under shirtwaists buttoned all the way up, or tunics that fit to her neck. No longer.

Then the twins stopped wearing any of each other's clothes, even made a fuss if their socks got mixed up in the laundry. And they no longer came to do their daily chores in the Director's office at the same time. Eula thought maybe after her chat with Linny about Beverly Rice, the twins had decided that she might confide more to them individually than as a pair.

Again, they were watching Eula in a way that suggested a concern with *her* welfare and the well-being of the rest of Drayton. Linny was relaxing the pose of distance, and Becca had been persuaded she should walk a separate path from her sister. They claimed to be sorry for what had happened to Beverly Rice, and the first step to an apology was to renounce, once and for all, the habit of deception. Julia Crane came to Eula jubilant, reporting another step in their separation.

"It's happened!" she said. "They've asked for separate rooms." Becca would share the upper front with Jodie Shiflett, who was two years younger. No longer troubled with rashes; now the only thing bothering Jodie was her beetle dreams. Julia couldn't get it out fast enough: "Erica Cochran made a full apology, begging on her knees.

Can you imagine it, Eula? 'You're no more colored than I am,' she said. She's moving in with Linny. It's done!"

"And what else?" Julia said. "They'll try not to use their own bad words. I doubt they'll hold themselves to that. The thing is, you wouldn't even think they were friends anymore, much less sisters. They're pretending they don't even know each other."

The following noon Becca came to Eula's office before her sister, furious about something. She refused her usual lemonade. When asked to dust the bookshelves, she made a perfunctory pass with her rag, and plopped down in a chair.

"Is that all?" she said, glaring.

Eula didn't know which was worse. This, or Kerstin's "You asked for it, Mummy," that evening. There had been no turning back. After motherly concern in the details of their lives, she would not be the cold authoritarian, though she did say, "Sit up straight, Becca. Tell me what's the matter."

"Why don't you ask my stupid sister?"

"You're going on fifteen," she said. "Aren't you ashamed of yourself?"

"I'm not ashamed of who *I* am," she said.

"Who *are* you?" Eula asked her.

"You should know."

Enough.

On her way out she walked right into her sister, who had been listening at the door. They bumped into each other hard, purposefully, and passed on without apology.

Linny went right to work pretending nothing unusual had happened. She was moving quickly and efficiently around the office, as if she enjoyed each task she set for herself. She made a show of elbow grease, putting excessive energy into the light work. Her replies were curt—"Nothing," "Yeah," and "No."

Eula had to beg her to take a rest.

"What did my sister tell you?" she asked at last.

"Not much of anything. Not much more than you're telling me."

"She told you something, I heard her."

There was nothing to tell her. She sent Linny back to her cottage.

Eula wanted to report all of it to Otto. There had been a month when he was unable to see or even talk to her, maybe afraid she'd try once more to rekindle his interest in her own therapy. He'd been so pleased when she agreed to deal with her own double, and to separate her problems from those of her children. The rest he said was up to her. She had to take off her masks.

She had gone to him originally just as Tess herself had, full of skepticism, ready to do battle with the modern therapeutic jargon. There was no jargon. He robbed her of an enemy, asking her to accept the existence of a dark sister. Confessing to an acquaintance with this other self was the main thing. If she got that far, he thought, she would eventually be able to will her recovery from her depression. And she would begin to understand the Careys' use of each other as behavior that was often beyond their control.

It was a lot to ask, but she'd said, "Yes, I see her, she exists."

For her it was like religious faith, maybe professed, but in the inner heart, in doubt. In what way was she really separate from the second self he wanted her to shake hands with? Was there a useful distinction to be made between Eula, and Eula in a bad mood? Was it just as logical to say that for every degree of dishonesty or hypocrisy she recognized in herself, she must name a separate sister, another alter ego? There could be dozens of her. The one who told the white lies, for example. The one who deceived gentlemen, the one who deceived ladies. A dozen for all the vanities of her career. One for the woman who hired and fired Beverly Rice. One for the high-handed goddess who balanced the Drayton scales of justice, and took it on herself to destroy the Careys' racial history.

She tried again to contact Otto, but he was away for two more weeks, gone to Boston this time. Before the details could slip her memory, she wrote to explain the new Carey drama:

This is not about me.

Our twins have split apart! And hooray, you may say. But we never expected such venom.

I've told you about our Saturday socials with the Flourtown boys. And a motley lot they are, from swells in the fanciest knickers and straw boaters, to a milk-wagon boy in thread-bare secondhands, and goody for democracy.

The twins, I believe, had decided on a strategic break with each other before the event. It was something we all admired. Becca is making a daily display of her birthmark. There's been a complete separation of wardrobes. And they've moved into different rooms. All pretty much as you predicted, and we assume it began with their recognition of the dangerous path they were on.

All very well, except that the separation has become a war. Their last time in front of me, Linny lapsed into the private language again, and called her sister "groose goosh." A wet movement, in case you've forgotten the translation. I pretended not to understand.

The night of the social arrived with high anxiety. I had talked Kerstin into bringing a gentleman, a Dr. Tupperman from her clinic, to join us as an extra chaperone for the evening. By the way, Kerstin wrote that poem about the twins from things that came from your talks with me. Her poetic vanity got the better of her good judgment. She's very ashamed, and not just for the quality of the verse.

Sorry. At the social I meant to have Kerstin keep a closer eye on the halls and the ladies' room, too. At the last dance there was a lip rouge passed around and some of our girls painted themselves like regular trollops. The twins used one of the bathroom stalls for their endless changeovers, but not this time.

Linny was wearing a remarkable dress of her own design, with beautiful fluting, and the piping sewn without a flaw. Remember, she's just gotten on to fifteen, and this was finer work than anything from our handiest seniors. You'd have thought she'd been fitted for the garment by a professional couturier. The other girls made a terrific fuss over her.

There was a row at the door. One of the layabouts from our woods, much too old for our girls, claimed to be there as the Careys' escort. Several of the younger village boys helped turn him out. Meanwhile I was keeping a lookout for Becca, thinking she'd have

difficulty matching Linny's gown. The boys were shifting nervously on the side, waiting for the signal to choose partners. Our musicians, the couple who run the school laundry, play the accordion and fiddle, and act as dance instructors, were warming up. And still no Becca.

"Don't worry." Mother Crane told me, "She's coming."

The fiddle played a two-step; there was a call for dancers, and through the door, on musical cue, head high, and with a skirt of engine-red flowing, Becca came gliding into the room. She was wrapped in primary colors top to bottom. Hair bound up in a blue turban, bright lapis lazuli. Her yellow blouse was so tight that her shape was in full relief, and the neckline so low it showed half the cherry birthmark on her breast.

She spun around once, and then again, in case anyone had failed to see that she was now the room's cynosure. As she turned, the crossed straps of her sandals were visible on her bare calves. A half dozen strings of bright glass beads were hung around her neck, and each of her wrists held as many shining bracelets. It was a costume of her own creation, mixed and matched from our theatrical trunk. Her lips were tinted with purple, which gave a dusky accent to the normal copper cast of her skin.

Odd to say, the whole effect, though provocative, did not seem cheap but thrilling, as if we were being introduced by a foreign princess to her tribe's ceremonial fashions. The presentation was so out of character with our normally taciturn Becca, and hardly suited to our modest ball. Mother Crane asked if she should send the girl back to change her costume. I said no, leave her alone, hoping to see if she'd learn something from this display. Though she looked quite stunning, it wasn't likely to win her a dance partner, much less the serious admirer for which these young hearts pine.

In fact, a brave fellow did ask her to dance right away. She refused and sat down. It was that way most of the evening. Becca sitting with a few other girls who were either dissatisfied with their offers or not asked at all. Occasionally all were called to their feet, boys and girls asked to circle past each other until the music stopped and a chance partner stood in front of everyone. Even then, Becca refused to take part.

At the end of the evening with a slow waltz in progress I was watching half the couples trying to make the fox trot work to the triple measure of the music, and telling Kerstin we should do a better job here on rhythm and movement. Becca walked up to her sister, who was struggling to follow her partner. I couldn't tell if she meant to instruct them in the step, or steal the young man for a dance of her own. She said something in his ear.

Immediately there was chaos, girls screaming, and boys backing away from the most violent struggle. Mother Reilly ran across the floor to separate the twins, but was knocked aside as they went at each other. It was the most awful thing. It made me ill. It was horrid for everyone there, really inexcusable, and it wasn't just pretend. They were hurting each other, swinging with full strength and audible impact. Their lips and noses were suddenly swollen and bloody. Their eyes were venomous slits for each other. When they had no more energy to swing their arms, they locked themselves together, scratching and pulling hair, all tangled on the floor. Mother Reilly and Kerstin had a hold of them by this time, and eventually pulled them apart. The beautiful clothes were ruined. Kerstin had to wrap her shawl around Linny to have her decently covered, and Becca ran out of the room holding her torn skirt around her.

I hoped the others would recover and finish the evening peacefully, but the Flourtown boys wouldn't dance. They were gathering around the one who'd been with Becca, wanting to know what was said to set off such a battle. He wasn't talking.

So, it was *Good Night Ladies.*

My question for you, Otto: Was this the final act that sheds the second self?

∞

It was several weeks before she had an answer to her rambling account, long enough to reproach herself for her garrulous letter. Meanwhile, she changed rules for the twins. At first sign of rudeness,

or any antisocial act, they were sent to their rooms for an hour of silence and introspection. All the staff were told to follow this plan.

And Eula took a more radical step. She moved Becca out of Thatch and into Stork, where she'd have the vigilant Mother Reilly keeping tabs, and her new roommate would be Melanie Kott, the oldest, toughest-skinned girl on the campus. She, too, had been directed to Drayton by Tessie Croft, saving her from the reformatory in Chester, where she was about to be sent for repeated thieving, though it had only been for food, well, mostly candy. Melanie gave as good as she got, or more, in verbal exchange, and the fainter-hearted steered clear. She wouldn't tolerate abuse from a younger sister without reprisal.

Linny didn't need extra attention. She was doing her best to become inconspicuous again after the outburst at the dance. She was keeping away from her sister as best she could. She was polite, she was quiet; she hid herself in the commotion of small groups that offered cover. She was going back to that shy silence she'd practiced when she first arrived at Drayton, reading alone in her room when optional activities were in progress. It was another way to avoid her sister through the day.

Becca was louder, even raucous in speech, all her habits more provocative. She was acting the part of someone new among them, as if the princess she had presented at the dance was now going to teach them the mores and manners of a rougher society. Most troubling of all, Eula thought, was the way she made over her wardrobe. She wore tops so low, they might slip to show the whole cherry mark on the upper half of her breast. She raised the hem of her skirts to bare the skin above her socks. The staff discussed a new dress code, but Eula thought it was the wrong remedy, letting one girl spoil the general freedom enjoyed by the rest of the community.

Her efforts to pry loose the secrets of Becca's belligerence were met with a childish sarcasm, beneath her age and development.

"You should know," and "Are you writing a book?" and finally, "Why don't you ask Linny. She's the white one."

When Eula sent her off for another "quiet hour" in her room, Mother Reilly said she spent much of the time pacing the floor, and cursing again in her fugitive language. That and making further alterations to her clothes.

Eula closed another report to Otto with "Becca shows off everything she's got, that is to say, the very developed figure which she shares with her sister. As if Linny and the rest of us were hiding ourselves in a false and shame-ridden modesty. And now she's turned our driver and groundskeeper into a surrogate father."

It was true. Becca had begun to spend all her spare time with Mr. Henry, the one who held the humblest position in the orphanage, the one who responded with a polite nod to the orders and will of everyone else on the campus, even the children. This was the parent she was choosing for herself, shunning the attentions of the popular Mother Reilly, who said Becca seemed to want him for kin, though Mr. Henry's light-brown skin was a good deal darker than her own.

Becca helped him rake leaves and stood with him at the incinerator, anxious to help. Eula assumed they chatted away about nothing in particular, though Becca was picking up the inflections of his speech, and bits of his poor grammar, and his accent.

The talk was sometimes whispered, as if she suspected her new friendship, however innocent, might not be acceptable. Eula had full trust in Mr. Henry; his circumspection was not deceitful, though he was careful to project a distance from the girl, when their talk could be overheard.

As Becca came out of her cottage to join him weeding in the flowerbed on a Spring morning, he saw Eula coming toward them, and she heard him say: "Child, you better cover that fruit, before somebody steals it."

It was his way of showing he was as critical of the way she was dressing as any of them, a worthy guardian, his genuine affection disguised by the way he fussed at her: "And get yourself busy, girl! Or go on back to your lessons. I don't have time to be fooling with your nonsense all the day."

He did have time. They'd be gabbing again as soon as Eula was gone.

∞

At last, a letter from Otto, postmarked Chicago. The sealing wax was red this time. But again, no matter which way she held it, she could see no pattern or figure, denied again his imprimatur. She'd learned from Tess that the carnelian, the crystalline red stone, was one of six given by Dr. Freud from his collection of antiquities to those he called his adopted children. Each, carved with its unique intaglio, had been set into gold rings and presented to this committee of six, who were expected to protect and carry the doctor's teachings into the world. Eula saw that Otto, though an outcast from that group, continued to wear his ring with pride. Depending on the angle of light, the carving might disappear in the translucent gem, even when the ring was right under one's eye.

She did a messy surgery on the envelope, and read that he was in Chicago for a week-long conference on the Freudian imperative and competing therapies. He was defending himself, he said, against some picadors who were trying to bleed him before their chief, Earnest Jones, arrived at the end of the session to finish him off. Once again he was being called "uncured," and thus not fit or entitled to cure. He and all his analysands were again publicly defrocked.

"So I go naked without shame," he wrote. "Nor will I charge their red cape, and this infuriates them. To the open-minded these men look very childish."

Otto said he was catching up with the correspondence he had brought with him from Philadelphia:

You and the twins are first on my mind, and I'm afraid I must disappoint you. This break between them isn't the separation you've been looking for, but something else entirely. When a double is truly shed it is not with premeditation, but desperation, and the act is final, in the sense of a gunshot and a death. I believe your twins are circling around each other for another confrontation. Look more carefully and you'll see their object is not final separation, but the opposite. They're determined to combine again, but on terms so far unacceptable to each other. The violence is only aimed at reform. The quarrel

is born of devotion. It must be settled before a rational separation is possible.

As you know, I don't admit children into therapy; however, I'd be pleased to see each of the twins for a single session when I return to Philadelphia in May.

Julia Crane wanted to know if others noticed a new fussiness and formality in Linny Carey. It was like nothing she'd seen before in any of their girls. Such careful attention to diction. And accurate to a fault in her use of pronouns.

"Have you noticed all the *whoms*?"

"Yes, and all the *shalls*," Eula agreed. "And so affected with the conditional."

"I shouldn't be at all surprised if it were so," Mother Reilly said, and they all had a chuckle.

Linny wanted to introduce a new social grace into their lives, a formal tea each week for all of the older girls, say, those between fifteen, her own age, and eighteen. Appropriate dress would be a formal frock and dark stockings. Perhaps even gloves. As for her regular habit of dress, Linny, too, had undertaken a makeover. From corset (Where in the world had she gotten one?) to the new matronly guimpe that covered her neck and throat, she was as tightly laced and buttoned, as morbidly modest, as any girl they'd raised. From head to heel, wrapped flat as the prairie, hermetically sealed.

She told Julia she didn't care to be trained for kitchen duty and motherhood, or a trade, or even to be a teacher or a nurse. There was nothing especially wrong with those careers, she said, but they were not for her. In this respect, a true child of Eula, she didn't care for the assumption that Drayton girls might be denied the privileges of the Flourtown schoolgirls. Julia said she didn't think of it as Linny putting on airs, so much as standing up for a right, maybe for a life which she now feared could be snatched away from her.

Eula saw the sisters were not living their parts so much as acting them. As if each was obliged to perform at an opposite end of the social scale. Julia reported that Linny had called her sister a slut. Becca's

retort was "high-cunt snob," which made Susan Bailey cry. With this venom came Otto's renewed warning that without intervention there might be a larger tragedy waiting for them:

"Nothing sharp lying around?"

"It's not like that, Otto."

"Oh? That's just the mythological extreme?"

"Yes."

But then came the discovery of another razor on the campus.

There was occasional trouble in Stork in spite of Ellen Reilly's watchful eye. Eula might have burdened her favorite housemother with one delinquent too many. There were actually three girls living on the upper floor of the cottage who might as easily have been in reformatories. Not just Melanie Kott, but the innocent-faced Clay sisters, Barbara and Julia, orphaned by the flight of embezzling parents, which made their own habit of thieving more understandable.

This was the cottage Kerstin called Mummy's Borstal, or sometimes The Reformatory, when teasing Eula about her Mother Goose fantasy village, and the house where Eula was most apt to pay a surprise visit to keep an eye on which way the influence was running between the willful Becca and the recovering delinquents. When she wandered upstairs and into the Stork lavatory several days after Becca's move, she found Barbara Clay with her leg raised and resting on a sink, shaving herself with a man's straight razor.

"No need for that," Eula said, taking the forbidden blade from Barbara's hand. "Look, you've cut yourself."

"Don't you want to know where I got it?"

"No," Eula said, "you can tell Mother Reilly about it."

"No one gave it to me," Barbara said, as if feeling her way toward a plausible story, maybe hoping no one would have to be punished. "I just found it in here."

The girl was sixteen, with the normal cover of light hair on her limbs, but determined to be shorn of it before the excursions to the swimming creek began again in June. She was ignoring the advice the housemothers passed along to all the girls to accept nature's way and live with this barely visible fuzz rather than cut it and cultivate a

troublesome heavier growth. No razors were allowed in the girls' toilet kits. Eula gave the blade to Ellen Reilly, who immediately searched all her cottage rooms for others. During her inspection she came across a news clipping torn from the city paper in Becca's bureau:

> Trustee Says Drayton College Mixing Races. Colored Twins At Center of Controversy. Race of Sisters Not In Question, Administrator Says.

The story began:

> A trustee of the Drayton College Orphanage in Flourtown brought suit in District Court last week, seeking the permanent closing of the institution.

The twins were mentioned in the second paragraph, and the article went on to quote a Drayton trustee who said the girls' grandmother was a Negro. Eula was the named administrator who told the reporter, "I don't know what the girls' heritage is. It doesn't really matter to me. They were deserving candidates for our home, and we took them in. They're part of our family."

Since the article had been written, Renee Drayton's manipulation of the orphanage investments had been exposed and her suit against Eula and the college had been dropped. The twins were still stewing in the news they'd created. The appearance of the story had coincided with the transformations in their personality and dress.

If Eula had been willfully ignorant of what was happening between the Careys, she could no longer deny the truth. The young man who had been dancing with Linny when the fighting started told his parents what Becca had said, and this had been passed along to the orphanage: "You're dancing with a nigger."

A note from Eula to Otto dated May 21, 1931, says:

> Several of us knew before we quite admitted to ourselves that Becca was convinced she and her sister were Negroes. She was determined to have Linny accept this. Linny was equally certain they

were white, and nothing was going to change what she could see with her own eyes.

Can you believe this, Otto? Identical twins, one black, one white. I think when they look in their mirrors, each sees an exaggerated color of skin. Their eyes deceive them. Of the two, Linny seems the more pathetic to me. She's asking everyone, "Don't I have the palest skin you've ever seen?" She's the one who needs reassuring. But if she asks us, what should we, in good conscience, tell her? The idea that one can be schooled for social work is such a laugh.

Where nothing could separate our twins, race has succeeded, and now they run from each other in opposite directions. If I understand your reasoning, one of them must win this contest before a more elemental separation of their lives can take place. Mother Reilly thinks they'll come to the right conclusion without our influence—right meaning either one they agree on. Our duty is to give them the facts. I wish I could believe it.

For the first time since she came to Drayton, Becca was showing an interest in religion. All her plans began with "God willing," another way of talking picked up from Mr. Henry. On Sundays he took a half dozen of the children to churches of their choice in the station wagon. Catholic, Episcopalian, Methodist, and Lutheran. These were girls who had been introduced to faiths by parents later lost to accident or disease. If they did not want to attend the nondenominational chapel they had this option of returning to their own religions as they grew old enough to make a decision for themselves.

Mr. Henry—Becca now insisted on calling him Mr. Davidson because it was more respectful—made this round of the local churches, handing the girls into the care of their various clergy for Sunday morning while he continued on to his own Gospel Corner Assembly across the river in West Conshohocken. Becca was demanding to be taken on this Sunday excursion. She wanted to test all the stories, she said, "to see which one I believe."

"A religion without a church," she told Eula, "is no religion at all."

This, too, would have come directly from her Mr. Davidson.

"Becca, dear, I have nothing against a church, unless it claims salvation for its members alone. When you came to us, remember, you renounced religion completely. You were never made to sing a hymn or say a prayer, and no one thought the less of you for your silence."

She thought about that for a moment, and said, "That was wrong. Look where it's taking my sister!"

And before Eula asked where, she said, "Straight to hell!"

"I don't believe that, Becca, and I don't think you do either."

"You don't believe in anything. None of you do. You don't believe in anything but yourselves."

Shocking from a child of fifteen. Eula understood this must be the dark glass through which Mr. Henry saw her world.

"That's rude," she said. "How can you know another person's faith? And what business is it of yours, anyway?"

But she told Becca, "Of course, choose your own church. Any church would be pleased to have you as a member. Just don't choose a faith for anyone else, not even your sister."

Becca was shaking her head. Out of the blue, she said, "You aren't supposed to take Negroes. We were never supposed to be here in the first place. You knew what we were."

"But you came here as a white child."

"My grandmother is a Negro," she said. "And you can't make me ashamed of it. My lossy aunt wouldn't even let her come in the house. She wouldn't even let us know her."

"Is," she'd said. "My grandmother *is* a Negro." Eula had never allowed herself to think of the grandmother as alive. In fact, she'd helped to dispose of her imagined remains, discarding the record of her existence.

"Becca," she said, "you'd been living as white children with your aunt when you came to us. You had gone to white children's schools. What kind of a person would I have been to deny you on the grounds you were a Negro? Why would you expect us to disrupt your life that way?"

"This is why!" she said, pulling the article out of her pocket and pushing it across the desk. "It was against your rules."

"But what do you think of those rules?" Eula asked her.

"They're yours, not mine."

"No," Eula said, "I didn't make them."

"You use them."

She couldn't deny it.

"My grandmother lives in Philadelphia, don't she?"

"Doesn't she. I don't know."

Becca's mood couldn't be salved with gentle logic because logic was on her side. Had she ever met her grandmother, Eula asked, did she even know her name?

"No," she said, "I was ten when I come here. You're the ones should know it. You could ask these city people." She was pointing to the newspaper article again. "These social-working people."

"Came here, Becca. What's happened to the way you talk?"

"You mean the way my sister do?"

"Does."

It was a sorry act, she thought: Becca, perfectly capable of good grammar, taking up the speech of the spiritual, but untutored, handyman, in response to the fancy new English of her sister. Eula wasn't going to deny Becca the company of her new friend, Mr. Henry. And it would have been cruel to ask her why her grandmother had not come forward to claim her and Linny when their parents had died, or when her aunt passed away. Eula did think it was her duty now, however risky, to ask Tessie Croft if the identity and address of the grandmother were anywhere in the records in her office. The answer came back, the same stark fact: "Grandmother: Negro."

Eula explained this to a disappointed Becca, who began her Sunday church outings with Eula's blessing.

Mr. Henry said the Lutheran minister had foolishly put Becca in with the kiddy group to learn her Bible stories, and the father at St. Mary's had been too grumpy about her religious ignorance to encourage her. The following week she was going to see what the Methodists had to tell her. Mr. Henry said a child looking so hard for the light was going to find it somewhere.

Soon afterward Mother Reilly reassured Eula with the news that Becca was now charged with bliss all day after her Sunday outings, and that by the end of each week the church trip was the thing she

most looked forward to. Eula was pleased with this bit of happiness Becca had found in contrast to her sister's indifference.

But that season, Linny, not to be outdone in standing with the angels, became the Drayton chaplain's assistant, performing as many chapel duties as he'd allow her, lighting and snuffing candles, turning pages for the Sunday pianist, keeping fresh flowers in the altar vase, and sweeping the floors. It was more than her share of community service, and much as Eula hated losing the daily opportunity of talking with her, she released Linny from the office chores.

Linny was more frightened than Eula at the prospect of a family member who might claim her rights as the twins' guardian. With Mr. Henry's help Becca had gotten a three-line personal item printed at the bottom of a column in the second section of *The Inquirer*:

> Seeking Grandmother of twins Linda and Rebecca
> Carey. Contact Drayton College Orphanage.
> P.O. Box 174, Flourtown, Pa.

Eula was annoyed with him for interfering. Again, it was Mother Reilly, the contrarian, who said, "Maybe we should have done it ourselves. Years ago."

∞

They came through the summer of 1931 unable to admit any new orphans for the coming year. The ad for the twins' grandmother ran without response. Becca, dissatisfied with the search, begged to have them try again that winter. Eula, with misgivings, placed another three lines in the city paper, this time at the bottom of a front-page column. When it appeared, she showed it to both of the girls. Becca said, "You could have made it bigger."

Linny cried. "Why are you doing this to us?" she asked. "You don't want us here anymore. You don't like colored? Well I'm not colored. Can't anyone see it?"

"Of course."

"Not Mother Reilly. She told Becca she should be whoever she wants to be."

"Isn't that fair?"

"No! It isn't!"

"Do you remember your grandmother?"

"No," she said. Except that she was always turned away by Aunt Gwen. She'd come back once or twice a year to ask for something and the door would be closed in her face. Linny recalled how the spurned lady would stand outside the house mumbling to herself. And how Aunt Gwen was certain the old lady was putting a curse on them.

Mother Reilly was the one who brought Rabbi Posten to a school assembly in March of that year to speak on Jewish life in Philadelphia. And Mother Greene found Frederick Wu, the testy little Chinese scholar and businessman, who lectured to them on American interference in the Orient. He was hoping to start a work-and-study program for one of the graduating girls, a fellowship in China. Then Ellen Reilly got Eula's approval to invite the Jubilee Choir from Mr. Henry's Gospel Corner congregation in West Conshohocken to make a Sunday afternoon appearance in the chapel. Music, she promised, at religious intensity the girls had never seen.

Eula needn't have been worried about the children's response. The whole orphanage, girls and staff, sat agape at the white-gowned singers from the moment they came single-file through the chapel door, to the final rolling hymn, and all their calls to praise in between. They watched the swaying heads and bodies of three ranks of singers. Supple as reeds, they bent before the hand of their Director. With heads independent of shoulders, and shoulders independent of hips, it was a suggestive kind of dancing-in-place that left Eula wondering if she should have exposed her children to such an erotic approach to salvation. She looked around for the reaction of the housemothers. They were rapt as the children.

Harmonies swelled and diminished with the diction cut sharp in syncopated phrasing. A soprano's solo rang up to the steep chapel ceiling, and the reverberation of two bass voices answered an alto's question: "Where was Daniel?"

"In the Lion's Den."

And still a lower rumble, "In the Lion's Den."

There was a squeal in the audience, not rudeness, but surprise at the magic of the thing, and a gasp of appreciation. The choir, all of them, were grinning. It was only then Eula saw that the light-skinned woman in the second rank of dark faces looked just like Becca Carey and *was* Becca Carey. Not a black woman, but the twin Becca, swaying with the others, mouth wide and joyous in her first public performance as a Negro gospel singer.

Eula looked up and down the pews for her sister. She had to turn completely around before spotting Linny way in the back, scrunched down, hands over her face, trying to disappear. It was worse when her sister was signaled to come forward and stand by the piano by herself. Becca spread her arms wide, making wings of her robe as if they were going to lift her—blessed vision of their own Becca—into the air, and words clear as glass began to pour from her mouth:

> *One bright morning, when this world is over,*
> *I'll fly away.*

It made the housemothers teary, the words and the voice. Becca did want to fly away, and with her sister, too. Maybe farther than a dollar would send a postcard. That she'd found a destination, someplace out of this world, brought Eula close to tears as well. Not for Becca's religious devotion but for the disappointments the twin had gathered to herself in her years at the orphanage.

As Becca sang for salvation, her voice, in its soaring grace, began to separate itself from the words, lifting Eula's spirits. It occurred to her there was another just like it in the chapel, an exact match, though hiding in shame. And afterward, she proposed to Linny that singing lessons be arranged for her. There'd be opportunities for her to perform here, too.

It only annoyed her. Didn't Miss Kieland know she'd had her tonsils out, and adenoids, that she was not an identical twin, that she couldn't sing the way her sister could? Hadn't the music instructor told her as much?

"And I'm not a showoff like you know who. Anyway, why do you pay me so much attention?"

"Why do you think?"

"I asked you," she said.

Instead of ordering her to an hour of isolation, Eula let the impudence pass.

"You know we all have high hopes for you and your sister?"

"What about the other girls? Why don't you ask them questions?" This was too much.

"I don't like the way you're speaking to me, Linny. I don't like your manners today."

Taking refuge in authority, she was wondering if Linny had seen more of her correspondence with Otto, if she was aware how recently Eula had shared more of the twins' story with the man who worked on dotty people, the man who so recently advised Eula in the matter of her own neurosis.

∞

"What comes first, Eula," Otto asked her, "first in any successful terapy?"

She smiled without risking a reply.

"Isn't it obvious, dear? Honesty. Trust."

"Too obvious," she said.

"So why did you withhold these?"

She guessed where he was leading her, and turned her head away. Suddenly this woman who might bend in sadness, but never melted in tears, a woman he had never imagined breaking down, who had not cried since the death of her adopted son, began to weep again in memory of his bright face, his cow-licked hair, and stolen years. "He was darling," she said. "Someone tried to tell him he was going to heaven." Eula stopped and wiped her eyes. "He told them not to lie to him. He was only nine."

"This doesn't have to be now, Eula. Come to me sometime when you want to talk about it."

"No. Now."

"I was embarrassed," he said, "and so sad when Tessie told me of your poor little Tony. Of course I was a fool when I said your terapy was complete, but you fooled me. How could you be finished when this was missing?"

"Maybe you know why I didn't tell you."

"You couldn't live in this sadness again."

"No. What woman adopts a child, thinking someday she'll marry? That's what you would have said. That's what you're thinking right now. But I did believe I could marry. I still do."

After their sixteenth birthday the twins made a special effort to be civil with each other again, though they were still living in separate cottages, still exaggerating their differences, committed to two dictions, two wardrobes, and two attitudes to the world around them. Mother Crane and Mother Reilly had both overheard them discussing their Grandmother Carey, contesting whether her skin had been dark or light. This, and the question posed to them like a hardwood thorn by Mr. Henry: Where had the Grandmother come from, and had she been born a slave, or a free woman?

Otto, fascinated with all this, said again it was time for Eula to bring the Careys to him. She thought not, not until they gave up the extreme parts they were playing. It was a wonder to her that they could keep it up, like actresses in a long-running play, enduring such a tedious charade, the daily effort of manufactured selves.

She wrote to Otto explaining how Becca's membership in the Negro church had escaped their notice. In fact, Mother Reilly had known about it, but kept it to herself, she said, because she did not want to rile the community, or cause more pain to Linny, and possibly set off another battle between the twins.

Becca and Mr. Henry had kept her Sunday destination from the other passengers in the van by suggesting that hers was the last stop, a phantom Presbyterian church where he supposedly dropped her before crossing the river to his congregation in West Conshohocken. And of course that would make her the first to be picked up as he made his rounds homeward. In fact, under Mr. Henry's sponsorship, he explained later, she was welcomed immediately into membership in his Gospel Corner Assembly, and her voice discovered when she first opened her mouth to sing.

Otto wrote back in that cold, pinched Winter of 1933. Still no image in the sealing wax. Her sorrow. He congratulated her for the more lenient rules for the senior girls and those who had reached seventeen. If properly chaperoned they could leave campus for evenings with their local suitors. No chaperone required if they went in pairs or more, and were back by ten p.m., a terrible mistake she decided later; it brought village gossip on their heads. And she was letting them ride their bicycles into Flourtown. The rule was, stay on the sidewalk where one was available, and walk the bike at the edge of the roadway where no footpath was provided.

His note was scolding, too: "I've seen the maze of telephone wires that run down Bethlehem Pike. Surely one of them runs into your campus. Or at least into that cozy house you share with Kerstin. I want a face-to-face talk with you, but a phone conversation would be better than this. We can spend some time on your own development if you like."

Later he wrote that he'd been pleased to hear that the budget, though drastically reduced, was not expected to go lower. He said his imagination was very busy with the twins:

> Have you stopped to consider the remarkable influence they have on your life? Or why? It's not just the paranormal stuff, the things that always get exaggerated with twins, or the striking physical beauty you describe. Or even the cussed stubbornness that frustrates your devotion.
>
> This business they've been up to in recent weeks is more phenomenal to me than their early telepathies. It suggests a single mind in separate bodies, but a mind in conflict with itself. Their battleground in the end is a moral one. This is a spiritual struggle. And religion, such an easy target for our scorn in the selfish and dogmatic particulars of individual faiths, is the field where the twins have met. Again, I tell you, the easy observation is that they are pulling apart. I

believe, on the contrary, they are making an heroic and soul-honest effort to combine.

∞

Mr. Henry was the first one to see the old woman. He was clipping the forsythia hedge along the Bethlehem Pike when she turned into the gate, limping along with a cane, right down the center of the driveway. He said he knew right away who she was, and came loping up to get the station wagon to save her from walking all the way to the buildings. She would not accept his ride, but struck the side of the automobile with her cane.

"Get out of the way!" she told him. "Where's the one put the notice in?"

She was holding up a little piece of newspaper, he said. And she was still waving it in front of her like a ticket that conferred a right of immediate admission as she came into Eula's office. She stopped in front of the desk, with Mr. Henry behind her, announcing, "This is Mrs. Jenny Carey. She saw your notice in the paper."

Her skin, Eula thought, what incredible coloring!

If this was the twins' grandmother, she was nothing like anyone could have imagined.

There was no doubt in Mr. Henry's mind about who she was, though he was staring as rudely as Eula.

"Must I go and tell the sisters?" he asked, almost out the door and on his way to Schoolhouse.

"No," she said. "Let's find out what Mrs. Carey wants."

He looked at Eula doubtfully.

"You want me to stay?" he asked.

"If you've got nothing else to do."

This wasn't quite fair; he couldn't admit to idleness. He backed out of the room, ashamed. But whatever happened, he would eventually tell Becca, and this forced Eula's hand. This was no frivolous thing; it was no time for a whimsical choice. But the driver and gardener would be hovering outside, making work for himself under Eula's window, keeping watch on the meeting.

She could do the daring thing, the natural thing, and introduce the twins to this Mrs. Carey immediately. There might be more wisdom in delay, but the situation was moving itself along, sweeping past her fears.

"Mrs. Carey," she said, "won't you sit down?"

"I ain't sat all morning, did I? Why should I sit now?"

The dishevelment and discomfort of the woman was too much for Eula. She pulled a chair across the room and forced her to sit in it. She had a wicker creel meant for fish slung over her shoulder for a handbag, and her legs were wrapped in white cloth fastened with strips of sheet tied in granny knots. Her outer garment was a purple terry bathrobe, the nap worn nearly smooth. It was held at the collar with a blanket pin. Her hair, reddish brown and wild, made Eula want to scratch her own scalp. It seemed not just unmanaged, but unmanageable, coarse and matted in frightful strands, as if congealed without oil into a powdery dry tangle.

And the skin! She'd seen nothing like it before. It was more pink than white, but freckled everywhere with little brown islands, something gone terribly awry in the pigmentation leaving this alteration of color. Her first reaction had been pity for what seemed an unfortunate disfigurement, as cruel as a pox. But now she rebuked herself for falling so carelessly into that unholy army against miscegenation, as if the skin could have been the penalty for a forbidden copulation. Her sympathy, she knew, should have been with the poet who praised God for creation of a dappled thing, for the glory of a trout's speckling, for the uncommon achievement of the woman's variegated coloring.

All very well, but the twins and their sister orphans would find no beauty here, only deformity, and their own repulsion. Soon enough, Eula saw the two colors, unmixed, as a presentation in the flesh of the futile argument others had made for the girls. From her creel Mrs. Carey pulled a document, yellow with age, which she waved in front of the Director.

"In case you doubt it."

"What's that, Mrs. Carey?"

"Look at it! You tell *me* what it is."

She pushed it toward Eula. It had the appearance of a legal paper, badly worn. It had been folded and unfolded for the better part of a century. Drafted in the elegant hand of a legal copyist, it was dated November 20, 1858, made more official by a toothed gold circle fixed over a black ribbon turned and crossed, and imprinted with a notary's press in Carroll County, Virginia. It was signed by Callard McKinty, Esq., a witness, and a notary.

"To All in these Precincts and Beyond."

"No," Mrs. Carey said, "read it so's I can hear you. Out louder."

"Be it known," Eula obliged, "this Negro girl, mottled roan . . . "

"Ain't that me?" she interrupted, holding her chin high for a better vantage of the stippling that followed under her face to chin and neck and, Eula assumed, over her whole body.

". . . the same who carries this testament and is called Jenny, was born on the McKinty Orchards in 1847, a free person. On this day she is released from all indenture. Orphaned, she bears no lien of service to any man or woman. She is free to pass from these premises, and beyond the jurisdiction of this county and state."

"There!" she said. "If I was free to walk out of Virginia 'cross Maryland and into Pennsylvania, who's to stop me coming through your gate?"

She was compressing a lifetime of wandering into her last few minutes. If the bit of newspaper had been her ticket to the Director's office, this was her passport to the world, and apparently had been for the last seventy-five years. She pulled it quickly away from Eula. Back into the creel it went. It had the stilted tone of someone pretending to a lawyer's knowledge, and Eula wondered if the document had ever had legal standing, or was simply the gallant or guilty gesture of the man who must have held her life—slave or free—in his palm, a gesture offered after his misuse of her, his way of coaxing her to leave the community of his embarrassment.

Eula guessed the woman was past eighty. Not so wrinkled as gaunt and wiry. There was ample spirit but little flesh to drive her.

"Go on. Look at me." she said. "I'm a jumble, ain't I? And why shouldn't I be?"

She meant her coloring. She was jabbing a finger at herself, pointing as if the Director was among those responsible for her predicament. And Eula, already fixed on the mystery of her skin, was wondering how the twins would respond to it.

Mrs. Carey was anticipating her questions, taking Eula where she would never have presumed to push her.

"What did he think he'd get? Wasn't he a chalk-face with white eyebrows if he had any at all, Mr. McKinty? He got me on my mother, who was his house girl, and she didn't belong to him."

She raised her hand to stop the woman.

Mrs. Carey paid no attention, hurrying on: "When she died—my mother—he give me this paper and sent me away from there."

She stopped and patted the creel, making sure Eula was following her story.

"How could that man expect yellow," she asked, "when he was throwing color like a pinto pony? Not just me. He got three polka dot children. And all on different ones. Told my mother if she ever held me up to him, he'd have her sent down the state . . . you got nothing to say?"

Eula shook her head.

"The twin girls you got here, you show them to me."

"Do you think they'd recognize you?" she asked her.

"How could they? They wasn't allowed to see me since they was two years."

"And how would you recognize them in that case?"

Eula hadn't meant to argue with her. She was trying to think clearly, looking for a way to deny all this in her own mind.

"I know their names, don't I? What you trying to prove? Have I got to tell you all of it?"

Eula could only guess at her duty here, not just the right thing to do legally, but the right thing. Mrs. Carey took a breath and went on: "It was my child, William Carey, who is their accurate father. He was got on me by a white man, too, Mr. Oliver Carey of Poolesville, Maryland. Mr. Carey married me in black night in the Summer 1877, and no one was meant to know it. So he could use me in conscience according to his religion. Our hands was on the same Bible and our

feet in the Potomac River, and he swore sickness and health and all the rest of it. He kept me hid in his house until the Fall. Until he was sick of the sight of me, and sent me on up the state again, in the neighbor's wagon, me already showing William. And I told you, William was the girls' father. Maryland disappeared in the week, and here I was in Pennsylvania, and already swollen."

"Did you have any other children?" Eula asked.

She laughed heartily at this delicacy.

"Is nine any other?" she said. "Four dead and five in the New York where it snows. I'm asking you, is colder people going to be better people in toleration? But mine had to be all the time moving up the map."

There must be lots of grandchildren, Eula suggested.

"Why must there be? What if there is?"

But she smiled and said, "Oh yes, there is more."

Eula was embarrassed again for the woman, whoever she was. There was no reason to question her word, except a fear that she was, indeed, who she claimed to be, and might be able to pull one or both of the twins away, whether by their preference or by law. At the same time she could see the woman's brave front hid a larger fear, an assumption that Eula would be judge of her honesty and would rule on her claims.

"Please," Eula said. "You don't have to tell me any of this."

"You got the children, don't you?"

"Yes."

"You going to show them?"

"Yes, we have twins here named Linda and Rebecca Carey."

"Those are the ones!" she said. "Now hear the rest of it. My boy William, he went and passed on the white side, and that's the way his missis wanted it. She didn't want to be hearing about any parts of me. And I never bothered them, did I?"

"Please, Mrs. Carey."

"Let me finish! After William and his wife got taken by the influenza, that's when I came back at them. When the Aunt Gwen put the lies in their head."

"How do you know that?"

"You taken a side already? Of course I don't know it by the fact. How could I? I know it by the reason. The same way you know I am the grandmother of those two girls."

She looked at the Director scornfully. "If she didn't let them see me, what else could she be telling them but lies?"

Eula walked to the window behind her desk. Only ten yards away on their hands and knees in the flowerbed Mr. Henry and Becca were chatting away. He hadn't told her yet or she'd be in the office already. Eula turned her back on him.

She was insisting that Mrs. Carey not tell any more of her wretched story.

"You want proof those girls are kin to me, don't you?"

Eula thought the woman was about to cry, and she thought of what Kerstin had told her the night before, that she, Kerstin, was tired of being a strong woman. She meant a woman who wields influence over other people's lives. She only wanted the world to run equitably, not to run it.

What Eula did here might signify little, or alter the twins' lives. She felt forced to a decision that should never have been hers. And what was right for Becca was not necessarily right for Linny. Eula chose impulsively for Becca. Linny would just have to accept it. She took Mrs. Carey to the window.

"There," she said. "There's one of them. I'll send the gentleman for the other."

"You got no better clothes for her? You let that girl go around here like that?"

Eula knocked on the glass, and motioned for the two of them to come inside. Mrs. Carey sat again in the cushioned chair. Her legs wrapped in the white sheeting, as if done up in bandages. With the ragged robe she might have been a patient in a charity ward, but she was preparing for her audience, hiding the cane behind her, running her fingers through her wild hair, pulling herself up straight.

A moment more and Mr. Henry was at the door with Becca.

"Missy," he said, "who do you think that is?"

"Becca," Eula said, "this is Mrs. Carey, who says . . . "

Her voice broke.

". . . who says she's your grandmother."

Becca couldn't believe it.

"She isn't," she said. "How could she be?"

Mr. Henry, still standing in the doorway, said, "Go ahead, Becca. Hold onto your grandmother," and then he was gone to get Linny.

Mrs. Carey reached behind her chair for the cane.

"Girl," she said, pointing, "shamed of yourself."

She began to move the cane back and forth, as if undecided where to direct her irritation.

"If I'd knowed they would let you get yourself up like that, I'd not have let them have you." As if she had ever come forward before, or been involved with the twins in any way. Eula made it clear this was the first time she'd known Mrs. Carey was alive.

A moment later Linny was standing in the doorway, coaxed forward by Mr. Henry. She was speechless and no more inclined to believe this was her grandmother than her sister had been.

"Stand beside the other one there," Mrs. Carey ordered. And when they were lined up together, pointing at Linny, she told her, "And get that thing off your neck before you suffocate yourself." She meant the guimpe, which in another day might have made her a Victorian lady, but only looked ridiculous on a girl her age.

The scene Mr. Henry must have hoped for, with their arms thrown around their grandmother's neck, the emotional reunion, never happened. Mrs. Carey made sure of that. The handyman was fidgeting next to the wall. Eula knew it was only goodwill that made him suggest something so natural but so awkward to the moment, so disloyal to the institution he worked for.

"Isn't she going to ask them?"

The question was for Eula.

"Ask them what?" Mrs. Carey said.

She turned her cane on him now, waving it slowly against the next irritation. In the presence of kin and the gardener, all her fear had vanished.

"Aren't you going to ask them, Mrs. Carey? Ask them if they want to come to live with you?"

"Come to live with me! How they going to live with me when I got not enough place for myself, only the one room? Come to live with me? Who are you, asking such a thing?"

Mr. Henry turned, shamed again. Eula was equally upset with herself. She never should have allowed this meeting without some assurance of the outcome.

Becca, finally convinced the woman was her grandmother, came up to embrace her. Their cheeks were almost touching when Mrs. Carey snapped, "Look out, girl. Look out!"

There was a horrid suction noise as a dental plate loosened and was pushed forward like the jaws of a protrusive fish, not something made by any ordinary dentist. She looked around at all of them, then sucked it in again and closed her mouth, clicking it back in place. It was something practiced and repellent.

Becca backed away. Her sister took her arm. The two wiped tears from each other's cheeks.

Eula, wanting an end to it, asked, "What *could* we do for you, Mrs. Carey?"

"You listen here. I didn't come for these children. God no! I barely got room for myself. I come for the silver frame."

"Frame?"

"Silver, and I don't care about the picture."

The twins took another step backward.

"The one the aunt got out of my boy William's place when she went in there and took what she pleased. After he died. You ask those girls if she didn't. She told me way back, she said she give it to one of them and wouldn't know which."

The sisters were sobbing. Eula could only imagine the long struggle of this woman, whose first concern was a piece of silver, more likely chrome, forgotten by all but herself, while two beautiful children wept in front of her, clinging to each other again.

∞

The twins' peace held. They begged to be allowed to share a room again. Eula's records show Otto advised against it, but she wouldn't

deny them in the face of their new harmony. Stork, the Borstal, was calm that month, partly because Becca's presence had charmed the recovering thieves into an admiring sisterhood. They had adopted her as mascot sibling from the strange land of Thatch, the girl with the fugitive vocabulary, a little of which she shared with them so that now they swore almost innocently, and without reproach.

And the twins' choice was to be in Stork Cottage together under the care of Mother Reilly. She had the rougher honesty they liked, with none of the soft soap of the others. And who wouldn't prefer the house where the nightly reading was from one of the modern romance novels rather than Julia Crane's interpretation of *The Pilgrim's Progress*? Poor Julia. She still hadn't learned that one of the easiest ways to the contempt of children of emerging sophistication is by reading to them with expression.

Julia's approach was too hovering for the Careys. After the anger of their time apart they needed a little distance from adults while they repaired the damage. Linny didn't want anyone remarking on the relaxation of her self-denial, or the more casual appearance she allowed herself. And Becca's return to the orphanage chapel for her religion in tandem with her sister was her own business.

Mr. Henry was no less kind to Becca on this account. He forgave her defection from the Gospel Corner Assembly and its choir in sympathy for the disappointment her grandmother had been. He still let her work beside him in the flowerbeds. Taught to pray for a reunion jubilee, and rewarded with the old lady's scorn, Becca was haunted by the sight of the woman, and by the idea that she and her sister were only one generation removed from the mixed coloration. There was the frightening mouth, and the insulting document, which Mrs. Carey had unfolded again, making *them* read it to her, as if it were a declaration of independence from them as well, from their white standing, from all the enemies who stood between her and the silver frame.

The twins might still deceive, but only through the staff's blindness. The occasional confusion now seemed to bore or annoy them, and the punishment for the staff's mistakes was the sisters' indiffer-

ence. If someone got the names wrong, too bad. Their collusion, if it was that, was more subtle than before. There were no more mirrored answers in their schoolwork. In the public school they were often in separate classrooms, apart through most of the day though they took the same courses. At lunchtime, Eula was told, they took refuge from their popularity with the boys, keeping their own whispering company, never dawdling in the halls, acting as one when approached for flirting.

"I suppose," Julia Crane said, "they must have been cheating after all. Beverly must have been right all along."

"You don't know that," Eula told her. "It wasn't cheating in their minds," defending them like a mother.

Rank called her.

"Eula, Otto," he said with a new, flattering familiarity.

If the twins had been shaken, she told him, they were once again a loving pair. Better twinned and indistinguishable again, she thought, than bitterly estranged.

Otto was certain it was time to bring the girls to see him in Philadelphia. "Not for terapy, of course, for evaluation."

"If you want," he said, "we can give a few minutes to your own recent behavior."

"My behavior?"

"Eula, I tink you have to tell these people who float around in your orbit, the ones who are drawn by mutual gravity . . . you have got to tell them who you are."

"I thought we were talking about the twins," she said.

"Tink about it, Eula. I will see you all on Wednesday at half after ten, yes? A half hour for each of the girls, and for you, perhaps, fifteen minutes. I have no secretary to greet you. You'll have to ring from the lobby."

Mr. Henry drove them into the city, with the girls growing more reluctant by the mile.

"You think I'm crazy?" Linny asked Eula.

"Tell me again," Becca said. "Why are we talking to him?"

"He's an expert in many things," Eula explained. "Art. Literature. Life. We might learn something from him. Most people have to

pay a great deal for the privilege of his advice. He's talking to us for nothing."

"Well, we're not charging either," Linny said.

Mr. Henry, from the front seat, told her, "Miss Linny, you watch your smart tongue."

Eula saw him smiling in the mirror.

∞

Rank was immediately taken with the girls; Eula could see he was a little startled by their beauty. Now seventeen, they were fully figured. The extra flesh of childhood was shed from cheeks and limbs, and their copper skin glowed with health. They were so notably the tall beauties in the annual orphanage photograph that this year Eula kept them off the front row, so the other children would not feel so upstaged.

The twins' news had been shared with Otto for so long, she almost forgot he'd never seen them.

"Hello, Becca," he said, looking straight at her. He could only be guessing, but Becca didn't know that. He had caught her by surprise. She blushed and nodded. "Let's start with you," he said.

Linny was sent into the apartment's kitchen to have fruit juice and be entertained by a young Negro cleaning woman who was put out by this extra duty. Eula sat at a far end of the living room, where she could overhear bits of the two conversations that ensued, the one in the kitchen as intriguing as that between Otto and Becca.

"How can I be dusting if I got to make lemonade?"

"Please," she heard Linny tell the woman, "you don't need to make anything for me. I don't want anything."

"You don't look like no orphan to me," the maid told her.

From the other direction she heard Otto ask Becca to make herself comfortable in the seat opposite him. He told her he had often imagined what it must be like to be an identical twin. "Tell me," he said, "is it like being outside and inside yourself at the same time?"

Eula was surprised at how quickly he was able to engage her.

"No," she said, "not really. It's more like watching someone who's always making mistakes for me."

"Explain," he said.

"She's always just ahead of me, or just behind. I can tell you what she's saying to that lady in the kitchen right now."

"Really?"

"She's saying we don't want anything to drink, but she knows we do. She doesn't want that woman to do anything extra for us, and neither do I."

"Is there something wrong with that?"

"Nothing wrong with it except I'm the one who should be telling her."

"Why?"

"I don't have to tell you why."

Eula almost called across the room for manners, but she wasn't supposed to be hearing any of this.

In the kitchen, Linny raised her voice.

"I most certainly am!" she said.

"Go 'way from here!"

"You can ask my sister."

"Why should I when I can see she looks the same as you?"

Eula, on her way into the kitchen to tell them to lower their voices, saw Linny holding her forearm up to compare it with the white paint on the wall.

"There," she said. "Does that look white to you?"

"Missie," the woman said, "you about as colored as a stick of chalk."

They still didn't know she was watching them.

"You should see my grandmother, if you want to see something different," Linny told her. "You'd believe me if you saw her."

Eula hushed them, and Linny spun.

"I don't want her getting me anything to drink."

Eula closed the kitchen door, realizing Linny had become a Negro, too. This was the twins' furtive compromise. Now the two of them were only passing for white in their white orphanage. She sat in Otto's parlor, wondering how to change their minds, how to save them from themselves, and from the world.

Otto was doing most of the talking at the other end of the room. He was telling Becca about *The Student of Prague,* not even sparing her the fatal ending, the attack on the double, which turned out to be a suicide.

"That's right, he tinks he's only killing his tormenting double, but of course he's killing himself."

This was way beyond the evaluation he'd promised.

He handed Becca a pen and piece of paper and ordered her to make a single black dot on the sheet.

"Please hold it up in front of you," he said.

She obeyed.

"Now, move it close to your nose. You see what happens?"

Becca wouldn't say.

"And move the paper away. Now what do you see?"

She smiled.

"Yes, Becca," he said. "When you see the two spots it is no more than anyone sees under such stress. This is not healthy. This way we would imagine obstacles for ourselves all the time; we would avoid things that aren't there, and bump into things that are. To prevent accidents we must keep some distance. You are seventeen, yes? And very clever. You will decide which way it will be."

Becca started to tell him about her first bathing suit, but he was finished with her. It was the sister's turn.

Otto wanted no more eavesdropping. He sent Becca and Eula down on the lift to take a couple of turns around the block while he went to work with Linny.

When it was finally Eula's turn, the girls were asked to wait downstairs in the lobby.

Had he had any success with Linny and the little game of double vision, she asked.

"With these girls," he said, "it was not just the dot, but the color of the dot that had separated and then become one again."

"What are we going to do about it?"

"With regard to their color," he said, "We can only accept the will of nature. You have to say a willing yes to the *must.*"

This was a favorite lesson of Otto's, but it always left her confused.

"Yes, yes," she said, "but it begs the question. Who knows when this *must* appears?"

"Don't be stubborn, Eula. We know when we are confronted with the heartbeat or the stopping of the heart, with sunrise, sunset, with death, and the will of the universe."

"But shouldn't we encourage them to be white in a world so unfair to those who aren't?"

"It's not so simple. What about the truth they see? Perhaps the *must* in this case is that we have to accept them as nature made them. As outsiders. You know, whichever way they turn, they will always be outsiders."

"You used to be more hopeful."

"Please, accept given evidence. They're subversives twice over, once as imposters who play each other's parts, and once as self-identified Negroes passing for white."

"But they aren't," she argued with him. "They are patently white children, whom some would penalize for the choices of their mixed ancestors."

"That's our view. Tink of the confusion of color the grandmother's skin left on their retinas? The evidence of their own eyes, as you put it. And now you offer them the gift of a guilty privilege, a secret to carry with them when they walk off into the world. Which will happen," he reminded her, "in just one more year."

Otto had the last word, tying her to the twins again with his insistence on the existence of her own elusive second self, the one she had difficulty recognizing, and never really acknowledged unless she was speaking with him.

"I have a full hour for you," he said, sending her into a fright, thinking of his analytical mind at work on her, afraid she couldn't fill the time with self-observation he'd find worthy or useful. She needn't have worried. He did most of the talking, covering new and riskier ground. This time he wanted her to define herself sexually, though it might be difficult to lead her in that direction. He'd

been a target for moralists, along with all the other analysts coming out of Europe, and their apostles. Little more than pornographers, according to the would-be masters of the new Europe, and to the men he had betrayed, a sexual neurotic who had never come to terms with his father-hatred. Eula supposed he was healthier in this regard than the Freudians who condemned him.

"Society's problem with sex," he explained, "is really its problem with women and birth. In early art there is very little reference to sex. Do you understand? Ever since man recognized the connection between sex and pregnancy he's denied it with myths—virgin births, the migration of souls, what-have-you, anything to belittle the womb."

Did she agree?

"And women's part as the womb of mankind, the bloody reality of reproduction, made them suspect. It allied them with the negative forces. The real enemy was death. The pregnant woman could only be introducing another death to the world. Where else could this unnatural repression come from?"

His eyes were holding her fast.

"Explore the repression, Eula."

He wanted her to confess that her celibacy was a willed truth, that she was secretly content with it, though she might profess a longing to the contrary.

"You talk about a future that includes a husband," he said, "but nothing could be further from your daily concern."

He'd gone too far this time. She gave him what was on the tip of her tongue: "You know, Otto, I could live with someone like you."

Just mischief? Infatuation with his learning? The smell of tobacco, and the shambling way he fussed with his pipe? The way his hands played with each other? All the artless mannerisms that denied guile, asking innocently for affection? Whatever the provocation, all the intellectualizing and their earnest preparation for this talk crumbled. They both began to laugh. Not because she hadn't meant it, but because she had, and because it was not only incongruous, but impossible. Not that she would have cared a whit that a tall and striking Nordic woman like herself would look lost or ridiculous on

the arm of the soft, charming, learned little Viennese Jew, but because he was married, though unhappily, and separated by an ocean from his wife, and she was Director of the Drayton College Orphanage, a pilgrim in the progressive movement, held up by her colleagues as a paradigm for girls and women moving forward in the century, mentioned in the same breath with Tessie Croft, Miss Perkins in Washington, and closer, the nest of reformers over at Bryn Mawr who were sending a committed cadre into the settlement houses wherever they sprang up.

She had just thrown herself off the pedestal, and Otto, kind soul that he was, did his best to restore her dignity with a fulsome declaration. She was not imperious, he said, but imperial, and a saint among educators. By genetic strain, favored over the norm in height and athletic line.

He hesitated and then dared to describe the graceful way she carried the long double curve, breast to hip, given to attract the seed, then nurse and bear the child, which she'd never done.

"Otto!"

He ignored her protest.

A face that made men stare in admiration. A composure that unsettled them. An analytical mind that did not preen with self-important flourishes, but humbly sought truth and the pragmatic path. And all in the service of social equity. In social fact, more man than woman, but in any artist's view, a fecund vision of aesthetic and maternal grace.

"A foster-mother-superior," he said, calling unwanted attention to her presumed virginity. Leaving her ample room to deny it, accepting her silence, and moving on.

And Kerstin's "Mummy," she thought to herself.

She couldn't say she wasn't pleased by all his flattery. Or even its confusion of beauty, intellect, and social purpose. But eventually he would come to the other Eula, the one who might desert the cause for marriage and children of her own womb. Or the Eula who might simply give up in frustration with all the obstacles beyond her control, and melt in her own depression. Would she submit to the mold,

and be the woman who had been hired to raise orphans up to the distaff, to train women according to the precept carved into the wall—*une femme doit plaire, c'est son bonheur?* Or would she be the one he had come to admire, the one who had quietly undermined the will of the founder, looking for the potential rebels in her care and nurturing their rebellion?

∞

In their last year at the orphanage the twins were advancing rapidly into womanhood. Ellen Reilly and Eula discussed their case every week, watching them mature physically and socially, at last accepting friendships among their peers. Becca was now willing to walk into the village hand-in-hand with girls other than her sister.

The school's sewing instructor came to Eula, and said, "The Carey girl, Linny, I can't teach her anything. Her mind is fast, and so are her hands. She's finished before the others get started. She hardly pays attention to me, and why should she? She's designing her own line of clothes."

Linny shared her sewing skills with the other children. Though the instructor lectured, it was Linny who actually led the class by default. Becca was proud of her sister, though she spoke dismissively of the matronly talent, and invented a new name for Linny. Spider. "Always hanging from a thread."

If Becca was just waiting to be eighteen, waiting to escape the custodial hold of Drayton and take her sister as far away as possible, she no longer spoke of it. Eula missed the mischievous joy they had once taken in each other's company. That had been lost, or given way to a gravity of purpose between them, which had something to do with the color of their skins. They were often so quiet in their conversation it was difficult to know whether something had pleased or disturbed them.

The natural communication of twins passing adolescence? Eula knew this much: For the time being, they were each the black girl and each the white girl, accepting or resigned to their white fortunes while they remained at Drayton. They were taking part again in the

functions shared with the Flourtown boys. The episode at the dance wasn't forgotten by the village visitors, but the same boys still came to the socials. The Carey twins, though more reserved, were too intriguing to be ignored, no matter what had been said about them.

A further sign of the twins' new maturity was the remorse they felt for their part in Beverly Rice's departure. Eula had allowed Beverly to continue living in one of the Drayton-owned houses for a modest rent after her resignation. It was another small cottage on Bethlehem Pike, a half mile from the house Eula shared with Kerstin. The twins, after years of reflection and guilt, finally went with Eula's blessing to apologize on their former teacher's doorstep. After that they were used to riding two bikes down the avenue to visit with Miss Rice, and help her around the house.

"Your twins have turned out wonderfully," she told Eula. "I'm so ashamed of myself. I love their visits."

The Flourtown High School, ignoring Beverly's mathematical training, had made her a social studies and American history teacher. She was going to have the Careys in her classroom once again, for their last semester. And, for Eula, she'd be a useful reporter on the behavior of all the older girls away from their Drayton home.

Before the Fall term was over, Ellen Reilly reported a new development. Becca had her cap set for one of the wood newts, who had charmed her at the soda fountain in the village drugstore. It was worrisome enough to hear about her forwardness with an older boy at Flourtown High School, but now she'd been seen with one of those lost young men who played cards in the woods just beyond the Drayton boundary. It was a twenty-four-hour job for the constables to keep them moving, and if they weren't in the woods, they seemed to Eula just as dangerous hanging around the village. Really, her girls ought to have more sense.

There was another boy after the twins, Jason Coates. A horror, Ellen said, not just because of his vile tobacco habit, but haughty airs as well. He called the twins Raggle and Taggle, which they didn't know, and Ellen didn't tell them, referred to their Gypsy skin. Coates was only a middling student at the high school with no apparent

ambition. His father did advertising for the Pennsylvania Railroad's passenger service, and the boy thought this a significant badge.

Beverly Rice, reporting from the school, said Jason was a boy whose culture must have fallen off since he'd learned his cradle songs. *The Raggle Taggle Gypsies?* At the Fall social, Eula was introduced to his cavalier and conceited manner. He was slumming among them with the basest motive, and pursuing the Careys, either one, or both; it didn't seem to matter.

∞

Provoked by Otto, Eula told him, "I'm not a libertine."

"No, Eula," he said. "No danger of that."

He thought she should move faster in the sexual education of her orphans. Especially after one of them went into a panic, thinking she had injured herself mysteriously on a walk, her first experience with the monthly inconvenience.

"My housemothers," Eula told him, "don't think we should introduce these things before their time."

"Very American," Otto said, "very naïve."

"As a country," he told her, "America is in the early anal stage of its development. Or that's what Dr. Freud might say."

Once her girls walked into the village, or got on the public school bus, Eula could only hope their training and good sense would carry them through. At the Autumn Ball she was shocked by the casual familiarity between the Coates boy and Becca. And then Linny. It disgusted her. Nose to nose, and staring into one another's eyes, teasing the carnal prospect. Again the chaperones had to correct their dance embrace.

The situation became more serious in November, when Linny tattled on her sister that Becca and Jason were discussing sex. Becca's reluctance had more to do with doubts about opportunity and secrecy than moral restraint, or fear of the consequences.

After Eula brought the matter of the young couple's involvement to the Flourtown principal, he told Beverly Rice he wasn't surprised that one of the orphan girls was so forward and shameless. He wondered if any of the other Drayton wards, "girls without the moral

core of family," were corrupting the ordinary village children. "Do they give them adequate moral instruction over there? Are they able to absorb it?"

When Eula took the matter to Otto, he reflected only a moment before saying that the submission of Becca might be equivalent to the rape of Linny. If the feared event took place Linny would not only feel violated herself, but might actually imagine she had experienced the same shock of penetration, giving her ample cause for reprisal against the boy and her sister.

"That's going too far, Otto."

He cut her short: "Eula, counsel the child against promiscuous behavior. Keep a close watch on both of them. You don't want a tragedy when they're so close to achieving honest compatibility. When you're only months away from releasing them."

"By the way," he said, "you can assume the other one has a favorite of her own, and no doubt Becca disapproves of *him*. Twins seldom care for their sibling's choice of partners. I can tell you this: With these two, if one takes up the sexual habit, the other will not be far behind. In revenge, raped by her sister, so to speak, she may rape in return."

"They're very strong-willed," she reminded him. "Both of them."

"Exactly," he said. "And not afraid of life, only a little abandoned. In search of new anchorage, as all your girls must be."

"My God, Otto! You're siding with that Mr. Smug in Flourtown!?"

"Are these your own words, Eula, or mine—*concupiscence, consummation?*"

"All right," she said, "so what exactly do I do?"

"Don't moralize. Counsel that abstinence at this age is only common sense. I told you. Don't stifle pleasure. Let people encourage a simulation."

"What?"

"Whoever speaks to the children; if the desire will not be denied; let your older girls be told there is no harm in simulation."

She'd never heard the term and didn't care for the sound of it.

"What?" she asked again.

"Himmel!" he said. "Manipulation. The fingers. The hand."

She turned the conversation to compensation for his services.

"I can't be paid for this anymore," he said. "Not even by Tessie."

Tess was preparing herself to write his biography one day, and Eula envied her rapport with him. She'd seen a note from Otto that began, "Dear Tessie," and was signed, "Huck," in homage to her and to his American hero, Mr. Clemens. The impression of his intaglio ring, if he ever revealed it to her, could no longer seem important to her. In any case, there was nothing in her budget to provide him with a retainer, even if he'd demanded one. As for the twins, she asked Ellen Reilly to have another session with Becca, emphasizing self-respect and the pride that would come with patience and self-denial.

"If you have doubts about her willpower against these urges, maybe you should suggest simulation."

She flinched at hearing herself.

"Oh, they've been up to that already," Ellen said. "They're not just sucking each other's thumbs anymore."

She'd told them both, men would line up to marry them soon enough. But they wouldn't be spending their virginity here. Not while she was their housemother. Eula had nothing to teach Ellen about moral hygiene, and it was Ellen who lived with the twins, not Eula's wise man from Vienna.

∞

One evening Kerstin called from her bedroom down the hall. Already tucked in for the night, Eula groaned inwardly, not in the mood for another long evening chat at the end of Kerstin's bed, commiserating about the fools she'd suffered during the day. Not the nurses she worked with, but the men who made the rules for them, the infallible doctors, many of them too busy to travel to their patients, yet afraid that visiting nurses might be usurping their work.

"Who was it today?" Eula called down the hall.

"No, no," she called back. "None of that. I was going to wait till tomorrow, but I can't sleep. Come in and say good night, won't you."

"Kerstin, I'm so tired."

"This can't wait, Eula."

She slipped down the hall in her stockings and a bathrobe.

"Come here," she said, "sit next to me."

Kerstin reached for her hand, and Eula dreaded what might come next. She looked so flushed and excited. In all their years of living together there had never been the awkward moment of an aggressive affection, never a grasping for more than a sisterly embrace. She was fearful Kerstin was about to cross the line, that her devotion would become a needy pleading, and Eula's only response could be a signal of mutual desire or a long and difficult explanation, a rejection.

The pressure on her hand increased. She looked into Kerstin's eyes and her head began to shift ever so slightly from side to side, the merest hint of a negative reaction to the movement of Kerstin's hand that was now caressing the back of hers. Eula was still hoping she'd stop short of embarrassing herself.

"Come here," she said softly, moving forward to fold Eula in her arms.

She felt herself stiffen as fingers spread and began to knead her back.

"Oh, Eula," she said, "this is so difficult. But if I don't say it now . . ."

"Yes?"

"Eula! Dr. Tupperman has asked me to marry him and I've told him yes."

Kerstin let go, and drew back for a better view of her response. Eula was stunned. Kerstin clasped her again, tighter.

"I thought this might be hard for you; that's why I was putting it off, dear. Will you be all right?"

"I will, Kerstin. But what's happened? You told me Tupperman was one of the oppressors. Have you gone a little soft?"

"Eula, dear, is that all you can say? I never thought he was the worst. Far from it. You know he may be the best urologist in Philadelphia. There are four procedures named for him. Probably a record."

"Did he tell you that? How old is he? Do you realize you called him doctor? Are you allowed to use his first name?"

"Alex is only sixty-one, and very vigorous. What's a difference of years, if all this makes him so youthful? It's quite shocking, the things he dares to say, the things he's suggested. I couldn't repeat them to you."

"No?"

"Do you have a smile?"

Kerstin's announcement was so peculiar, so clearly freighted with a lusty excitement, her bosom rising with pride as she confessed her joy. So unlike Kerstin. And what were the shocking things Dr. Tupperman dared to suggest? What was she in thrall to? Coming into season at this late date.

"I know what you're thinking," Kerstin said. "What about my work?"

"No. Not at all."

"Yes, that's what you're thinking. Alex agrees my career will come first. Before the demands of the marriage. What man do *you* know who'd concede that? Of course, this could change if there were issue."

"Issue? Kerstin! Have children become issue? What kind of man calls a child issue?"

"Eula, dear. I was afraid you'd take this badly. It's a horrid abandonment and I'm sorry. But you'll be standing beside me at the ceremony. You'll be our regular guest in the city. It's going to be soon. We didn't want to wait until the Spring. Will you keep after the garden for me? He's in a hurry, and, well, I admit I am, too."

Stand beside her? Of course. But a regular guest? Not likely. Maybe she knew better than Kerstin what was in store, the domestic design, the surgeon of renown, this future father of "issue," intended for her.

"Eula," she said. "Your fear of marriage has the best of you. You don't even know Alex."

Eula shuffled back to her room, thinking she was probably meant to live alone.

∞

Behind the high spirit and expectation, December is a sad month in an orphanage. As the darkness deepens, morale walks backward with

the religious advent in the shadows of diminishing days. The season of obliged grace and joy collides with the parentless reality of the orphans' lives. The children hang roping, string lights, and go into the community to perform carols, manners, and genuflections. They know they're being patronized, they know they're singing for their supper. No one has to tell them. No fee changes hands; their whole lives are rocked in a cradle of alms.

"Aren't they lovely this year? Look at their sweet faces."

In the fantasy village on Bethlehem Pike, in the kitchen of Greystone, Kerstin's Bakery, flour is everywhere: in the girls' hair, on their clothes, the floor. Gayle Mackety, so chubby, Laura Baker's little personality gal, old enough to know better, threw the first handful. Then two others joined in the white battle. There was only a moment between delight and tears. They were coughing and blinking in the dust. Blame and denial. Mother Greene in the doorway; anger falling on Christmas puddings and pies. Only minutes ago, the chatter of a half dozen pastry chefs, thumbs in the batter, tongues licking the wooden spoons. But the hilarity has gone up in white powder; no one is happy in Greystone. There is only shame and sorrow. A house in mourning for the approach of Christmas.

Up the lane in Thistle, Kerstin's Bedlam, the girls talked of the coming present exchange. They were splayed about the living room, just more of the clutter, along with pieces of construction paper, coloring wax, little bottles of mucilage leaking through cracked rubber lips, dripping on the floor, along with some India ink, permanent. Card making. Mother Greene arrived, surveyed the mess with fox eyes, and wasn't angry. All she said was "Who's going to clean this up?" No capital threat. Still, the question hung over the room, a melancholy cloud growing for the new child, Janice Paine, into a gray cover over the holiday.

In the Borstal, where Linny and Becca had taught three thieves to say "shit" in the safety of a foreign language, it should have gone better. If the Borstal family skin was tough enough to withstand the season's rain, why the soft sobbing of the tough Clay sisters on their Christmas Eve pillows? Eula knew all the preparations might do more

to remind the children of their disconnected families than it ever could to fill them with the joyous combination of altruism and expectation, birthright of the home-nurtured at Christmastime.

Every girl in Drayton College had an outside family to visit from Christmas afternoon to New Year's Day, volunteer families who opened doors and arms to the children. It gave respite to a tired staff over the holidays, and was a chance for the children to take a new perspective on the world free from the crotchets of their housemothers. The twins had been taken over the Winter breaks and Easter holidays by a childless couple in Chestnut Hill, the Carpenters, Jacques and Marie, wealthy and retired, and instantly and completely devoted to the two girls.

Both of them liked their pro tem guardians but had taken a careless advantage of their hospitality. The previous year they had frightened the older couple, riding a bus into Philadelphia and roaming the city. In this, the year of their reform, they promised Eula they would go nowhere out of sight or calling distance of the Carpenters. They had each sewn a lavender sachet as a gift for their Christmas hostess.

Eula supposed they made their pledge with honest intentions. That was before Becca gave the Coates boy the Carpenters' address, before he came calling and lured her from the house. Linny knew what was going on, and followed after them with a prescience for Becca's evasions, the twists and turns that took them through the backyards and over the lawns of handsome houses. The trail led in several circles before the cold weather and the urge to hide a cozy tryst from the eyes of the world took Jason and Becca back into the Carpenters' house, through the cellar door, and into their basement guestroom. They couldn't escape Linny.

She reentered the house soon after them and followed down the basement steps. She found the cellar room locked, but heard mumbling behind the door.

"Go away," Becca called. "Leave me alone."

"You're not alone," Linny answered. "What are you doing? What is he doing?"

"Linny, it's all right."

"It isn't."

She banged on the door, and kept talking. Becca was angry, but Jason more so. He started in on the Raggle-Taggle thing. Becca was calling for her sister to shut up and go away.

That week Eula came into the Schoolhouse basement in time to see the latest verse on the "Slate," before Becca erased it:

Jason is a dirty flirt,
A filthy hand beneath a skirt.
Stop him now, I don't mean maybe,
'Fore he makes a dirty baby.

There was no case against the boy. He was a year younger than Becca, and up till then she had only encouraged him as far as anyone could tell. After the holiday, Linny's account was full of stammering contradictions, and tears. She broke down altogether when Ellen brought her to Eula's office for a confession. Or accusation. She wasn't sure what she wanted to tell them, and cried out in her confusion, "I don't want to have a baby!"

She had always shown more sense. Mother Reilly grabbed her by the shoulder and ordered her to stop. But there was more wailing, and finally Ellen took the girl in her arms, rocking her gently until she calmed and began to explain herself again, still without much coherence.

"He was calling us those names again, and it hurt."

"What, Linny? What hurt?"

She was confused, pointing down to her groin.

"But you weren't in the room with them," Eula reminded her. "You were never in the same room with Jason, were you?"

"She was!" Linny came back. "Becca was!"

She said Jason suggested they should let her join them. Didn't Becca always tell him she liked to share with her sister?

"That's when we pushed him away."

"Linny," Eula asked her again, "were you in the same room with them? Did he touch you?"

"You don't understand" is all she would say.

A visiting doctor said he couldn't be certain, but doubted either of the girls had lost their virginity. Becca wouldn't say any more about it. Eula's order to stay away from Jason wasn't necessary. Both girls despised him for his vile proposal that they share him. And it disgusted Eula that the twins had been introduced to this side of men so crudely, and simply because they were residents of an orphanage, considered fair game for village boys and wood newts. Otto called again for a course on marriage and family for the girls, and Eula was inclined to agree.

Tessie was all for it, too.

"But imagine me presenting *that* idea to our board, a course of sex education!"

"It's coming," Tess said. "Who better than you to put it forward?"

But should she lead in these matters because she ruled over a population that could be used experimentally, children without parents? Her girls were not laboratory animals.

When Tessie visited Drayton in mid-January of that year, she told Eula to stop devoting so much time and emotional energy to the Careys: "What will you do when your matched pair is tossed off to the world next summer?"

Eula rattled off a list of other concerns—Denise Carlson, the child who had brought Drayton head lice in 1928, measles in 1929, and ringworm in 1931, each epidemic or infestation after a different trip to a cousin's house in Norristown, the same girl whose scalp was being treated that week for impetigo. Medicated shampoos for every child in her cottage. Then there was Melanie Kott, in trouble again for a proposition she'd written to the garden boy who helped Mr. Henry on weekends. How could she deny it? She signed it with her own name. And Phyllis Long, who wrote her name in other people's clothes in indelible ink; and Mary Sanger, who lied about cousins who spent summers in Europe.

Tess saw through the list, which could have gone on and on, but in no way monopolized Eula's interest or time the way the twins did.

Eula was creating a problem for herself and for the Careys, Tess thought. Unless she meant to adopt them, she should draw back. They'd be helpless when they were forced to leave. They might become the celery children Eula warned against.

Adoption seemed a wild suggestion at this late date, with the twins only three years from twenty-one, and hardly fair to the other children. They'd be incredulous themselves if she proposed such a thing when they were only months away from escaping Drayton. Tess thought she might be surprised by their answer. But Tess didn't know how resourceful these two were, how consumed with secrets that had nothing to do with Eula or Drayton, nor how dangerous they might be to themselves. Otto had convinced Eula of that. He saw passion hidden beneath the present calm, and easily transformed into a kinetic danger.

Unlike the other girls in the graduating class, they kept their plans to themselves. Even if they'd wanted to, there was no way they could continue living at Drayton. The rules were clear about that. Eighteen and gone. As long as a child had finished her senior year of high school she must step into life. This might mean nurse's training, teacher training, or for those who were slower academically, service in one of the Chestnut Hill homes, a community where the same condescending admiration still stuck to Eula's graduates: "Oh, her girls are very clean."

She'd made some progress in placements since her first graduates had been loosed on the world. For a favored brainy one there was now a scholarship offered at Bryn Mawr or the University of Pennsylvania. Eula encouraged several of her best to go down to a settlement house in New York—Richmond Street or Henry Street, where she had contacts—to get some firsthand experience helping families less fortunate. If they had the talent for it, Tessie might eventually give one or two scholarships in the School of Social Work.

Now there was another position for an adventurous soul—the China Scholarship, in its second year, an opportunity for which Eula couldn't really vouch with great conviction. Jennie Alexie, the first girl to take it, had been in China for almost a year. Jennie, who came

to Drayton as a foundling without a relative in the world to fall back on, had been eager for travel. Professor Wu, who introduced the fellowship to Drayton, had asked for a girl interested in piano (he didn't say accomplished, and he never asked her to play), and bright enough to learn his language.

Mother Greene had brought Wu to the school after hearing him speak to an assembly at Swarthmore on justice for Chinese peasants. Just the man to take part in the series of political lectures Drayton offered the older girls and citizens of the Flourtown community. His fellowship, open to only one each year, would not be an option for inseparable twins.

∞

Eula warned Becca there would always be girls who made the great mistake, girls lured into early sexual experience, unplanned families, unwise marriages, babies too soon, and divorces. When the twins graduated the first week in June, their birthday would still be more than two months away in mid-August. Looking ahead, this gave Eula a little grace period to deal with their placement. Reminded of the day of reckoning soon at hand, Linny asked if she meant to put them out in the street.

The twins, who had sworn to put distance between themselves and Drayton, were now defensive about their drift. Their plans were dreams, Ellen said, and their dreams were secrets. She didn't think they had a notion how they'd support themselves in the still-wretched economy. Eula could imagine them gone one day without a "by your leave," never looking back, and, for that matter, never looking forward.

Early that Spring, Cyril invited Eula to another luncheon at his club. She expected him to fuss with her about Drayton security. Her little community of parentless girls now seemed to the outside world like a society of privilege, a little wonderland of stone cottages on rolling meadows protected by the largesse of a small fortune, received before the great fall.

They were only short miles from the darkest heart of city tenements, not far from the empty, window-shattered industrial decay of

Conshohocken, or even from a few of the fancy homes in Chestnut Hill, now bank-owned and empty, their young squires on the road with the rest of the country's destitute. There was no knowing the background of the unfortunate young men passing the grounds, not just on Bethlehem Pike but in the hedgerows and tree lines that marked the orphanage perimeter. Every day there were men sidling along their border, peeking at the orphans' lives, maybe even looking for a weak salient to advance on, or some vulnerable door to be breached for a bath, or food, or a more dangerous appetite.

Cyril disapproved of the rule that allowed girls to go about the wide and wooded acres of the campus, even though it had to be in groups of three or more. One of the Drayton neighbors had written to the trustees, suggesting that the orphanage ought to be registered as an attractive nuisance.

"I have something to tell you," Cyril said.

She braced herself to defend against one of his probes at her parietal rules. He put his hand on hers, settling with affectionate pressure. She stiffened again. No, she thought, not this. He's reversed his field. He's going to ask me. She had to pull hard to free her hand. It didn't stop him; he was already saying, "I've asked Mary Newbold to marry me. Yes! Chestnut Hill. And what do you think? She said yes. Eula, I wanted you to be the first to know."

∞

Otto, who had taken Kerstin and Cyril as unfortunate suitors of her ambivalent desire, was not alarmed by their abrupt departure from the field of play. But he could see she was depressed. One could hear it in her voice. He supposed it a transferred anxiety when she told him the twins were up to something. She thought they were naïvely confident, each counting on the other to know which way to turn when they walked out the Drayton gate.

"They're leaving with a balance of regret and ingratitude," she said, "as if I'd stolen their childhoods for myself, and now they're making sure I don't steal their futures."

Otto had no reply.

Part 2

Departure

It is the phantom of our own self which casts
us into hell, or transports us into Heaven.

E.T.A. HOFFMANN

Departure

"Because you made a secret with Japan. That's why China is full of communists."

Dr. Frederick Wu, the professor from Peiping, looked down from the podium right at the twins sitting beside Eula in the front row. As if they or any of the audience from town or the orphanage might have control over America's foreign affairs.

The little, bespectacled man, whose European inflections were at odds with his yellowish skin and his Asian idiom, bared his teeth.

"Yes you did!" he said. "Oh by golly yes." A grin spread across his face.

The twins met his stare, uncomprehending. One of them whispered, "Goosh."

"And you gave support and ammunition to the gangsters in Shanghai."

He was looking straight at the sisters, and still they did not blink.

"Your League of Nations was a League of Lies. Your fourteen points like darts in China's eyes. But you didn't blind her. And you won't keep her as the white man's mistress, your concession forever."

Eula cleared her throat, and he caught himself, nodding in her direction.

"So. Very sorry."

But clearly he wasn't. This was far different from the lecture he'd given the previous year, when he'd spent the hour pointing with a yardstick to a large map of China, major rivers, cities, and seaports, and the cultural springs of her many dynasties. It was an ancient civilization still waiting to be understood by the Western peoples; in particular by one of the Drayton girls, who would soon win the second China Scholarship.

This time his lecture was all about exploitation, and a coming retribution. The leader of this revolution was gathering strength in the hills, living only for the day of reckoning.

Eula didn't mind her girls hearing this, but there were complaints from her Flourtown neighbors in the audience. The village's weekly paper reported, "Communist Speaks to Orphans." What sort of views were taught at Drayton? Were these children, with no parents to defend them, being led into radical politics? Eula answered in the same newspaper:

Dr. Frederick Wu is a professor at the University of Peiping. For a second year he has visited Drayton for one day to speak to our girls about China and Chinese culture. It is part of The Drayton World Lecture series. These talks are open to the public. We welcome a wide range of views without endorsing them. Dr. Wu was invited as a scholar and as the donor of a fellowship now available to one of our Drayton graduates each year. He travels here with the approval of our government. His political affiliation was not stated, nor was it asked.

It suggested more confidence in Dr. Wu than Eula actually felt. She'd encouraged the first China scholar, Jennie Alexie, to accept his offer on the strength of his presentation, and the recommendations from two people she had never met, one an assistant secretary in the Department of Commerce in Washington and one a piano exporter from Baltimore. She did know that the professor had business connections with the piano man. That he had spoken at Swarthmore proved she was not alone in her presumption of his qualifications. His references are documented in her journals of 1933 and 1934,

both of which are in the Drayton archive. The only material deleted from these papers before they were placed with the other school records concerned her personal life and medical history.

∞

If the twins' lives at Drayton were full of mystery, their high school careers were transparent and flourishing. Both sisters graduated with distinction, surprising everyone in the final months after the holiday indiscretion. Becca achieved extraordinary marks in French and history in the last semester, while Linny had long since turned away from academic niceties on her way to taking top school honors in the domestic sciences. She had a professional's eye for design in fabric, according to her new instructor; she had drawn and sewn a marvelous dress, and reproduced it three times, for a school dance program.

"Not something I taught her." This teacher was as full of wonder and admiration as the Drayton instructor had been. "Born with the gift. Dance costuming is especially difficult. The child brought some of this from a previous life. I know that seems impossible. But then, so does her talent. Karinska's hand, Karinska's eye."

Eula wasn't sure what that meant. Linny seemed to know, though she shrugged it off.

The teacher said she could find her a job in New York with no trouble, but how could she go without her sister? Eula was sure she'd never do it. There were other things going on the twins' lives, hidden things. Their recent school triumphs brought them more freedom; it was harder to put a rein on them. The two of them had full senior privileges, which meant frequent unchaperoned trips into Flourtown, and more contact with young men anxious to keep company with them. There was one they both admired, the wood newt named Grayson.

Grayson was a wily charmer, whose threadbare wardrobe included the plus fours, sporting jersey, and winged brogans of a down-at-heel golfing dandy. He told them about the railroads west, and his stirring service in a Conservation Corps camp in Washington state, tales in which he was always champion of the underdog. They couldn't keep

their admiration for him completely to themselves. Much of it was revealed later, passed along by Erica to Ellen Reilly and from Ellen to Eula, after it was too late to do anything about it. He had taken them into his confidence, turned their heads with his experience of the whole American continent it seemed, though this had been limited to the tableau visible from railroad cars.

∞

When Eula finally sat down with the twins to talk seriously about their futures, they held each other's hands, and became a little weepy. Becca spoke first.

"I want the China Scholarship," she said. "I earned it. I got the best grades, didn't I?"

As if Eula would argue against her going.

"It's all right with me," Linny said. "We've decided. Whatever we do, we're starting opposite."

This was wonderful, Otto told Eula. "What you've been working toward for eight years. It comes at just the right moment."

He encouraged Eula to put Becca's name and credentials before Professor Wu first thing. She thought of the accusing way Wu had stared at the twins during his lecture, insinuating their complicity in American foreign policy, and the girls' initial cold reaction. She cast aside her doubts, accepted Otto's advice, and pushed ahead with the plan. Best to be completely honest with the fussy little Wu, she thought. He was pleased with her choice.

Eula did her best to describe for him the sisters' unusual sojourn at Drayton—the trials of twinship—and she made sure he understood what having a Negro grandparent had meant to them. Wu told her of his own experience with prejudice, being half-bred himself, half German and half Chinese. There were taunts in the Munich streets, called behind his back, or spit directly into his face.

She sat with the little professor as he interviewed Becca, warmed by the excitement and trust that passed between them. Becca promised to work hard to please the man, and he promised her an experience she would never forget. She would come home with stories of a

land magically different from her own, he said. She wanted to learn Chinese, starting right away she told him. He chuckled, maybe at the conceit of a girl with such ambition.

Eula had many questions about Jennie Alexie's progress in China. It might be useful to ask them in front of Becca.

"We have given her every chance to learn and improve herself," Wu said.

Eula was especially concerned about Jennie's failure to write more than one early letter, though she knew what a lazy hand she'd been at composition in spite of her intelligence, and how shy she'd been about expressing herself. It was her interest in the piano that Wu remarked on. This, he said, had made her a success and celebrity on the beautiful island of Gu Lang Yu, the Western concession where Becca might find herself one day if she was lucky. On the island, he said, Jennie was giving music lessons to the youngest children of the European businessmen who had built villas there for the vacation months.

"Perhaps Becca will be a better correspondent," he said.

Becca was nodding her approval of everything he said, afraid that any hesitation might disqualify her.

In this, the second and final year of Jennie's fellowship, she was her own boss, Wu reminded them, no longer obliged to work in his university office. This was the great opportunity of the fellowship, his own generous contribution to the young women "fellows," he made them understand, and so it would be for Becca, if she agreed to come to China. Why not decide right now? And Becca was nodding her head again, like a regular dodo bird, and smiling at him, and at Eula. What could she say to a strawberry child but, go, with God's speed.

"What was all that about Jennie and the piano?" Becca asked her afterward. "She always wanted to, but she couldn't play a nickel's worth. Just the same notes over and over again."

Eula saw nothing out of the way in this. If the academic Wu had some secondary interest in taking a Western instrument to the Orient it seemed a plus on his ledger. The more pianos in China the better, she reasoned. Her records say Wu made Becca's travel arrangements and helped her with her passport application. He brought her travel

papers to Drayton in early July of 1934. As with Jennie before her, the passage would be on a cargo steamer in Wu's care. To Peiping by way of Tientsin, leaving Philadelphia the following Monday.

That week the sisters went everywhere together, hand-in-hand, up and down the driveway, into the village, through the halls. They worked in the flowerbeds together with Mr. Henry. Ellen said they slept in the same bed the last week, folded in each other's arms, as they had done in their first days at Drayton. A regression more endearing than troublesome, and Eula asked her not to interfere. At mealtimes she watched them staring silently into one another's eyes. A communion, she supposed, beyond her comprehension.

Would they need help from Eula in dealing with the separation?

"No," Otto said. They had already separated. What she was witnessing was a period of mourning and apology for the injuries inflicted on each other. They were sweet as doves together, bumping gently as they strolled between buildings, or up and down together.

There was a small good-bye supper at Eula's house the night before departure; with Kerstin, Ellen, and the two girls. No river of tears, not even from Linny, who, after all, was the one deserted. When Ellen and Eula gave their toasts, neither child seemed the least emotional, or even appreciative, preoccupied with something else. The women might have known something was not quite right.

"You have free will," Eula told Becca, though she'd never really been sure this was true. "Listen to your better half," she said.

"That's me!" Linny said, putting an arm around her sister, kissing her on the cheek. "Miss Kieland means me."

Ellen's toast was for Linny, more eloquent, and longer. She praised the remaining twin for the gift she was giving Becca, the gift of letting go with goodwill and affection. She said Linny's travels would begin soon enough, and needn't be rushed just to keep pace. It was clear to them later how patronizing all this must have seemed to the girls, whose plans had gone far beyond the adults' presumption.

Eula stood and took a sip of sherry with her last words to Linny: "She also serves who only stands and waits."

And then thought better of it.

"Linny, dear child, I don't mean you're going to be stuck here, as if blind and helpless. Really, I'm only repeating what Mother Reilly told you."

They asked if they could be taken back to Stork Cottage. Eula imagined them lying in each other's arms, perhaps for the last time. Again, this didn't bother her. In fact, she was envious of their last hours of closest sisterhood, a union beyond her own experience. The nearest things to it she could imagine were the times she had caressed herself.

At the docks the next afternoon Becca didn't want anyone coming onto the boat with her—only Mr. Wu. Linny had agreed with her sister that she would not come to the pier. Becca went up the gangplank backward, waving as she went, with the same leather satchel at her side that she'd carried the day she arrived at Drayton. But this time an emigrant. A strawberry child on her way to China! If Eula had to lose a daughter of her very own, she thought, let it be this way. Tears? Oh, yes!

On the way back in the station wagon with Mr. Henry, she told him what Otto had said. That the two girls had actually gone their separate ways some time earlier, and had recently been grieving quietly for the hurt they'd done each other. Mr. Henry rolled his eyes.

"What?" she asked him.

"Excuse me, miss. We don't need anyone to tell us what the girls told us their own selves."

"What was that?"

"You know what," he said. "What the use of playing 'round it?"

She was silent.

"You know," he said at last, "one of them knows she's colored. The other one says she isn't."

When she came back from the docks, Ellen Reilly was waiting in Eula's office.

"She's gone!" Ellen said.

"Yes," Eula said. "With no regrets and not much by way of thanks."

Ellen bowed her head. "No," she said. "Linny. Linny's gone. I've called the Flourtown drugstore. I've called Beverly. I've called the village police office. I know she's gone."

No, Eula said. She was probably just wandering, walking out past the gate, and forgetting to turn home, dazed by the loss of Becca. It was getting dark. Darkness would turn her around.

"Her satchel's gone from her closet," Ellen explained. "There's no underwear in her bureau, no socks. She's gone."

The next morning the housemothers converged in Linny's room, all hoping she might have returned in the night. Eula gathered the children after breakfast in the Schoolhouse basement, and asked for their help.

"Linny Carey has run away," she told them. Had any of them heard her discussing such a plan?

No one had. Eula wasn't surprised. As far as anyone knew, the twins had shared conversation with no one but themselves in the last few days. Ellen confessed she knew that both of them had recently been in the habit of hiking off across the grounds on their own, or together. She knew the rule was "three," she said, shaking her head sadly.

Eula was thinking again of all the shadowy people who roamed along the edges of the campus, men who had little or nothing, not even shame. They might cadge any sort of favor—food or a blanket or matches or even a hurried affection—from the girls, some of whom, like the Careys, were old enough, advanced enough to be intrigued by the Gypsy style and rough charm of this declassed society of nomads. Eula had asked the town police for protection but she couldn't expect the two Flourtown constables to spend all their time in her woods.

In fact, there were dozens of these lost men—women, too, for that matter—wearing their only shelter on their backs, usually no more than a dirty overcoat, going by every day and, she supposed, through the night as well. All the orphanage could do was lock up extra tight when it went to bed. Sensing the danger, and without being asked, Mr. Henry had got in the habit of rousing himself twice during the night to walk a patrol of the service road and around each of the cottages.

Two weeks went by with no sign of Linny. Legally she was still a ward of Drayton, and would be for two more months, until her eigh-

teenth birthday. Police in five jurisdictions assured Eula they were looking for her, but she suspected Tessie was right; they should get used to the loss. They'd have to get on with their lives.

But Ellen Reilly had kept something from her.

"I didn't want to frighten you," she said, "and Linny wouldn't have told me any of it if I hadn't promised my silence. She was afraid she was going to hurt her sister badly, mortally. And she suspected Becca might likewise be thinking of ways to be rid of her."

Eula told her Otto had spoken of this possibility. She discounted it then as overreaching analysis, and she told Ellen now, "This is too melodramatic. Didn't you see them? A couple of lovebirds."

"No," Ellen said. "Linny told me the same day she left, while you were taking Becca to the boat. She said, 'It doesn't matter what I do, Becca's watching everything; she won't let go. We fight and we cry and we hug and we fight. It never ends. We want it to end.' Did you know they were breaking the rule? Riding their bicycles in the traffic on Bethlehem Pike. When they went to visit Beverly?"

No, Eula hadn't been aware of that. And she was annoyed not to have been told sooner.

"Yes," Ellen said, "I followed them out in their last week. I saw them turn off the curb into the street. They were arguing. On the road they were shaky, maybe a little frightened, trying to hold a straight line next to the traffic."

"Yes, yes." Eula didn't like the sound of this, and Ellen had only begun.

The twins were passing back and forth, she said, swiping stupidly at each other. The front of Linny's bike began to shimmy as if she were suddenly spastic. Becca bumped her from behind, and Linny veered into the traffic lane. Instead of turning back, she veered further into the road. The car behind her ran up onto the curb and came to a stop just before colliding with a pole. Becca rode into a hedge, which held her there frozen as she watched the scene in front of her unfold and unfold and unfold.

Ellen said she could never reconstruct it all. She couldn't possibly remember the order of it. Too many things happened too quickly.

But autos were weaving back and forth in all four lanes of traffic. Linny drove right across the path of a car coming toward her, and then back across the same lane as if she were in a do-si-do of bike and machines. One car turned all the way around and just kept going in the same direction it had been. A milk truck swerving to avoid her also crossed the line of oncoming traffic. Instead of braking, everyone seemed to be using their speed to avoid collisions, and Linny, careening over and back across the center line, could only continue to dodge and weave. She must have been a quarter mile down the Pike when she finally brought her bicycle to the side of the road.

Without pause, life and traffic went on as if nothing out of the way had happened. Becca caught up with her sister. They were laughing stupidly as they walked on beside their bicycles. The car that had run over the curb pulled back into the road and was on its way. No one else even stopped.

"You didn't need their permission to tell me this," Eula told her.

Ellen brushed the irritation aside, and went on: "While we were getting the girls ready for the swimming trip, Linny told me something else. You were already on your way to the boat with Becca.

"The two of them were so scared of what they might do to each other they were putting themselves next to danger, to prove, over and over again, that neither would take advantage of it. You know at the end they were sleeping every night in each other's arms. And the kitchen knife, the one missing from Thatch, was right under their bed."

"You didn't tell *me* that?"

By the time Ellen knew it, she said, Becca was already on her way to China. Safely apart.

They knew nothing of what had happened to the twins in Flourtown after the misadventure on the bicycles: the trouble that met them in the drugstore, sitting on either side of them at the soda fountain, the Coates boy who trailed them in, just to taunt them, and the wood newt Grayson, already there, handsome as ever, washed clean for once, out of the dingy plus fours in a new suit of clothes, apparently flush and offering to treat them. He was about to leave the state again, he said, going west to rejoin the Conservation Corps in Washington.

Jason Coates, listening to all of it, spun on his stool and asked Grayson: "Do you know who you're talking to? Do you know who these girls are?"

All conversation in the room stopped.

"They let anybody come in here now," Jason said. "I could be Little Black Sambo." He twirled again. "No, I'll be the tiger who turns to butter. How about that?" He spun on his seat again.

"Shut up!" Grayson told him.

"I'm turning into butter," Jason said, knocking Becca's legs as he turned, forcing her attention. "You can put me on your pancakes."

"They wouldn't have you on a left-handed toothpick," Grayson told him calmly.

"How about on a colored toothpick?"

Grayson climbed off his stool, walked behind Jason, and pulled him off the stool. There was no fight; Coates was no match for Grayson. He was grabbed by his collar and rushed out the door, onto the sidewalk. That was the end of it.

When Grayson came back in, he was too honorable to talk about it. The twins, as pleased with his modesty as his mastery of the situation, listened to more of his railroad travels. He'd just come back from Chicago, but was turning right around and heading all the way to the Coast this time.

"You're old enough to go yourselves," he said. "That's where people with real ambition are going."

"I'm going to China," Becca said. "I've won a scholarship."

"And I've won a trip to Timbuktu."

He turned to Linny.

"What about you? You could get work. It's not like here. But you can't go alone," he warned. "You need someone to watch out for you. There are plenty who'd take advantage, if you know what I mean."

∞

On the way to the pier Dr. Wu was all smiles, well pleased. Becca didn't know why he'd come to Drayton to gather her for the journey rather than just meet her at the boat. As if she might change her

mind at the last moment, or Miss Kieland might refuse to let her go if he weren't there to reassure them. Wu rode in the back of the station wagon. He was eager to get her on the boat. She was up front with Mr. Henry, and turned halfway around in her seat not to miss the things the professor was saying about whales, and porpoises that would weave a path for them to follow across the ocean.

"You wait, Miss Becca. You just wait."

She was afraid of disappointing him, wondering if she could perform for him as well as Jennie had. Like her, she'd be working in his office at the university in Peiping for the first year, helping with his English correspondence. He spoke English, Chinese, and German, he said, but only wrote English with difficulty.

Mr. Henry stared straight ahead at the road, and would add nothing pleasant to the conversation. Becca supposed he couldn't know much about what was happening in the world, because he'd told her China was a land where people got hungry enough to eat dogs while they let Christians starve. He said gangsters ran the big cities, and the government let it happen. How could he know these things about a place he'd never been?

There'd be time to learn the real story from Professor Wu once they were safely on the ship. Meanwhile, she was glad Mr. Henry was keeping his notions to himself. Anything could ruin this. They could get a tire puncture, and the boat would leave without them. She might get a fever, and Wu, not wanting a sickness in his care, would refuse to take her.

Worse, Linny could change her mind about going to California according to their plan. She might show up at the boat, and refuse to let Becca go to China. Linny's plan was a secret because they knew Miss Kieland would never let her go across the country with a young man she knew nothing about except that he was recognized by her older girls as one of the wood newts, a man at risk himself in the world. No matter how gentle and kind he had been with the twins, no matter how understanding and protective.

On the way to the boat, Eula could tell Becca was already missing Linny. The longest they'd ever been apart was the week Linny had

her tonsils out, and the most they'd gone without speaking was for a few weeks after their fight at the dance. She never believed that twins always know when something bad is happening to the other. It was incredible enough that they'd agreed to go in opposite directions.

Eula didn't know how to say good-bye. She was shouting at Becca to make herself heard over the noise of the ship's engine: "Drink boiled water! Stay with Dr. Wu! When you get to Tientsin, don't leave the International Zone till you get on the train!"

Here at the end she, too, was losing confidence, making China sound like a frightening place: "In Peiping, don't leave the university by yourself! Look, it's a German ship!"

On the side they read, *FREIDA SCHWARTZ, BREMER-HAVEN*, black letters on a band of red that ran around the boat like a painted ribbon. Eula was right next to her ear, still shouting: "I want you to write us every week. You tell Jennie one letter in two years is shameful!"

Becca threw her arms around Eula's neck, the only way she knew to make her stop. She had to raise her hand to keep the Director from following as she backed up the steep platform onto the ship.

"Do you hear me, Becca? Are you listening?"

Becca was both thrilled and frightened to be getting on the boat. It had never been so clear to her why she wanted to escape. To put an end to their study of twins, to flee the people who cared too much for her, the people who hovered over her life with so much concern. But now the fact of her singularity, never so stark, settled over her; she felt herself stripped bare of her lifelong armor, her sister.

The ship's officers were Germans who stopped and clicked their heels when they passed each other. They saluted like soldiers, throwing their flat hands at the horizon. Were they serious, or just playing at being Germans? Professor Wu told her to stay in her cabin; the sailors onboard were not to be trusted. He told her their behavior and language in the dining room were too coarse for a young woman, and right from the start meals were brought to her cabin, usually some

kind of sausage, cabbage, and boiled potatoes with a small dish of a bitter yellow paste, which she supposed was German mustard.

After her first dinner, Wu brought the captain of the ship and two of his officers to visit in her room. They spoke German, leaving her out of the conversation. No one was introduced; it was more like a display of what Wu had found in America. They set their jaws appreciatively; the captain spoke something behind his hand, and at last said something in English: "Ya, the little orphan *Schwarze,* eh?"

Was she to be ship's mascot then? She thought herself clever to have noticed, and a little special for them to name her after their boat. They clicked their heels for Wu, and left.

The window of Becca's cabin looked over the upper cargo deck, toward the bow. She was in a row of quarters just under the wheelhouse; Wu's cabin was right next to hers, with a door between them that could be locked from either side.

"For your protection from the seamen," he told her before locking her door to the companionway as he left. She looked in the mirror over her tiny sink, and saw Linny looking back at her, shaking her head. Her lips were moving slowly, "Lock the other door." Becca understood she meant the door to his room, and she did as she was told.

The sea was smooth that night. Even so, she slept poorly. The morning meal was brought to her cabin, again by the steward. He could speak some English, and she made him talk to her for a while. It didn't help; the door to the passageway was locked once more from the outside.

Dry toast, herring, and apple juice.

Later she saw Wu through her window, walking with the captain like an officer of the ship on a cargo deck below. In mid-morning he came to her cabin and gave her permission to take a chair to the railing at the side of the boat until lunchtime, but she was not to leave this deck. It would be dangerous, he said, to wander further.

She had learned something of their route from the steward, but was still full of questions. Why was she going around America on this cargo steamer instead of straight across the country on a train?

"The sun sets over there," she said, pointing to the west. Had the navigator forgotten the promised destination? She knew it would take several weeks to reach San Francisco, and another five weeks to Tientsin. All this before they got on a train for Peiping. But only if they started off in the right direction.

"These things are not your concern," Wu told her.

She was looking in the glass again, for another glimpse of her sister. And she was persistent in following Eula's advice: "Don't let anyone shame you out of asking questions—not anyone!"

"Can you tell me what's in the crates? Why are we going first to Baltimore?"

"You continue to ask? Why do you stand there looking at yourself? Are you so vain? Have we chosen the wrong girl? Read your book. You will not be ready for China."

Professor Wu called her the mascot name again, *Schwarze*. She looked at the book he'd given her. *The Asian Claw: Japan in China*, and her heart sank. The book was thick, with long words and no pictures. On the cover it said the author, Carlton Farrow, an Englishman, had risked his life in the Orient gathering information for this masterwork. He had been accused of spying by both Japan and China, and had been jailed in both countries. This was offered as proof of his fair approach to his subject.

Becca fell asleep with the book unopened in her lap. A horn startled her—loud and long. Men were shouting. She ran to her door, still bolted. She knocked, took off her shoe, and used it to bang louder. She yelled to be let out. A moment later the steward opened, and stood in her way.

"Be quiet, *Schwarze*," he said. "The Customs are onboard."

She didn't care who was onboard. He had no business calling her this name. She pushed him out of the room, and slammed the door, which was locked again from the outside.

The commotion was all about their docking in Baltimore. Later, she watched through her window as cranes lowered huge boxes into the hold. More wooden crates marked BALDWIN, and KUHN & RIDGEWAY. She knew they held pianos. Who would believe the

Chinese played pianos? A prisoner, she made herself a spy, keeping track of everything odd that was happening on the ship.

Supper was handed to her through the door again. She demanded to see Professor Wu. This time the steward would not speak to her. She cried for a while, and went to her mirror again. No Linny. She frightened herself, staring into her own face, and promised her sister anything if they could be together again, for the first time wondering if they ever would be.

Anything, she promised, she'd be white again as Linny wanted. Always.

∽

A few nights later, her door was left unbolted, and she snuck out after dark for her first tour of the ship. She went silently down the first stairway she could find. Her foot had hardly touched a lower deck when a hand fell on her shoulder. One of the Germans turned her around and marched her back to her quarters. Wu said nothing about this. The whole ship's company must have been told she was a prisoner on their boat. There was nothing to do but eat her meals and wait.

Several days passed before the professor showed his face again. He behaved nothing like the man who encouraged her to come to China. He came into her cabin without knocking, looked her up and down like a rude wood newt, and said, "We are feeding you too much."

Without asking, he began to search the room, going through her bureau, her closet, and the cabinet over the sink. He took a red ribbon off the dresser, and the red from her box of colored pencils.

"You should know these will be forbidden," he said, and he began to page through the travel atlas Miss Kieland had stuck in her bag.

"In China," he warned, "maps will put you in trouble," snatching it away.

"Are you ready for your quiz?"

"I didn't know there was going to be a test," she said.

"Let me see." He found *The Asian Claw* on her bunk-side table, noticed its pristine cover and crisp clean pages. Her handling hadn't even broken the book's spine. He assumed she'd never opened it.

"You didn't read this," he said. "Maybe we have to find other work for you in Peiping."

He was searching through the pages for questions: "What is the life span of the average man in China?"

"Twenty-nine?" she said, as if she were guessing.

"You are very lucky, eh?" He went leafing through the book again.

"Why is the Red boss called 'The Twenty-Eight Stroke Gentleman'?"

She looked at the ceiling, like a schoolgirl asking for an angel's grace, as if she needed help.

"Because it takes twenty-eight strokes of the brush to write his name. Why does he write it with a brush?"

Wu looked at her in wonder.

"You didn't think I could read?" she asked.

Becca knew he was trying to embarrass her, and she was spoiling his pleasure.

"You don't ask the questions," he said. "Feng Yuhsiang is . . . ?"

She answered slowly and carefully, provoking him with another correct answer: "A northern general who does not cooperate with Chiang."

This information had been in the back of the book, in the appendix. There was no way he was going to stump her, but he wouldn't give up.

"The Autumn Harvest?"

"That was the peasant uprising in Hunan in September 1927," she said. "They ran from Chiang's armies to the hills in Chingkanshan."

She was even surprising herself. Wu could not believe she had mastered his thick book.

"The Follow and Obey Service?" he went on.

"Chiang's people," she explained, without a notion of what this meant. "The Red boss calls them China's sheep."

He flipped backward through the pages.

"What was the Chinese reparation for the Boxer Rebellion?"

"Three hundred and thirty-three million dollars," she said. "What is a reparation?"

His eyes narrowed.

"Leighton Stuart?" he asked, a name she remembered from a footnote.

"The American missionary who started your college in Yenching. Because there were so many scholars of revolution at the university in Peiping."

She hadn't a clue what any of this was about, but thought she had earned the right to ask: "Where is the left wing of China? Can you show me on a map?"

"This is very interesting," he said at last.

He took her hand, his first friendly gesture, and smiled on her.

"I must be careful with you," he said. "If I wind too tight, you make a sour note, or maybe a string breaks and goes, kabom!" She was an instrument, which he had just discovered could be tuned to the key of his choosing, or perhaps broken by his carelessness. Her head was full of *The Asian Claw*—violence and betrayal, exterminations, gangsters, and fearsome things she'd never heard of before— warlords, the Terror, whoremasters, generalissimos. When Wu was gone, she looked at the last words again:

> China is a land of intrigue and sword, a land of uncounted ways to die, political traps, jails, fields of battle, floods, provinces of starvation, and a struggle for life behind the gates of ten thousand villages, a vast territory of lives uncounted and uncountable.

She had a change of heart, though not one she cared to reveal to her sister. In spite of her confinement and Wu's ugly turn, she was content again to be on her way, never mind what it would cost to send Linny a postcard, if there was any mail delivery at all.

∞

Becca was gone, and Linny was on her way, too, convinced that Grayson could be trusted. Becca had made her promise. They had judged the young man, not by his clothes, or his words, but by his protective kindness. Linny left Drayton in broad daylight, a couple of

hours after lunch, just after cleaning Miss Kieland's office for the last time. There was a note on her desk from Mr. Knows-What's-in-Your-Head, Mr. Otto Rank, who wrote that he was leaving her on her own now, going back to Paris to start another Institute for Psychiatry there.

Miss Kieland had warned Linny not to read her office mail, but what did that matter? Linny wasn't going to be her maid anymore, and besides, she knew they wrote back and forth about her and her sister. She was looking for her name, but this letter was mostly about his reasons for leaving:

> Most psychiatric institutes are like Sunday schools where the Old Testament (Freud) and the New Testament (Jung) are taught mechanically. That's why we need another institute, since you ask. Of course, I would admire to carry on a regular correspondence with you while I'm away.
>
> I've thought about your request for another consultation on the Careys, your anticipated depression at their departure, this period of their new vulnerability, and your assumption of fresh guilt. I still think they could be a mortal danger to each other, or even to themselves. Destruction of the double can play out as suicide, and you mustn't forget that, remote as it seems.
>
> Time is short. We'll have to use the telephone. In the meantime, Himmel, Eula! Don't anticipate depression. You know it can show up soon enough uninvited. A prompt from you may be all the fillip it needs to knock you down. Call me.

Linny dropped the letter and her dust rag on the desk. If she needed a final push, this was it. They were not just twins to these people, but an example of twins. Linny did like Miss Kieland. The woman had been like a mother to them, whether they behaved or not. She had given Linny fashion magazines with pictures of the most elegant gowns. She wanted to make the Director a dress like one of those, but one of her own design, cut low and long, using a newer French method of construction. With cloth cut at angles to

the seams for stretch, a stylish sheath that would fan out when she turned. She knew Miss Kieland would howl at the extravagant use of material. Then she'd hire Linny as the new sewing mistress of Drayton. She wouldn't have to look any further.

But Linny had no shiny material, no silk thread, and she had no time. And she'd promised Becca she would leave immediately. Grayson was waiting for her in the woods. For all her bridling at her guardians' smothering concern, Linny knew Mr. Rank was right about one thing. She and Becca could be a danger to each other. They were separating before one of them made a terrible mistake.

Fresh in their minds was something else the adults didn't know—the way Becca had cut her hand. Not in their fight at the dance as everyone thought, but afterward, striking at the mirror in the upstairs lavatory of Thatch, smashing the image of Linny's insolent face staring back at her.

∞

Grayson was in the woods as promised. So fit, Linny thought, for a man out of work. It couldn't be his fault. Dark-haired and tall, no longer in the tattered plus fours, but his new blue suit, something to be worn to work in an office. The pants and jacket were both a little too large, as if borrowed or poorly hired. Most of the wood newts wore the same suits every day, which only meant they had fallen on hard times, and who were the girls of Drayton to hold that against anyone?

Grayson always showed them the manners of a gentleman. When he told the girls' fortunes, he read their hands without holding them, without touching at all. Erica Cochran thought this was a certain sign of class. She was sure he had fallen from a high place in society. The twins, recognizing his hard luck, would take him apple butter sandwiches and fruit. And he told their fortunes for nothing, though sometimes he charged the others a quarter. Sure enough, he said, one was going to China, and one would be heading west on a train. With him!

Grayson said he was thirty, not too young, Becca thought, for a dependable chaperone for her sister. Going back to Washington state

to work in the Conservation Corps camp at Sunset Falls was only a temporary thing, he said. The camp had been built the year before with trees cut on the spot. He'd seen squirrels too many to count, and a place where a man with a rifle couldn't starve unless he was blind. He was a man who had fallen into the romantic life of a pioneer, a man who could survive in nature.

He'd show Linny how to do the same, if it came to that. Linny would be safe with him. He'd take her west on the Pennsylvania Railroad, and she wouldn't have to pay a thing. He wished he still had his guitar, he said, but it had been stolen, and he had since seen it in a pawn shop. He sang them a verse without it:

> *When the north winds blow, and we're gonna have snow,*
> *And the rain and hail come bouncing,*
> *I'll wrap myself in a grizzly bear coat,*
> *Way out on the mountain.*

The man who sang that for money, he said, wouldn't know a gondola car from a Pullman, but had the nerve to call himself a singing brakeman.

Becca said it wasn't as if Linny was going west to be with him, only that he'd escort her past danger, to the West Coast. He was sure he could get her kitchen work in the camp in Sunset Falls. But why should she settle for kitchen work? After all, wasn't she double master of sewing rooms—at the high school and at Drayton—already handier at a dozen stitches than the women who should have been teaching her? Linny had shown one of them how to make a stronger binding with an overlaid backstitch, and had taken the other's job by default, but with enough tact to keep the woman from losing face; she could help the slower members of the class. Linny was overseer of all the machines at Drayton, and was the only one the company man cared to speak to when they needed repair.

It was when she demonstrated what could be achieved in flexibility and design by cutting materials at an angle to the cloth's grain that the Flourtown High teacher came to Eula raving about her. She

had shown she could make a dress that held a shape, ignoring the pattern books, designing clothes herself. She was sure to end up in New York, famous. For Linny to give this up meant something else to Becca, who said her sister was making white women's clothes. And why would she want to decorate all that vanity?

∞

After reading Mr. Rank's letter, Linny went straight to her cottage. It was hot, and all the Drayton girls on campus were being taken to the swimming hole on Wissahickon Creek for the afternoon. Linny begged off, telling Miss Reilly her trouble had come early. Nurse Jean came and fussed over her, and said she must lie down for the afternoon. Instead, Linny waited for the housemothers to gather the other children for the walk to the creek, and then began to follow Grayson's drastic instruction.

She cut her hair back, right down to the scalp. She put on the bib overalls she'd taken from the garden shed, and the work boots. Against his orders, she packed her old satchel, mostly with underthings. Miss Reilly had taught them that much about travel hygiene. She set off across the meadow and found Grayson in the woods, impatient.

"I told you, no bags."

He took the satchel, spun, and hurled it away. The bag struck a tree and her underwear went flying over the ground. She felt herself blushing, violated, but he'd already turned his back on her, heading for the road.

"Are you coming?" he called over his shoulder, leaving her no time to gather her things.

"Don't worry," he said after a while. "We'll get you another satchel. And there'll be a lot more than your unders in it."

It seemed just a lark at first, fooling the busman on their cross-county way to Paoli, then dodging several conductors on the way down the Main Line into the Philadelphia station. They were put off trains at two stops before reaching the city station. Waiting for a second local in Ardmore she worked up the courage to ask why they were heading east to go west. She said she hadn't expected to be traveling like a bum.

"Sunset is that way."

She pointed out the obvious, wondering if he were steering them toward a place and purpose of his own. Moments later she had her answer. A train shot past them, a west-winging streak that sucked them toward the track. She was thankful for his bracing hand on her shoulder, the first time he'd touched her.

"You wouldn't want to jump that one, would you, mister?"

She was "mister" now, and she understood their direction. Anything going as far west as they were would be flying through the local stations. But when Grayson said the journey wouldn't cost her a cent, she didn't know he'd meant they would cheat and steal their way across the country, or that he'd defend this as a free man's right. Linny was already a fugitive, a minor about to move from state to state with a man close to twice her age.

He wanted her to know he was in far greater danger than she was. He wanted her strapped tight and flat as a boy in her overalls. And if they were ever stopped and questioned they should pretend to be strangers to one another, traveling in the same railroad car by accident. Linny, thrilled for the moment by her delinquency in the company of a righteous outlaw, felt safe enough with this athletic man who would keep his hands to himself, while he took her all the way to the Pacific Ocean. She was on her way, with no intention of turning back. She hadn't imagined that freight cars would be their Pullman coaches. Or that for porters they would have brutes with clubs, who, given the opportunity, wouldn't mind breaking their heads. But there'd be no sniveling; Becca wouldn't have to be ashamed of her.

They sat on a wooden bench in the huge waiting room for most of the afternoon like legitimate passengers with tickets for a late train. They were pretending to read newspapers. Grayson explained the order of things. Wait for dusk. Then run along beside a passenger train as it pulled from the station. Use it as a shield to reach the freight yard unseen. Then look for a freight train already made up. Find an open car that was going beyond Harrisburg. He knew how to read the code chalked on the side.

A policeman had his eye on them. Grayson nudged her, a signal for her to walk across the concourse to the ladies'. Meanwhile, he found them a meal of two rolls on a table in the cafeteria. In the ladies' she glanced up at a troubled image of Becca over the sink as the two of them washed their hands. Her face was dirty, and her hair chopped off in a ragged pattern that left some patches almost bald. She felt better when her silly-looking sister began to grin back at her. They each said, "Good-bye," at once. They raised their hands to touch each other's lips, but could get no closer than their fingertips.

Later, outside and crouched behind a switch in a maze of tracks, Grayson found a piece of coal between the ties, and told her to rub it over her face. She refused. He did the job himself. He wasn't at all the same young man who invited her on this journey. She struggled free of his grip, and stared at him.

"You don't understand," he told her.

He was disgusted. A few minutes later he was pointing to a line of cars.

"There," he said, and then they were trotting easily along beside the moving wagons.

"You first," he said.

She thought he might watch her climb into a car, and then wave good-bye and be rid of her. She wasn't turning back.

"Not that one," he yelled from behind.

Too late. She was already halfway in the car, her legs dangling, and the train gaining speed. Her foot hit something with force and went numb. She crawled into the car, alone, on her way west, and frightened out of her wits. She was cursing herself and Becca for trusting a wood newt. She sat for several minutes, her head between her knees, a failure at running away, intending to get off the train at the first chance, to give herself up to the police, and beg to be taken back to Drayton.

Still in despair, she heard a whoop, looked up, and there was Grayson overhead, like a hero in a comic book, swinging down from the roof and through the open doors of the boxcar. She wanted to grab him, and shake the devil out of him. He was full of himself, how

he'd climbed the ladder of the car behind them, jumped to a handrail at the end of the boxcar, and made his way along the roof to the doorway. Her head was turned again; she was on her way with her protector, Grayson.

"How instant is salvation" came to mind from the hymn Becca used to hum after singing with the colored women, when she'd been religious, and colored herself.

Grayson didn't seem angry now, but he said if she didn't follow orders he'd push her off and let the bums do as they pleased with her. She had got them in a pickle, he said. He could put things right but there was no more room for mistakes. This car would be sent north at the end of a black snake, he said. A coal train going to Scranton. They'd have to jump before the yards in Lancaster, where the rail bulls were especially vicious, where a man might be clubbed to death just for sport. He was scaring her into complete submission. She could only think of the coming jump from the moving train. Rubbing her painful ankle, whimpering, she confessed all her doubts to Becca.

Grayson was showing off his train lingo again. As they flew through the night, he said the engineer had the throttle at company notch— fast—and warned her again about the cinder dicks, the railroad police, who would hound them all the way west. He did seem more comfortable here than in the woods at Drayton. He wouldn't touch her. When she leaned against him for support, away from the rattling wall of the car, he pulled himself away. She regretted her butchered hair. How could anyone look at her with respect or kindness?

At dawn the transfer to another train went more easily than she could have hoped. Grayson eased her jump, and she was able to lope along on her own with not much pain. They climbed into the very next train that came by, which was hardly moving. As it came alongside them, the engineer was looking directly into her eyes, waving his finger at her. He gave a blast on his horn, and she jumped backward.

In their boxcar Grayson taught her another trick—how to climb the slats on the inside wall, close to the door, to get themselves off the floor so they weren't seen when a patrol looked in. The car was

shunted once, reconnected, and finally traveling at pace again. When the sun dropped close to the horizon, he said, time to eat. He was looking for farming landscape, corn. And listening for two long blasts and a short on the whistle, the signal of a grade crossing and reduced speed.

They tumbled off in country completely flat to the horizon, and wandered along the tracks till they came to a river. Climbing down the bank under the railroad bridge they came on a group of two dozen or more men standing over a fire roasting a goat on a long spit. Further down the stream there were several lean-to structures built between the trees.

Grayson said they should approach them slowly, and not ask for anything before these men had eaten their fill. She thought it was a little miraculous that one of them recognized him.

"Professor," the man said.

This man wasn't dressed like the others in a lost-and-found of baggy overalls. He had a suit like Grayson's, still creased, and he seemed to be a recent arrival in the company of the poor. He was introduced to her as Gerald Cormack. Tall, with a long sad face, and drooping eyelids that might have closed completely but for continuous effort. He had just buried his daughter, he told them, a victim of typhus. He looked down at the valise in his hand, all that was left of her, two dresses and such as she had traveled with. He turned aside in a shame of tears.

Grayson put an arm around the man. He told Linny to find a private place downstream and wash herself in the river. When she came back they were sitting on some paper on the ground, in conversation, already sharing some of the roast goat. They gave her a small portion. She was ravenous, ready for gristle, fat, or lean.

They had found themselves a little village on the plains. It had everything, they explained to her—transportation, the tracks and slow moving rolling stock; a river, the Mohican, Gerald said, and you could get sick as an Indian from drinking it, full of cow piss and so forth; small farms to plunder; and constables scarce for miles in any direction. Though that would change quickly, he said, in a day or two when they were spotted and farmers began to complain.

What's your buddy's name, someone asked Grayson.

He called her Joe-Joe.

"He's got a sissy voice for a boy." Had she been cut, or what?

They weren't fooled for a minute by her flattened figure and ragged haircut. Grayson nudged her and told her not to worry; they wouldn't be camping anywhere near these men.

Gerald had extra blankets and a tarpaulin, which his daughter had used, and they were welcome to them for the night, he said. The three of them made their own fire upstream from the others. She felt like a regular pioneer woman that first night on the plain, sitting between two protective men. In fact, her safety from the other men seemed to be their first concern. When the campfire conversation turned to plans and destinations, Gerald seemed surprised.

Didn't Grayson know that his camp at Sunset Falls had been closed, that it was no use going back there, that all the camps in the Cascades Range in Washington were shutting down that year? They were letting the older men go, and turning new ones away. It was in all the papers.

Grayson stood up as if stunned by the news. She shouldn't worry, he said, but everything had changed. She went to sleep thinking again she might have to turn back to Drayton. She'd need their help. She slept on the ground between the two men, close enough to feel the warmth of their bodies, and neither one of them put a hand on her.

In the morning she saw that Gerald showed Grayson his wallet and the green bills in it. And he had silver in his pocket. This is why they had eaten without argument the night before. He spent another quarter on some scraps of meat for their breakfast. They gave her a sheet of newspaper, and told her to find a place in the woods to do her business while they did the same. When she came back they were arguing about a number.

She heard Grayson say, "Eighty."

Cormack said, "Seventy-five, and that's top."

"Look at the goods!" Grayson argued.

"Seventy-five," he said again, "just like last time and don't try to pull anything."

Cormack's eyes were no longer sleepy, but wide and angry. He'd forgotten about his daughter. When the two of them saw her listening, their dispute was over. They all sat down to make plans. They were trying to talk her out of going back to Pennsylvania. What did she most like to do? Gerald asked. She was best at sewing, very good at sewing, she told him.

That's wonderful, Gerald said, because he knew the very woman in California who would give her all the sewing work she could do, a friend of his sister's who made clothes for the kind of families that had their own tailors. No, she said, she thought she ought to be going back to Pennsylvania.

That wouldn't be smart, Grayson said.

"Listen to what he's telling you. The work you like. It's a sure thing."

She was shaking her head, no.

"San Francisco," Gerald said dreamily, "what a city for a young woman."

"No," she said, "I'm not going there. I'm going back to Drayton."

"No, you're not," Grayson said. "You ran away. They don't want you anymore. Anyway, I wouldn't let you go back where they use you like their private maid."

"It wasn't like that," she said.

"Of course it was," he said. "Listen, Gerald, you'll help me, won't you? We can't let that woman have her again." They walked away, along the river, discussing the situation, and came back with everything settled. She heard an engine coming. From the west, they said. Grayson was climbing the bank to see what sort of cars it pulled. Others were climbing the bank with him.

Cormack opened his valise to show Linny his daughter's frocks, two showy dresses, poorly made with frayed seams, and some machined lace at the collar. One was lavender with puffed shoulders, and the other a blue satiny thing with long sleeves. Both of them too cheap for her, the hemlines way too high. Hardly traveling clothes, but he was insisting that she take one of them into the woods and try it on.

The train came rattling slowly over the bridge, shaking the ground, while Gerald was explaining the dresses were going to be hers. She understood some deal had been struck between the men. She scurried up the bank to see the last of the freight cars disappearing down the line, with someone hanging from a handrail. Then gone around a bend. There wasn't one man left standing by the tracks. Grayson on his way east with all the others who had gone up the bank.

She imagined him in his own car, a huge private compartment, and richer with a wad of Cormack's money. Those other men, where did they think they were going? Scattering like trash blown backward across the country, going back to whatever mischief they'd come from. And she saw herself being blown as the wind might take her, no better than one of them. All up to their own tricks, claiming their place wherever they found it.

She sat on the ground for a while, silent. If she were going to use Cormack, she shouldn't show how angry she was.

"I won't have you looking like that," he said.

"Like what?" she said. "Who said I was going anywhere with you?"

"You want to be left with them?"

He gestured toward a half dozen filthy faces, the remainder of the camp, all looking her way.

He said that from then on, she must pretend he was her father, and for the time being she did as he told her. He made a shelter for her with the tarpaulin draped over two saplings, and she obliged him, changing into the blue dress. Cormack reached into the valise again, and pulled out the very thing she needed, he said. It was a cloche hat that could be pulled down over her ragged hair.

The men across the clearing began to whoop and cheer as if she'd been dumped into camp for their pleasure.

"Never mind them," Cormack said. "They're common."

She could only follow him down the river, valise in hand.

"What about the blankets, the tarpaulin?"

"They can have them," he said, looking back over his shoulder. They were the price of escape. He was running now and she struggled to keep up. She was exhausted when they came to a highway

bridge, and made their way up through the underbrush to the road. An automobile was sitting at the far end, much too convenient, like a taxi service. The driver said he was only cooling his engine, and would be cranking soon. Would they like a ride? A lift, he called it. He was going north to Chicago.

"Too lucky!" Cormack said, and for one of his five-dollar bills the man gave them the lift all the way to Chicago, driving until he had to turn on his headlamps, even delivering them to the rail yard. But first thing in the city, Cormack ducked into a bookstall next to the station. He sent Linny to the back of the store while he chatted with the merchant.

Everything was falling into place for them, Cormack said, arranged by a favoring fate. If the first half of her trip had been stolen, the second half would be paid, full fare. With Gerald Cormack, she was going to travel with tickets. Before they talked anymore about where she was going, he treated her to a roast beef dinner, and lemon pie. While she ate he began to talk about the wide reputation of his sister's friend in San Francisco.

"They wanted her to go to France," he said, "but she was just too darn happy in California. And that tells you something."

Not much, Linny thought.

He said she might be surprised by how much he knew about the last thing in sewing and fashions.

"Listen," he went on, looking around the cafeteria, in case others should hear. "Have you ever heard of these people?"

He pulled a pencil from his pocket and wrote his secret on a napkin: "THE CALLOW SIRS."

"Heard of them? The very ones who wanted my sister's friend to come to Paris, France. And she turned them down!"

This Cormack was a complete fool. She knew very well he had got the name from the man in the bookstall. She knew who the Callot Soeurs were. Marie, Marthe, and Regina, her heroines from the fashion magazines Miss Kieland used to buy for her, the ones who made the Charleston dance possible for ladies of class. She thought of the short chemises with flared vents and the most intricate embroidery.

This man was an idiot. But she was scheming, too, and would use him, as long as it was convenient.

The next morning she was surprised again. The coach they boarded was not going east. The conductor told her it was one of three that would be switched in Kansas City, and pulled all the way to Oakland by way of Salt Lake. She considered getting off the train in Joliet, and fending for herself. But she had nothing; she'd have to turn herself over to the police, and she wasn't ready for that. She wasn't scared anymore.

Linny had her mind made up for adventure. And when she looked in the lavatory mirror she saw Becca agreeing with her. Let this idiot Cormack pay for her first trip across America. Every few hours he was asking if she wanted another meal in the dining car. She was well fed when they reached California two days later. On the way, she'd made and lost two friends—a nurse and her travel companion on their way to Oakland. They were worried that a beautiful and polite young woman should be traveling with such a boastful talker. Their warnings became a nuisance.

"The dress, dear," one of them said, "it calls too much attention."

When they became meddlesome, she stopped speaking to them. None of their business that she hadn't a shred of interest in the man who was paying for every little want of her journey, though he never let his hand stray to familiarity, while they sat all day and all night right next to each other, sleeping and waking, in the coach.

She decided to accept his introduction to a woman he referred to as Mumsy, who ran a rooming house close to the San Francisco waterfront and knew his sister and the seamstress. He was sure she'd give Linny bed and board in return for house chores. This would carry her over until she had met and settled into her sewing career.

To make sure Linny didn't feel trapped he was going to buy her a rail ticket back from San Francisco to Pennsylvania which she could carry with her at all times. When she was more comfortable with her situation, she could cash in the ticket and keep the money. For all his blather, Cormack seemed as much like something for nothing as the

orphanage. It was flattering to think she was getting all this just for being herself, not for being the perfect double of a sister.

Close to Oakland, she went into the train's lavatory just to use the mirror, just to say: Becca, look at you! Look at me!

Mumsy Crider was nothing like Linny expected. Everyone, not just Cormack, called her Mumsy, including the boarders, and if she knew Cormack's sister, she made no mention of it. She was short and stout like Mother Crane, but with flaxen hair and a face which shifted in an instant from twinkling pleasure to a grimace of disgust. Linny saw that her humors were not feelings but decisions of stunning speed.

"Welcome to The Sea Tossed," she said, "and isn't that what all my girls look like when they first arrive? Tossed by the waves, just like you, dear. Take off your hat, and let's have a look. Lordy, look what he's done to this one. Well, it'll grow back, won't it?"

She was looking closely at Linny's scalp, the same way they checked at Drayton, for lice. Right away, Cormack explained to Mumsy about the sewing, and that if Linny were going to stay, there would have to be the introduction to the sewing lady. And it was all yes, yes, yes with Mumsy, all in good time.

It was cold and foggy on this low street of the city. Maribon, a downcast chambermaid, cheered a little when she was told to take Linny to the attic room to see if it would suit her. Maribon had a pretty mouth but horrid teeth. She was full of chat, trying to tell Linny everything at once: "The Sea Tossed, ha! Mr. Williams and them calls it The Sea Toast, because every morning the toast under the eggs is soaked in the poaching water. You think this is cold, you wait, the heat don't make it to the third floor, and you're in the attic, no, it's not like the pretty rooms downstairs, just the wood supports and the outside boards. You better complain or you won't get an extra blanket. Anyway, if she likes you, you won't be here long, you'll be working at the house on Carter Street. Not me," she said with pride, "she says I'm too valuable right where I am."

They'd hardly got to the second floor when the arguing started in the kitchen. Linny wanted to hear what was going on down there, but Maribon wouldn't stop chattering: "That dress you think so

much of, it's nothing to what they wear over there, so you can bring your nose down out of the atmospheres. I'll be teaching you your chores, what you'll have to do every day. And how to keep yourself clean, where have you been, anyway, whew! She'll want you to take a bath first thing. The tub's on the second floor, towels in the cupboard, end of the hall, and she might walk right in anytime and check your pootie so don't be careless." Her conversation was breathless. A lot like Mumsy's.

Maribon went right on: "Sundays you can't go anywhere, though you might want to. Reverend Charlesburg comes to the house and gives training in the Scriptures right here. The Body Rapture. You know, the Holy Sensations? And in the afternoon there's personal instruction, and guilt washing. Guilt is just another dirtiness, isn't it? Dirt that's got to be washed off before there can be the true sensation."

At the time, Linny only thought the girl was a little mad. No stranger to religious blather, she knew if this was anything like Reverend Light's congregation in St. David's, it was money that made it run.

Maribon stopped at last and cocked her ear to the loud voices below them.

"You old cow!"

"Get out!"

Cormack and Mumsy were arguing numbers the way Grayson had with Cormack, but this time Cormack was on the larger figure, all in favor of one hundred and fifty. And she said she was damned if she'd tolerate this every time he showed at her door with another poxie slut.

"Foul with impetigo and ringworm, too, by the look of her. One hundred, and you're taking me to the poor house. Take it, or leave it, and get out!"

"She likes him, eh?" Maribon said. "I can tell."

Linny couldn't.

"Oh, yes, if she didn't like him, you'd know it. You go down and take your bath now, and I'll call you for supper. Broth in the evenings, you know, so we don't start beefing up like cattle, Mumsy

says. Can you read? There's Reverend Charlesburg's booklet on the Holy Sensations there by your bed. After dark's too late to read, there's no gas up here. After supper, don't wait too late for your last trip down to the johnnie."

"How old are you, Maribon?" she asked.

She looked at Linny for a long moment as if deciding what might be believable.

"Truthfully," she said, "almost thirteen. But Mumsy says I'm ready as I'll ever be, if I'd just learn to keep my mouth shut."

"Maybe you talk so much because you're afraid," Linny said. "You don't have to be scared. You could probably go somewhere else."

"Oh, no," she said. "All the doors are locked tight. You can't go out. At night, even the bedroom door."

"Why is that?"

"You don't know much, do you?" she said. "About the central sensation and all."

"No," Linny said. "What's that?"

Maribon was indignant. "If the door was open any man in the house could come in and practice the body rapture anytime he pleased. Mumsy doesn't let anyone get away with that."

Linny had heard enough. She was on her way down the stairs. But Mumsy was on her way up. The woman knew exactly what Linny had in mind. She backed her up the steps, scolding her "little blabber-mouth," Maribon.

"Get down there and run your new sister's tub, and just a little hot, there won't be any left for the others."

"Never mind the bath. I'm leaving," Linny told her. "I'm going to the police. I want the ticket Cormack bought for me."

"I've just been talking to the police," Mumsy said. "If they catch Mr. Cormack it'll be the last time he crosses lines with a child. The sergeant on the street knows all about you. We're not going to let that woman in Pennsylvania get hold of you either. Nobody's going to make you a slave again. You'll be safe as Snow White right here."

Linny went past her, but at the second floor landing found a doorway bolted in front of her. She ran down the hallway to a fire door. It was locked, too. She cursed the woman.

"You'll get over it," she said. "Wait till you see what's coming in the morning."

Linny submitted to her capture for the night, took her bath, had her bowl of soup, and put on a shift left on her bed by Maribon, and a pair of long woolen socks that would keep her legs warm. She even took a look at Reverend Charlesburg's pamphlet:

The Body Rapture

The skin is the first layer of resistance to the Holy Word. On top of this there is almost always a patina of guilt, which must be cleansed before the first communion of the inner spirit and the Purpose can begin. We trust to Science here. Consider the Epidural, and then the Middle Layers, each with its degree of Laudable Penetration, and the Subdural, and after these, the Sacred Cavities, through which life itself is carried, seed and infant, and where the Central Pleasures are celebrated. There is a curse on the ones who turn from these with a shameful face.

It is worrisome that the men have taken to the faith more readily than the ladies. Our Mission is to gather women to Testimony, turning our efforts to the Campaign for Conversion and Salvation.

Ahead were chapters on Laudable Guilt, Inconsequential Guilt, Guilt as Barrier to Completion, and Guilt as Ordinary Dirt; then The Holy Sensations, The Body Rapture, The Central Pleasures, and an appendix of Dermatological Terms of Religious Significance.

She saw that Mumsy's business must depend on girls as dim as Maribon, not just destitute, but stupid and gullible as well. When it got too dark to read, she felt her way down to the second-floor bathroom, where a dim light was still burning on the wall. She wanted to look at her sister, face to face. To let her know what was happening

to her sorry twin, locked up for the night, while Becca sailed free across the world. She would have promised Becca anything, even changed color for her, if only they might be together.

∞

One of the Drayton girls found Linny's leather satchel at the edge of the woods on the south border. It had been opened, and her white underthings scattered on the ground. To Eula they were the sodden evidence of assault and struggle. Her little community was petrified, all of Flourtown as well. The girls were gathered and questioned, first in an assembly, then individually. If they knew anything they dared not open their mouths. Their fear was palpable, and so was Eula's.

They passed a miserable week. Village and city police promised a wider investigation. From their grunts and silences, Eula imagined the worst; if they found Linny, it would likely be her defiled corpse. The girls didn't have to be told to be careful. They wouldn't even walk in the meadow in groups. A picnic in the woods, out of the question. The seniors stopped riding their bikes into the village. They were hunkered down and waiting for graduation from their suddenly fearsome acres, even children with a year or two left at Drayton. They couldn't go on this way.

Eula tried to be happy in deference to Kerstin's wedding, which was to be held at their cottage later the same month. But Kerstin was despondent herself, sick with Eula over the loss of their twin. There was more; Kerstin was having second thoughts about her doctor-lover.

Every night one of the women sat on the other's bed to commiserate over the lost child. Over both Careys, really. They gave each other what they called eye massages, holding the other's head between their hands as they rubbed their thumbs gently over the closed lids. Lovely relief from headache and care. And they could manage it simultaneously with their forearms on each other's shoulders, in whispering exchange. Yes, like twins. It came to them more often, how much of a matched set they were. They agreed they were red-eyed more than was seemly for women of leadership.

There was time to get a message to Becca when her ship arrived in San Francisco, before it left for the Orient. But what should they tell

her? The truth would bring her off the boat and across the continent in a Union Pacific minute. Should they tell her all they knew? They had to, Kerstin said. Becca would never forgive them if they didn't.

"Do you suppose she already knows?" Eula asked.

Kerstin had no patience for telepathy. But there was something else still on her conscience.

"I should never have put that silly verse on your 'Slate,'" she said, and her eyes began to water under Eula's slowly revolving thumbs.

"I was more worried for you than for the girls," Kerstin said. "Anyway, it was wrong."

"For heaven's sake! That was ages ago."

"But just imitative stuff. And look what it's brought us."

She was blowing it way out of proportion, Eula told her.

"No it was self-indulgent and cruel."

With her eyes in full flood, Kerstin leaned into Eula's arms.

"I'm not going to marry him," she said. "I can't. I won't."

Eula wasn't really surprised. Instead of confessing her relief, she asked, "What are you going to tell him?"

"I made a mistake. I'm already settled."

Eula put a finger over her friend's lips. Her balance with Kerstin was back where she liked it—with mutual affection and respect for the privy details of their lives, their sniffles, the management of their hair, their pesky cycle, which had long since come into synchrony— and perhaps a little floating tension between decorum and desire, which Otto thought so unnatural.

∞

In the third week of their mourning, Erica Cochran came into Eula's office. They had a placement for Erica in nurse's training in the city. She had graduated from the Flourtown High School in the twins' class, and was only in residence at Drayton till the new training sessions began at the Lying-In Home. One of the girls had reported to Ellen Reilly that Erica knew more than she was telling, and Ellen, unable to coax anything from her, had ordered her to the Director's office.

Her head was down; she was barely mumbling, "I saw her leave. She had the suitcase."

Eula was amazed.

"But she always did," Erica defended herself.

"Did what?"

"She always took her suitcase with her sewing to show Miss Rice. She always took the shortcut across the meadow."

Eula had Erica sit in the soft chair, and told her to wait for a moment before saying anything more. No one was going to punish her, she said. Wait till everything was clear in her head.

"Now, begin again."

She did, and more came tumbling out: There was a young man that many of the girls had seen on their walks across the fields and into their woods. His name was Grayson, and for small change, and for keeping his name and business a secret from the Drayton guardians, he would tell their fortunes. He predicted there was another world war coming and that Erica was going to become a nurse. He told her one of the twins would find her fortune on the West Coast. He couldn't say which twin. They didn't believe any of it, but they liked him. He told Erica he could get one of them a train ride all the way to the far ocean. They would have to decide which one it would be.

"Erica, child, didn't you think we should know this?"

"But I didn't know it. I didn't think she would ever go with him. I thought she was visiting Miss Rice again, taking the shortcut. I know she was planning to make a dress for you. For a surprise. Even though you said she had to leave."

Eula, rattled by her own part in the horror, tried to make Erica go on, but the girl had nothing more to say, except for this: "He's in the woods again."

∞

The police had Grayson James in custody two days later. When they finished with their interrogation, Eula was allowed to see him. Better they should have let her talk to him first. Beating the story out of him got them only so far. His face all bruises, he stared at Eula hatefully. Not a class hatred, she knew. He was from a Main Line family, which had lost its home. He and his siblings were on the road.

Grayson had been discharged for theft from a barracks of the Civilian Conservation Corps in the Northwest. He wasn't up to the tent life or army-style discipline. He had confessed only this much to the police: that a girl whose fortune he had predicted would be made in the West had followed him off the Drayton campus and into the city. He had told her it was against the law for her to travel with him. He begged her to leave him alone, but when he had jumped into a boxcar at the Thirtieth Street yards she had followed him in. At first opportunity he found another open car for himself so that no one could say he was traveling with her. Still worried that she was fastened "like a tick" to his journey, he jumped train somewhere in Ohio. She was watching, and jumped off as well. At that point, rather than risk further travel in her company, he caught the next freight train east, and that was the last he'd seen of her.

It was a mystery why Grayson had admitted any connection with the girl at all, beyond his meetings with her in the woods, which others had observed. For all his story's unlikeliness, Eula saw, between the flourishes of invention, a girl surviving. After hearing him twice, she felt sure that Linny was alive. By then the police thought so, too. Grayson was released, and the Drayton girls said he never showed his face in their woods again.

One companion in her need—Kerstin—had been thrown to her, and her counselor, Otto, withdrawn. He was in Paris again, and the news of him was a worry, more for Tessie than for Eula. Tessie was having to defend him against another attack by his professional enemies. This time they said he had indulged in more than friendship with a patient, a young French writer and libertine, then preoccupied with her diary of sexual encounters with her own father.

In a letter to Tess, encouraging her to visit his new institute, he had not denied any of this. Rather, he said Tess must come and meet two of his new patients, trainees in his open method of therapy, a man and woman who had broken out of their sexual prisons, and were ready to counsel others. None of this reassured Eula, but even if

the worst of the gossip were true, it did nothing to diminish the monument of his work. He stood above the original Freudian troop, buoyed all the higher by their pompous gassing. She wanted to scold him. Instead, she wrote, "What are you up to in that intriguing city?"

∞

Miss Kieland had promised she would have mail waiting for Becca when she reached the Embarcadero in San Francisco. But no, nothing; Wu was sure of it. Easing this disappointment, he took a new approach as they started across the Pacific. He still would not leave her cabin unlocked overnight, but with the cargo of pianos safely in the hold, he had more time for her. No longer the testy businessman, he spoke to her again as the thoughtful professor who had lured her with his fellowship. At times his instruction was like a romantic vision.

"In a great Chinese city you will not know how to cross a street. The traffic at a corner is like a thousand journeys woven into a single moving sheet. You look no one in the eye, you touch no one; no one touches you, but so close. Soon you are on the other side."

"In America," he said, "people are expected to give you room. In China your room stops at your skin." She was grateful to be warned ahead of time. What would poor Linny think if people pressed close as the hair on her arm? Wu explained Chinese food to her. To say the people lived on a starvation diet didn't mean the Chinese were starving, only that a history of famines had taught them to accept certain foods which she, as an American, would only eat if she were starving. Pleased with her close attention, he gave her atlas back. She would have to surrender it again when they reached Xiamen.

With the Farrow book as familiar as her palm, she began to work on the maps of China, four pages in the little atlas. With only this for amusement, she set herself a goal—to draw a detailed map of the whole country from memory. By the time she docked in Xiamen, she could reproduce a freehand border of the country, with two hundred cities placed with some accuracy, plus rivers, mountains, and the paths of several railways.

"You traced this," Wu accused when she showed off her accomplishment. He tore the work to pieces, took the atlas back, and threw it into the sea.

"You must never again," he warned her. "For your own good."

Everything for her own good. Her door was locked the whole time they were in the Xiamen port. For her own good. She watched as the crates swung off the boat, all the pianos. Wu would say nothing about them. From her forward window she saw him screaming at the crane operator. One of the crates fell from its harness the last several feet to the dock. It sounded like a giant kettledrum exploding, with Wu waving his arms like an angry conductor.

She hoped it had splintered into a thousand pieces. Her mood low, she slept until the ship's horn woke her as they moved out of Xiamen, up the coast toward Tientsin. Her door had been unlocked; she was free to roam anywhere on the empty boat. Was there no longer danger to her from the German seamen? She was making her first real tour of the ship, and again one of them called her Herr Wu's Schwarze.

At last they were on a train to Peiping. Wu was watching her closely. He said there would be men everywhere waiting for an opportunity to snatch her away. The train was overcrowded, teeming. They were lucky to have a seat. Pressed together on a narrow bench, so crushed they could have been canned fish, his indifference was insulting. The air in the car seemed all garlic breath and unpleasant gas, some of it his.

They reached Peiping with Becca famished. Her first impression was of small yellow people who stared. Everyone stared at her as they made their way with the hand luggage, looking for a restaurant. The first one Wu pointed to had dog carcasses, skinned and hanging over the entrance. She refused to go in. He laughed and pushed her ahead of him down the street. When they finally found a place and sat down to eat, he ordered something unrecognizable, some sort of meat with a reddish, bubbled surface.

"Is it liver?" Becca asked him.

"No," he said, "not liver, but very close by."

She settled for a bowl of rice flavored with a salty brown liquid.

As they ate he explained that her duties for him would not begin for a month. In the meantime she would stay at the old Palace of Dance as the guest of a very important man who now owned the building. Wu spelled his name for her with his finger on the greasy table.

"In your letters, GAO TSE-SHING." He looked around him, and whispered it.

"Me," he said, "you should call me Chiang Professor of Social History." He implied that he had little respect for Mr. Chiang, emphasizing the name with a wink that distorted the whole side of his face.

"Everything will change soon," he said.

Would he please explain?

"No," he said. "You listen and don't ask questions."

He looked around, saw that no one was paying attention to them, and began to whisper. Chiang's people, he said, were selling the country, province by province, to the Japanese. For now, they must salute the forces of Chiang. But never mind, the Twenty-Eight Stroke Gentleman was preparing a surprise.

"Now are you happy you have read Mr. Farrow?" he asked her, very pleased with himself.

"For my real students," he said, "the ones with imagination, there are special books. The others read from the usual list. Will you be special or ordinary?"

She wasn't ready to say.

"Yes," he said. "Very wise to keep the mouth closed. But, I think, special."

He took her to a large concrete building in the middle of a rickety neighborhood. Her trunk had already been delivered to her quarters. She knew this place was wrong for her as soon as Wu showed her inside. The floor held a pattern of peacocks and blossoms inlaid in the parquet. The bed, large enough for four of her, was covered with red satin pillows, and made up with blue silk sheets. Mirrors everywhere, all the walls and ceiling, too. She opened the gaudy carved doors of the wardrobe, and saw that her trunk had been opened, and all her clothes put away.

She said, "You won't believe this, Linny," and there Linny was, looking down at her from the ceiling, in equal amazement.

Becca excused herself to the bathroom, bigger than any she'd seen before. The walls were decorated with finely painted tile murals. Sitting on the oddly round commode, she saw that the little blue figures in the murals were naked women in a public bath. When she pulled the chain to flush her business, a little bell sounded on the tank overhead, and the clay figure of a woman, bent over and presenting her hind quarters, popped out the door of a miniature bathhouse. Becca pulled the chain again to be sure she hadn't imagined it.

When she came out, Wu had disappeared, and the room door was locked. He was on the other side, explaining as usual this way was best for her. He said a tray with rice, fish, and some rice wine would be brought to her. He had left a pamphlet for her on the bed. She used it to beat on the door.

"Read it carefully," he said.

It was all about the extermination campaigns of Mr. Chiang's glorious armies, the people he had recently told her he despised. Which side was he on? She threw it aside, and sat down at the writing table to begin a long-overdue letter to Miss Kieland. On the boat, she'd reasoned, there was no use writing till she reached San Francisco. When she found no mail for her there, she was too hurt, too stubborn to begin the correspondence. Now, she was ready to tell of her adventure to date and all her misgivings.

"Mr. Wu has this notion that I'm in danger from everyone but him."

She tried to explain what a two-faced person they had put their trust in. She said Jennie's name was never mentioned, that her questions about the first scholarship girl were ignored:

He calls me *Schwarze*, and thinks I could be comfortable in a pleasure palace where he's found a room for me. And no telling what they expect of me here. Yes, I think we made a mistake about Professor Wu, but I am only just arrived here and already

complaining. I am sorry for that because you taught us to make the best of a situation. And I promised to be a strawberry girl so I will.

Becca

She sealed the letter, and addressed it.

They had forgotten about her supper. When it got dark she heard men laughing in the hallway and someone trying the handle of her door. Retiring that night, and waking the next morning, Linny looked down at her from above, as scared as she was.

Wu came for her in the morning. She asked him how to mail the letter. He tried to take it from her.

Was she so naïve? No mail left China, he said, unless it had been approved. In this zone of the city, it would be best to give it to him, and he would pass it along to one of Gao's men. Then perhaps it would travel to America, perhaps not. He tried to grab it, but she tore it in half, and again, and again, until it was all scraps, scattered on the floor.

With a new sense of isolation, she understood Jennie's long silence.

"Think about it," Wu said, as if logic were all on his side. "If words about China leave her shores, should not China know what is leaving? Are you so ashamed of what you write, you tear it apart?"

Taking her to his first class of the morning at the university, he tried to reassure her, but only made it worse.

"We have a saying: 'The good news sails, the bad is read by the fish.'"

He tried to convince her of her good luck in being given the room in Mr. Gao's Palace of Dance, "where the finest artists of movement were trained." It was a privilege granted to only a few.

"I'm not living there," she said. "You can tell Mr. Gooey."

Raising a warning finger against her impudence, he asked. "Where would you go? Remember who you are, *Schwarze*."

"Don't call me that," she told him. "We're not on your German boat. I would go to Mr. Leighton Stuart at Yenching."

She started, ahead of him, across the thick traffic of an intersection.

"Come back!" he yelled at her. But she continued, weaving through bicycles, people, and carts, like a native, looking into no one's eyes. Wu caught up with her on the other side, and grabbed her arm.

"Forget that name, Stuart," he warned her, and he gave her a Chinese thought, this one to be written in her notebook when they reached his classroom, which wasn't even on the university campus.

"To know too much is to know too little."

Wu introduced Becca as the second girl from America who would work in his office. She was asked to read the first lines on Wu's chalkboard. "To know that you are ignorant is wisest; to pretend to know is a disease."

The boy sitting behind her was asked to follow: "Honor comes to me when I'm least known."

Wu said they must talk about this in English. A girl raised her hand and began, very slowly, "Noisy person does never go ahead. If she quiet, she does go."

He corrected her grammar, ignoring her acceptable interpretation.

Next came "The stiffest trees fall to the ax. The supple live to rise above the rest." More discussion.

After the class Wu had one of the girls, Han Ling, take her to the cafeteria.

"What did you think?" she asked Becca.

She didn't want to insult, but had to say it was a very sorry history lesson.

"Oh, not history," Ling said. "This was English conversation," and she explained that "Professor of History" was only a title Wu had given himself, not a description of his work.

Wu took Becca into his tiny office, and assigned her first task. She was to compose a letter advertising his China Fellowship, which could be sent to any university in America. She should add the endorsement of Miss Kieland and Drayton College, and her own. If she did a good job, he would have something exciting to tell her. There was so much she could say.

"This is very nice," he said when she was finished.

But it wasn't. It was full of double meaning intended to subvert the message: "Your Future's Locked Up, Surrender to Professor Wu's Orient."

He was very pleased, and began to explain their real work. He would speed things up for her. Becca was to join his master class in political thought the very next day. This was outside the university's curriculum and must be secret. Some of the ideas could get one thrown into jail by Chiang's people, the Kuomintang. He taught these lessons in the evening, when the students were through with their regular classes on the central campus.

"Do you agree, Becca, that truth demands the witness of our whole life? Do you agree that old ideas must fall before the modern evidence?"

She didn't know what he was talking about. There was no reason to deny it. While his friendly side was toward her, she asked again, "Where's Jennie? Are there other American girls here?"

He slammed his fist on the little table that was his desk.

"*Schwarze!*" he said. "You, who know our map and the size of our country, ask such small and selfish questions? You know nothing of China. You ask about one life, when thousands are hunted and killed. And all they ask is a bowl of broth."

Was it selfish of her, too, to wonder if this broth would be flavored like hers with the single claw of a chicken's foot? While this man who had plenty to eat was trying to make her thinner? He thought she was heavy, and could make herself more beautiful by eating less.

Han Ling accompanied her back to her quarters, and cooed like a dove at the sight of her room. She agreed with Wu that the American's door should be locked tight. She left, and Becca was alone, brooding. No matter which way she turned in her chamber of mirrors, there was Linny staring back at her, imitating her mood. She slapped at the glass wall, which only stung their hands.

Again, there was commotion during the night, the sound of men carousing, and again her door was tried. It was locked on the outside, and bolted by her from within.

Ling came for Becca in the mornings to let her out, take her to breakfast, and walk with her to the classroom outside the university grounds. Wu had assigned Ling to be the scholarship student's guardian.

"Why does he risk teaching his dangerous politics?" Becca asked her.

"For him it is a passion," she said. "He cannot help it. His heart beats with the Twenty-Eight Stroke Gentleman in Chingkanshan."

The girl spoke these extravagant lines with no more feeling than she recited her lines in the conversation class. Everything was rehearsed and repeated without emotion.

"He writes to so many universities in America," Becca said, and the girl answered with another of the professor's phrases: "To catch a single crab, we fix a dozen baits."

If Linny lasted two years here, she might be speaking only in Wu's translations of Chinese proverbs.

The lessons went on in his secret class, the one held in the evenings after most students had gone home. A class for Becca, Han Ling, and five young men, who bowed to Wu like students she'd seen in the martial arts arena, repeating lines in a monotone: "If the people have no fear of death, what use to threaten them with it? The executioners might as well cut off their own heads."

As the days passed Wu was asking more frequently for sacrifice and bravery. One evening he set a new course for the seven special students. They were going to sharpen their minds with a feat of memory, a list of names to be kept in their heads. They must not risk writing them down, the names of those who agreed with them. One day it would be a Grand Directory of Peiping, a book of heroes, all the friends of the Twenty-Eight Stroke Gentleman, "all who sleep with one eye open."

"You will go in many directions," he said, "and who will come home the winner? Who will unwind from the tongue the longest list of names?"

"You are the American," he told Becca. "You will be welcomed at Yenching University."

Two times a week she was to monitor a class there. She would have her own bicycle. The others gasped over this extraordinary

good fortune. At last, she thought, she could write a letter to Miss Kieland. She would lie only a little to be sure her news did not go to the bottom of the ocean. Linny, look at me now.

∞

"I'm not what you think I am," Linny told Mumsy.

"Don't make me laugh," she said.

"Look at me close."

"You look all right to me," she said, but she was right up next to Linny's face, and concerned, her finger on Linny's protruding lip.

"If you let someone interfere with me, you'll be sorry you did."

"This isn't a place like that, dear. This is a house of praise where we worship from the outside in, from the skin to the heart, as God intended. The only thing you have to worry about is your patina of guilt. Reverend Charlesburg will explain it to you. Maribon says you're a twin. I think you miss your sister. There's no reason she couldn't join us here."

"No reason except she's in China."

"You little scamp. You little liar!"

"I'm going to make big trouble for you."

"You, by God, are not!"

The next minute she was making up to Linny again with a lot of sweetness, promises about a sewing machine, and enough fabric to put uniforms on a regiment, all this, and an introduction to the famous sewing mistress of San Francisco.

Locks were Mumsy's specialty. And keys. She had a steel ring loaded with them. Double locks for every door in the house. And the front and back doors had iron gates outside them with their own padlocks. The windows on the first and second floors were barred against burglars.

Mumsy found a sewing machine in a secondhand shop and had it carried up to the attic room. But the treadle shaft was broken, and the foot was bent, useless. There was no needle, and no bobbin. She called Linny ungrateful and a spoiled pup.

A week went by. And another. Linny was learning more about the house from Maribon as she helped her clean the rooms and make the beds. She was looking for her chance, studying the faces of the tenants as she helped serve their meals. She thought one of them might help her get away, but soon found they were all beholden to Mumsy in one way or another, living here at her pleasure. They all had something to do with the Church of the Holy Sensations. They were sent out on the street at the same time each morning, sent off to their mission work. And at five in the afternoon they lined up at the door, waiting to be let in. They weren't about to help one of the precious ladies in training leave the house.

At the evening meal they discussed the successes and failures of the day. Sometimes Mumsy stood over them as they ate, scolding and demanding greater effort. It was understood that the work of recruitment at Sea Tossed was supported by Mumsy's more profitable house on Carter Street, where the ladies in training went after they finished their cycle of instruction from Reverend Charlesburg.

The Reverend came to see Linny a month after her arrival. She wasn't sure why Mumsy waited till then for her indoctrination, unless she thought her spirit had been broken, that she'd be ready for any change in her routine. The only thing she'd had to read was the reverend's pamphlet on the Order of the Holy Sensations. She wasn't eating much, and Mumsy had changed her mind about that, thinking maybe Linny was trying to starve herself.

Promises about the sewing lady were not kept. Linny understood this woman never existed. For her introduction to the reverend she was taken down to the second floor, to the instruction room. Maribon brought in a tray with teapot, cups, and saucers, and Mumsy said she was to receive the reverend as a lady would, who had asked her pastor to tea. The reverend arrived, Mumsy whisked Maribon out of the room, and the session began.

He was very young for a minister. It would be all right if Linny called him Reverend David, he said. Too much formality, he explained, bred a sense of inferiority, and right next to inferiority in the chain of error came guilt, the enemy, the thing he wanted to discuss first. The selfsame thing, he said, which held her back at that moment from smiling on her blessings.

"You don't trust me," he said. "It's obvious from the way you look at me."

His hair was long and black, but no darker than his eyes, which followed Linny's without release, unblinking.

"No! Don't look away," he said. "Look right at me. I see what's behind those eyes. Primary guilt. It's spreading right now over your whole body. The patina of guilt. Look at you!"

It was true. She was hot all over, blushing, thoroughly embarrassed by his unyielding inspection.

"You needn't pour the tea," he said. "This will take all your concentration. Did you read my pamphlet?"

"Some," she said.

"Shame!"

His gaze fell from her in disappointment.

"We'll see how lazy you've been, how much ground we have to make up."

She thought, Becca, he's going to give us a test, but no way to accuse us of cheating.

"Who founded the Order of the Holy Sensations?"

"Pastor Reginald Johnstone of Winnipeg."

"When?"

"Nineteen seven."

"Where was the Revelation given?"

"In the Wood of Tamarack in Manitoba."

"To whom?"

"Seven virgins and three men. One of them was Pastor Johnstone."

Reverend Charlesburg was impressed. It was nothing but a sorry joke to her, and she played along, containing her scorn and laughter as best she could. She'd read through the pamphlet three times, the third time in hopes that her sister might be gathering some of the nonsense with her. What else was there to do for a month?

He went on: "How did this group happen to be together?"

They were members of a sect looking for a new path. They had gone into the woods together to share among themselves equally.

Each was to give himself, in body and spirit, to all the others. Without embarrassment.

"Where was the truth finally revealed to them?"

"On the Stone of Seven Virtues."

She was barely able to hold it in now; Becca was tickling her inside. Charlesburg came to her rescue with another question, trying to stump her.

"How was the group saved?"

"Sunlight fell from Providence and blinded Pastor Johnstone. He couldn't see the virgins' glands of nourishment."

She couldn't help herself. She began to giggle.

"Linda," he said sadly, "this is nothing to laugh at. Perhaps we should have you wait a few more weeks."

"No, no, of course it's not funny. I'll stop. Pastor Johnstone read the lessons from the stone. They all bathed in a stream before gazing on each other."

She began to recite the first of the seven virtues: "The use of water alone is insufficient to the purpose. Without intent . . . "

"Never mind, never mind," he said. "That's enough. Perhaps you're ready after all. I want you to close your eyes. I'm going to face the wall. Now I want you to place your hands on the glands of nourishment. Yes, are you doing it? All right."

She said yes, but she wasn't doing anything of the kind.

"Push gently. Now apart, now together. Five times. And when I've finished counting, all sense of shame will have left you. I'm going to turn around now, I'm going to look at you. Your hands should still be on the bosom."

But of course they weren't, she assured Becca. They never had been.

"We'll try again."

Another failure.

"Do you want to go on?" he asked. "You're showing no progress. You're too hot. You'd better remove your sweater. That's better. No wonder. This time you're going to close your eyes. That's it, and mine will be open. Now place your hands as before. No, on the glands."

She would not.

"Do as I tell you, Linda. Will I have to show you?"

He raised her arms, took her hands and pressed them against her chest.

"Hold them there."

She let them drop to her sides.

"Like this," he said.

He put his own hands on her breasts. She tried to push them off, but he was strong. He grabbed hold of her shirtwaist, and pulled open the top button. She struggled to free herself, and the blouse was torn open at the top.

"Look at you! Just as I thought," he said. "Look at the guilt. You're covered with it."

She swung at him, tried to hit his face. He was too fast. All she could do was cover herself. But the moment had come. She looked right into his angry eyes and said, "I'm a Nigger! She didn't tell you that, did she?"

"What are you saying?"

"I am. I'm colored."

"Be quiet, girl. There are other people in the house. You're no more colored than I am."

"Look closer," she said, getting next to his face and pushing her lips slightly forward. "I can prove it. My grandmother is all speckled with it."

He led her downstairs for a conference in the kitchen.

"The girl says she has Negro blood."

"Don't make me laugh," Mumsy told him.

"Our order takes no colored."

He raised his voice. "How many times have we discussed it? No shape or part."

"She isn't," Mumsy said. "Look at her."

"I am looking at her."

He grabbed Linny's arm, pulled her across the room, right under the woman's nose.

"That's not pure white," he said. Their faces were right next to her arm. She could have poked their eyes out.

They pulled her back the other way, to the window, for better light.

"Is that white?"

"Yes," Mumsy judged.

"No, it isn't."

He took Linny's hand, and turned it over and back, over and back.

"Pink and that," he said, "pink and that."

"That?" Mumsy said. "What that?"

"I should have known it from the start. Her attitude. She's covered in black guilt. Nothing's going to wash that off. I'm not working with her. I can do nothing for her. It's a shame. Her mind is quite good."

Mumsy was in a crimson fury, watching Linny's usefulness disappear before her eyes. And the money she'd given Cormack.

"You black bitch," she said, slapping Linny across the cheek. A minute later she was running up to the attic room to make sure Linny was putting nothing from the house in her satchel. She was taking back all the clothes she'd given her, even the dress she'd arrived in.

"This is mine, too," she said, and Linny didn't doubt it. "And this. And this!"

Mumsy put her out in a trashy shift and some sandals. She turned for a last look at her shabby prison with paint peeling from its porch and siding. There was a splintered plaque over the door with SEA TOSSED burnt into the weathered wood in ill-formed letters. She looked up at the corner and saw for the first time she'd been living on Mission Street. Fifteen minutes later she was in a police station, thinking how stupid she'd been all that time. She could have been free a month earlier just by declaring the color of her skin.

Eula was disgusted with Becca. She assumed the girl would have posted a letter from the Baltimore docks after her first couple of days

on the steamer. Six weeks later, when nothing had come from San Francisco, she could only think of it as the rudest sort of farewell, the careless omission of an ingrate. Mr. Wu had promised to make her write. He wouldn't get another of her girls anytime soon.

She had written Becca the bare minimum about her sister's disappearance, the secret departure on the same day Becca had sailed. That they had traced her as far as Ohio. She didn't mention the open suitcase in the woods and the scattered underwear.

The secondhand news of Otto, passed along by his more special American friend, Tessie, brought Eula lower. More special because she, Tessie, was receiving repeated invitations to visit his new Paris institute. Not Eula, who was envious and confessed as much to Kerstin. Tessie was the first of them to hear of his affair with the young French woman, or was she Spanish, the diarist, who had come to him for advice—bad behavior, an ethical lapse, that even his gymnastic mind could not vault. It would take some plastic wizardry of the language to extricate himself from the shame and save Tessie's support.

His news arrived at last. Eula's own letter, and suddenly she was number one. That is, he wrote that of all his American friends, she was the one he was most concerned about, knowing that she would have heard about his Paris adventures secondhand. She looked again at the envelope. Running her letter opener through the top fold she had almost missed the figures in the green wax. She had been taken into the circle, shown the intaglio design.

It was a carefully stamped impression, closed in a circle no larger than a thumbnail, and required her magnifying glass. Though small, it was perfectly formed. The tiny detail put her in awe of the Greek artisan who must have carved it before Jesus walked in the Levant.

Two male figures in the center of the work were well muscled and naked to the waist. They were leaning on each other. Their hair, full and long, covered the position of their hands. She couldn't really tell if they were resting on each other's shoulders in fellowship, or closed on each other's throats in a death struggle.

Otto wrote:

Maybe now you'll understand my reluctance to show you the message in the ring. The story of these Greek twins, Tripto and Lezzor, seemed too dark a model for the Carey pair, even more frightening than *The Student of Prague,* where the tragedy was accidental. You know the Greek and Roman myths are full of tangled versions of similar characters and events. These two boys may be confused with Castor and Pollux. The two sets do have this in common: One of the boys dies and the other must go back and forth from earth to a nether world to keep company with the sibling he mourns. And these boys, too, were assigned the Gemini stars. But in the case of my twins, the death is a fratricide. Lezzor kills Tripto in a birthright argument, and is sorry ever after.

Don't try to find their story in Bullfinch. It isn't there. Their names are scratched on the back of the stone. I searched for a long time before a classics man from Berlin told me they show up in the monograph of a scholar from Messene, and his citation is only "oral folk tradition of the Peloponnese."

In considering this I want you to remember what I told you about Dr. Freud's modern gang. When they describe symptoms, they always like to think they've explained the myth. Oedipus and so on. Don't fall into this self-deluding trap. The stories are just guides anyway, not inevitable outcomes.

I believe the only thing Lezzor and Tripto predict with certainty about your Careys is this: If one of them is lost, the other is certain to visit or be visited by her on a daily basis on this earth for as long as she lives.

He went on to his own life:

From my correspondence with Tessie I know you received a version of "Otto and his French patient" that is misleading. The beautiful young lady is a French diarist, a novelist manqué, thirty years old. I think she may have bobbed her nose. Yes, there's a little nubbin missing from the tip, and a shiny flat circular end. Curious. Back to the point:

The lady is mischievous, manipulating, incestuous (her father, and completely mutual, and recent), charming, dishonest; a liar about her liaisons. She keeps the most profound philosopher of sex in her elegant household for her physical and intellectual pleasure, all paid for by an adoring banker husband, who plays the fool out of pathetic necessity. He calls ahead rather than arrive home to find rumpled bedclothes.

These are not my adjectives; this is not my description. They are her own. She came to me for help in breaking her diary habit and turning it to fiction. She had already seduced a previous analyst. Why would I make room for her on my couch? You know my marriage is all but finished, and she is so honest with me about her dishonesty. Thoroughly beguiling. One wants to believe. Her diaries are completely self-indulgent, intricate, and perceptive. She and her barbaric writer friend are quite under my influence in psychiatric therapy. For all her storm and thunder, she is capable of helping others. I am training her in that direction. Condemn me if you must.

This woman is a shocking example of self-aware doubleness. This should interest you. For all her faults, she points toward freedom. She has one name for herself as a diarist, another for the person living the life she must write about. She calls her self-observed life *"dedoublement."* A spy on herself, on the street and in the bedroom, with nothing too sacred for confession. As journal keepers, the two of you couldn't be more different. She is totally fearless in the practice of life and on the page.

Why do I go on this way? Because she's coming to New York later this year to take some clients into analysis after my instruction and introduction. I want you to meet her. I don't expect you would follow her all the way into strangeness. But, Eula, a little way wouldn't hurt you. I don't hesitate to tell you this much about her, because I know she'll spare nothing in telling you yourself.

Tessie has informed me of twin Linda's disappearance. My hunch is she'll come home, and sooner than you think. What will you do then?

If he was trying to cheer Eula, he succeeded. Fantasizing Linny's return was happy work. She discussed the letter with Tess, who said Otto didn't need their pardon, only their support for his therapeutic method, which she still believed the best available. Eula had hardly rung off with Tess when one of the children dumped the morning mail on her desk. At the top of the pile, a shock. A familiar envelope in her own hand, the letter she'd mailed to Becca addressed to the San Francisco dock, returned to sender. If this had never made it onto her boat, perhaps a letter from Becca had never made it off.

Whispering across the continent and ocean, she asked Becca's pardon, turning her anger on an incompetent postal service, which, with its afternoon delivery, surprised her again with a communication from Washington, the Department of Commerce. Her contact there, Mr. Forbes, regretted he must withdraw his favorable referral for Mr. Frederick Wu, who traveled on German and Chinese passports. Wu's U.S. visa had been withdrawn. If he returned to this country he would be taken into custody and prosecuted for a forged signature on a letter of export.

The same afternoon she began her effort to retrieve Becca from Peiping, but she found the Chinese, through their embassy, were in no mood to cooperate. They disputed the American charge against their citizen Wu. A subordinate officer, weary of her hectoring, said, "Who need the piano, anyway? Stupid big elephant for wrong music."

She switched her attack to the American diplomatic service. Within a few days she found to her disgust that her own government was no more equipped, or disposed, to tangle with Mr. Wu and his friends on their shore than the Chinese themselves. She was told that if Miss Carey had traveled to China, she had done so at an ill-advised time. If the girl was a minor, her guardian had been negligent.

Eula's cable to the university in Peiping was answered:

THERE IS NOT YOUR PROFESSOR WU STANDING ON THIS FACULTY. HE SHALL BE STANDING OUTSIDE. STUDENT CAREY ALSO.

OUR REGRETFULS

Kerstin made a feather-light prediction, as airy as Otto's: All would be well for Becca in a country where the manners were much superior to those in America. In fact, that both of her strawberry twins would prosper, transplanted. Kerstin was threatening to sleep in Eula's room if she didn't stop calling down the hall every night, her imagination lit with Chinese horrors.

The twins' eighteenth birthday had passed in private mourning. The Drayton board was familiar with Linny's story as far as it went, that is, as far as a hobo village in Ohio. Eula wasn't revealing her misgivings about Becca's situation. It wasn't so much cowardice or self-protection that kept the girl's name on the list of graduate honors as "China Fellow, Peiping," but a comforting denial of her suspicions. Eula simply couldn't accept that anything untoward was happening to her.

Then, before the end-of-month board meeting, God Bless Western Union, Hooray for Union Pacific, and praise any other link to the West Coast. A telegram! This time from San Francisco's public welfare office:

> Your Linda Carey in custody here at Seldom Street Settlement House. Wire contribution and RR fare? Transfer assistance provided in Denver and Chicago. Meet her at Philadelphia Station, August 28, 6:35 P.M. Reply.

Eula's journal says that when this news arrived she and Kerstin danced together like a couple of newlyweds. Take that, Madame Frenchie. They twirled, they kissed, they were overcome. Otto had been right, and he always asked the right question. What would she do when Linny showed up on her doorstep?

∞

Linny was reed-thin, and so shaky. Eula was horrified. The girl had lost all self-confidence. No strawberry child, she was celery, skin to core. Eula didn't care what the charter or the mission statement said. She was changing the rules. Linny was going to stay at Drayton under Eula's supervision as long as she cared to. The staff understood

that, and what the trustees might think of it didn't matter to her. Who would dare challenge her?

With her first step off the train, Linny begged to be allowed to stay at the orphanage. She was ready to do anything to persuade Miss Kieland. On the way home from the station she kept looking down at her arms and hands.

"You know I'm colored, don't you?" she said. It was both declaration and question, though almost whispered. A little neurotic, Eula thought.

She was turning her palms up and down, comparing back and front.

Eula was better prepared this time.

"You're going to be whatever you choose to be," she told her. "You look quite beautiful to me."

"I'm not going to be," she corrected, "I am."

She grabbed the Director's arm and held so tightly Eula went soft again with full maternal devotion.

"What has Becca written to me?" Linny asked.

She couldn't believe that they'd heard nothing. Not a word from her sister to be passed along to her.

Eula eventually told her board she was hiring one of the graduated girls in the new position of Sewing Mistress, as if the title were her idea. Linny still thought of herself as a dependent orphan. She wanted to move back into the room in Stork where she'd lived with her sister. Eula wouldn't let her do that. She put her into the cottage on Wissahickon, shared by the school nurse, Jean, and Jessie Stein, the new alternate housemother. Linny was apprehensive about living with adults, about the Director's presumption of her maturity.

Otto, not surprised at the return, wrote, "Of course she wants her old room. Just as a dog holds to the place it last saw its master."

Otto's letters were always more insulting than his spoken words, which could be softened by inflection and his elemental kindness. It was hard, but an apt figure for Linny's perseverance, sticking to the scent of the essential other in her life, refusing to be pulled away.

And from his long distance, Otto began to soften Linny's aversion to him and his influence on the orphanage. He sent a letter just for her and, more surprising, sealed it with the impression of his ring. Then a most unusual gift arrived. The crate was six weeks coming over the ocean, arriving a month after the letter, which had been confusing without it. The large wooden box had to be retrieved from a warehouse at the Delaware pier.

Mr. Henry muscled it into the Schoolhouse lobby, where they all watched like customs officers as Linny opened it. She knocked at the crate rather fecklessly with Henry's hammer before he took it from her impatiently, and pried it apart himself.

"Did you tell him I was going somewhere?" Linny was looking at Eula, whose mouth went slack as the contents were revealed. There was the finest sort of weekend case with brass fasteners, and covered in blue and green brocade. Ellen recognized the name of the Paris shop it came from.

"So heavy," Linny said. "If it was full, I don't think I could lift it."

"Open it!" the women said at the same time.

Perhaps they shouldn't have. It *was* full, packed with the most incredible wardrobe. On top was an evening gown of pale green silk in a box labeled Vionnet.

"My God!" Linny said.

She held it up against herself and several of the girls standing around covered their mouths in shock. God knew how much all this had cost him.

Next out of the bag came a tea dress in a tiny floral print with the most elaborate smocking and embroidery around the neck. It might have been Victorian for all its fussiness, but for its skirt, which was short and free enough for the dizziest flapper. The contents became more unbelievable as she went deeper. Filmy underthings, and on the bottom, a lacy negligee. Packed in the corners were toilet water, creams, powders, and a perfume.

Outrageous! It looked like a fast woman's ensemble, with accessories, for a house party weekend in the company of Europe's wealthiest libertine. Eula tried to put it in the best light she could.

Maybe all of it together was meant to remind her of the freedom she still had to move on in the world, along with Otto's affirmation of the style he expected her to carry with her, head high as her sister's. In spite of the excess, so generous in its intention. All Eula could say was, "Linny! Look what he's sent you!"

Then they remembered the letter she'd received from him.

First he'd explained the image on the envelope, Tripto and Lezzor in the sealing wax. She was old enough now, he said, to understand their story as a kind of warning, and without fear. One day, perhaps, she could explain it to her sister. Then he'd written: "I understand you're going to be teaching sewing to all the children of Drayton. This is your syllabus for the year, all in a suitcase."

He said he was pleased she'd been smart enough when in trouble to return to the people who loved her best. He'd been told that if she took all these garments apart, piece by piece, every last stitch, and then sewed them all back together again, she would understand what had happened in women's fashions over the last twenty years. In the process she would be learning how to make them herself.

What could any of this have meant to Linny before the box arrived? And when it came, Eula thought, ripping out all that smocking would be a man-hour crime of the first order. And the negligee! He must have been unaware of all the extras in the elegant case. Was the negligee to be unstitched, too? And what about the creams and perfume? What was he thinking? What Eula thought, or wondered, didn't matter to Linny. She was thrilled with all of it.

"Vionnet," she repeated softly. "Marie Gerber. Do you think she made this herself?" She might have been whispering the names of goddesses, whose charms and powers were beyond her heaven.

Otto had set Linny in motion again, after weeks of perfunctory daily ritual. If she was going to wear any of these things, she was first going to tear them into their parts, and restore them herself, never mind how long it took. His masterful therapy was needle, and gown. The hours she spent waiting for her sister could be measured out in spools of thread, unreeling slowly as the turning days that brought them closer to the news of Becca.

And news finally did come from Peiping. What they'd all been impatient for. Linny couldn't believe the letter was addressed to Miss Kieland and not herself. The postmark on the envelope was obliterated, and the return address on the letter itself was inked over.

"She doesn't know you're here," Eula reminded her.

"She should," Linny said with no shade of doubt.

The letter was childish, too simple to be Becca's actual words:

Mr. Wu is very pleased with me. Mr. Wu is very kind. China is a very fine country. Two times a week I can ride my bicycle to the university in Yenching. I am following a course for foreigners. I am learning the brushstrokes of five hundred and seventy Chinese words. What a wonderful writing this is! They can't believe how quickly I learn. They say impossible. I must have learned it in another life. Many of them have come from other lives.

I can count to a hundred in Chinese and say the first three poems of Lao Tzu. You must be proud of me. Linny is right beside me all the time, whispering the answers. With her I have twice the memory. She won't let me forget. If you ever see her, you can show her this.

Professor Wu is famous. They like him because he brings the piano to China. With the piano they can study our music. This is very good for America and China. We study hard and leave politics alone. This is best for students, don't you agree? Did you know the piano has ten thousand moving parts? Can you blame Professor Wu the piano is so expensive here? This letter is gosh.

Linny said she didn't mean "gosh," she meant "goosh," and she suspected the letter was false, start to finish, something Becca had been told, or forced, to write.

∞

Becca used to think Drayton was the prettiest place in the world until she rode her bicycle through the gates onto the campus of the Yenching University. She went over a marble bridge, over a stream, and the first thing she saw was a lake around a small island with a bell tower

in the middle. The trees were all clipped and tended like pets. Cherry trees, and willows, acacias, and plums. Peonies and roses were planted along the paths of crunchy white pebbles. There was a rock-lined lotus pool and beyond, a great pagoda with dozens of curving roofs.

Many students were speaking English. A few were Westerners like Linny. There were small groups here and there. They seemed excessively cheerful. So much laughter. There were couples on the paths, girls and boys walking together, something she hadn't seen around the Peiping campus. It was a little Chinese wonderland made to invite, to make you forget where you'd come from, the way Drayton tried to do.

Right away she wanted to be there always, away from the changeable Professor Wu. There were friendly people all around her. One touched her hair, another admired her bicycle. Two of them, a Chinese boy and an English girl, insisted on helping her present her papers to the admissions office, showing her the way, and waiting while the questions were asked.

She wasn't sure what was written on the documents she handed to the secretary, but things happened quickly for her. Before she left the office she'd been accepted as an auditor of Professor Moore's course, "Faith and Duty: A History of the American Missionary in China." She was told she could enroll as a full-time student if it suited her. She had an offer to spend that night in one of the women's dormitories, and in the off-campus room of a rude Dutch boy.

She'd been warned by Wu that the Follow and Obey people, the followers of Chiang Kai-shek, would try to recruit her. One of them did ask her to sign an endorsement of Chiang and to come to weekly meetings. She pretended not to understand him.

"Better for students to study hard, and leave politics alone," she said.

She delayed her return to Peiping, hoping to meet someone Linny could admire, a friend just for herself. She was sitting alone, staring into the lotus pond at her shimmering face, when a young man trying to control an armload of books plopped down at the other end of the bench. Notebooks and papers fell to the ground. Several sheets went sailing into the pond. She jumped up to help him.

"No," he said. "I'm so sorry. I don't need."

But he did. The books were still sliding around and onto the gravel.

Collected again, he introduced himself: "Huang Don." He spelled it for her in her letters, speaking English with only a slight accent. He was more clumsy than shy, apologizing for the inconvenience, for disturbing her. She liked him right away, and started asking questions, afraid he'd get up and leave.

"Are you a student here?"

Silly things like that.

He was patient. It was rude to tell him he looked different from the others, but he understood. Though his father was Chinese, he explained, his mother was Belgian. His European eyes and nose were a problem for him in China, but accepted without prejudice at Yenching University. It wouldn't be the same at the university in Peiping. She thought he looked wonderful, and was trying to tell him so.

He turned away, in modesty, and Becca apologized. He told her he had graduated the year before. He was allowed to keep studying because he was preparing to be an instructor. He asked if she was interested in politics. One of the texts in his pile was the Farrow book, the one she had read for Wu.

Instead of answering, she said, "I read that."

"Everybody reads that," he said. "It's for beginners. Very obvious. Very simple. The first thoughts of a man from the West."

He asked her again, "Are you interested in politics?"

She was not sure what to say, afraid of disappointing him. She took a chance on "Yes."

He moved a little closer, to the middle of the bench.

"What have you read?" he asked her.

Very little, she explained. She was just getting started, studying with a man in Peiping, who was letting her come to Yenching, to broaden her understanding of China.

Huang Don liked the sound of this.

"This is a wise man?" he said.

When she failed to answer, he said, "You were talking to the Follow and Obey. I saw you."

"Just to say I am a student and don't have time for them."

"I think you are more than a student. I think you have time."

She was being too careful. He made a move to leave. If she wanted to hold him there she was going to have to declare herself.

Linny was advising, no, no, no. But only because she wasn't there to see for herself that Huang Don was going to be all right. And she said, "Yes, I am. How could you tell?"

He took more interest when she said she wanted to learn more about the men in the hills of Chinkanshan. He moved closer still, almost right next to her. He pointed to things in his pile of papers that she should be reading, things it was dangerous to publish, mimeographed sheets stapled into booklets. She saw the titles *After Japan, The Self Comes Last,* and *Extermination, The Last Campaign.*

"Why are they all in English?" she asked him.

"You are at Yenching. Here we speak Chinese but many of us know English. For us it can be a secret language. The wrong ones don't know what we are reading."

When she let him put one of the pamphlets into her book satchel, he said, "You are very brave."

In fact, she was a little frightened, wondering if she would get the pamphlet back to Peiping, before someone stopped her on the road and found it.

She asked Don if she would see him again.

He touched her shoulder.

"You don't like me," he said. "That will be best for you."

She was still on her bicycle after dark, gliding down the long incline into Peiping. There was no motor traffic, only pedal vehicles and carts as likely to have trotting men in the traces as oxen. She went slowly, standing on her pedals from time to time, gazing at a horizon of twinkling lights, the candle-lit city lying in front of her. There wasn't anything for Linny to worry about.

Wu was waiting in her room.

"How did you get in here?" she asked him.

"Where were you?" he asked. "Everybody was worried."

He was only pretending to be angry.

"Did you bring any names of our friends?"

She tapped her skull with a finger.

"Very good," he said.

She told him the people at Yenching were not afraid of their own ideas the way his students were. She didn't care if he was insulted. She wanted to say something her sister would admire. If it bothered him, he kept it to himself.

All he said was "*Schwarze.*"

When he was gone she took *Extermination* from her satchel and read about savage executions, and the people's justice gathering strength, the power of sacrifice, surviving one bowl of rice at a time. She fell asleep filled with a spirit of revenge for the downtrodden.

After two weeks of the long ride back and forth, Wu encouraged her to enroll full-time at Yenching. She would come home only on the weekends, for a class of instruction he was giving to the Sisters of Tomorrow, secret supporters of the Twenty-Eight Stroke Gentleman. This way she could do a more thorough job of gathering the names for the Grand Directory, without forgetting the duties of a woman in the coming revolt. She would not lose sight of the great generosity of Mr. Gao, who kept one of the finest rooms in the Palace of Dance empty just for her.

"Make many friends," he said. "Go with them to the dormitories. A Sister of Tomorrow is not afraid of tonight. Do you understand, *Schwarze?*"

The women's instruction group met on Saturdays in the little room next to Wu's office. There were three from his other class, and the rest were girls he had brought up on the train from Tientsin who were kept as Becca was, under key in Mr. Gao's building.

They were all quite beautiful, and dressed in the same black pants, white blouses, and embroidered vests. They wore black-cloth-topped shoes with roses stitched over the toe. None of the girls was pure Chinese. The clothes, she discovered, were the uniform of the half-bred ladies of the Palace of Dance, and she was one of them. Wu's

Schwarze, the one American in the bunch. She'd been given the same outfit. It was hanging with her own things in the wardrobe when she first arrived.

Wu was annoyed with her for avoiding this costume he'd provided in favor of the bib-topped jumpers she'd worn for years at Drayton. He ordered her to wear the pants and blouse to his sessions for the Sisters of Tomorrow. But what would her new friends in Yenching think of her service to the common cause if she appeared in this frivolous style? She continued to dress as she pleased when in Yenching.

As the Sisters of Tomorrow, all English-speaking, continued their weekend studies with Wu, a new ideal was proposed to them. Wu's friend, Instructor Tsu, who wore a suit like white pajamas, and slashed his arms through the air when he spoke, explained to them that all things were political, even love, no matter how selfishly they had practiced or imagined it before.

"You will be too young now to understand. I am thinking you are all in virtue," he said in their second session with him. His arms flew around.

"I am right? I am right?"

He was looking for a response from each of them in turn, his hands flashing by their faces.

Perhaps Becca was slow to respond, thinking of the pain she had caused Linny last Christmas.

"You are not sure, *Schwarze?*"

His arm flew around in an arc so that his fist might have struck her between the legs if he hadn't turned aside at the last moment. The rest of the class covered their faces in shame.

"Good!" he said. "Very good."

And instead of scolding Becca, he turned on the others in an arm-waving fury. Again, one at a time, forcing them to meet his gaze.

"Are you not thinking how selfish you are?" he asked each of them. "What does it mean, this pride in your virtue, this love of yourself? What is it for? You say you will be sisters of the Twenty-Eight Stroke Gentleman. Ha! You ask him to save you from extermination with your families running across the fields. We bring you

here, and what do you offer him? Your virtue? Ha! What is that worth to him and the Men of Tomorrow? They fight for you in the sunlight, unafraid, and under the moon you hold yourself against their need, your hand over this thing you call your virtue. What is that? Who are the cowards here?"

Tsu said he was disgusted with all of them. No more class that day.

"You also, *Schwarze*, you who are not sure. Go back to your rooms now, all of you. And think what to say when the Man of Tomorrow turns the key in your door."

She went back with the others, and lay shaking on the huge bed. There was Linny, overhead. This time Becca was happy to have her watching, and repeating with her, "Keep it locked."

She waved to her, not a moment before Linny waved back. She understood her sister thought she might let the wrong man touch them.

During the night there was screaming and sobbing in the room next to her, then silence. The weekend passed with no one trying her door, and she was off to Yenching again. She started at dawn, and got there in time for noon classes. The muscles in her legs had never been so strong. For the first time she pedaled all the way to Yenching without once getting off the bicycle.

∞

These were the happiest weeks, the time she spent at Yenching. Walking to the teahouses with Huang Don and his friends after the lessons. Don spoke Chinese to them. She followed anyway, showing her admiration with smiles and a nodding head. The others were quiet when he spoke, and she knew by the way they glanced around furtively this was all about things that the wrong people must not hear. She liked to listen to his voice rise and fall. Even in Chinese there was no mistaking his passion.

After these sessions, if she waited for his attention, he would explain all over again in English, for those who had not understood. It might be the number of people exterminated that month in Shanghai, or Chiang's bribery of another warlord with money from a German businessman, or the long suffering of another hundred rebels

who slipped through the lines of the Kuomintang to join the opposition in the hills.

She'd been surprised to learn from Wu that these honorable soldiers in the hills were the same ones he was calling the Men of Tomorrow, the ones whose need should not be denied. The day was coming when Wu would test her memory again. If she failed maybe he'd pull her out of Yenching. She wasn't going to fail. She meant to win the naming contest, to show Wu and the others something they wouldn't have believed possible. She hadn't been idle in her hours with Huang Don's people. She was composing a poem of nothing but their names. It was growing longer each week, the stanzas expanding as new members joined his group and were introduced to her. She wanted to tell them of her secret effort in their behalf, but was afraid they'd resent her.

She kept it all under her breath, repeating the sounds over and over again. In one cell, Dou Ping, Chou Deng-win, Han Suyin, Hu Wei-ling, Rachel Chin, and two dozen more that rhymed with these. In her Yenching dormitory she fell asleep each night, with her lips moving through the same exercise, one cell after another.

She began to follow Don further off the campus. Sometimes he spoke to groups in the countryside four or five miles away, even beyond that. Here were more names for her silent rhyming. She could think her way through all of them if she didn't stop, but when something interrupted her she'd have to begin all over again. She didn't know how many names there were, only the pattern they made in her head.

She wondered if Don could tell how much she admired him. And she thought about why she preferred the Western angles in his features to the softer surface of the pure Chinese face. His mixed blood could be a problem for him. He admitted as much, but his chain of information ran all the way to Chingkanshan and back, and none of his followers could match that. He preferred not to speak English in front of his followers, and Becca kept her distance during the long political meetings, where he held forth without contradiction or interruption.

After one meeting he explained to her that he had just called for a gathering of all the members at the same farm on the following

weekend. He told her he had asked them to come prepared next time to declare their full commitment to tomorrow. How much were they willing to give? A trinket? Their money? Their lives? She should tell no one, but they would be sending a messenger to Chingkanshan, for the first time declaring their number and their allegiance to the Twenty-Eight Stroke Gentleman.

"I trust you," he said, his hand lightly at her waist.

She looked into his face for a sign of communion beyond political passion. She felt favored, alive with secrets, so charmed she lost track of the time.

Becca was due back in Wu's classroom in the morning for her first recitation of names. She had stayed with Don's people much too late. It would be long after dark before she reached Peiping. As shy as he was in her company, he would not let her go back alone. For the first mile or two they walked, she beside her bicycle, he on the other side of the road, like a stranger. When dusk fell and no one was left to recognize them, he asked her please to get on the bicycle seat. He would stand in front of her on the pedals while she held onto his belt. If Linny could see this, the beautiful young man with China's future on his shoulders, pedaling just for her.

She put her hands on his back and felt a shiver run through him, not the pleasure kind, she thought, but as if afraid of what was happening behind him. Instead of loosening her grip, she held on tighter as he rose and fell on the pedals. He was like a carousel horse, up and down, working so mechanically for so long the sweat began to come through his shirt. She could offer him a bath in her room, but Linny was against it. Though she begged him to rest, he wouldn't stop till the ride was over.

They reached the long incline where they could glide the last miles into the city. They were gaining speed, passing horse carts and the more cautious cyclists. She thought of Don with all the students around him, blabbering their politics. She didn't have to know Chinese to understand they all vied for his esteem with their own political virtue. A rare and perfect thing to have him to herself where he could be unashamed of her company. She thought again of asking him into her room.

As they gained speed, her hands slid down his sides, and she wrapped her arms all the way around him. Her fingers pulled against his muscled abdomen, and he screeched like an owl in the darkness, warning the timid traffic that flew past as if moving in the opposite direction. He never used the brakes. If they were out of control, she wasn't afraid, but blissed by his courage. She pressed her cheek against the warm, wet place between his shoulder blades, and drew her arms tighter around him, her breasts snug against his back.

They raced ahead, weaving through the walkers, dodging the oncoming wagons. Don let their momentum carry them as far as it would into the city, until the bicycle wobbled, and their feet reached for the ground. Without asking directions he'd come gliding right to the front of her building.

"Let go," he said.

Someone was watching them.

"Where do you stay?"

"Here," she said. "You found it."

"Not possible," he said. "This is Gao's building. They are all Gao's women here."

When he saw that she was serious, he dropped the bicycle, looked around him, and began to trot away, out of the light. Becca called but he never turned around.

∞

Becca was in her room, surrounded by mirrors again, her sister scolding from every angle. Why did you hold him like that? He's going to talk about you to the People of Tomorrow. You can't go back there now that he knows where you live. You were cheap. Say your names before you go to sleep. Get ready for tomorrow. She looked angry, scornful, bossy. But Linny didn't know everything; Becca thought she had nothing to be ashamed of. If Linny was hiding in the glass, waiting for daylight, she didn't know that the hard pillow next to Becca was Don Huang, his shoulders rising and falling as he rode with her through the night. She whispered her long list of rhymed names in his silk ear and they fell asleep together, contented.

It was easy. The other students in the conversation class had been satisfied to gather a few names each, and then wasted their time in the teahouses, boasting of their intelligence. Wu saved Becca's performance for last. He must have known she was going to win. He nodded, and tapped his foot to the rhythm of her recitation. One hundred and thirty-eight names he counted in her poem of ten stanzas.

Wu asked for it again, but slower. Against his own warning he was putting the names into his notebook.

"Names are one thing," he said when she was finished. "Where we find these people is another."

Nothing satisfied him. One by one, she identified the dormitory rooms and the houses in the villages beyond the Yenching gates where her People of Tomorrow lived. The others in the class were amazed, and maybe shocked by the way she showed off in front of them. Wu was writing fast as he could to get it all down; committing the list to paper, he said, because the time had come to deliver the Grand Directory. They weren't the only ones who were taking part. All over Peiping groups like theirs had been preparing for this time. All these brave people, he said, would be set down on one scroll to be hidden in a beggar's cart and pushed all the way to the leader in Chinkanshan.

"You are the winner," he assured her. "The rest of you, aren't you ashamed to let the American *Schwarze* be first Sister of Tomorrow?"

Her prize was no prize at all, though Wu said she would no longer have to wear herself out pedaling the bicycle to Yenching and back each week. In fact, he said, she had completed her duty there, and to return would now be forbidden. Not just against his rules, but foolhardy and against the law. It would be like asking to be put in jail. The police would be stopping everyone on the road. Students especially would be watched, and foreigners would be trusted by no one.

Becca's world had shrunk again to the room of mirrors, where her sister couldn't leave her alone. Of course, she understood it wasn't Linny's fault. Wu said he would bring her something else to read. For all her good work she could relax until the weekend, when Mr. Tsu would be continuing her instruction with the other Sisters of Tomorrow.

Someone had taken Huang Don's pamphlet *Extermination*. She assumed that Gao or one of the men who worked for him had a key to her room. She already knew that Wu did. And now she realized the lock she thought she controlled from the inside could not keep them out. This, and the prospect of Tsu's rapid hands and strange arguments, left her no choice.

Before first light on the following Saturday she was on the road again, pedaling slowly up the long grade toward Yenching, on her way to the meeting at the farm, where she meant to pledge her political heart and her life to Don Huang and his cause. She was ready to please him in whatever task he asked of her. In return, she imagined Don might find a way for her to stay close by him in Yenching, a way for her to leave Peiping for good, and eventually find a new way home to America that would not require Wu's favor.

Wu had been wrong about police on the road. There were only the usual wagons and carts moving vegetables, and chickens, and goats from farm to village. They stared but did not speak, and she was reassured she was doing the right thing. Wu had exaggerated the danger, she supposed, to frighten her into obedience.

She reached the farm at noon, wondering if she were early or late. No one else was there. There was only the farmer by himself, raking his hay into bundles. She sat on a warm rock and watched the Chinese grasshoppers, copper and red-eyed, half jumping, half flying over the tops of the stalks, thinking if she could do that, she wouldn't need anyone's help to get away from Wu or his friends. An hour later she knew something had gone wrong.

Eula didn't fully understand Linny's obsession with her sewing project. She took the gown apart and found seven kinds of stitching, two of which she'd never seen before. Hidden in the seam between two panels of the bodice she discovered a name she could treasure, stitched in red cursive on a white tag, Vionnet, Callot Soeurs. As perfect as the lettering was, it couldn't be read unless the dress were taken apart as she had done. She was intrigued by the modesty, and

set it as an ideal for herself. That so much could be said so quietly. If you needed a tag to identify it, you would never own the dress in the first place. Callot Soeurs' sophistication surpassed the need or desire to advertise. All of this made Linny wonder more at the gift, and her special place in Mr. Rank's estimation.

Eula explained it as best she could in one of her frequent letters to Paris.

Instead of putting the dress immediately together again, Linny was using the pieces, spread around the living room floor of her cottage, as the pattern for a duplicate garment to be stitched in tandem with the first, and saved for Becca's return to America, maybe two years away if all went well. In the meantime Linny was making an intramural reputation as a very stern sewing mistress. In spite of her previous experience instructing the younger girls, she was really too young for this. Eula had only been trying to restore her confidence until she could be hired away to the city.

One afternoon there were angry voices in the Schoolhouse common room, where the sewing class was being held. Mother Reilly heard one of the intermediate girls sassing Linny, who had lost patience.

"Stop the machine!" Linny told her. "It's all wrong, what you're doing!"

"Mind your own work," the girl said. She turned her head to give Linny the tongue, and the Singer's needle went not just once, but twice, through her finger. Before the surprised child had the wit to stop pumping her treadle, she had sewn the linen placemat she was decorating to the side of her thumb. There was a terrible scream as Linny turned the machine by hand to extract the needle. The panicked child flung her arm about trying to shake the mat from her finger. Blood flew over both of their clothes, and Linny grabbed the girl's arm.

The staff were too kind to say the obvious, that Linny was still too much a child herself to hold the respect and obedience of other children. There was a reason for pushing her beyond her maturity; she had to have a job in order to stay, and Eula was damned if it was going to be menial. She talked with Linny about the tone and attitude she took with the students. She enrolled her in Tessie Croft's weekly

seminar on personality, a class meant for older women training for social work. Again, she was pushing the girl ahead of herself.

Tess allowed Linny into the course with reservations, thinking
some of the weekly discussion would be useful to her, though the
texts might be beyond her reach. As the weeks passed, this experi-
ment began to take hold. At first, getting Linny to speak in the seminar was near impossible, and when she did open her mouth her
contributions were vague and never more than a few words. The
other women, though disposed to be friendly, were put off by the
girl's indifference to them, unaware that she was studying this material with an absent partner.

"We forget," she'd say, or "We don't know," trying Tessie's patience. Toward the end of the seminar, Linny couldn't recognize the
progress she'd made in self-possession and confidence, though Tess
had forced her to begin her recitations with "I."

"The women weren't very smart," she told Eula. "They spent six
weeks trying to figure out what makes people laugh, and six weeks
on what makes them angry with each other. In the end two of them
were crying because they didn't pass and one of them because she
did. I don't think any of them can sew a button on a collar."

Miss Croft said Linny had passed. She was suddenly very proud of
the twin, especially for what she called her "horse sense." Eula insisted on a little celebration, a supper with wine at the Director's cottage on Bethlehem Pike. Kerstin was chef for the evening and Miss
Croft was invited with her own housemate, Celly Harrison. Eula was
more excited at the prospect of the evening than Linny.

She had a surprise in mind, something in the tone of the gathering, a promotion for Linny without change of rank, an affirmation of
her emergence as a woman, a kind of coming out party, at which independence would be celebrated rather than eligibility, an introduction of the twin into their sisterhood of social service. Not that she
expected Linny to be swallowed into this honorable coven overnight,
but that the pleasures of their commitment, their joy in each other's
lives and professional success should be on display for a young and
worthy seeker.

Eula thought it was the moment for them to be Eula, Kerstin, Tess, and Celly, that a bottle or two of wine shared five ways, should help Linny, so full of talent and the desire to share her gift, past any embarrassment of first names. There was nothing starched or overly mannered about the group. They were all fine-looking women, well figured, who had been courted and offered marriage, all but Celly— perhaps the most strikingly pretty—because she, of all of them, had made her disdain for the prospect of double harness so clear: "It's not a harness. You can remove a harness."

None of the others were so adamant in their freedom to work and entertain themselves without masculine restraint, so insistent on independence; nor were they close to forsaking it. As Eula watched her company arrive and imagined what Linny, standing beside her, would be thinking, she saw how similarly they had all dressed for the occasion. Every one of them in a white blouse with rounded collar, nothing puffy or exaggerated in the sleeves, and every one decorated high in the center; one with a cameo, another, a silver saint, a round of red amber, and her own, a tiny, glass-covered locket of her grandmother's woven hair. They could have been sailors lined up on deck for inspection; so minor were the differences in their costume, the uniformity was all the more apparent. And each had a rich head of hair, ranging from light brown to black, pinned up modestly in a soft curve or bun.

Their skirts were all dark, and hemmed to the same ankle length, neither confining nor full, and the shoes—practical, night and day— leather pumps, dark brown or black, whose style was the lack of it, no cosmetic stitching, only that which attached the uppers to the soles. Celly and Kerstin, who were on their feet so much, swore by the new hard rubber heels, the same that left black marks everywhere.

"Look at that," Eula said, pointing to a new line on the floor. "When she's in her scuffling mood I have to follow her around the house with cleaning fluid and a rag."

"I know," Tessie said, "Celly's just as bad."

The nod to paired lives, the revelation of time apart from the academy, and the trivia that filled a shared day did little to relax Linny. In fact she seemed more nervous as she shook hands with Miss Harrison.

"Please, call me Celly, dear."

It was the sole bits of jewelry they allowed themselves, the broaches, that were the giveaway to their forsaken roots, little Victorian and Edwardian anchors, the jewelry of mothers and grandmothers, which had not held against the drift into radical lives as social and educational progressives. Perhaps, if Eula could reduce these to the informality they deserved it would calm the jittery twin.

"You're wearing my favorite pin," she told Tessie, reaching to turn the amber piece into the light. "Do you see the star in it, Linny? It was her aunt's. Tell her the story, Tess."

"It's very pretty, Dr. Croft."

"*Doctor*'s just for the classroom, Linny. No need for that tonight. This is your party."

Eula could have hugged her distinguished guest, but Tess immediately turned attention away from her amber to the glass locket at Eula's neck. "That's very interesting," she said. "People have always made such a thing over hair, but it's odd to think it was so common in a reliquary." Eula saw all the introductory repair disappear in a single word, and the girl's glance of panic. Eula was too tactful to offer a definition, and Linny, too nervous to destroy the presumption of her understanding. She drank down her first glass of wine exactly as if it were her first glass of wine, as if it were grape juice.

Eula explained it was her grandmother's hair in the locket, and allowed that we're all tied to forebears in ways that repay study of the connections, though these might be forever beyond comprehension. She couldn't explain, for example, why she wore these little, intricately plaited strands in spite of other symptoms they provoked in her, tying her to a grandmother whose mean tutoring produced a father, successful in business, liberal in public posture, yet so miserly in family finance that he turned common comforts into luxuries, and Eula's mother into a beggar at his throne.

After her second glass of wine, and before Kerstin's cheese fondue, Linny said she wasn't feeling well. The women reproached themselves for allowing her too much to drink, too quickly. Eula took her upstairs to lie down for a while. She fell asleep immediately

and her party continued without her. She woke to their loud happy sounds below her, and went to the head of the stairs. They were having a grand time, conversation, bursts of laughter, interruptions, their voices shoving back and forth at each other, good-natured pleading. They sounded like grown-up children.

Kerstin was explaining to the others how Dr. Tupperman had lectured her on the expectations of their marriage bed. "He didn't want me to worry too much. The sword shouldn't frighten me, he said. He knew the anatomy very well, and was sure I'd be adequate to the requirement."

"My God, Slue, think how close you came."

"What about you, Mummy, you and the moist-eyed Cyril?"

"He never mentioned his sword."

Miss Croft interrupted the laughter: "Bunny, didn't your last man want to know if anyone had ever 'interfered' with you? Gave you his purity test, didn't he?"

"Oh, Skins! You're horrid, dragging that up again! I never should have told you."

Mummy, Slue, Bunny, Skins. Their wild conversation was nothing to these revelations. They might have first names Linny was now encouraged to use, but there was another degree of familiarity between them, which she'd never reach, and supposed she'd never want to. Still, she felt some kinship with them. They were hiding in their own way, as she and Becca were hiding, their intimacy masked from a world that wouldn't understand or tolerate it.

They were toasting Mr. Rank.

"Once again," Miss Croft said, "to the most intelligent man I've ever known. And the most generous spirit. To Otto."

"Tessie! In one gulp?"

"He needs a little extra help just now."

"The French woman? How do you explain that, Skins?"

"It's about courage and will. He admires that side of her."

Linny heard Miss Kieland begin to argue, but Miss Croft wouldn't listen.

"Do you know," she went on, "from one conversation with him I had the whole syllabus for my course on personality? He condemns

classification and then spins out a model that contains us all. Try this, he told me. Divide personalities into three types in ascending order of moral worth.

"First, the lowest, the adapted, the sheep perhaps. They learn their will; that is, they live by society's code and control their impulses.

"Second, the neurotic. Their will is stronger; they fight against domination, and win, but waste their victory with guilt about being willful, repressing the natural.

"Third, the highest, the productive, the artist, the genius. They accept and affirm themselves. They create an ideal and a new world."

"Where do we fit?"

"Eula dear, I'm surprised you have to ask."

"You mean the French woman is . . . "

"I'm afraid so. Isn't it obvious."

"But no artists? No geniuses here?"

"Oh yes! That girl upstairs. That Linny of yours. She's on her way. I'm quite sure of it."

Linny retreated from the top of the steps, back to the bedroom, with a whole new estimation of herself. These extraordinary women downstairs thought she was an artist, a genius. And if she was, then Becca must be as well. She thought it was simply bad luck that brought Miss Kieland tiptoeing upstairs to check on her sleep just as she was going through the bureau drawers. After all, she was only looking for what was hers. All she could think to say was "I could smell your sachet. You have so many pretty things."

∞

Otto was encouraging Eula again to meet the lady friend from Paris. He'd trained her in his analytic technique. She was lining up patients for therapy in New York in the coming Spring.

"Just meet her," he wrote. "And don't get the wrong idea. I'm not dumping you in her lap. I'm not trying to get rid of you, though you might find yourself opening yourself, maybe more trusting of a woman's perspective. I've told you she's an artist, who suffers from the twin demons of longing to write something that will not only be worthy in her own estimation, but widely admired, while thumbing

her nose at those who marry in churches. In this latter attitude she's not so different from you. Don't ignore her invitation.

"To save herself the embarrassment of the reputation that will follow her name over the ocean she might introduce herself to you as Linotte Culmell. Linotte is the name she used years ago for the one who kept her diaries, the impossible one who had to be locked away from the public. Her real name, her father's, is the one she may withhold from you."

Before closing, he wrote, "So I've introduced you to another double. Are you keeping a list?"

Before she heard from Linotte, there was a visitor from Washington at Drayton, a Mr. Walsh who was in the Philadelphia region to speak at several colleges on cultural exchange with China. With support from Tessie, Eula had raised such an unholy fuss that he'd been asked to come to see her in person, maybe to keep Becca's situation from public attention. Walsh had a letter his department had received from a prominent American in Peiping, who knew of Becca's case through the consulate there. Beyond that, there was nothing very useful.

A girl had been traced but her name was Schwarze. Dark-skinned but blond, an American, she was a sudden foreign hero of the Follow and Obey movement supporting China's generalissimo. She had provided a list of well over a hundred names of communist students, and these unfortunate naïfs had been rounded up and probably eliminated. Of course the girl would now be in great danger. It was no wonder she was out of sight, probably in house confinement. If she ever surfaced in one of the American concessions, it wouldn't be a secret for long. She'd stand out like a gold-topped mountain on any street or road in China.

As for Mr. Wu, Walsh said the man had strong associates in several Chinese cities, that the Americans, even if they could find him, were in no position to arrest or question him. One of his backers was Gao Tseshing, a man of such influence he was able to keep a private police force. Gao was known for his operation of two party ships, which plied the Chinese coast between Tientsin and the concession island of Gu Lang Yu. They were known informally as the Piano Line because the

piano importer Wu used the cruises to demonstrate and sell these Western curiosities to the leisured Chinese and European businessmen.

Mr. Walsh ran ahead on this wild tangent till Eula finally asked why he was telling all this to her.

"Aren't you concerned?"

"Why should I be?

"Didn't you place a half-bred girl in Mr. Wu's care?"

"Half-bred?"

Anyway, her name wasn't Schwarze, and Eula was certain she knew little or nothing of Chinese politics, and would not involve herself.

"But I was told your child was dark. Colored."

She thanked Walsh, for coming out of his way, and told Linny nothing about his visit.

In early May, when the forsythia made a yellow shield along the Drayton border on Bethlehem Pike, Mr. Henry told Eula he had seen the Carey twins' grandmother again, bent over in the hedge's thick undergrowth. When he called to her, she had ducked and fought her way like a trapped animal to the far side. He walked all the way to the Drayton gate, and then along the hedge, by the roadside, looking for her. She had disappeared.

By the end of the month, when the overgrown forsythia was green again, he insisted the Director give him a week or two to prune it severely, so it couldn't be the hiding place for useless men who would bother their girls, or a polka-dotted woman who might jump out from time to time and frighten them. It was a huge job. He persevered, day after day, clipping away. The cut branches hauled together made a pile the size of a house. When he was done, he was so proud of his accomplishment he called Eula out to see what remained of the hedge, a thin line of stalks along the property line. If it made him feel safer, fine, though they could now look all the way through to the flickering silhouettes of traffic on the Pike.

She clapped and put her arm around Mr. Henry's shoulder. His pleasure was brief. He turned to the forest line, the adjacent boundary where they had found Linny's bag. "She could be in there," he said, as if it were up to Eula to have something done about all the

woods in case the polka-dotted woman should use these, too, for cover.

∞

Linotte Culmell knew when Eula would be in New York for a conference, and asked her for a meeting at the end of her trip. Eula went with a feisty self-assurance, the same way she'd first approached Otto, ready to brush aside flattery and pounce on nonsense. They met in a tea room on Eighty-sixth Street, across from the Adams Hotel, where Otto had arranged rooms for Linotte.

She was alluring, if self-consciously turned out, in a tight black dress with a party décolletage, net stockings, and high heels. Eula's high-buttoned blouse seemed sadly conventional, even a little comical. The bolder garments Linotte wore were a reproach even before Eula opened her mouth. The heart-shaped face described by Otto was certainly that, framed by jade circles that hung from gold earrings.

"Otto said you were pretty," Linotte began. "You're much more. Your eyes are honest as stone."

She shook Eula's hand, holding on an extra moment.

Linotte was very quick off the mark, noticing right away Eula was staring at the end of her nose.

"It had a little turned-down tip," she said, touching it. "I had it taken off."

There was no apparent scar, but a shiny little flat circle, which, if it had been powdered like the rest of her face, might not have been noticeable at all.

She ordered sherry for herself, tea for her guest.

"Otto has told me . . ." Eula began.

"Let's not waste time with pleasantries," the woman said. "He's told me a lot about you, too, and that takes us nowhere useful. I know I'll have to convince you I'm more than a self-involved little bitch out for money and success. What else could you possibly think from the bare outline you've probably been given?"

She stopped to let Eula consider that much, and went on: "In the end you'll still think so. But maybe there'll be more, and that will

make my acquaintance worthwhile. You stare so much," she said with sparkling charm, taking Eula's hand again. "Don't you speak?"

Eula withdrew her hand. The woman patted it lightly, as if forgiving the rude retreat. This time she'd caught Eula looking at her ring. Anyone might have stared; it was large enough to be a man's with a round red stone, and worn disconcertingly on her first finger.

She told Eula she had just finished writing a book about the double, really about herself and her father. Or, more precisely, herself looking at herself as she carried on with her father. She didn't have to say she'd slept with this man. Eula already had that from Otto.

"Otto is so wise," Linotte said, ". . . and so foolish. He saw my obsession with this as a path away from my diary habit. And he explained what my indifference to my father really means. What I'm actually doing when I scorn his pretense of faithfulness to me. A double cannot deceive me," she said, winking. "I have to hurt my father. Do you understand that? To deliver him from his guilt."

Eula felt herself succumbing to hokum, and she pulled herself up straight: "What about your guilt? What about the child you made but wouldn't finish?"

This was the most ugly thing she knew about the woman, far worse than seduction of an analyst or her deceitfulness with lovers. Not just her determination to have a stillborn baby, but her cold indifference afterward in the way she'd written about it. Otto had sent Eula a copy of the shocking pages to convince her of Linotte's honesty.

Her face lost its animation. A tear drew a line down her powdered cheek.

"I have more work to do with you than I thought," she said calmly. "I might even be able to help you. But not if you despise me."

Eula had gone too far. She reached out and touched the sash at Linotte's waist. The woman took her arm and held it tightly.

"You have twins," she said with new life.

"Not mine. And not anymore."

"Oh, yes," she said. "Much too late to abort those two."

"One's gone," Eula said. "And the other soon will be."

"No," she said. "I'm sure Otto wouldn't fool about this. One is with you now and forever. The other will be back. They're yours."

When Eula didn't argue, she said, "Yours for good."

Linotte didn't want to hear about Eula's work as the Director, her career, her orphanage, any of that. Eula understood from the moment the woman looked into her eyes, she was trying to seduce her, and not just intellectually. She wasn't repulsed. Linotte was quite charming, quite pretty, and Eula was flattered. She could afford to be because she was onto the game.

Linotte finished her sherry in several gulps, and said Eula must come up and see her living room, which Otto had furnished for receiving her therapy patients. "Society women from Connecticut," she said, distancing herself from them. Eula followed her without qualm, ready to counterattack if the need arose.

"Go ahead, sit down over there."

Linotte pointed to a softly upholstered chaise longue.

"Let's pretend you've already asked for my help."

Eula did more than sit. She lay back and closed her eyes, almost hoping Linotte would do something forward, something that could be condemned outright. She had lines ready if needed: Do all you modern analysts entice your patients sexually? Is that part of the therapy?

"It's the doubling that interests me," Linotte said from the chair behind the couch. "If you'll forgive me, I think Otto perceives you as two people, the one who gives totally—your life to your cause—and the one who stands back, withholding. I think for you a full integration would not only mean full mental health, but a crushing normality, and that's why you won't dare it. No neurosis, no art. And you are an artist, whether you realize it or not. You paint children, but without a brush.

"Now let's pretend you've confided in me, all the way to the bottom," she went on, "and already I have some advice. Stop thinking of yourself as the good sister and the bad sister. You're probably more like me. Your twin isn't an evil sister; she's your editor. Though for me the problem is more acute. I know I'm an actress playing a role for my second self to observe and write about. I lie like the dickens, and my reasons for it are always stronger than any inclination to reform."

"I can't hear very well with you behind me."

Actually Eula could. She was trying to make the woman sit closer, and she did, right beside her, nestling her hip comfortably into the curve above that of her own.

"Your reasons for lying," Eula said. "What are they?"

"To give the men hope. If they can believe for a time, it's better than a constant despair. It makes the next moment possible."

Eula had never heard anything like this mixture of candor and depravity.

"Your claws are clipped a little shorter than mine?" Linotte said, "though perhaps not as short as you think."

"Your twins," she went on, "they can't help mutual observation and imitation. They were born to it. They don't need to find second selves in their own skins to haunt them. For you and me the observation of our second selves must be willed. It must be a duty."

Eula sat bolt upright, almost knocking the woman off her perch.

"It's not really your business to analyze the twins. You've never seen them."

"Listen to yourself," she said. "You're not disputing what I'm saying. You're doubting my competence."

"Why shouldn't I? You're ashamed of your own name."

That stopped Linotte only briefly. Quickly she was loaded again and on the hunt, cunning.

"I was aware that you knew. Call me Anaïs if you prefer. It won't change anything for you. For me, it will make you seem more a friend."

"I'm not your friend," Eula reminded her. "I've just met you."

Linotte was making herself comfortable beside Eula again, and once more she caught Eula staring at her, and at the ring.

"It's carnelian intaglio," she said, "carved in Greece way before Christianity got people worked up. I want you to relax again, and please, stop thinking about me. Think about what I'm saying."

Eula lay back sighing, closing her eyes tightly, making a little display of submission, giving Linotte all the rope she'd need.

"You're not fooling me," Linotte said. "Let's talk about your distrust, your contempt. It will be difficult. You may hold my hand. I'm not going to reach for yours again."

Eula sighed.

"Let me start over. I began with my father maybe as a little confession, a little play for your trust. If it seemed irrelevant, there was this behind it: Otto's insight that revenge rules us underneath all. It keeps equilibrium in our emotional life. I have to punish my father to make his recovery possible."

"And who punishes you?"

Without hesitation she said, "I punish myself. There is constant examination, with confession of the smallest sin. Your question is useful but your antagonism shames you. You won't be happier for it when you leave here."

Eula imagined the beautiful woman holding onto her like a crab on bait, an appetite incarnate that might betray itself if it didn't let go in time.

"Your good works are well advertised," Linotte said. "Your life is a social cause. But you deny yourself pleasure. Even in private you follow society's expectation."

"Did Otto tell you that?"

"Of course not. He wouldn't have to."

"How would you know? What expectation?"

"You make me say the obvious? All right, I'll say it. Sexlessness. The forced frigidity of the professional woman. The busy woman. The woman with authority."

Eula started up once more, and softly she was pushed back again, against the sofa. Linotte rearranged herself, and went on.

"These sighs of yours," she said. "They aren't reflexive. They aren't from your heart. They're premeditated. What is this superiority you feel? You admit to mistakes, but you're sure the foundation of your life is above reproach. If the role you play is so pure, what of your constraints? Compare them to my freedom and the honesty of my work. If my life is full of lies, it is all confessed in my art. Believe me, I hold nothing back. Can you claim the same?"

Before Eula could answer, Linotte said, "Of course that isn't fair. If you told all, as I do, I mean everything, you'd have no job. No one would tolerate you. You'd be forced as I've been to live as a dependent, to beg for extras. My husband is very generous, but not infinitely wealthy."

Eula wasn't sorry for Linotte or for herself. She was reeling from all the presumption, the extrapolation from what Otto must have told her, and all the inferences, the endless nerve of the woman.

"Let's talk about Otto," Linotte said. "He's the one who matters here. Admit it. You take a magnifying glass to everything he says. Why wouldn't you? I do as well. Doesn't your friend Miss Croft tell everyone he's the smartest man she's ever met?"

No longer in a mood to duel, Eula made herself more comfortable against the woman's side. She had decided to let Linotte be Anaïs now, more honestly her double self. And she felt the woman's hand, falsely innocent, at her waist again.

Anaïs became softer, more reflective.

"Otto met me in Paris," she said, "and lost his head. Of course, I encouraged him. I went to him for help, and immediately fell all over him. It was evil. He was helpless. The seduction became material for my therapy. Of course that's useless as long as the sex continues. There were presents, then my betrayals, and his recrimination. It was all over within a month. In spite of it, he encourages my writing, instructs me as a therapist. He even pays for these rooms. Otto has a big heart, but a bigger brain."

She was right about that; Eula shared the same respect. Anaïs was pulling her hand away slowly. She said Otto had given her diary back to her, that is, his therapeutic permission to keep writing in it. Though he'd once called it her opium, he now considered it significant feminine introspection, and certain to be published.

"You know very well what it's like to have Otto's blessing," she said.

With that, Anaïs said they had reached honesty, and now they could begin.

Eula wanted to hear more about the presents.

"It was last summer," Anaïs said. "I was supposed to meet Otto on the Mediterranean, after one of his meetings. He gave me travel money, and a brocade suitcase stuffed with a vacation trousseau. The fanciest outfit in Paris. You wouldn't believe the dress, the negligee, accessories, everything. It was *de trop*. As soon as he was gone I took it all over to my friend Henry's. I gave him the money to publish something, and wore the clothes for him."

"What happened?"

"Otto was furious. He's no masochist. He took it all back. He was going to send the suitcase full of clothes to America. To someone more deserving."

Eula was almost certain something more important had changed hands. She was afraid to say so. Instead she asked if Anaïs would show her the impression her ring made. They rang down to the lobby for some sealing wax. The boy at the desk offered a rainbow of colors. Anaïs chose copper.

She scalded herself on the wax and sucked on her finger like a simpering schoolgirl, while Eula made the impressions. Four of them, as if each repeated a lie, the little copper men, hanging at each other's necks. She didn't want to believe that Otto would have given the ring away to this woman or anyone else.

"Yes," she said. "He gave it to me."

She was pointing to the pairs Eula had pressed in the wax, one at a time, and named them.

"Tripto and Lezzor. Anaïs and Linotte. Eula and . . . Eula. Linda and Rebecca."

"Do you like it?" Anaïs asked. "Yes, just look at your greedy eyes. Perhaps someday I will give it to you. Of course it would have to be earned . . . to have any useful meaning for you."

Given the opportunity, Eula would have stolen it from her.

Anaïs asked her to lie down again. She didn't protest, but decided to actually lay herself out as a subject, and put her guilt for the twins' predicament at the woman's disposal. She couldn't deny she was thinking, too, of the ring, of getting and keeping it. The little talisman that spoke out of antiquity to modern mysteries that entailed her life. Think what others would have given for one of Freud's rings. And how much more intriguing, the apostate's? How could he have lain it down in lust? That Eula might rescue it, maybe even return it to its rightful hand, was more than a worthy grail, and less, the quest almost childish in its romantic modesty, taking a martyr's part in restoration of his honor.

Anaïs was gentle with her, probing and retreating, exploring the history of the Careys. She swallowed hard on Eula's explanation of

what had happened to the brocade case and its contents. With Anaïs Eula made a scene she would never confess to anyone. In the middle of their honesty, Eula surprised herself, reaching for the warmth of the woman's hand. Anaïs was pushing back Eula's skirt making it seem the most natural thing in the world, and placing her warm fingers high above her stocking, against her thigh, and there they stayed for the rest of the hour. Kerstin had never dared such a thing. Eula would never have allowed it. But an audience with Anaïs was like being in a foreign country, beyond the pale of domestic decorum.

They talked and talked, past Eula's grief for Becca and Linny, into a future in which Anaïs predicted the twins would meet again at Drayton, and that one of them might stay forever.

"Look, you're happy," she said.

Eula was not aware she'd been smiling, though she was giggling on the inside, thinking of the way Anaïs might describe what was happening for her diary, "from my exploring hand, the message of pleasure traveling in the dark, creeping under each wall of self-denial, reaching all her extremities."

It was as reckless as Eula had ever been. She thought the woman must know this. If this wasn't enough to capture Tripto and Lezzor, she would never have them. The ring, on Anaïs's finger again, remained there, and nothing more was said about it.

Becca tried speaking with her hands. She tried a line of stones in the road, then sticks upright in the mud to suggest a crowd of people. The farmer looked at her doubtfully and beat his arms up and down as if he were shooing a cow.

She rode back to the Yenching campus to look for Don Huang and the others there, but found only a few scattered students rambling aimlessly, their heads bowed, and their lips moving in a somber prayer. Professor Moore, her first teacher at the university, came out from the faculty offices and threw his arms around her. He was crying.

"It's awful," he said. "I didn't think we'd see you again."

He pointed to sheets hanging from the windows in the women's dormitories. They were painted with black ideograms and English letters.

FOR SHAME CHIANG
FOR SHAME KUOMINTANG
FOR SHAME JAPAN
FOR SHAME CHINA

"Where were you hiding?" he asked. "The Japanese soldiers came in the night with a Chinese officer. They surrounded the campus. No one could get away. They stood here on the grass, and read the wanted people from a list. Don Huang and his followers were taken away. All of them except you. Where were you?"

She fell to her knees on the lawn. All classes had been suspended. The only political faction left on campus was the Follow and Obey. They were too stunned by the destruction of their opposition to show themselves. Moore took her, sobbing, to his faculty apartment. She didn't know what to tell him. He couldn't convince her to spend the night on his guest bed. He couldn't make her stand. She sat all night in misery propped against his living room wall. He put a blanket over her during the night.

Before daylight she snuck away, and pumped her bicycle furiously back to Peiping. She meant to grab a few things from her room in the Palace of Dance, and escape into another zone of the city. Wu was waiting for her, sitting on her bed. She flew at him in a fury, swinging wildly, calling him goosh, and every other shitty name in her head.

"What?" he said. "You don't understand? You are only a *Schwarze*, but still a hero in my country, a patriot of China! You followed. You obeyed. There can be a parade. You can stand up in a carriage. Soldiers will salute you. You only have to pledge. You only have to thank Chiang for his protection."

She spit at Wu, whose politics were now perfectly clear. She kicked him away. She sat on the bed and cried into her hands.

"This is very selfish," he said. "To suffer alone is to suffer in vain."

She told him to shut up and get out of her room.

She should think of what had happened, he said, as no more than a box of red pencils confiscated by the police. If red pencils were against the law it should have been obvious to her that red ideas were as well.

She spit at him again.

"No parade, then? Tomorrow you go to Tientsin."

"Anywhere away from you," she told him.

"I will do what I can for you," he said. "No one will bother you here."

She was locked in her room for the night, and at daylight an older woman, who did not speak English well, came to take her on the train. They were handcuffed together.

"For you safety," she explained. "The thing you say, police take you jail, and no more you."

Wu said if she did not make a problem she might prosper on one of Mr. Gao's luxury ships, which carried businessmen from Tientsin to the island of Gu Lang Yu in Xiamen and back again. The People of Tomorrow were no longer of any interest to Wu. They were only paying for their mistakes, and this was as it should be; she was too young to understand.

She didn't know Wu was on the same train to Tientsin, not wanting to be seen traveling with a handcuffed passenger, one who might start screaming at him. He met them at the dockside and took her onto the boat himself. When they were safely onboard he said, "You are not in America. You are not in China. On this boat you are in a separate country. A country with laws of its own. You are a citizen of this country now. You have duties to this country."

Wu unlocked the handcuffs, paid the woman who had accompanied her, and sent her down the gangplank. He knew his way around this boat as well as he had around the cargo steamer. He took her down three stairways, somewhere below the waterline. There was no window or porthole in the cabin he showed her.

"This is where you stay. You see there is already a dress for you. Madame Suyin will give you a clean one every day. And shoes, see, shiny."

The cabin was tiny. The strange little dress of green velvet with no sleeves and stuffing in the front hung on a hanger over the bed, puffed out like a second body in a room that was hardly big enough for one. There was a toilet bowl, already smelly, and a sink in the cramped space between the end of the bed and the wall. At least she would be alone in here. No one else would fit. But there was Linny, as panicked as she was, standing in the mirror on the back of the narrow cabin door. With the door open two people could not pass between it and the bunk. Her sister would be thinking the same thing she was—they'd go crazy cramped together in this room. There wasn't enough air for one, much less two.

Wu pulled her back into the passageway. She kicked at him. She was crying again. He wanted to show her the other important places on the boat. Several doors opened along the passageway, and girls peeked out to see what the fuss was about. Two of them she recognized from the obedience classes Mr. Tsu had taught to the Women of Tomorrow. Then she saw Jennie Alexie. The beautiful skin she remembered, all a rash now. Jennie looked dreadful. She called to her. But Jennie wouldn't answer. When she recognized Becca she ducked back and snapped her door shut.

Wu pushed Becca up the stairway, and into a little dining area.

"You eat here, *Schwarze*. Do you want to see where you will dance?"

"No," she told him.

He dragged her along the corridor anyway, up several more steps, through swinging doors into a large ballroom with chandeliers. There were couches all around, and between these, along two sides of the room, were pianos. All kinds of pianos. She counted seven on each side.

"One of them plays itself," he said. "You can pretend."

Becca spit at him again. Her nose was running with all her crying. It was a mouthful of phlegm she blew on him. It stuck to his shoulder, and began to run down his front, toward a pocket. There were stewards watching. Wu yanked her next to him, and used her hair to wipe the mucus from his jacket. She kicked hard, and caught him

square in the shin, enough to make him double over. He recovered and was about to strike her, but thought better of it.

"You belong to Gao," he said calmly. "There can be no bruises. You should be grateful Gao is already protecting you. Did you know the police onshore are already asking for you? Imagine what they would do with you if I let them have you, a *Schwarze* whose heart is in Chinkanshan with the Twenty-Eight Stroke Gentleman. Stupid girl!"

She sat on one of the sofas, crying into her hands again.

"The men will buy you sweet drinks. You must only pretend to drink. You only pretend to play the piano. You will sing for them. You will dance with them. On the long journey they require comfort. Behave well, and you will live well."

She was sobbing. She understood the boat was a prison, and her cabin, a cell to be locked or opened at the steward's pleasure, that her only escape would be into the sea.

"Aaach!" he said. "A *Schwarze* with no family, a *Schwarze* with blond hair. What did you expect to find in China?" It was finally clear to Becca this wasn't a name Wu had chosen just for her. There were other *Schwarzes* in the world, all of them despised. He left the boat, saying he was going to write to Miss Kieland in America. "Better we just tell her the good news. So short a time, and already her child behaving like a hero who should have the Order of Chiang around her neck. So clever a *Schwarze* she has provided us."

He wasn't going to send any letter. Becca tried her best to spit on him again. He was out of range. Madame Suyin was called to take her again to her cabin, and instruct her in her performance for the first night out of port. The men would all be in a mood for the party, she said. The first night was always the busiest, the men always the loudest. After that they would get tired. By the end of the journey only the best of the girls would be able to coax them out of their lethargy.

She led Becca into the ballroom again, to show her which piano would play itself. All she had to do was pump the pedals.

"Get you warm up, eh?" she said, pinching her buttock. Becca slapped her hand away.

"Never mind," she said. This was the one Becca would demonstrate. Madam Suyin told her how she should hold herself against the
man when she was dancing. How to wear the dress in a way to cheat
with the breast. Becca supposed the woman thought she had graduated from Mr. Tsu's class. She showed her all the places to put the
perfume, even below. She pushed herself into Becca's cabin right beside her, and Becca imagined Linny watching this too, the two of
them disgusted, listening to Madame Suyin go on: "When you are
finished with a man you come to my cabin for the proper washing the
business. You don't come here. You don't clean yourself you will be
smelly. No one pay attention."

Becca told her to get out.

Once more she was locked in for her own good. She wept on the
bed with Linny. Not for herself, or what might happen to her on this
boat. But for Don Huang, and all his followers at Yenching, for her ride
against his back down the long road into the city, for all his friends, who
would be cursing her name and face if they were alive to curse.

What were these piano boat people to her but scum on the water
she would have to dive through if she ever wanted to see America
again, or her sister outside of a mirror?

Two nights later she was locked in her room. She was not to have
food for two days. The false velvet dress with the cheating bosom was
torn and on the floor. She was using it for a mat next to the toilet.
She felt decent again in her oldest clothes, a worn tunic and scuffed
shoes, her own American costume of labor that gave her solidarity
with the missing members of the Twenty-Eight Stroke order.

What she wrote that night was more a letter to herself than to
Miss Kieland, since she was using stationery that would never cross
the ocean, the note paper of the Piano Line:

> Jennie Alexie is on this boat. You'll be sorry to hear you have raised
> her up to be a hired lady. The nice skin she used to have is all red
> blotches. Jennie says it is from the paints Madame Suyin puts on the
> girls' faces, and if I let it happen to me for a year, mine will get that
> way, too. Don't worry.

Jennie plays every night on a Tribune piano. That's one with the keyboard on top and strings you can see down to the floor. There is a little stairway up to a raised seat so she can look out over the top and be seen by the men as she plays. You're surprised she's playing the piano? Well, they've taught her to play "Für Elise," which you probably know is one note at a time, so it's not that much harder for her than "Chopsticks." God, if I hear it one more time!

The first night I was supposed to demonstrate a player piano. It has two rolls. One is "Everything Is Peaches Down in Georgia." I am supposed to sing while I pump the pedals. The other is "Momma Left the Window Open, and I Got Caught in the Draft." Get it? I can tell you the Chinese don't. While we play we're supposed to let the men touch our shoulders, et cetera. When they're tipsy from drinking, the gambling tables are opened. After they lose, they are allowed to choose whichever girl they want.

I told you, don't worry about me. Just ask Mr. Big Shot Japanese, whose finger was hanging by a scrap of skin when I opened my mouth. That's why I'm locked in my room, and writing to you while they decide what to do with me. Madame Suyin says, turn me over to the police in Xiamen. If the man's hand gets infected, which it already is, they are going to have me tested for four diseases, one, the madame says, is carried by white people, and three by blacks. She's just trying to scare me. The steward wants to put me on the Gu Lang Yu ferryboat to see if I like that any better. He smashed my nose.

There was a noise in the passageway. She stopped writing and looked over her shoulder at the door. In the glass she could only see her sister's face, as bruised and swollen as her own. She had a pair of scissors stolen from Madame Suyin's room after they had beaten her with a strap. She stood up ready to stab whoever came through the door. It was Jennie Alexie. She had a key that worked in all the doors on the hall because she was trusted as Madame Suyin's assistant and informer. She closed the door, leaving without a word, and Becca took up her pen again:

They have used Jennie on this pleasure boat for more than a year. She looks thirty years old. Her face is made up like a theater woman with red paste and powder. She is supposed to change my mind, to make me happy here. It's for my own good, she says.

Her mind is silly with alcohol. She couldn't convince me, but she told me how the business works. Wu supplies the comfort girls, so Gao allows him to sell his pianos with no charge. The Chinese buy them for half the price they would pay onshore. None of them can play the piano anyway. It's only for their wives to decorate their houses.

There are two piano boats, Jennie says, which pass each other going back and forth between Tientsin and Xiamen. The food is better on the other boat but the madame is meaner. I should stay on this one, Jennie says.

When she saw I didn't want her friendship or her advice, she asked me, "Why did Miss Kieland let you come? Didn't she get any of my letters?"

Becca added a postscript to her letter that would never sail:

Jennie is so used to this she doesn't think anymore about trying to get away. I should tell you Wu is not a professor. He is lower than a snake. He supports everything he does with a proverb. "The loudest rooster is the first to lose its head."

That's all.

In the two remaining days of the cruise Becca was allowed to reach the fresh air of an upper deck only once, accompanied by the steward's aide, who spoke no English, and poked her in the ribs to guide her. They used this time to search her cabin. Jennie had tattled on her about the scissors, which were gone. And Becca was locked up again until the boat reached Xiamen.

In the middle of the night she was wakened and led off the boat, down a stairway hung from the side. She was shoved, and fell the last few steps into the bottom of a dinghy. A man on a platform in the

rear pushed a single paddle back and forth. They were turning away from the lights of the mainland.

Why not drown her right there?

She answered herself: They didn't want a body washing ashore in their city. But why would they care? Huang Don had told her there were bodies floating on every river in China. She remembered very little after falling into the dinghy. The next morning a fog hung over everything. She was on the deck of yet another boat, curled like a baby in the womb, pulling her thumb from her mouth. Cold and naked, she recognized the underwear under her head as her own, and she began to remember the night behind her. Linny passed over her, telling her to jump overboard.

She had been helped up out of the dinghy onto the rope stairway of a large boat, a ferry. Someone climbed behind her, pushing and prodding. At the top, a shrunken little man said, "I am captain," pulling her onto the deck.

"Stand up! Look! You are nobody! Look at you. Who care? You stay shut up, you hear? You want rice, you shut up. All the time, shut up. Come with me."

He led her across the deck and down a companionway. There was a small boy sprawled in the passage in front of them. The captain kicked at the child, but the boy was quicker, pulling himself out of harm's way, and scurrying off.

"What you good for?"

He meant her, not the boy. She was pushed into a cabin, the door shut and bolted behind her. Another tiny room with a single cot. In China, she decided, small room or large, she would always be locked in. And for every order of awful man in China there seemed to come a lower order creeping, and she was still spiraling down among them. There was hardly time to sort this out or consider why Providence had chosen her to test this country rather than her sister, because the goosh was already opening the door again, and fast in his demand.

"Clothes off!"

She dashed by him, and up the companionway. A chase began around the main deck, a race she couldn't win. She knew none of the

hiding places, and he knew them all. She had not gone twice around the rail, when he spun into her path. She tried to punch him. He struck back and she fell to the iron deck, and was still.

Now, in the morning, through her swollen eyes she saw the blood between her legs. The thing had happened. She thought of the face of the vicious little man and the horrid smell of fermented fish sauce on the hands that had beaten her till she hadn't strength to fight. It was all coming back, the vile stick, his yellow worm, forced between her legs, squirming inside her, while he yelped and kneaded her breasts like a madman with his fishy hands. Now she was screaming at the violation. Her hatred had no target but the vile syrup inside her.

"You couldn't help it," Linny called to her. "Jump in! Wash!"

Roused by Becca's voice, the Chinaman stood over her again.

"Get up, big whore girl!"

He turned a hose on her, stinging her face with salt water, and soaking the clothes that lay beside her. He pointed the hose between her legs, right at the patch of hair there.

"Put on clothes!"

People, many with bicycles, were lined up to come onboard. They were pointing and laughing at her nakedness.

"*Schwarze,*" he called to them, as if they could understand, as if this explained his part and justified her humiliation—why she was naked and why she was there. They began to throw things, pebbles and dirt, not hard to hurt her, just to show their contempt.

She learned later that she was on the ferry that ran between Xiamen and Gu Lang Yu, the foreigners' concession, the Piano Island. Police were everywhere, the ferryman said, to protect the expensive homes.

"Don't get the funny idea."

If she got off the boat at Gu Lang Yu, he said, she would be arrested immediately. If she tried to escape on the other side, in Xiamen, she would be shot as the friend of the Twenty-Eight Stroke people.

When she was dressed he gave Becca her day job, handing out cards to any on the ferry who were not Chinese. If she did this to his satisfaction there would be rice for her at night. That first morning she wove up and down among the passengers, almost comatose, her

eyes streaming tears. Her work identified her as the boatman's slavey, with no right to a seat, no right to any space on the crowded deck. The people, swaying side to side with the shifting sea, pushed her left and right like a bit of trash.

The first cards she was given said, "SATISFACTIONS" on one side, and "I CAN PROVIDE" on the other. When she understood she was advertising her own availability, she threw them over the railing into the water. She was slapped for this, and given another set of cards: "PIANO LESSONS—ENGLISH YES AND NO." On the reverse side there was a teacher's address in Xiamen. If the people dropped them on the deck, she was expected to pick them up and hand them out again. If any were left in her hand at the end of the day, or found on the deck, she would get nothing to eat.

In the middle of her first morning the boy who had been chased down the passage the night before reached for her hand and left a crust of bread in her palm, a secret between them. He said nothing and ran off when the captain yelled down from the wheelhouse at him. She never saw the boy again.

The ferry made the round trip six times a day. On the Xiamen side the water was full of trash and floating sewage. In the evenings they docked at Gu Lang Yu, where, if she ran, it would be easy to find her. The water around the island looked clean as Wissahickon Creek.

In the evenings the captain ate his supper at a rice stall next to the dock. He brought Becca's portion to her in a child's bowl. Given nothing but rice and fish sauce, she was losing weight. The man had not tried to use her again. She made it clear he would have to knock her silly, or kill her, if he didn't want his nose, or something else, bitten off.

He came after her again in nightmares, but her daydreaming was a continual vision of Huang Don and his followers. She thought of her rape as punishment for her part in the disaster at Yenching. Horrible as it was it could never be adequate penance. Nothing could. She promised her sister over and over again that she would be white

forever, if Linny would relieve her of confession, if she never had to know these things. And this played over and over because she knew she was asking the impossible.

There was no mirror on the boat. She caught a reflection in the wheelhouse window when she took the boatman his tea. Was her sister so thin as that? Another week. She looked down at her scrawny arms. She thought the man might be starving her until she had no strength left to fight him. One night, long after the captain had fallen asleep, she snuck to the deck and went over the side.

∞

Miss Kieland said it might be best for Linny to leave Drayton, but then she made it so easy for her to stay. Linny hadn't told her yet, but she was there for good. Or until Becca came back. There was therapy available to her in the city. Miss Kieland would pay for it if she cooperated with the therapist. She said it would help get her over the fear she brought back from California. It would make her more forgiving of the children's behavior in her sewing classes. Linny knew what therapy really meant. It meant separating herself from her sister, and wasn't China separation enough?

Someone wrote on the "Slate," "There's a colored teacher here."

Linny thought it was Melanie Wetherholtz, the one who ran the machine needle through her finger. The words were erased the same day. Not before everyone saw them. Miss Kieland wanted to talk about this, but Linny wouldn't. She wished Eula would forget about it.

Instead, Eula went out of her way to tell her, "Linny, I don't care what color you are."

Other people cared. Linny cared. She thought the Director of the orphanage should care, too.

"You didn't understand what I meant," Eula said.

She was unaware Linny wouldn't be home at Drayton if she hadn't declared herself colored. She'd still be in California. She'd be working for Mumsy at The Sea Tossed, and taking instruction from Reverend Charlesburg.

Linny was in love with the gown from Callot Soeurs. It didn't matter if she never wore it. She might try it on now and then, but she certainly wouldn't wear it before Becca was there to put hers on, too. Eula warned her that might be a long time coming, or perhaps never.

No use reminding her, "It's only a dress." She looked at the gown the way Miss Kieland admired the painting by Martin Head, the picture of haystacks in the marshes, which hung in the hall in School-house. And perhaps for the same reason; it came from someone's head and hand, and there wasn't another like it in the world. Linny saw the startled look come over Miss Kieland when she learned the dress was worth more than the painting, that it would cost over a thousand dollars to have Madame Vionnet make the dress. And the dress was only part of Mr. Rank's gift.

At first, when Miss Kieland took the underthings away, Linny didn't argue with her. They weren't appropriate, she said. But Linny changed her mind. The night of her party she had gone looking for them in Eula's bureau. The two pair of panties with paper-thin waist-bands were lacy, more holes than cover. How could Linny help thinking about Mr. Rank now, even if he was nosy? He, too, said she was an adult now, almost twenty. Linny had a job and was ready for counseling, which meant he thought she was an adult. Miss Kieland, who had a letter from him about a woman in New York who could help, said it would be a freezing day at the middle of the earth before she let that one get her hands on one of her twins, or any of her girls for that matter.

If Linny loved the dress so much, Mother Greene asked, how could she cut it up into pieces? She wasn't cutting it up, but taking every last stitch out and studying it, the way Mr. Rank advised, and then putting it back together the same way, first using the pieces as a pattern for Becca's copy, which would require identical stitching.

Mother Reilly bought her the material in New York—silk from Thailand, which looked maroon in one light and shimmered close to black in another. The orphanage paid for it. Eula said she wasn't going to let Linny waste her time on a piece of calico. This was another lesson for all the girls who'd be watching the project go forward.

Linny understood the Director was doing unusual things for her because of what happened in California, and because she couldn't forgive herself for letting Becca go to China. Not just the job as sewing mistress, but the graduation party after Tess Croft's class, when the women had encouraged her to use their first names.

The naughty thing, Linny explained to the girls who watched what she was doing to the dress, was that Madame Vionnet put two layers of interfacing in the bodice so what's pretended about the bosom is hidden between the outside material and the lining. It stands out like you're full, and no one's the wiser. Wait till Becca comes home. She won't believe it.

When Eula made Linny the sewing instructor, she got more than she'd expected. Linny wasn't satisfied having things done the old way, people going off in their own directions, quilting this, embroidering that, knitting a cap, or taking all year to sew a silly sampler and never getting past the capital letters. The old instructor wanted it to be fun, and if something useful got done, so much the better. Some of the girls made dresses, mostly the simplest sort of shifts. A front and a back of the same shape, sewn up around the edges and turned inside out. The majority of the girls at Drayton couldn't even overcast a loose selvage, and hadn't considered why you'd want to.

Linny intended to run her classes "from the beginning."

Eula thought she meant taking charge right away, but what she meant was first things first. No one would use a sewing machine until she'd proven herself with needle, thread, and thimble. Eleven basic stitches and a tailor's buttonhole. Linny had taught herself most of what she knew from the sewing books and taking things apart, just as she was doing with the dress from Callot Soeurs.

Did Linny understand, Eula asked her, that she was different from the others, that no one else at Drayton had the same skills?

Just get her the supplies she needed, Linny told her, a bolt of plain white muslin for the class, and five spools of black cotton thread for every girl in the school. Everyone would have to prove herself to Linny with a neat display of handiwork before she'd be allowed to even whisper Singer. Whipstitch, backstitch, diagonal basting, slip-

stitch, felling stitch, blindstitch, hemming stitch, herringbone, and more. The black thread against the white muslin gave away every unevenness and fault. Linny could point to the problems and show how to correct them. Eula suspected this would lead to trouble; the standard was far too high for most of the children. But she wanted Linny to figure it out for herself. She did tell her, "Not everyone is planning a career at Callot Soeurs."

It was much easier making the younger girls mind her. They'd climb in her lap and play with her hair when they tired of the sewing exercises. Sometimes they asked, "Isn't your name Becca?" and she told them, yes. That got others going. The senior girls, who had been only a year or two behind her when she went west, rolled their eyes and stuck out their tongues. They started calling her Becca, too. It was a joke to them; they supposed it hurt her feelings. Even Mr. Henry got confused and changed her name now and then, until she asked him please to just settle on Becca. He was so kind, and after all, Becca had been his favorite. Linny learned how much fun it was to work beside him in the flowerbeds, as Becca had, charmed by his gentle subversion: "Have the ladies decided what color you are? . . . Pay no mind to me, girl."

Sometimes he would reach over and touch her nose or her lips, as if the same question was on his mind, or he wasn't sure who they belonged to. He didn't mean anything by it. It was as if he was trying to figure out who she was the way a blind person would.

After a while, the only ones who still called her Linny were the housemothers and Eula, and once she even heard Miss Lambert call her Becky. She didn't mind at all. After all, she was the one who had been so changeable.

When Eula had sent her into the city for the seminar with Tess Croft, it was supposed to teach her to work with personalities of all kinds, even Melanie Wetherholtz's kind. Something Linny had heard repeated in Miss Croft's class—"unrealistic expectation"—made her give up on the mandatory sewing exercises for the older girls. Miss Kieland had been right about that; most of them just couldn't do it, even when they tried.

After Melanie sewed her finger to the placemat Linny gave help only to those who asked for it. There were girls who called her "colored," and made big lips at her, whispering behind her back. It took all her patience just to keep order in the room.

In the evenings she worked on Becca's dress, sewing with a stitch that wasn't in any book she'd ever seen. One might think a machine had done the work on the original gown, because two threads were intertwined along a single seam. But the little irregularities in length and line proved to her it had all been done by hand. Madame Vionnet's seamstress had used the stitch to connect the long panels of the skirt. Linny puzzled over it for a long time before she could reassemble the first gown to her satisfaction.

It came to her partly as a gift of her own imagination, a discovery that the seam had been achieved in two passes, and in opposite directions. The first was a simple whipstitch, from the top of the panels to the bottom. Then, working upward, a thread had been woven into this in small, crossed diagonals. The result was a line of tiny knots, which you could see closing tighter as you pulled the material against them. Double stitch, she called it, demonstrating the method to anyone who would pay attention. And she gave all of Drayton something to think about, diagramming the technique on the "Slate" with a bewildering swirl of arrows and instructions. Under these she wrote:

> You can't find this in the *Encyclopedia of Sewing*. Materials bound with the double stitch will tear before the seam gives way.
> Linda Carey

Eula was as fascinated by the action of the tiny knots, as by the work they held together. Later that year, when things calmed down in the sewing classes, she said, "Linny, you're sewing yourself into Drayton. You're like Madame Vionnet's label. I'm the only one who notices you're hiding yourself away from the world, because I put you here. I let you stay here out of sight. It's not right. It's not appropriate."

As if this was all her doing, and none of Linny's own.

Appropriate? Linny didn't want to have another of these discussions. She knew it was mischievous to ask, "What did you do with the underwear from Mr. Rank?"

"Do you remember?" Eula said. "We decided it was unsuitable."

"Yes, but why? Who else would ever see it but me?"

There was no good answer for her.

"Why do you suppose he sent them to me? He wouldn't signify to a young girl, would he?"

"Of course not. It was a mistake," she said. "A mistake in judgment. Sometimes men lose their sense of proportion. Even the smartest men. For all we know some salesgirl convinced him."

Eula thought this had put an end to it.

"What do you think? Is it time to talk about what's next for you?"

"Do you still have them?"

She tried not to lose patience. "I thought it would be imprudent to just throw them away. Wasteful."

Linny didn't ask where she'd put them. She imagined the underthings still kept somewhere in that funny bungalow Eula shared with Kerstin, with scuff marks on the floor. Had Mummy and Slue put on matching silk undies? Women with secrets; Mummy who'd had her head examined by Mr. Rank, and Slue, who had decided not to live with the doctor and his sword after all.

When Linny tried on her Callot gown, her own underwear made a visible line through the soft lime-green silk. Perhaps Mr. Rank's salesgirl had known her business after all.

"We won't talk about it anymore," Eula said. But Linny had shamed her. To keep them would have been a thieving hypocrisy. She had Mr. Henry deliver them to Linny's cottage securely kept from his knowledge in brown paper, hoping her twin wouldn't notice that one pair had been worn and laundered, that she had given way to the temptation to wear them once herself.

Linny tried them on with the Callot dress. The difference was more than invisibility. As she moved in front of her mirror, the pleated panels spread for a moment into a thin cover of silk, and a dark triangle flickered across the glass in front of her. It was Becca she

recognized in the mirror, shameless Becca, quite pleased with herself. Why should Becca be ashamed? She'd been sent off to China, where she would surely be unavailable to any man. Maybe that's why Miss Kieland had been so pleased to let her go. Becca's own pair of elegant underwear was only waiting for her return.

Eula was obviously happy that Kerstin had thrown the doctor over, and Otto wrote that it was feeble not to tell her so, to reveal all it meant to her. Kerstin could see it, but Eula suspected he was right, that her reticence was in keeping with a practice of evasion, which Otto found to be a staple of her neurosis. Having one of the twins back was relieving this strain of self-observation.

Since Linny had taken a more lenient approach to her students, the staff was more comfortable with her continuing as sewing mistress, the title she'd invented for herself. She now preferred her class to be listed in the schedule as "Sewing with Linda." Eula wouldn't allow Becca's name to be printed there, though it threw the younger girls into confusion again.

Linny thought it would be best if sewing were no longer a required subject. Eula couldn't agree with that either. The older children had to fit it in twice a week in the early evenings, after returning from the public high school. The younger girls, who studied on the Drayton campus again, sewed three times a week, from the day they first arrived. It didn't matter to Eula if they were all going to be aviatrixes or steam fitters, when they left Drayton they would know how to thread a needle and hem a skirt, not because they were women, but because they wore clothes.

It made a long week for Linny. She had four classes a day including Saturdays. Eula was sure the drudgery of it would be enough to drive her out into the world. But again Otto had been right. For Linny, the scent of her sister was still on Drayton. When she wasn't sewing, or hanging around with Mr. Henry, she roamed back and forth over the grounds and through the cottages and Schoolhouse, skirting the older girls as if they carried cudgels against her, but engaging the little ones in games and conversation. The smaller children adored her, and she returned their love in full measure. Sometimes a favorite would find a new frock, perhaps appliquéd with a rabbit or a turtle, on her bed, an anonymous gift. For the time being the talent in Linny's hands and the designs in her head were the intramural secret of Drayton.

∞

Eula's exchanges with Otto that season were brief but frequent; many by way of penny postcards. Tessie was still receiving his correspondence signed Huck. And Anaïs had shown her a sample of the same endearment. Eula was relieved when it happened for her. And she answered him in kind after he wrote:

Did Linda get the big package?
Huck

Hasn't she thanked you? The dress is a great success. It's all in pieces on the floor. I think she's forgotten how to put it back together. Why the scanty stuff?
Becky

Sorry. No harm I trust. I'm told you can't wear the regular thing under a gown like that. Oops, should this be under cover, too?
Huck

Linotte was everything you advertised. You must have known she wouldn't keep any secret that flattered her. Don't worry. The history of the suitcase and its contents is safe with me, though Aunt Polly may never let you cross her threshold again.
Becky.

Postscript: You might have remembered to take the undies out of the suitcase. Oops, yourself!

I concede. We'll use envelopes from now on. I never expected Linny to wear the dress. I can't believe it fits her anyway. You know my idea was for her to find inspiration there. In case you didn't know, it was very dear.

Huck

Enough with brevity. There was too much to tell him:

Thanks in part to your lavish gift and her persistence, Linny is caught here in a web of her own design, unspooling thread, yard by yard. She's inventive and eager to share her handiwork, though silent about the thing that most haunts her. I'm certain she's wandering up and down the coast of China in her imagination, seeking telepathic news from her sister, who was never shy about sending it, even when they were in the same room.

The older children here are envious of Linny's beauty and her skill. They whisper about her color, and the talk spreads to the younger ones. I believe bringing this into open discussion would cause more trouble than it saved, though I've tried to engage Linny on the subject. Do you agree? Ellen Reilly isn't so sure. I was hoping the nonsense would disappear by attrition as the older children graduated. Instead, it's passed down to the younger ones, an endless contagion.

Linny is mute and stoic about it. She's discovered, or maybe invented, a new way of binding material. She calls it double stitching, an intertwined line of two threads, which knot themselves tighter as you pull against the seam. She showed me proudly that if her thread is as strong as that used in the material, the fabric will tear before the seam gives way.

You don't need to reply with your interpretation. I've guessed it already. A question for me: Is Linny now bound as tightly to Drayton as she is to Rebecca? If so, what if Rebecca never returns? I have a nightmarish figure to offer you. In separating them, we tore each of them down the middle because the binding held.

Mr. Henry has become the kind of pal for Linny that he used to be for Becca. In fact he calls her Becca, as does most everyone else around

here. I don't like it, but there's not much I can do. Henry tells me Mrs. Carey, the ancient grandmother, made another pilgrimage to our gate, but declined to show her face. It has the poor girl wondering again.

Fondly,

Eula

If she drowned, Becca would owe nothing more to Huang Don or the Twenty-Eight Stroke order. She was no swimmer. Her dog paddle was hardly adequate for crossing the wider parts of Wissahickon Creek. As she went under she was hoping the Great Light promised her at the Gospel Corner Assembly would come shining through the water, and Huang Don would be riding along beside her on his bicycle, not angry or even ashamed of the girl from America. He'd ask her to get on the seat behind him for the long ride to Chinkanshan.

She came to the surface, gasping, and thrashing. The pier shone black, a sheer, slimy wall, impossible to scale. Pushed mainly by the current, she had bobbed under the waves again before she was carried into a sea break of rocks. She crawled up the massive stones to a walkway and lay on her back in the moonlight. She rolled herself over, vomiting water and a little rice. If she really wanted to drown she could jump in again on the other side, where the undertow and tide would carry her away. When her heart stopped pounding, she stood, and staggered over the huge stones to land.

A road rose in front of her, lined with tall trees and large houses. Along the shore ran a darker lane, perhaps safer, but its shadows lasted only briefly. Around the first bend, a long masonry building stood blocking the lane. It was lit in front with gas lamps, a one-story structure that stretched backward, into the night. Under the lamps was the painted sign: WU & SON

She walked around the corner to a side entrance and into a tool room. Two Chinese men were sleeping on the floor beside upended liquor bottles. She walked past them. The inner door gave into a warehouse filled with pianos of every description. The place was dimly lit with gaslights hung at wide intervals along the walls. Perhaps eighty or

a hundred instruments were opened for display, their tops raised, fronts open. Their strings of copper and steel, glowing in the half-light, ran left, right, and diagonally as far as she could see. There was a bench in front of every one. All set, she imagined, for a sales exposition.

Becca thought of them all being hammered in concert. The noise that rang in her imagination was not some grand concerto, but the monotony passed down to the world by that succession of anonymous fools who played "Chopsticks." Fools like Jennie Alexie, who beat away at the keyboard in the Drayton common room while others tried to study, and in the ballroom of the Piano Line where whores danced.

Becca had seen what she needed as she passed through the tool room, and she went back for them, the metal shears that must have been used to cut the steel bands off the packing crates. With these in hand, she started down one wall of the warehouse with no care for where she began. Every piano string in the building was her target. Right away, she discovered the base strings didn't go Kabom! as Wu had suggested. They went Thwang!

The snap of the thicker strings began to vibrate through the neighboring instruments. As she moved along down the line, echoes were bouncing from wall to wall. Using both hands and the full length of the shears' jaws, she could cut several strings at once. The racket passed to the end of the building and back. There was thunder at the bass end of each piano and the clamor of sparrows at the top. She continued for perhaps two hours or more, and the drunken watchmen never stirred. It was a "Chopsticks" to irritate heaven. Before she finished, the whole warehouse was ringing a pain in the ear for one man, along with two lines she repeated as she moved down the line:

Professor Wu, Professor Wu
This is the song I'll play for you.

She wandered out of the warehouse and back the way she'd come. Before first light she was walking up the residential hill of Gu Lang Yu with dogs barking on all sides, and candles being lit in the win-

dows. She came to a path lined with shrubbery cut in the shape of large turtles on one side and rabbits on the other, some of Linny's favorite creatures, and this was the path she chose.

A houseboy would not let her in the front door.

"Mrs. Fleming say, no more laundry girls, you go away."

But then Mrs. Fleming was at the door, too, pulling Becca inside, asking, "What's your name, child? What are you doing on the island? How did you get here?"

Becca could tell she was English.

"I don't know," Becca said. "I'm lost."

She was cold. Her hands covered a pain between her legs.

"Someone's been at you, haven't they? They've dumped you here. You'll have to go back to your people. Who are your people?"

Becca glanced at her filthy face in the front hall glass, disgusted with her sister's image. Her clothes, still damp with seawater, felt glued to her.

"I worked on the boat."

"Oh, Jesus!" the woman said. "That man! Something's got to be done about that man! I'll put paid to him, believe me. I'm going to speak to the colonel. But you can't stay here. Why did you come here?"

"The turtles," she said. "And the rabbits."

"How old are you?" the woman asked.

"I'm not sure," Becca lied.

"One of those?"

"Those?"

"I don't know why these people think we want to take in every lost soul they throw our way. I mean, you don't have any parents? You don't even know your age? Are you going to tell me your name?"

"Linda Schwarze."

These were the first names in her head, and she said them. Anything to avoid her own.

"German, are you? But not that fair. Just the hair. Half-bred? What have they done to you? Why are you holding your hands there? Do you have to use the toilet?"

The woman didn't know what to do with her. There was no phone line between the island and the mainland. Messages traveled on the ferry by bicycle courier. Anyway, her husband, Colonel Fleming, she said, wasn't at his office in Xiamen. He was away in Lushon.

She told her housekeeper, ShenShen, to draw a tub of warm water in the servants' bathroom, and stood over Becca herself to make sure she was properly washed. When she saw that the girl was a good deal more than a skinny child, she left her to her modesty in the washroom. She had ShenShen finish the job and bring Becca some clean things to put on, the white slacks and jacket her servants wore.

Her questions were less friendly after she'd seen Becca naked. Maybe she deserved everything that had happened to her, though Mrs. Fleming actually thought someone had left her at her door to work for her. It had happened before.

"The same way they leave kittens," she said. "Oh, they know where the soft hearts live. Don't think they don't."

She was giving Becca a provisional place in the household until the colonel came back. Then it could all be sorted out. There was precious little left each month to pay her help, she said. Now, there'd be one more. And the food.

"I can't afford another thief in the kitchen. Don't try to take advantage. The last one was feeding her whole family. Sending it over on the ferry by the crateful. Straight from market to the boat, on our tab, if you please. I put paid to that, I can assure you. Skinny, but I'll bet you eat your share when you get the chance. Eh? Speak up. I don't like a mousy sort!"

From what Becca could tell, Mrs. Fleming's staff understood just enough English to survive her impatience. It didn't take her long to judge the woman garrulous out of boredom. She told Becca she was in residence on the island year round because she disliked the mainland, the city of Xiamen, and especially the house she and the colonel had been assigned there. Both of her children were at university in England.

"The girl, too," she had Becca know.

Mrs. Fleming lived here alone most of the time with just her house staff.

"You can't find anyone with a decent reference. Nobody lets a good one get away. Clean is all I ask. And honest. Just don't waste food. Are you clever with your hands? Have you used a mangle?"

The last laundry girl had hurt herself dreadfully. Two fingers.

"I don't want any more scorched curtains. No daydreaming at the ironing board. You can't just sit around the house doing nothing till the colonel gets back. You can do the wash, and help ShenShen with the cleaning. She's not very good about the dust. You have to rub her fingers in it."

ShenShen spoke scant English, and that was the problem, Mrs. Fleming said. The insults were only a relief to Becca, proof she had gotten past the door and into the household. It was quickly made clear that her facility with the language made her a godsend, and turned Mrs. Fleming's head.

"So bracing to have someone who understands me. Most of them pretend they don't know what you want."

What Becca withheld from her in the next few weeks, and how much the woman pretended not to know, were mutually convenient. She must have figured out by then that the new girl's initial innocence had been a play for sympathy and entrance to her home.

"You'll have to tell us everything," she said. "But all in good time." She was delighted with the range of Becca's vocabulary, and came into the laundry for conversation she couldn't find in any other room. As Becca pressed and folded her tablecloth and napkins, Mrs. Fleming asked, "Have you read the good poets?"

"The good ones?"

"Not those Irish devils. You know. The ones who worship Parnell and believe in fairies."

No, Becca confessed, the good poets must have been beyond her education.

In the first week of her service, a Chinese official from the mainland came to the door. He was investigating felony vandalism in the

piano warehouse, looking for an American girl. He had no right to be there; he was only hoping for the islanders' cooperation.

"In point of fact, they're looking for a black girl," Mrs. Fleming told Becca afterward.

No, Mrs. Fleming had been happy to explain to them, the only newcomer there was Linda Schwarze, a perfectly respectable German type, and sorry for their trouble.

The small island population had a single constable and one assistant. It was understood his investigations would be limited by the private interests of the little international community that paid his salary. Of course, everyone on Gu Lang Yu had heard about the destruction at Wu & Son. And according to Mrs. Fleming, most of them thought Wu had it coming.

The homes on the island already had their pianos. The people were tired of outsiders referring to their concession as Piano Island. It made their resort a musical joke. Wu's horrid business was responsible for much of the disrespect, along with the party boat cruises, the infamous voyages of the Piano Line. He shouldn't be allowed on their island anyway. It was only that he claimed to be half German, and carried a German passport. They despised the way he fawned among the Chinese for business favor.

The colonel's return was delayed. Becca's position in the household grew stronger. Mrs. Fleming had her passing orders to the cook and gardener. She took Becca off laundry duty, and put her to work in the solarium on the south side of the house, which looked down to the sea. The glass room was full of delicate flowers. Every one of them had to be given a French bath, the lady said, that is, sprayed with a vapor bottle morning and night.

"The colonel brings me something new whenever he travels." She was especially pleased with "this one from Nanking," a large purple plant that snapped its huge purple blossom shut on trespassing insects, and then digested them. "A flesh-eater," she said, with a breath of scandal. "Phew! Linny, the smell!"

"Oh, you've been naughty," Mrs. Fleming told the plant.

She berated another for a pale lack of effort, and congratulated one for a new leaf. If Becca could bring herself to talk to the flowers she might prosper here. But the silly household could only be a resting place while the awful thing she had done to Huang Don and the others retreated further into the past. The trouble was it had not retreated a single step. She couldn't pass a day when the memory did not torment her. What had happened to her that first night on the ferryboat, was slowly losing the hands and face that made it the ferry captain, though she still ached with the knowledge of it. A doctor was brought to the house to examine her. She wouldn't cooperate with him, which made Mrs. Fleming angry. The man had to be paid. And for nothing.

The woman was looking for a confession. She took Becca into the servants' bathroom and showed her the cracked mirror in the cabinet over the washstand.

"How did this happen?"

Becca didn't know.

"But I'm sure you do. ShenShen says you did it."

And there was ShenShen standing behind them in the bathroom door.

"Oh yes, missy, please no deny. You wake everybody talking name, name name. Then so angry, you slap-slap very hard."

Becca, who liked ShenShen, couldn't understand why she would lie.

"Everyone innocent?"

Mrs. Fleming, uncomfortable with the standoff, led Becca to the library. She said the glasses prescribed for her in London were far too weak. They made the little letters all a straight line, and the large ones tremble. She wasn't going to let a Chinaman play with her eyes, she said, and there wasn't a good English eye man in all of Xiamen.

"So you'll be my eyes," she said.

It wasn't poetry she preferred, after all, but books about English women of an earlier century, lives of leisure, and finery, especially the clothes. The books were forwarded by her son, she said, through the Foreign Office and delivered to her husband with the commercial

communiqués and letters of introduction that sailed in the embassy pouches. She was proud of her private mail service, which worked free of Chinese interference.

The books she liked so much were full of colorful illustration, and samples of the most sumptuous costuming. She was fascinated with the luxury they entailed, and she touched the glossy color pages as if the texture of a brocade, or embroidery, could pass to her fingers.

∞

Becca wasn't sleeping well. The horrid dream repeated itself, coming early and late, not the rape, but the other. She was watching herself standing proud in the classroom, Dr. Wu's obedient *Schwarze*, amazing the others with the tumble of names, the pledged friends of the Twenty-Eight Stroke Gentleman, until she threw her fists wildly at the prattling mouth, the lips that betrayed Huang Don.

Becca was sure Mrs. Fleming knew that her Linda was hiding from something. The woman never asked why her new girl didn't want to go outside, why she didn't want to stroll with her to the island's perimeter road. And she never suggested that Becca accompany her when she went down to greet the arriving ferry, Gu Lang Yu's only regular social event. The woman, too, was afraid, almost from the start, of losing her reader, and she saw the colonel's return looming as a dangerous time.

"You can't put anything over on him, Linda, whatever you've done. How far did we get last night?"

Becca was holding out a different book, large and brittle with age. It was printed fifty years earlier, and concerned a courtship a century before that. It had lavish color prints of a princess who was having a dress fitted to her body.

"My sister would like this," she said.

Mrs. Fleming was onto the blunder right away.

"What's her name, Linda? Where is she? Is she anything like you?"

"Rebecca," she said.

They got on with the book. As the story progressed the English gown of lavender-ribbed silk was transformed from unlikely shapes into a tailor's masterpiece. The story was for a child, but the illustrations might have been the pattern book and instruction manual for a seamstress. The story was not about whether the princess would get the prince, but whether her gown would be ready in time for the ball. And the princess, making daily trips to the sewing room, knew exactly what was happening. So did Mrs. Fleming, and therefore so must Becca.

Becca had to pretend she cared that the gown's skirt was sewn with twenty running stitches to the inch; that the bodice and sleeve seams were lapped and backstitched, and that for more strength under the arms, there was French seaming in the armscye. She was supposed to see significance in the bodice style, which took its shape from the center back and side seams, and from the pleats that tapered to the waist in back with linen tapes drawing the skirt high over the hips in polonaise fashion. Blah.

The woman was absolutely childlike in her delight.

"Oh Linda, the travail! Look at the smocking!"

∞

The colonel came back in April. From Mrs. Fleming's description Becca was prepared for a strict and clever man, with time for business only. He was Becca's height, a little shorter than his wife. His hands and face were soft and puffy. He wasn't much more polite to her than his wife had been. He'd heard enough in Lushon and Tientsin to make him suspicious.

First, from the embassy in Peiping, the story of an American girl with blond hair from an orphanage in Pennsylvania, out of touch with her sponsors. Her name was Rebecca Carey. From Chiang Kai-shek's bodyguards, the report of a swarthy American girl who had supplied the people's government with many names of student traitors. She was wanted for decoration, and return to her country.

From the authorities in Tientsin, a wanton double of the same girl, a dark American with blond hair who had fallen under the influence of

student thugs, plotting with them on behalf of the Twenty-Eight Stroke outlaw. From the police in Xiamen, a whore off the Piano Line, a black woman with blond hair, probably a wig, the most recent half-starved castoff of the Piano Island ferry captain. And in his own household, Linda Schwarze, a German girl with straw blond hair, who spoke English with no German accent. And hadn't spoken a word of German since she'd been there. A girl who could read English with wonderful expression, by his wife's account.

The colonel finished his list, and asked Becca, "Do you see what rumors can do to a woman's reputation?"

There was nothing she cared to tell him.

"You can sit there until you decide who you're going to be," he said.

He didn't have all day to wait, he told her, though she knew very well that he did. And would.

"Well, are you black or white? Rebecca or Linda? Schwarze or Carey?"

She was a child again, being questioned like a child, forced to answer the same unanswerable questions.

She'd been sitting in front of him, silent for several minutes at least. Mrs. Fleming came into the room, and told him to stop.

"Go away. Leave us alone," he said.

She paid no attention to his orders, until he said, "Shall I let the Kuomintang have her?"

"No!" she yelled. "No!" And went hurrying out of the room.

"You're all of them, aren't you?" he asked her.

"Yes," she said.

"That's a start. We'll talk again tomorrow. No more fairy tales."

∞

In May of 1935, before Drayton had any further news from Becca, Eula had word from the British Embassy in Washington that Rebecca Carey was in service to the British Economic Minister in Xiamen, actually on the Island of Gu Lang Yu. She was comfortable and well

cared for. Sending her home to America was not immediately advisable. It would be very dangerous because two serious charges had been lodged against her. She was wanted as a political criminal and as a vandal. As soon as she stepped off the foreigners' island onto the Xiamen ferry, her only exit, she would certainly be arrested. Only two crimes, but three factions wanted her, and none of them could be trusted, not even the Kuomintang, which claimed it only wanted to reward her for her bravery. In the meantime she was serving as a housegirl and reading companion to the British diplomat's wife.

An exchange of mail began in August, all of it through the British Foreign Office pouch, which had to go first from China to the British Embassy in Washington. One or two notes a day without fail, but six weeks behind their posting date. Linny and Becca wrote daily. After a first excited flurry, Eula relaxed into once or twice a month. It seemed curious to her that the English could deliver a letter safely—that is, without manhandling or censorship—but could not deliver a human being with the same guarantee of safe passage.

Becca's first letter started with the big news:

I'm here. Please write to Linny at the conservation camp, or wherever she has got to, and tell her my address is care of Colonel Fleming, the British Economic Minister in Xiamen, China Pouch, care of the Embassy of the British in Washington. How are you, Miss Kieland? I'm well enough. You don't have to believe all the stories you will hear, and I will tell you the genuine thing when it is safe to come home.

Don't ask them to send me back right away. If they could put me in a crate like a piano, maybe, but how would I breathe? I can't explain everything. The things I told you in my first letter were not the complete story, far from it. I just wanted you to know I was ok, if not all right. Do you see the difference?

I am all right now. Frederick Wu is no professor. He sells names to the Kuomintang, and sells pianos and women to the Chinese. He teaches Chinese sayings in English, and that's the only thing he

knows how to teach. How did you ever hear about him? I would like to know, and I think Jennie would too.

Eula made Linny promise that if Becca ever wrote anything about a plan or prospect of traveling home, she would share it with her.

"Don't let her do anything foolish," Eula said. She should let the British make the plan for her. Linny did promise, but she never let the Director see what Becca wrote to her. She shared some of the contents but not the letters themselves. Eula didn't expect her to.

Eula began a correspondence with Becca's British guardians. Her first letter was addressed to Economic Minister Fleming:

> We're relieved to hear that our child Rebecca Carey is in your house-hold, and that you are pursuing the diplomatic formalities required for her return. She is a willful girl, but whatever untoward circum-stance has met her in China follows from my own poor judgment in sending her there, and perhaps her own naïve political enthusiasm. We expect she is being treated with all the respect a British citizen would receive from an American Embassy.
>
> Please inform us of her physical and emotional health, and pro-vide a description of her daily life there, and opportunities for contin-uing her intellectual development while she is forced to wait for a guarantee of a safe return.

Fleming must have turned the letter over to his wife. She's the one who wrote back:

> Your orphan was less than honest with us, though I find no fault with her behavior in our home. She is clever enough for the work we give her. She came to our door calling herself Linda Schwarze, and seemed to be hiding from a past that shamed her. Whatever her transgressions in China, there is no prejudice against her in our household, though her appetite is unseemly for a young girl in service.
>
> Linda (we still call her that out of habit and because she prefers it) is capable in the laundry, though not enthusiastic, and actually

better at housecleaning than our regular girl when the spirit is willing. You'll be pleased to hear she is able to read and comprehend very advanced material. I allow her into the colonel's library to help with one text and another as my eyesight is failing.

Though we don't consider Linda indentured, her bed and board while she waits for her opportunity to travel cannot be offered without compensation. There is a debt of service to be paid for the safety we provide in her difficult time. Perhaps you know the Chinese government is looking for a girl of her description, wanted for espionage and for the destruction of eighty-seven pianos. The financial damages would be far beyond a lifetime of labor for her. Maybe you will account for her time with us as her partial payment to society in general if not specifically to the Chinese, and you will understand how much better off she is than if we surrendered her to one of the several groups in this country who are eager to take her into custody.

A point of information. We have asked Linda if she is colored as some of the bills for her arrest have described her. In this matter she has taken an insolent look-for-yourself attitude. She claims she doesn't remember her parents, so how could she possibly know. We can't argue with that, and I have not punished her for her attitude. We have looked closely but cannot be sure. When our cleaning girl ShenShen asked her, "Are you nigger?" Colonel Fleming heard Linda say, "Yes." Was this a foolish and self-destructive insolence? I doubt you allow blacks in your college. If we receive confirmation that she is Caucasian, it might clear some of the barriers to her return.

With admiration for your efforts on behalf of such as Linda,
Mrs. Patrick Fleming

Eula showed this letter to Linda because she wanted her to see how privilege could be turned to abuse, and because she wanted to make common cause with her on behalf of Becca against these contemptible people. Also because she was still uncomfortable with her own pained reactions to the question of race. It hadn't been quite right to tell Linny she didn't care what color she was. It left Eula

groping, and unsettled, and Linny testy: "What else did you find out? What else haven't you told me?"

Eula didn't say she was sending an immediate reply to Mrs. Fleming, which was "Yes, Caucasian, of course."

And didn't tell Linny about another letter that was waiting there at Drayton for Becca. An onionskin envelope bore the return address of a Mr. Leighton Stuart in Peiping. Eula hadn't forwarded it through the diplomatic pouch because it had the look of official trouble about it, maybe some further embarrassment for Becca in China. Besides, Eula could open her desk drawer now and then and take comfort in its promise of the twin's eventual return.

Linny was saving her money. Eula helped her open a bank account, showed her how to keep a checkbook, and encouraged the savings habit. Immediately, Linny took it to the extreme. Every other Friday she rode her bicycle into Flourtown and deposited her whole salary. She ate lunch and dinner at one of the cottages on campus and had only a plain roll and coffee for breakfast. She made her own clothes as demonstration projects for the other children from material supplied through the sewing program. Her Buster Browns had been resoled and reheeled until the threads in the uppers were giving way.

After four months with the bank, she showed Eula with pride that the next check in her book was only number three. Both of her purchases had been under three dollars. After that she kept the size of her young financial empire to herself. Eula used her birthday as the occasion to present her with a new pair of oxfords.

Anything extra that came Linny's way went right into the bank. It seemed miserly. She never gave gifts, and there was no evidence she spent anything on herself. It wasn't her nature to be selfish, and Eula was flustered when Mr. Sampson at the bank asked if she knew what the young Miss Carey was spending her money on. It was a revelation that Linny was spending on anything at all.

It was not Eula's business to ask, "How much has she spent?"

And against his bank's principles to tell her, "Almost all of it."

Eula was puzzled. She asked Linny how her savings plan was going, and was told, just fine.

"No unexpected expenses?"

"Why should there be?" with the bite of 'mind your own business.'

And it came to Eula, the obvious, late arriving: She thinks she can buy her sister out of China. The money is going to Becca, who's paying some Chinese, probably no more honest than Wu, to get her out.

She came at Linny directly: "Are you sending money to your sister? Are you sending money to China?"

Linny denied it instantly. Too quickly, Eula thought, and she said, "If you are, it's a great mistake. If someone's taking money to send her home, they'll just keep on taking it; they'll never let her go. Why would they, if they thought the money was going to stop? Do you see? Do you send cash?"

"I told you, I'm not sending her anything."

Eula just couldn't believe her.

Linny went straight to Mr. Sampson to see if anyone had been asking about her account. Lying, he told her no, and he apologized to Eula, saying he never should have mentioned it, and never would again.

∞

Kerstin was curious about this Linotte Culmell, this Anaïs, who was sending notes to the cottage as frequently as Otto, though all of them in sealed envelopes. Eula answered one or two, not to seem rude. She believed Anaïs was as evil as she was alluring. She wouldn't trust herself again on the woman's sofa.

Anaïs said she was determined to convince Eula that the restraints she placed on herself were neither fixed nor unconquerable; the majority of them grew out of social expectation, and for Eula to be a complete and happy woman some of them would have to be shed. Anaïs said she was not suggesting that she be the one to initiate the Director (Wasn't she? Hadn't she already been?), rather that some intimate of her daytime soul be nurtured as a companion under the stars. Yes, the one who would deny nothing and be denied nothing in her bed. So outrageous, it couldn't be ignored.

"Otto," Anaïs said, "was only half right about you. You do have a double, but he should not have identified your two selves as the

straight-laced dame of social justice and the coquette, or even as the woman who would love a man and the woman who would love a woman. He should have called you the denier and the denied, the two halves of your sexual self at war."

What could come of this, she went on, but self-destruction, a life of mutual defeat for both sides?

Imagine if Kerstin had read that letter. This woman was far more presumptuous than Otto had ever been. She had to be stopped. But Otto must have told Anaïs that Eula was once again in contact with Becca. And this had set her off on another note-writing campaign, ideas for treating the pathology of the glued-together pair. Ways to separate the girls down the seam, so to speak, so that they didn't rip each other apart. And hadn't that already happened in a sense? As she understood it, one of them thought she had been raped in her travels, and the other wasn't sure.

Had Otto told her that, too? Where had he gotten that? Never mind that Becca was still in China, in service, as the British woman put it.

Eula wrote Otto more in a pretense of outrage than real anger. She couldn't send him the note from Anaïs; she had destroyed it. What right did the woman have to gossip this way about her or the twins? Had he given her any reason to say those things? And the nerve of her in criticizing Eula's sexual reticence. As if indulgence were the prerequisite of a healthy society. Wasn't that false on its face? What could she possibly know about Eula, anyway? It seemed to be all probing and revelation with her. Guesswork made to look like supreme intuition. The way a fortune-teller worked.

Otto scolded Eula for acting angry when she was only confused. He said if she had truly been angry she would never have written to him complaining about it. She would have written to Anaïs. He thought what Eula really wanted was approval from him to stop answering Anaïs's letters, and he wasn't going to give her that. That was up to Eula. If Anaïs was guessing, he went on, it was well-educated guessing. He knew as much from Eula's own confessions to him. As for the twins, yes, if she looked carefully at Becca's letter about her first night on the ferryboat, the abuse was patent in the

language. As for Linny, wasn't her description of the Reverend Charlesburg's methods enough to make Eula wonder?

Most of all he wanted Eula to consider this: There were people who lived excessively perhaps, but were creative; the artists who, instead of fighting against will, affirm themselves. "They create an ideal, and a new world; Anaïs for example. They suffer for it, but they learn, too, and have something to teach the rest of us. That's what artists do."

It was a carbon of Tessie's explanation at the party for Linny.

"Meanwhile, we're the neurotics, you and I and Tessie. We win the struggle against domination, but we fight against our own wills, too. We worry about being willful, and then we have nothing left to power the freedom we've won. It's an open secret. We're a nervous lot. Be careful who you cast away as unfit for your instruction."

∞

Everyone wanted to know why Linny was staying at Drayton when she could be off on her own somewhere, using her talent for making clothes in a big city, making a fortune. Cresswell House in Philadelphia sent a woman out to talk to her about a job as a seamstress. She thought this had come from Miss Kieland's boasting about her. The lady examined the Callot gown she'd made for Becca.

"You didn't design that," she said. "That's a Vionnet from Callot Soeurs," as if Linny had been cheating.

"No, I didn't," Linny said, "but if you'd climb out of those shoes, and take your corset off, I could make one for you. And Madame Vionnet doesn't work for Callot Soeurs anymore. She's at Doucet now, where all the mannequins go barefoot and without all the elastic like you're holding yourself together with."

Lucky for her, Miss Kieland wasn't there, but the woman never bothered Linny again.

Maybe she was scared, maybe she didn't want to go anywhere without her sister. She was happy around the little girls, who made her feel as important as a mother. When Mr. Henry told her, "Look out for the dapple woman. She's been here again," her grandmother

started coming into her dreams along with Becca. And one day it wasn't a dream. Linny was riding one of the bicycles into Flourtown to put her salary in the bank, and the old lady was walking along in front of her, her legs all wrapped in white cloth like before, and wearing the same dirty bathrobe that came above her knees. She was striking the path hard with her cane at each step, the cane still more weapon than support.

"I been looking for you," she said. "I know you come this way on a Friday. And your sister, where is she?"

Linny tried to make her get on the bicycle seat so she could push her the rest of the way into the village. That didn't work. They walked along on either side of the bike, and her grandmother told her that the woman who gave her the allowance had died, and at the end of the month she would have to be out of her room.

"Where do I go, now? Have you found the picture frame? The woman knew it was mine when she gave it to you."

"Becca's in China," Linny told her. "She can't get out. She's reading books to an English woman."

"Took it to China!" she said.

She walked right into the bank alongside Linny, still going on about the picture frame, but holding tight to her granddaughter in case she was accused of trespassing. When she saw Linny hand her check to the teller, her eyes rolled up to nothing but whites.

"How much is that you're giving him?"

"Twenty-five dollars," Linny whispered.

And the old woman whispered back, "Why would you give it to him when I got such a need?"

The teller looked at Linny. It made her angry that he was laughing. She thought he might be looking at Mrs. Carey's skin.

Linny told the man to give her the cash instead.

"Do you have identification?"

He knew Linny. He didn't need any identification. Her bank card with her signature was in her purse, but she didn't feel like showing it to him.

"You saw me two weeks ago," she said. "And two weeks before that. You know who I am."

"Miss Carey, all cash disbursement requires identification."

"The woman before me. You didn't ask her for any."

The man called for Mr. Sampson, the manager. They went behind the counter together, and talked with their backs to Linny.

Eventually they gave her the cash. Afterward, Mr. Sampson called Linny aside. He was sorry, he said, but the teller knew, as the whole town did, that she had a twin sister who looked just like her.

"For your own security, we have to be sure."

What kind of apology was that? Either they thought the muttering, polka-dotted lady, her grandmother, was going to rob her, or that twin sisters would cheat each other. She took Mrs. Carey down the street to the drugstore. They sat in a booth way in the back, and Linny gave her all the money but a dollar, which she used to buy two chocolate sundaes with nuts. Mrs. Carey was so pleased she stopped talking about the picture frame, and said this would keep her easily for most of a month, eating whatever she pleased. Then she'd come and visit again. If Linny's people at the orphanage were paying for everything there, Mrs. Carey reasoned, Linny didn't need the money. Common sense wouldn't have it any other way.

Linny wrote Becca, "Miss Kieland thinks I'm sending you money. She must think I'm stupid, that I thought you could spend United States dollars in China. Anyway I'm really giving my money to guess who . . ." By the time Becca got the news, Linny had met her Grandma Carey three more times, and when Becca finally got word back to say she was doing the right thing, they had met three more, and the old woman was letting Linny call her Grandma, which she wouldn't at first. It made her feel obliged, Mrs. Carey said, and she already had too much to think about. She took the bus out to Flourtown every other Friday and waited for Linny outside the bank. Each time she was given nearly all the money, which she put in her creel. They always kept a dollar for their sundaes at the drugstore, and the leftover change was used for her carfare to the city.

By then Linny had made Mrs. Carey a dress with a high collar, and two petticoats. Together they bought her some dark cotton stockings to keep her legs warm and high black shoes. The dress buttoned all the way up the front. Linny told her the last button should be left open so the high collar could turn over in a fashionable curve. She slapped Linny's hand aside, and did that button up, too. When she saw herself in her new things, the first thing she said was "Now we got to get your sister back here."

As if things might go doubly well for her when Becca came home. She still wouldn't allow Linny to come into Philadelphia to see where she lived, though she said with what she was paying now, she didn't have to let anyone else into her bathroom. She could lie in a tub full of hot water as long as she pleased, just so she kept the strength to get out of it.

Linny would push her ice cream aside, and stare across the table at her grandmother's skin, and then down at her own arms. The old lady told her, "No use comparing. You never coming back to where I am, and I'm never coming up to where you are."

Linny thought this might be another way of refusing visits at Drayton or in the city, until Mrs. Carey explained, "Child, I'm never losing my spots, and you'll never have any."

"Can you tell me how old you are?" Linny asked, sorry for what she'd started.

"You can do numbers. I can't."

Linny didn't believe her. She knew well enough the number on the paychecks.

"You do all right with the money," she said. "You can count that."

"It's the faces," she said. "I know the faces, don't I?"

One Friday when she'd had her fill of her own sundae and some of Linny's, she sat back, satisfied, and said to herself, "I got two grandchildren who do more for me than all my own children together."

It surprised Linny, who thought she was the only one supporting her.

"No," she said. "If it wasn't for your sister's say-so I wouldn't get nothing from you. Didn't you say you'd have to write her, see if you should be giving me anything?"

"What about your children?" Linny asked.

"They don't know where I am," she said. "They haven't been knowing for seventeen years. And they won't know for seventeen more. And that ought to finish it."

It didn't sound right.

They had all got too high on the map was the only way the old lady could explain it.

Linny wrote about all this to Becca after dozens of earlier pages about San Francisco and the house on Mission Street. The more Becca heard, the more eager she was to come home. But Mrs. Fleming had a whole shelf of books that had just arrived from Hong Kong. They had smaller printing than Becca had ever seen before, on the skinny paper she'd seen in Bibles, more than a hundred pages in a little fraction of an inch. It was an *Encyclopedia of Manners, Clothes and Customs* through history, and around the world, and Mrs. Fleming thought Becca was going to read the whole thing to her.

Imagine how smart we'll be, she told Becca. And maybe when that was finished, the Chinese would have forgotten about her case, and there would be a way to send her back to America.

Becca had figured out after the first hundred pages, that to read all the volumes aloud would take her seven years, if she read two hours a day, seven days a week.

"Can you help me?" she wrote.

Part 3

Reunion

Was that the double of my dream the
woman who by me slept dreamed,
or did we halve a dream?

W. B. YEATS

Reunion

Damn the Flemings anyway. Becca had no respect left for them if she'd ever had any. They had no love for each other, and no concern for her, other than to keep her in their house for their own uses. The colonel was always looking into her room at inconvenient times, standing there as if she might invite him through the door. He was never at home when he had an excuse to be on the mainland. Once he brought a Chinese lady from Xiamen into the house to take his dictation for several days, and Mrs. Fleming left on the ferry. That week Becca was told to help ShenShen with whatever needed doing around the house.

It did her no good to be impolite. If she complained, they would only keep her longer. She wrote Miss Kieland to find out what the people in the American government were doing to bring her home, and Miss Kieland wrote back that Becca must not lose hope. As far as Miss Kieland could tell, they had done nothing yet. They were neither polite nor sympathetic; they needed to be convinced that Becca was not guilty of the things the Chinese held against her. Eula said that if the subject came up Becca should be sure to tell the Flemings that she was not colored.

Later Mrs. Fleming showed Becca a note Miss Kieland had written her on the same subject: "Wherever you got the notion that the child is colored, please put it out of your mind. She is not, and as you

guessed, could never have been admitted to Drayton College if she had been, since our charter forbids it."

"Dear," Mrs. Fleming said to Becca, "I'm so relieved. I wasn't sure when you were so fussy about it. Why didn't you just tell me? It will be easier for me to relax now when you're reading. It won't seem like such a strain for you. And you know I like to think you're getting something from it, too, that it won't be a waste of your time."

Both of the Flemings told Becca how reasonable they were about the "other peoples of the world," though not about each other.

"I mean I live right among the Chinese, don't I," Mrs. Fleming said. "But he's quite horrid about it. With him, it's the wogs this and the wogs that until you find out he means everybody east of Calais."

She was always talking beyond Becca, saying things Becca had no way of understanding. This last about the wogs sent Mrs. Fleming into a great spasm of coughing and laughter, and she lit a cigarette to get herself breathing properly again.

Becca wrote:

> "Come on," she says to me. "Off to the library with you." It's always time to read to her. Yesterday she told me it was important for me to understand what I'd been reading about—the difference between the English notion of civilization and the German's *Kultur*. With the Germans, she said, it was how many symphonies did you compose, how many poems did you write, how many borders did you cross?
>
> I wouldn't know about that, I told her.
>
> "Of course, you wouldn't," she said. "Now with the English it's a matter of appreciation. Literature and music and our own country-side. You see the difference, don't you?"

Just then she had nothing but her books and Becca's voice to amuse her. She was so much easier in conversation now that she was assured it was a white voice. She wanted Becca's company all the time, in the library and in the solarium, giving the plants their French bath, until all Becca's clothes were permeated with it, until her nose no longer knew the difference between her bureau, bed, and closet,

and the solarium. Toilet water was to that household what saltwater was to the island, the pervading atmosphere inuring all nostrils.

Now that Becca had put some flesh on, Mrs. Fleming felt she was due some credit for the generosity of her pantry. "Such a lovely strong complexion," she said. "You've blossomed here."

When Colonel Fleming was convinced Becca was not a darkie of any kind he began to respect her privacy again. He no longer opened her door without knocking, and he began to ask her the same kind of questions his wife did: Did she know any lines from Mr. Shelley? Did she know any lines from Lord Byron or Lord Tennyson?

Miss Kieland was right. There was ample reason for her to be white here. The Chinese despised half-bred people even more than the English. Becca was sure she'd never get off this island, or out of China, unless she was all white, all the time. Linny would be pleased to hear that. But then she started getting letters from her sister almost every day about their Grandmother Carey.

She was a little desperate, a bit silly, when she wrote to Linny that someone might have to go to Washington and speak to Mr. Roosevelt about bringing her home. Mrs. Fleming was taking a new approach to Becca's case.

"You don't have to go back to America if you like it here. We could have some young men from the consulate over to the island now and then. Would you like that?"

She'd never spoken that way before. Something was going on. The mail stopped coming from Linny and Miss Kieland. Mrs. Fleming blamed it on the correspondents. She was a liar, but Becca had to be careful not to say so, or show that she knew it.

In the *Encyclopedia of Manners* they had got to behavior in the bedroom and the relations between men and women. Mrs. Fleming said if these chapters made Becca uncomfortable they might just as conveniently come back to them later, when Becca got older. How much older did she mean? Becca guessed that her service to the Flemings was stretching on without end.

No, she didn't mind reading this part, Becca told Mrs. Fleming, but she didn't think she would be with her much longer. Becca had

no immediate reason for saying so. They had been reading in the book of manners that in this genteel era, camping was the only way for a respectable writer to approach the subject of sleep. One could not mention a bedroom. Anyway, ladies and gentlemen did not go to bed at night; they retired.

"Child, you're not even blushing. I do worry about what's happened to you here in China."

Mrs. Fleming was fascinated to think that for two hundred years schoolboys had read in their Erasmus that they could speak of conception to a lady if they intended to marry her. And that the Benedictines in the sixth century were required to sleep with their clothes on, even their belts.

"Colonel Fleming is like that," she confided to Becca. "At least when he's home, but that's none of your business. If he ever interferes, you come straight to me."

They were reading about the change from nightshirts to pajamas when Mrs. Fleming burst out in a fury at ShenShen for interrupting them. The girl was tapping on the glass in the library door, frightened in front and frightened behind.

"Soldiers!" she said.

Mrs. Fleming was told to get Becca ready to travel. Becca was given a small bag with one change of her white servant's jacket and pants and a change of underwear. There were four British soldiers outside, each with a rifle. As she was taken out, Mrs. Fleming stood sobbing in the doorway.

"I suppose they're taking you for trial," she said.

The soldiers went two on either side of her, the rifles in hand, all the way down to the waterfront. A crowd of island families with children and Chinese staff were there to see what was happening, shaking their heads. Mrs. Fleming, coming down the road behind Becca, had to be supported by neighbors.

Becca was marched across a dock and onto the deck of a small motorboat, the armed guards still beside her, and a moment later she felt the boat lifting up on the water and they were flying over the surface toward the mainland, toward Xiamen.

The idea of the twins torn in half, right down their middles, instead of split at the emotional seam that bound them, was the worst thing the Culmell woman could have written to Eula. The image stuck and stuck harder each time she thought of what was meant. Rape, blood, the end of childhood, and all her fault for trying to separate them in what she thought was the most thorough and practical way.

Tessie was trying to get to the bottom of Linny's ordeal in California, that is, to make her relate the worst that had happened to her so that she might put it all behind her. Linny's attitude was "Mind your own business." If something happened to her, she wasn't going to let it happen to her again in the telling. Tessie thought Eula should find a qualified therapist, and be sure that Linny cooperated in her treatment.

"Otto?"

"Why not?" Tessie said. "He's already tired of his new institute. He'll be back here soon."

Eula was opposed, not so much to Otto as a mentor to the twin as to any further work for the time being on Linny's head, which seemed just then to be steady and well occupied. While she was anchored at Drayton, the biggest thing on her mind was bringing Becca home.

Linny had a long letter from her sister about the *Encyclopedia of Manners* she was reading to the British lady. She was not just passing along strategies for her escape from China, but the ideas she was forced to read aloud every day to Mrs. Fleming. Had Linny ever stopped to think, she wrote, that as they grew from children to adults they were passing through the same civilizing process that their society had?

"We started washing our hands before eating, we began to use knives and forks instead of our fingers, we stopped touching our private parts in public, we stopped farting where others could hear us. Aunt Gwen put an end to that. And we had to pretend to like people, even if we didn't. And we never knew it was civilization that was happening to us."

Linny let Eula read that much, then pulled Becca's letter back, which made her wonder again if money was being sent to Piano Island for ransom.

"You don't let me read your letters from Mr. Rank or the French woman."

No, Eula tore up the Culmell letters as soon as she read them. Which made Kerstin think she was hiding something. And of course Eula was holding back. The French adventuress said Eula *was* two people, sexed in her fantasy life and unsexed in her profession, the two of her at war. While the battle was on, her dearest friend, Kerstin, could live unmolested, in relative peace.

Linny came to Eula, and asked, "Do you think you could speak to Mr. Roosevelt about Becca?"

She actually thought the Director of Drayton could pick up the phone and get through to the president.

"No," Eula said. "He has other people who deal with these things. They're the ones we're talking to."

Eula supposed her voice sounded as false and empty to the girl as it did to herself. Something else was happening in Linny's life—contact with her grandmother. Mr. Henry had seen the two of them in the drugstore in Flourtown. He had no use for the old lady since she had denied her grandchildren. Now he expected Eula to warn Linny against her.

It was too late for that. The two of them were still meeting in Flourtown on paydays, every other Friday afternoon, before the bank closed. Mr. Sampson said Mrs. Carey would stand there like a sentry at his bank's door, guarding her granddaughter's deposits and withdrawals, clipping people who came too close with her cane, watching over the girl's safe exit.

"It's not that," Mr. Henry said. "She just comes for the money. And the ice cream."

Linny was still hoping to visit Mrs. Carey's apartment in Philadelphia. Mrs. Carey had finally told her where it was: on Fifth Street at the south end of the city. After a while the old lady ran out of excuses to deny her, and Linny said she was going in the following weekend to stay overnight. Afterward, Eula was eager to hear what had happened. She went to find Linny in the sewing room on Monday morning. But no Linny. The children were making a racket and a

mess of things, unspooling thread on the floor, and using the machines with no supervision.

Eula sent the class back to their cottages to clean their rooms for the rest of the morning, and went looking for Mr. Henry. He had nothing to tell her, only that Linny had gone to stay with the speckled woman, and he wouldn't be surprised if the old lady had got the girl into trouble.

Linny didn't return till the following morning. When she had cleaned up and changed her clothes, she came to the Director's office with an apology. Eula wouldn't accept it. Someone could have been hurt, and Linny had no excuse.

"Do you know when you're waiting for a train," Linny asked her, "how the two tracks come closer and closer together the further away they get? Do you think that's like Rebecca and me?"

If she thought this could lead her around Eula's anger, she was wrong.

"Don't be silly," Eula said. "You know that's an illusion, an optical illusion. Like the trick Mr. Rank showed Becca with the dot on a piece of paper."

"That was different," Linny said. "With this it's just there. You don't have to try."

"It's an illusion," Eula said again. "Where were you?"

"Yes," Linny said. "And remember what Mr. Rank told us. Most of the things we're so sure of are just illusions."

"Where were you?"

"I took the train," she said. "With Mrs. Carey."

The grandmother had never been on one before, Linny explained. She wanted to know if it was as smooth as the people said, or would it shake her as badly as it rattled itself.

"Yes, yes," Eula said, "but where?"

"Don't worry," Linny told her. "It was just a short ride and back."

She wouldn't force Linny to tell her. But she'd already guessed. My God, they went all the way to Washington. They were going to talk to Roosevelt.

Linny promised she'd never leave the sewing room unattended again.

∞

It was Mrs. Carey's idea to ride the train, but it was Linny's idea to go to the White House. She didn't really expect to see Mr. Roosevelt. She'd seen newspaper pictures of people carrying signs. Make a little fuss, she thought, get some attention. If they could find a room for seven dollars a night, the salary she was taking to the bank that Friday would be enough for two round trips to Washington, two nights' lodging, and maybe two meals.

They sat in the station at Thirtieth Street through Friday night, and took the morning train for the Capital. It was all right except for the conductor, who asked them to sit in the next car back. The second time he checked their tickets they still hadn't moved, and he asked them again, very politely. Mrs. Carey said she didn't mind, but Linny said, "No, why should we?"

He nodded in her grandmother's direction. The old lady was the reason.

"She's not colored," Linny told him.

"What is she?" he asked her.

"Leopard," she said, standing up to his face.

He walked off, punching tickets, shaking his head. A few minutes later he came back through the car, pointing them out to another trainman, and the two of them laughed and left, going off in opposite directions, going about their business. After Wilmington it wasn't mentioned again.

Mrs. Carey tapped the floor with her cane, celebrating.

"I got a grandchild now!" she told anyone listening. "I got a child and another coming just like her."

She was wearing the dress Linny had made for her. And she undid the top button the way she'd been shown, and asked, "Is this the way it's supposed to be?"

Over eighty, and carrying on like a child. Linny was proud of her, maybe more so of herself.

In Washington they'd have to be more careful not to get people angry. They weren't three blocks from the train station when she saw the sign: "Two for $4." She got directions for taking a trolley from there all the way to the White House without changing cars. Already

saving money; they could have all the meals they wanted. Linny bought a pretzel as long as a loaf of bread, and broke off pieces for her grandmother to soak in her mouth before she chewed them.

There were a lot of people, and all ignoring the two of them. The first day, walking back and forth with their sign outside the iron fence, they were just two of a dozen petitioners carrying placards, mumbling this and that, "Socialism is Communism Spelled Different," "Farmers Don't Just Feed the Pigs. They Feed You," and "Matthew III, 13." She could tell the passing people thought they were just as crazy as the rest. What good was her sign in a line like that? You couldn't stay still, even for a moment. The police would keep you moving, prodding you with their sticks. Mrs. Carey sat in a park while Linny went back and forth in this parade of coo coo birds, feeling sillier by the hour.

By Sunday afternoon she was ready to give up. She bumped into a man coming out of the iron gate. Actually she did it on purpose. One of the police saw this. He put his hand on her, but the gentleman said to let her go.

"What do you mean, your sister's a slave in China?" he asked. "What's the matter with you?"

Linny began to explain. The officer said he'd take care of it, but the man said, no, leave her alone. He walked her across Pennsylvania Avenue to a little house on the other side where he said she'd be welcome for tea. She could tell him more about Rebecca.

She went all the way back to the day they came home with identical bathing costumes. She must have talked to him for an hour or more. When she was through she asked, "Are you going to tell him?"

"No," he said, "but I'll tell his missis."

All that time with him, and the whole trip had been just that useless. She hurried down the street to fetch Mrs. Carey out of the park before it got any darker. Her grandmother was crying, thinking she'd been left there, abandoned by Linny with no way to get back to Philadelphia. They came home Monday in shame, making no fuss about the coach they were told to ride in. Mrs. Carey, feeling bad for Linny, let her stay overnight in the city for the first time. She showed Linny her private bathroom, and made her take a hot tub. That made the old woman feel better. She was behaving too much like a mother

now. She never talked anymore about the picture frame. Linny slept sitting up in her grandmother's rocker.

Tuesday morning she took the bus back to Drayton to face Miss Kieland. The Director was mad but she didn't say a word about punishment. Linny knew Miss Kieland had ideas about becoming her legal mother. She didn't tell her everything about where they'd been because the trip had been useless, and she didn't want to embarrass herself or give Eula the satisfaction of "I told you."

∞

The motorboat never got to the dock in Xiamen. It came to berth under the side of a much larger ship in the harbor, rolling dangerously close to the side. Looking up, Becca had to lean backward to see the edge of the railing high overhead. She could read *Alice Moreland* on the side, another woman. The men overhead lowered a metal stairway just for her.

"Can you climb this, miss?" One of the English soldiers was helping her onto the first step.

On deck, a steward took her up another stairway to a cabin with her own toilet and shower, and a window that looked out over the stern of the ship. The captain himself came down from the bridge to welcome her. He had a brown envelope full of papers he had carried across the ocean just for her.

One of the papers would be her passport, he said. The rest were information and directions. There was a confirmation card for a hotel reservation for one night in San Francisco. And railroad tickets.

She was free to go anywhere on the boat except the seamen's mess and quarters. The captain wanted her to eat at his table with his officers. If she didn't show up on time, he'd send someone to look for her. She was overcome with her new prospects, aware of the flag flying off the stern rail, on an American ship, going to America. The *Alice Moreland* had been waiting in the harbor just for her. She'd never felt so important in the world, and she never had been.

Not much to see, the captain apologized. Just boxes in the hold, most of them filled with painted china and vases, and stuffed with ex-

celsior showing through the cracks. She took his word for it; there was nothing much to see. On the way over it was a different story, he said. There had been stalls in the hold for thirteen thoroughbred mares and four stallions, all for one man who was bringing horse racing to a northern city. The captain could not impress her.

She took the first private moments in her room to stare into the glass on the back of her washroom door, looking like Linny looking like Becca looking at Linny. When she lined this mirror up with the one on the cabin door, the sisters sprang into a thousand copies that curved off into the future, or perhaps the past. Before they were a week into the voyage she noticed that someone had broken the glass in the door; the infinity of images were all split in two.

She made Linny mourn with her for Huang Don and his followers, and had her repeat as she did, "They may still be alive."

That evening at dinner the captain told her she could send a message of dots and dashes that would be radioed over the ocean from one ship to the next until they reached California. Telegraph lines would take them the rest of the way to her sister. When she was ready she could take her message to the radio room. One of the younger officers was looking across the table at her at that very moment, signifying his interest with a silly movement of his eyebrows. Why would she share her first words to Linny with any of these people?

At first she walked the decks for exercise, but did not care for the casual conversation of the officers, who could not pass without a little salute and a comment on the unexpected pleasure. She'd been so long apart from young men's company. All their efforts at friendship seemed exaggerated. When she allowed the ship's radio officer to walk out of the dining area with her on the third evening, she regretted it immediately. His fellow officers rolled their eyes as the man led her down to the boat deck. By the time they reached the stern rail he was in full throat in his admiration. Her copper skin, how radiant her hair, which had grown back to its shoulder length. The next September, he said, his ship would be in Philadelphia, and on and on. He'd be pleased to send the message to her twin about her new friend on the *Alice Moreland*. Would she like to tell her sister, she had a new

friend? He could show her how the Morse key worked, even let her tap on it herself.

What is the matter with this man? She wondered. Did these liberties follow from some presumption about her? She turned quickly, freeing herself from the man's hand, looked him in the eye, and said, "You ought to have your head examined."

In her cabin at last, she saw the broken image of Linny laughing on the back of the door. She had her split sister accompany her in everything she said.

"They're not sure who we are. They're not even sure what we are."

They had written each other about the meaning of *Schwarze.* There were no more illusions about that. *Black* in Germany, *black* around the world.

The ship's officers kept their distance after that, and now the captain seemed to think her company belonged to him. He invited her into the wheelhouse every day when he saw her on the bridge, explaining his charts and their path over the sea. The course they were taking back to Linny was not a direct compass heading, but a rhumb line, the shortest distance between them and San Francisco over the curved surface of the earth.

And why wasn't she happier on his ship, he wanted to know, so safely out of China and being delivered first-class to the homeland? She wasn't going to share her story with him. There would be some for Miss Kieland and more for Linny, but the worst would only be for herself, herself and the grave.

There were a few books in the small officers' lounge, all seamanship and tales of the sea, most of them sticky with mildew. No one had touched them on this voyage, and maybe not for years. She pried the fattest volume loose from its neighbor and took it back to her cabin. She didn't want to be humored so much as distracted from her worst reveries. She was resigned by then to her own company between meals. Now she had the occasional intrusion of Linda breathing over her shoulder as they read "Master Davey Jones, Storm and Tragedy on the Seven Seas." The first, a comical story, about frantic

signals to a lighthouse, ordering it to move out of a great steamship's way, was followed by five hundred pages of sailing misfortune.

All the way to San Francisco she diverted herself with drownings, wives' courage onshore and in the chapel, and endless verse to those in peril on the sea. Despite two heavy storms and seasickness, she never shared this sense of peril. She wanted to be frightened out of her wits, to be tossed about, maybe all the way down to Mr. Jones's locker, still determined to pay for her fatal part in the lives of the Twenty-Eight Stroke people.

Nothing scared her on the ocean. No man on the *Alice Moreland* frightened her, officer or able seaman. If one had attacked her she would have clubbed him, or bitten his finger off, or jumped into the ocean. She'd proven that much already. Never again would she suffer for a man's pleasure. She was sure of that. Miss Kieland's friend Mr. Rank would have said she had a stone driving her blood, a heart out of order, but Miss Kieland herself would understand. At mealtimes Becca kept a long face for all the men, declining all invitations to stroll the deck. Now and then Linny caught her passing in the glass, but couldn't really cheer her.

If Tessie was a little vain about her friendship with the wise Otto, she was discreet about her connections in government, who were many and high-placed. She never boasted about her acquaintance with Frances Perkins, and Eula knew she never presumed on that alliance for a favorable nod from Washington. Favors came her way automatically, by virtue of her steel character, her compassion, and her membership in that coven nurtured in and around Bryn Mawr College—women doing good work in the world, stirring their stumps in a forest of men. If they were a coven they were heaven's coven, and they gave each other strength. Eula was proud to think herself a member of the gang through her close connection to Tessie.

When Tess called, cool as you please, to say she'd had a little note from Eleanor, Eula was confused.

"Eleanor in Washington," she explained.

Eula made a greater fool of herself.

"What Eleanor in Washington?"

Before she recovered Tess was telling her that lady number one was pleased to learn from the Boss that the Carey girl had been successfully removed from China, and was then on a steamship bound for San Francisco. She was wondering if there had been a cable from the child to the orphanage.

That night was the second time Eula sullied her reputation with her board by serving alcohol in a Drayton building. It was long after lights-out on the campus, and again, it was only sherry. They were all in her office, all the housemothers, and Kerstin. Mr. Henry was outside patrolling between the cottages. Tessie was there, too, to celebrate. It was the second time Linny was encouraged to drink. This time it was only a drop of sherry Eula wanted her to share when they toasted her sister's return.

This time it was Eula who actually got tight. Maybe Ellen Reilly, too, but not so far gone that they couldn't see the worry in Linny's glances. Transformed by the news of her sister's coming, the twin was happy enough, but she sensed danger in the chance of adults' losing control. And Eula knew that Mr. Henry, watching them from time to time through the windows, wasn't comfortable with it either, though they raised their glasses to him as well.

The little party reached anticlimax. Something more needed saying, just to keep things going, something more in commemoration. There was a heavy silence. Eula wanted to congratulate Linny and her sister for something she couldn't explain, even to herself. It was more a presentiment than a fully formed idea, a shadow, painted into life, the way they had worn their copper skin through their short lives, and across continents, the glowing beauty of their skin along with the weight of its insult.

With another nod to the twins she raised her glass once more, maybe a little sloppy in the way she was citing their contributions. She was going to propose to her board that the only criterion for acceptance here be the female child in need of family.

If Eula expected congratulations and hoopla, there wasn't any. Perhaps a "hear, hear," and a bit of applause. The housemothers who disagreed with her kept it to themselves, and the rest of the company would have thought the move long overdue.

That week the board received the agenda item from Eula, and in return she had a note from Cyril.

Eula Dear,

You know since Renee's departure you are surrounded only by friendly advisers on our council, so you should take this as a kindly notice. Someone, I needn't say who, has passed word among us that alcohol has been used again by Drayton staff on campus and in your presence. I tell you only so that you may come prepared at our next session to defend yourself against the temperance diehards among us. You know the names.

We've all received your agenda item. It should make for lively debate.

With warm regards,
Cyril

Linny asked if she could cancel her sewing sessions for a day, allowing her a trip to the city to pass the news of Becca to her grandmother. Eula consented, but asked her to sit a moment and answer a few questions.

First, she wanted to know why Becca wouldn't have sent a message about her emancipation, if not before she left, at least from the steamship.

"She wants to surprise us. You have the ship's name. Why don't we send a message to her?"

"Did she give you any clue she might be leaving?" Eula asked. "Was there something we missed in her letters?"

"You didn't miss anything. She's afraid you won't let her come back."

"Did she tell you that?"

"No, she didn't have to tell me."

"Why would you say it then?"

It was the same old double dose Linny gave her—the look of irritation and resignation for another obtuse reaction to a truth that seemed so obvious to the twin.

"Because I'm afraid. For her."

"Where do you think you two will go when she gets here? Are you making your plans already?"

They wouldn't be going anywhere, she said.

"Not as far as you can send mail, and farther?"

One of them had already been that far, Linny reminded her. It hadn't worked. Didn't she think Becca would make a good instructor, too? And if not, why didn't she think so?

Eula hadn't answered her and Linny was arguing the point. That could wait.

"What should we say in our message?" Eula asked her.

"Tell her don't stop for anything in San Francisco."

"She wouldn't do that," Eula said. "Not with you waiting here."

"Oh yes, she would. She's planning to."

Linny was sure of it. Together they wrote a cable of welcome, which Linny insisted they close with "Don't go to the house on Mission Street."

"Stop," Eula wrote at the end.

"Don't put that in," Linny said.

The Western Union would put it there anyway, Eula explained.

"It doesn't really matter," Linny said. "We know she's going to stop there anyway."

"No we don't."

"I wasn't including you," Linny said.

∞

The sea was calm as the *Alice Moreland* drew closer to the coast. Nothing like the violent water crashing over the *Schooner Progress* as it washed into shore at Coney Island in eighteen seventy-five, with its cargo of oak timbers serving as the life preservers to a crew of fifteen,

all of them miraculously saved. Becca dropped "Master David Jones," and this final escape from the deep sea, let it fall to her bunk as the ship's horn blew for the wheelman's joy at his sighting of California.

Becca walked out to the bow rail and looked across the glassy surface of the ocean to a dim outline of land. From her pocket she pulled the cable from Linny and Miss Kieland, crumpled it, and tossed it over the rail. Not because she planned to ignore its advice, but because the radio officer had typed it out for her, and delivered it to her cabin with a bitter lip, like a spurned wood newt, and asked, with no apology for reading her mail, "Who do you know on Mission Street? You're not going there?"

The paper hit the sea, and a team of several dozen dolphins broke the surface as if summoned into harness to pull the ship the rest of the way to land. They wove in and out, up and down, racing along at the bow in a pattern beyond human dance. But their achievement could not break the pall over the impending landfall.

Her heart *was* out of order, and revenge was the balm she chose for guilt. She might have left well enough alone, but any bruise on Linny was a mark on Becca as well. It would be easy enough to find Mission Street, and the wood-burnt letters over the door: SEA TOSSED. Just to leave a little mark of her own.

They docked later that afternoon, a day and a half early thanks to favorable wind and fair weather in the last week of the crossing. An agent of the Southern Pacific was there to take her straight from the docks to her lodging on Essex Street. Before leaving her at the hotel desk, he looked over her tickets and papers.

"Aren't you the little first-class lady?" he said.

And she was, with travel orders signed by an assistant secretary of state, and Pullman and parlor tickets all the way to Philadelphia. There was just the stopover on Essex Street, two days and nights to ride up and down and through the tunnel, before the rail agent would come again to take her to the ferry for Oakland. Then another private taxi to the station, and she'd be on her way across the prairie. He promised.

Like the freedom papers that gave license to her grandmother's crossing from state to state, the documents Becca carried seemed to

her like a proclamation: Leave this woman alone. She may travel over any border she pleases. She happens to be on her way to Pennsylvania. Don't get in her way.

Before she stepped out of her hotel the next morning, on her way to Mission Street, she made sure the papers were in order in her handbag. The strap was securely over her head, the bag riding proud on her opposite hip. She missed the house on the first pass. A light mist was settling over the district. The weather changed. It was suddenly chilly, and her nerve began to fail. Crossing to the other sidewalk and turning back, she'd only gone a few steps when she saw the sign.

Blue paint had peeled from the steps and wide porch, leaving the wood cracked and gray, bare to the weather. She climbed to the porch, where she could see all the way to the back of the parlor. Two young women sat attentively on a sofa to one side. In the middle of the room, a man in a clerical collar stood gesturing to them with a sweeping motion of his arms. In a doorway, a woman with a broom had stopped her chore to nod at the lesson in progress.

Becca watched for a while, but could hear nothing. She tapped on the glass. The man turned. The woman flinched and came forward. Becca put her face right against the pane, and moved her lips.

"I'm white as a snowy dove," she called out.

The woman who stared back at the ghost of a hateful memory was speechless.

Becca had no doubt this was Mumsy, who was moving now, into the hallway. It must have taken a few moments to get all her locks undone, before she came charging out the front in a fury. By then Becca was on the sidewalk, and calling to her again, "White as a dove."

"Where did you come from? I knew it, you little bitch. Twelve weeks I fed you!"

She ran toward Becca, into the street, with her broom raised. Even going backward Becca was faster, moving up the hill. Mumsy was shouting for someone to stop the dirty little tramp who owed her room and board.

"Months it was! Stop her!"

There was no one in the drizzly street to hear, no policeman on the corner. At the end of her block she was finished. Becca turned her back on the rush of filthy language, and walked away, her passport to the world in the bag at her side. She was wishing there had been a policeman. Maybe an exchange of messages between Washington and San Francisco, with the woman in a raging confusion at the doubling of her defeat.

The next day the Southern Pacific agent accompanied her across the bay on the ferry, and all the way to the Oakland station. He stood beside her as she sent her cable to Drayton, listening to every word she said. And he stood waiting on the platform for half an hour, watching her in her seat through the window until the train was moving. In Denver and Chicago, too, there were men to shepherd her transfer. Unknown to her traveling companions, she was a celebrity to those delivering her to Linny. Nothing was too much trouble for her comfort.

For Eula to say her heart was full was evasive. Full of what? Love? Fear? The anticipation of unleashed affection? Recrimination, ultimatum, second departures? She prepared for her board meeting, not by looking over the accounts again, or making another list of deferred maintenance items, or the usual discipline cases, or even by preparing a rebuttal for the guardians of temperance.

She was preoccupied with Becca's return, the sisters' reunion, not just with each other, but with her and all the others who'd been charmed and troubled by their double life. In fact, she was primed for rebellion. Upset in her private affairs by Otto and the Culmell woman, challenged by Tessie for temporizing the last dozen years with the constraints of her charter, reproached and anguished by the recent history of the twins, she passed daily under the French carved on the wall—Une Femme Doit Plaire, C'Est Son Bonheur—with a superior toss of her head. And now her board chose the wrong time to cross her.

Month after month, one meeting after another, she was pushed to the limits of civility. She could predict the way each of the trustees would respond to any issue. There was far too much self-congratulation for this sacrifice of their time and their honorable

intentions. And always someone reminding them of founding principles, and one who barred any shortcut to action with his *Roberts Rules*. They bored her; she tolerated them.

Cyril, in the middle of his two-year tour as chairman, made a calm parliamentarian, though too ready to suffer a tangent. If a discussion of the food budget flowed off into the possibilities of some third cousin's vegetable farm providing the kitchens with asparagus for a month, or the outlook for farming in general over the next decade, he welcomed her help in bringing the meeting back to the point. He liked to open meetings with praise for some recent accomplishment of hers. Even this flattery was tedious.

Renee's place on the board had been taken by another family member as the bylaws required, her first cousin Landon Sears, a rather dim lamp, not a troublemaker, and not very articulate, but happy to attack a crippled argument when a dispute was all but over. A great improvement over Renee, Eula knew, though not someone she could count on if she were bleeding.

Two of the members had passed away since the founding and their places had been taken by a pair of fashionable women, liberals, by self-description, though they were the water-testing kind. They were like another set of twins, with like-minded probity, wool suits of the same cut, and the same hairstyles under round felt hats with veils raised for eye-to-eye honesty. And they never failed to second, or support, each other's positions. They, too, liked to compliment Eula, and usually sided with her when they could without controversy.

One, Connie Wetherall, had been put up by Cyril to connect Drayton to her family's retail fortune, though no penny of it had come their way, and because she had once made a feint at a teaching career before marriage and her family's objection saved her the indignity. The other was Mintonette Tucker, Connie's friend from childhood, who had presented a paper to the White House Conference on Dependent Children in 1919, and involved herself in social research before she was similarly restrained by a marriage. Eula might have liked her well enough, but for the one persisting tic, her obsession with alcoholic reform.

The four other members of the board had been with them from the start. All reasonable men, she thought. They had all been acquainted with Mr. Drayton, who left a note to his executors favoring these four for their young energy, and their commitment to his orphanage.

Eula hadn't known when she was hired that all of them—David Ross, Harris Newbold, and Roger and Carroll Ney—were members of the First Troop, City Cavalry, the quasi-military social club of Philadelphia's high-born, who gave their daughters' coming-out parties at their armory, and used the blackball to protect their ranks. If they rode into battle in wartime, they drank just as enthusiastically in their clubs in longer periods of peace. These four were fond of their evening brandy in the Union League, and no special danger to Eula if alcoholic consumption was on the agenda. Newbold was the stickiest of them, the legal dean of the board, his *Roberts Rules* always ready, against the chance of some informality jeopardizing the legitimacy of an action.

In truth, she thought of all the board members as friends in the cause. For all the posturing, they were a rather easy group to pull in her direction. They had probably saved her from excesses. And now they could imagine her as the master of a zoo in black and white, little inmates, wild and sorted by color staring balefully at each other from opposite sides of their classrooms, or totally confused by their own skins at the first social function they might be allowed to attend together.

That was the liberals' first fear, not miscegenation, which seemed out of the question, but the embarrassment of social encounter. Mintonette's question was really asked on behalf of them all: "Eula, what happens when you have a dance?"

"They dance" was more an evasion than the reproof she intended.

They weren't thinking of a black cheek against a white cheek, but the cruel use of children in a cause that had never been theirs. So unfair to invite them all to a gathering where half the invitations to dance were already denied.

Cyril opened the meeting, reporting the gift of new bedding for all the cottages and the staff housing, and a hundred glass tumblers, unbreakable, he was told; both gifts from the Wanamaker department

store, and both "thanks to our Director's cultivation of the store's friendship with the college."

No. The store president's sister had been a friend of hers at the Richmond Street settlement house. It gave Eula no pride, but led to a cryptic entry in her daybook: "Jenny W. pays a rummy debt of five dollars with a large gift. From her brother!"

Cyril read the first agenda item with eyebrows at full mast: "Increase in mandatory graduation age—policy or exception?"

He must have convinced Mintonette not to start a fuss about the second sherry revel, which was nowhere on the list.

Two voices, but Connie Wetherall grabbed the stage.

"I've heard good things about the sewing program from Julia Crane. I mean since the accident. Should we take it, this extension of time for the Carey child has been a good thing after all?"

She was looking to Eula for the answer.

Eula imagined an exchange of calls, and again, the conspiracy to save her from herself. Cyril was coming up short of her issue, allowing a bit of it through the back door, by way of the Careys' return. They all knew the other Carey twin was on her way home, and that Eula was making a place for her in one of the Drayton cottages.

The twins' mixed background, Connie called it. Wasn't this taking them close enough to this matter of opening the doors wider? Eula saw her proposal for open admission at the bottom of the agenda, along with four other items collected under "Issues for the Coming Decade," not something they'd get to this evening if Cyril held to form. Or even this year, if he could help it.

"I've seen those two together," Roger Ney said, "and I've seen them apart," as if this were a rather tricky and admirable accomplishment. "Marvelous human specimens."

"Very impressive, I'm sure," said Landon Sears.

"Let me finish," Ney cut him short. "I think we must know every misfortune they suffered as residents here. And I'll say this. With what we now know, I don't think we should have taken them in the first place. . . not just the disturbance they caused the others, but their own unhappiness. I don't think we can justify it. And the fight-

ing . . . the charter forbids them, and they came anyway. I'm not blaming you, Eula."

He, too, was looking for a response from the Director. But he hadn't asked a question.

"What do you think?"

"Think about what?"

"Well. . . their background, the commotion . . . all of it. You know."

Cyril, who must have seen trouble coming, interrupted.

"Maybe you could be a little more precise, Roger."

"Oh, very well. What color are they? It's as simple as that."

She could have said, their hair is straw blond, their skin is between gold and copper, their eyes are a blue-gray, their palms slightly pinker than mine, their nails are white-tipped, with white half-moons, their gums are a little bluish perhaps, and their tongues very much the same color as yours. She'd once said all that to Renee. She wasn't going to sit still for a discussion of the Careys' color.

"Cyril," she said, avoiding Mr. Ney's gaze. "What was the item? Could you read it again?"

He brought them back to extensions of residency, and Eula was able to win a consensus for "Director's discretion," though not without Harris Newbold's insistence on a change in the bylaws, and a motion that included "only as an exception where the immediate welfare of the child is at risk, and only as a temporary measure."

Only one negative vote.

"A nay from a Ney."

The roundtable obliged with a chuckle, but this did nothing to change the mood of Roger Ney, smarting from Eula's earlier evasion. As they moved along from perimeter security (never enough of that, and never enough discussion of it) and the proposed construction of a locked gate across their driveway at Wissahickon (consensus against, after Eula's adamant opposition) to an increase in the cap on petty cash expenditures to seventy-five dollars, and a ten percent increment for the food budget, she led the evening and carried each point with Cyril's cooperation.

It was past their usual closing hour. The session appeared to be over. "Issues for the Coming Decade" had been avoided. Cyril was asking for the motion to adjourn.

"No!"

Roger Ney again.

"What use are we here?" he asked everyone.

He was holding up the charter and bylaws.

"I read here on the very first page our duty is to lead the institution according to the seven points of its charter and the principles of the mission set forth by Mr. Drayton. I suggest to you, we're leading nothing. We're following and that's all we do, under the very persuasive direction of Miss Kieland."

He dropped the bylaws with the same drama she imagined him dropping a brief on a counsel's table. He grabbed the agenda sheet and shook it in her direction.

"And look what's hiding down here!"

He read from the bottom of the page.

"Open admission!"

He nodded around the table.

"Never discussed. Here this month, and I expect it will be next month, too, and the month after that. Until we're used to reading it. It's poison," he said.

"Perhaps," Cyril said, "this is for another evening."

"No! That's my point. This is for no other evening. This is for never!"

She saw Cyril back on his heels, at a loss for a way to close. Roger was way ahead of him.

"My point has been offered. Cyril, if you ask for adjournment again, I'll insist on a motion to table open admission for good."

"The floor is yours," Cyril conceded, and the game was on.

She remembered how her father would ask her mother, "Would you marry one?" whenever this discussion passed his tolerance. She couldn't recall her mother's ever saying yes outright, the way a child would have wanted a badgered parent to do. It was a question that shut her mother's mouth, and thinned her lips near to disappearance.

Her mother had managed "if I felt like it," on one occasion, and Eula remembered her father's thundering response: "Well, go ahead then!," stomping out the door, slamming it on his way. And whispering with her siblings in wonder, probably not so frightened by what they'd heard as fascinated by the thought of their mother with a colored man, and asking her more questions to keep this savory stew at a boil.

"Mother, would you really marry a Negro man?"

"I don't think so, dear, but it's not because that wouldn't be right."

An answer that disappointed, since they never believed it could happen anyway. Her father had his way again. If he didn't, he refused his civility. Roger was like him.

"The court could shut us down over this," he said. "If we accepted one single Negro child. . . "

"It's a good bet we've already accepted two," Sears said. He looked to his chief, Roger, for approval, wanting to help him, she could see, but Ney shook him off with a pained tolerance, and continued, "The charter says our cottages are for white children only."

"Would that be chalk white?" Mintonette asked him with a nod to Eula, striking a blow for her Director.

Ney brushed this off, too, as a comment of no standing from a woman ignorant of law.

"Estin Drayton never asked us to mix the colors," he said. "He had one color in mind."

He was holding up the charter and bylaws again, waving the pages slowly, in front of the board, as if hypnosis might succeed where common sense had failed them.

"He asked us to oversee an orphanage that would accept white girls six to ten with both parents deceased. His family would have every right to take back the whole estate if we broke faith in this iron document. This is a contract," he said solemnly.

"One last thing . . . I'd like again to state my confidence in Eula as our Director. It would be a great loss if she withdrew from service here."

So, she could stay on Roger Ney's terms.

"We have two Draytons on the board," Eula said. "Maybe we could hear from them." She looked to Cyril first. "Would the family sue us?" she asked him.

He doubted it. Not anymore.

Sears doubted it, too.

"Irrelevant," Ney said. "There are a dozen others who have legal standing here."

"Yes, at least that many," Sears agreed.

"How about it, Roger?" Cyril asked. "Have we had enough of this for now? Is there a motion to adjourn?"

"No!" Eula said.

Cyril looked betrayed.

"Well then," he said. "Your turn."

Mintonette, silent for most of the meeting, and biting the ends of her fingers in deep thought, dropped her hand to the table, and asked, "Eula, tell us, just exactly how would this work? Would they share the same bedrooms? And bathrooms? Would they sit on the same toilet seats?"

"Oh, I'm sure not," Connie said.

"We could have outhouses for them," Eula suggested.

This startled David Ross, who must have been half asleep.

"Oh Eula," he said. "We couldn't do that."

"Oh, I don't know," she continued with it, "it's not so far in their past. If not privies, maybe a trench along the driveway."

"You see? You see?" Ney chimed in, victorious. "What do we get when it comes down to the daily realities? Disbelief on the one side, sarcasm on the other. I rest. I rest."

Yes, he ought to, she agreed. He didn't understand what was happening. None of them did, if they imagined Eula loading the halls with black faces. She was no more ready for that than her mother for a Negro as helpmate. Search the Drayton diaries of those years, start to finish; you find no mention of a move to integrate the orphanage, tacit or vocal. If this was the board's shame, it was hers, too. The only ones working for that in that decade were the Carey twins, and they didn't know it, since they had come to Drayton innocent of color, and had left plagued by it.

Eula took the charter, which Ney held out to her. He looked pleased as a congressman holding the country's constitution under another representative's nose. And she gave him a little of his own, holding it under his.

"You should have another look," she said. "If this is iron, it's eaten with rust. We've broken it dozens of times."

Eight heads led with their chins over the table as Eula went on. She'd never kept it a secret. Most of her girls had a parent living, some of them, two, a father on the run, a mother addicted to a drug, or a court moving them from harm's way. Mr. Drayton was a philanthropist, not a student of child welfare. He didn't know who'd be knocking at the door when he made his rules. It wasn't the first time she'd explained to them that white girls between six and ten with both parents deceased were a charmed lot at the adoption and welfare agencies. Drayton would never fill its cottages if these were the only ones it received.

"Should we close down on that account?" she asked.

Cyril was relieved.

"If that's all this was about, Eula, I'm sure we can find the necessary language. . . ."

He trailed off, looking around for support, perhaps a motion.

All around the table they took to their pencils and legal pads. And when they were finished, nothing. She broke the silence.

"The most sensible restriction is the one I've already proposed. The female child under eighteen, in need of a home. Leave the rest to our common sense."

"I don't think so," Ney said.

What, then, did he propose?

On the instant, he wasn't prepared to say. But he would say this again: "The institution could crumble if we move to admit the colored."

"You mean those with black skins?" Mintonette asked him.

"Of course that's what I mean."

"Yes," Sears agreed. "All the support we've built in the community. I believe Roger's on the right track here."

But the track was the same inconvenient slope, from black to chocolate, to coffee, to tan. The devilish spectrum again, whose mention seemed to rile the gentlemen among them more than the ladies.

Exactly what portion of Negro blood would be enough to elimi-
nate a candidate: a half, quarter, eighth, sixty-fourth?

Ney said the question itself begged for a blanket restriction. "For
clarity's sake."

Connie Wetherall said she'd been told in college, "We all have a
few drops of Africa in us." She mentioned it, she said, not because
she was inclined to disagree with Ney; she just wanted to keep the
debate on a scientific footing.

Eula knew they were all waiting for her to concede something.
She told them she'd be willing to lead Drayton for another ten years,
but she would not follow them into the past. It was enough of a rebellion to bring them up short. After all, she was the institution. After a dozen years here, it never occurred to them she might walk
away without a push. Every article ever written about Drayton referred to the Kieland approach, or the Kieland theory, the Kieland
plan, the Kieland philosophy, melding school and life, and Drayton
with its surrounding community. The trustees had no wish to purge
all that. They began their retreat.

"No need for haste," on every tongue. Even Roger Ney repeated it.

They could have his "appropriate language," if one of them had
the nerve to compose it, or they could have Eula. She wouldn't allow
anything that excluded the twins.

Cyril asked her to prepare a motion for the next meeting.

"You already have it," she said. Roger Ney allowed the meeting to
close.

∞

Eula expected the two girls to sail into each other's arms. It was
nothing like that. They approached one another solemnly, touched
cheeks, and began to talk as if they'd seen each other the day before,
as if they'd never been separated—by time or geography. Eula and
Kerstin, Tessie, too, watched in wonder, before indulging themselves
in bear hugs and tears with the reunited sisters. Mr. Henry did, too,
though a bit more formally. It wouldn't occur to them that the twins
had seen and talked to each other every day of their separation.

Tessie left for her office, and they packed themselves into the station wagon. When all was ready, Mr. Henry turned to Eula: "Miss Linny says we must go to Fifth Street."

She wasn't sure what he meant. And then she was.

"All right," she said without enthusiasm.

At first glance, the south side of the city did not appear so full of problems as Eula knew it to be. It was just that as they crossed a certain line a shadow came down. Linny asked Kerstin, Mr. Henry, and Eula to wait in the car. As Linny and Becca walked up to the stoop of the row house, past the staring neighbors, Eula could only think of the two as pale pilgrims in a dark world of darker trouble than they could imagine. She waited with Kerstin and Mr. Henry for half an hour before they came out of the house again. As they passed out the front door, she saw the old woman opening her window on the third floor.

"Friday," she called down to them.

"How did it go?" Eula asked as cheerfully as she could.

"Fine" was all they cared to share of the visit. Now, Eula supposed, they could move on to happier times.

∞

This is the way they'd started at Drayton, Eula still confusing them with each other. Strangers couldn't really tell them apart. Not to look at fully dressed, not with their hair up, though Becca's speech had slowed a bit, and in the first day or two, as she went everywhere with her sister, her red-rimmed eyes were more apt to brim than her sister's. Whether it was sadness for her first exposure to the wider world, or an unimaginable relief, Eula couldn't say. Becca had regained her weight during her time with the British couple. She came home chastened and quieter than they remembered her. But so had Linny.

Becca moved right into the cottage with her sister, without a question to Eula, as if this were her right, and beyond debate. She was presuming the Director owed her something. Nurse Jean, eager to accommodate the weary traveler moved downstairs to the study opposite Miss Stein's room. This gave the twins the two upstairs bedrooms in the cottage. Otto thought this would be all right, so long as

they were not sleeping in the same room; not because he feared their intimacy, just the opposite.

Linny wanted the adults to leave and then come back to pick them up for the coming-home supper Kerstin was preparing for them. When Eula came to get them, she could hear them up to some sort of mischief upstairs. They called for her to come up. And she saw what it was—they'd been observing each other in the nearly invisible underwear. She found them posed like a couple of Paris mannequins in the pale green Vionnet gown and the copy Linny had made of Thai silk. They were admiring each other, standing on their beds, impish but fully developed women, their chests lifted, and hips thrust out, affecting disdain for their audience of one.

They'd already rearranged the furniture, putting both beds in one room for the first night together. Eula couldn't keep them apart, never mind Otto and the separate rooms. The other bedroom, in front, was to be Linny's sewing parlor, with two tables and window light for her work. That was the only time Eula ever saw them in the gowns. She didn't think Becca had much interest in hers beyond the remarkable achievement of it. She was happiest in a simple white blouse and one of the old corduroy jumpers she used to wear. And saddle shoes, and her sister dressed the same way.

Becca's first day back on the campus she took up where she'd left off. That is, with Mr. Henry. While Linny held her sewing session, Becca fell in beside him in his maintenance chores. On the second day of her return, unasked, she was trimming the shrubbery with him, and on her knees weeding, and deadheading the marigolds. She said this was all she wanted for a while.

Just as Linny had, Becca made a job for herself as she relaxed into her new residency. Mr. Henry now had two boys from Flourtown who helped when the mowing got ahead of him, or the fall leaves overwhelmed him in piles over his head. It was long past time he should have had a full-time assistant. And here was Becca, showing them the way it should be.

When she came to Eula's office to make it a formal job, she was told she could start at the same salary her sister had. Eula asked if she understood she and Linny were only here for an interim.

"How long is that?"

Eula wouldn't say. She'd almost forgotten she'd been holding something for Becca, the letter from China. Becca was fearful taking it from her hand, and even more afraid to look at it. She wouldn't open it in front of her Director.

"She isn't herself," Nurse Jean told Eula. It would take time. Living downstairs from the twins, Jean heard a lot of muffled conversations, full of strange words, sometimes in the middle of the night. Once, when it had gotten quite loud, and taken on the force of a drumbeat, she called up the stairwell to let them know she couldn't sleep with all that going on. They paid no attention. Jean went up to investigate.

"It was the most charming thing," she said. "When I realized it was all in their sleep, I didn't want to wake them."

It was like singing in tongues, she said, back and forth to each other, repeating the sounds, an urgent flow of alien syllables, and their soothing imitation. As if one voice called for help and the other comforted in the same poetic invention.

"It was lovely," she said. "They are so in love with each other. I think they're just keeping their demons at bay, so many horrid memories, whatever they are."

Piece by piece Eula heard more of Becca's story. Linny was telling more, too, now that they lived in tandem again. And the more Eula learned, the more shame she felt for her part in their first ventures into the world, and the more sympathy for this retreat into the strained safety of their childhood.

Otto was back and preparing a seminar for Tessie's graduate students on "Symbols of Government." He told Eula it wasn't the filthy swastika he was concerned with in this course, but the cant in Washington. He was calling, he said, to test a theme on her: "Do you see? The New Deal is as full of mythology as the old one?"

He didn't really want to talk about that. He was enchanted again by the Carey girls, the real reason for his call.

"A seamstress and a gardener," he said, "but sewing in the same row."

He paused to let his pun settle. Actually he'd grown more serious about them. He confessed that, before this, they were more like a well-known puzzle, one that had a published set of solutions, and he'd always felt a bit of a fake discussing their case. He was certain they could still be a danger to each other, but this came less from his reading and mythology than from their relentless intimacy. Now that they had established a history apart from each other they were more a phenomenon to him.

He was looking for a real consequence of their symmetry.

It was too easy pointing to the obvious, he thought, to the mirror images of their journeys, both walking so innocently into the same ancient perversion. The one who would be a Negro escaping as white, the one who would be white escaping as a Negro. And all the time they supposed they were on such different paths.

"For God's sake, don't let them sleep in the same room, in the same bed."

Hearing nothing in reply, he changed the mood: "Do you know what Tessie's students have been calling themselves? The terrapins. Because of the way I say terapy. Eula, you and Tessie are so terrible. Why didn't you tell me?"

"So," he began again, "they go to either side of the planet. And on opposite sides of the world, each has a looking glass to tell her, 'You think you have troubles?'"

∞

Becca told Linda she was wild about her gown. Eula knew she wasn't, and Linny could tell, too. When would she ever wear it? Linny didn't mind. The sewing troubled her sister. Becca saw it as the thing that might separate them. She was explaining things to Linny about China that she hadn't put in her letters, not all of it, though she showed her sister what Mr. Leighton Stuart had sent her from Peking.

Dear Miss Rebecca Carey,
    I have little idea of who you are, and no idea where. I only write to oblige my dear friend, your first professor at Yenching University,

Nelson Moore. He says the people at your old college in Pennsylvania may know how to forward this to you.

Professor Moore wants me to tell you what I know of the Chinese government's treatment of students who are opposed to it. He asked me if I could discover and pass along to you the fate of the hundred and more naïfs who were taken from the Yenching campus in October 1935. I have no sympathy for their political nonsense, but Professor Brown's obvious devotion to you calls on my sympathy and appreciation of your attachment to all those misguided friends.

I can't tell you where any of those young people are today, or if they are alive. I can tell you this. The Kuomintang at that time were not killing all the dissident students. I know they transported a number of them for reeducation far north in Harbin, where they could be a mischief to no one but themselves. You can be sure life there would not be easy. If they went to Harbin, it's likely they're still there because Professor Moore tells me not one of them has come back to him to explain what happened.

If they are not in Harbin, well, let's not think about that. You ought to write to your professor some day, and apologize for the rude way you walked out of his house.

With mutual concern,

Leighton Stuart (friend of Nelson Moore)

Becca said the letter was half a blessing, and that's all she cared to say about it. It gave her hope. Sometimes she twirled the globe in the Schoolhouse study and let her hand rest on the north of China. She couldn't find Harbin, but such a vast territory under her palm! Somewhere under her hand was all her sorrow. Linny couldn't help her. Listening at night, she was absorbing the misery, but passively. Sleeping head to head with her sister, she was hearing the Chinese names—Dou Ping, Han Suyin, Deng Win, Hu Wei-ling, Rachel Chin—sung out as poetry. Linny mumbled them to herself in her daydreams, and said them in her sleep. She understood they were none of her business, and tried to keep them to herself, but was no

more able to silence them at night than Becca. They came unbidden, and ran loops in her head.

∞

One afternoon, exhausted with her outdoor work, Becca came to the sewing room, and tried her hand at what Linny was teaching the others. She was hopeless. It made Linny still more tolerant of the other girls' limitations, the ones who got things so crooked and tangled. She didn't mind Becca calling her Spider anymore, or Thimble Witch, because she *was* always hanging from a thread. Or had a thread hanging from her, on a needle stuck in her blouse, ready for any child's loose button. And a red line around her thimble finger that began to form a callous.

"How do you do that?" Becca asked her.

Linny sat her at one of the Singers, but it was no use. How had Becca got the treadle going backward? How had she made such dreadful tangles around the foot and bobbin? The backwardness was as astonishing to Linny as the skill was to Becca, whose kack-handed way with a needle might mean they'd never work together.

"You're going to be a businesswoman," Linny said, in compensation, not because she had any real faith in that, but she'd heard Miss Kieland say it, and it seemed a kind thing to repeat.

Every other Friday they took the bus into the city to visit their Grandmother Carey. At the middle and the end of the month the old woman came their way to collect the money for her rent. Half from Linny and half from Becca, since the sisters were both getting the same salary, they had something to save again in the Flourtown bank. It made Mrs. Carey calmer when the checks had been deposited and the green bills were finally in her creel.

Drayton had taught them it was bad manners to speak of money unless they were shopping. The sisters understood Grandma Carey never had anyone to teach her that. She knew if you didn't have any you were lost. To her, there was no special honor in making it or even having extra. It didn't matter where it came from, and certainly if you had more than enough, you were meant to spread it around

you. As sharp as she was about their support of her, they never thought of her as greedy. It only made them grin to see the way she fastened the creel's lid so carefully after they dropped the money in.

When she told them she was ready to die, they didn't believe her. The way she tramped up the three flights of stairs to her apartment without their help gave no sign of it. She said she was more than eighty-five; how much more she wasn't sure. One Friday on their way from Drayton to the bank she got angry at something the bus driver said to her, smacked his leg with her cane, and walked off the bus, with them right behind her.

"Speckled bitch," the driver called her.

Becca and Linny went on either side of her, their hands under her elbows, all the way into the village. Between them, light as a bird, and chirping all the way about the bump she should have left on the man's head, and the ice creams she was going to buy each of them after the bank business, and she was never out of breath.

Eula brought Mrs. Constance Wetherall into the sewing room to observe one of Linny's classes. The gown she'd made for Becca was on one of the mannequins as a demonstration of her skills. Eula had asked her to show it off for this occasion. Mrs. Wetherall knew what it was, just as the sewing mistress from Philadelphia had. It was the duplicate of one she'd seen in her *Gazette du Bon Ton*. She also knew just what it would cost from Callot Soeurs. Linny heard her whispering the figure to Miss Kieland.

"Child," Mrs. Wetherall said. "That's not yours. It's from Paris."

Linny was ready to throw her hands up in disgust, but Eula explained, and Mrs. Wetherall took a closer look at the sewing, the lining's binding, and the way the panels were seamed.

"Where did you learn this?" she asked. "Americans don't cut cloth this way. It's far too wasteful."

She wanted to know if Linny could reproduce it once more, if she could fit the same dress on her, make her another one.

"Yes, of course," Linny said.

Mrs. Wetherall was excited.

"Connie," Eula said. "It's not Miss Carey's design. It wouldn't be right would it?"

"One dress? Good heavens! Callot Soeurs couldn't be bothered! Americans can't do this at the price. It's all hand-stitched. They don't even know how."

Though Miss Kieland didn't seem convinced, Linny was all for making the gown, perhaps with a variation, something to make it her own.

"Oh, no," Mrs. Wetherall told Linny. "Don't change a thing."

"You know," Linny said "I'd have to work directly on you. You'd be wearing nothing."

Mrs. Wetherall was silent. Linny wasn't sure what had made her say it. All part of a professional's pose, maybe. It's what she'd imagined a pushy Paris seamstress, someone at Callot Soeurs, telling a client. To put a little respect in the customer. To take control.

"I suppose we might do that," Mrs. Wetherall said, recovering.

"We would *have* to do that. It's the only way."

"Of course," she said.

All pretense. And all invented on the spot. It was all new. She'd have to take one of the gowns apart again, and work from enlargements of those pieces. And Mrs. Wetherall would bring her some silk taffeta she already had in mind. She'd do it within the week. No money was discussed. Linny was flushed with pride for the impression she'd made on the trustee, one of the women who made decisions about Drayton. She hadn't considered Mrs. Wetherall might be more pleased for herself than for her young seamstress, having just found a bargain-rate couturier who was going to make her a Vionnet gown, and who knew what after that.

When she was gone, Eula asked Linny, "Aren't the dress mannequins adjustable?"

"But it isn't the same thing," Linny said, which was true to a degree. Eula suspected she was already up to mischief in her new career. Becca thought Mrs. Wetherall might be taking advantage of her sister.

"How could she?" Linny asked. "We're already paid for what we do here. Anything more is extra."

Becca still wasn't satisfied. "We'll never get ahead that way," she said.

"Get ahead of what?" Weren't they staying at Drayton?

∞

When Mrs. Wetherall brought Linny the material she was bubbling over with more scheming. Did Linny know, she asked, that her brother, Walker Trowbridge, was the president of Trowbridge and Ranier, the department store?

"Well, yes, he is," she said, "and my friend Mrs. Tucker's cousin buys in Europe for him. When you're finished with this I'm going to show it to her."

Linny still hadn't the nerve to ask what she or the woman at the store would be willing to pay. And this time Becca was angry about it. She said she doubted Linny would ever get away from Drayton because she didn't have the nerve.

And she didn't have the nerve the next time either. When she'd cut the silk and pinned the first pieces together, she had Eula call Mrs. Wetherall so she could come for a first fitting. She arrived, keen to begin.

"Can we lock this?" she asked. "I suppose nobody's around at this hour. This is so exciting."

Linny looked across the room and saw the woman was starting to get undressed for her, and asking if the room wasn't a bit chilly.

"Mrs. Wetherall . . . "

Her bra was off and a girdle coming down with some difficulty, while Linny stood there, agape at the woman's satisfaction with her middle-aged body, as if, unsupported by the foundation garments, she was now a more satisfying natural wonder, and about to be transformed again by Paris fashion.

"Please call me Constance," she said. "After all . . . "

"Mrs. Wetherall!" Linny said again, blushing fiercely, stunned as much by her own part in this as the woman's unlaced flesh. "Miss

Kieland thinks it would be more appropriate if we worked from the tailor's form."

The woman's face went slack.

"That's silly of her, isn't it?" she said.

"But I can't disobey her."

"Well, I suppose she makes the rules. What did you want then?"

She had an arm across her breasts now, and her free hand covering the center of her shame from Linny's sight, but Linny had already turned her head away.

She said they just had to see if the form was adjusted properly for her waist and so forth. There would be some measurements. It would only take a half hour or so. Mrs. Wetherall, who had come all that way from the city for what she anticipated as a real Paris fitting, was rather cross when she left, not pleased at all with the number Linny had taken for her bust.

∞

All this dress business had turned sour for Eula. It was wrong of Connie Wetherall to propose it in the first place. She was a trustee, not a client of Drayton. From the start Eula thought it was an abuse of Connie's position. Then, when Eula heard what Connie had paid Linny for the dress—three hundred dollars—she was out of her head with anger at the excessive patronage, the lost perspective. It spoiled Linny's proper progression into self-sufficiency. The sisters were on a modest salary. The woman never even asked Eula, just went ahead as if this was going to be a wonderful surprise for her and Drayton, an immediate success for the girl.

It was worse than that. With a nod from her brother, the Trowbridge and Ranier store had ordered three more dresses, all for the same price. Linny said if they were only to be ready-to-wear, and required no fittings, she could deliver them in four months.

It was an outrageous interference. What time would she be devoting to her work at Drayton? The money alone was absurd. She'd be making more in those four months than Drayton's highest paid housemother was paid for two years.

She called Linny into her office.

"Do you think it's right, what you're doing?"

Linny wouldn't answer.

"I don't think you do," Eula said, "or you'd have something to say about it."

First of all, Eula told her, it wasn't right to be working for someone else while she was paid to work here. Not on this scale. And what about the dress itself?

"It's not your design," Eula reminded her.

"I've changed it a little," Linny said.

"The money, Linny. It's way out of proportion."

"It would cost more than three times that in France," she said.

"You're just starting," Eula argued. "You're not a Paris fashion house. You're not worth that much. You're not Madame Vionnet."

"Who am I?" she asked. "How much am I worth?"

She was looking at her arms, at her skin.

Eula hadn't meant to belittle Linny, or define her. She only wanted a promise that she'd return Mrs. Wetherall's money. That would put an end to it. She was wrong about that. Linny told her she'd already taken an advance from the store for more silk, and signed a paper about it. Becca thought it was all right, she said.

"But what does Becca know about contracts?"

Linny was crying. Drayton could have all the money, she said. She didn't care. If the Director didn't want her to make the dresses here, she'd find somewhere else to make them. She had moved the debate sideways, out of Eula's grasp.

Otto was back in Philadelphia after a series of lectures in Buffalo. His Anaïs, he said, was behaving like a transatlantic butterfly, if not in her actual migrations, at least in the scatter of her emotions. At the moment she was in New York, in mind and body, because her Mr. Miller was there, too. At the same time there was a younger man out west she was deceiving.

"Better another than her father," Eula suggested.

"Stop it!" Otto said. "Eula, you have no idea what's involved here. Look beyond the surface behavior. Explore!"

According to Otto, Anaïs was anxious to see Eula again, but too proud to ask after all the unpleasantness. He told Eula once more to put aside the bourgeois orthodoxies.

"You don't have to give them up," he said. "Just give them a day off, and have a look at the world through her eyes."

Anaïs had been following the twins' story through him, he said, and Eula wasn't pleased to hear it. If for nothing else, she thought she should visit Miss Culmell for a pledge that their names, real or pseudo, would never appear in her diaries. Of course there was the other lurking reason—to take back the ring—though she didn't intend to spend any more self-respect on it, not even a little of her tidy reputation. She could at least pretend she didn't want it for herself, only to rescue it from this perversion of its history. She wanted it by guile or reason. Even more so when Otto told her, "Eula, I've been ambivalent, and I may have confused you. But the past *is* important. They *are* sisters to Tripto and Lezzor, who, after all, were a mortal danger to each other."

He reminded her of the phenomenon of their conception and birth as antecedent of all the telepathic wandering that would follow, the one seed and one egg halved, doubled if you prefer, the forced entanglement in the amniotic bath, imprisonment in the same tissue, and a combat for equal nourishment before they ever knew they were in a blood war, before they could ever understand that this loving embrace they were bred to was also a lifelong struggle, if only an accident of their conception and birth.

"What could we expect would come of that?" he said. "And if you still think the similarity of their late experiences is some kind of miracle, remember what the Irish fellows say: 'We all have the same stories running around in our blood.'"

∞

Eula still played with a different ambition, more a fantasy. If she could take the ring from Otto's Anaïs, perhaps she would not keep it,

but give it back to Otto. She imagined a solemn moment in which she placed the ring on Otto's finger, in a marriage of principle, their heads bowed in a mutual devotion to history and fellowship beyond the need or reach of words.

Eula called Anaïs.

"May I call you that?"

Anaïs was cordial. They made an appointment for the weekend. Eula packed for a two-day trip to New York, encouraged by Tessie, whose faith in Otto was strong as ever.

"As far ahead of the Freudians," she said, "as they are ahead of the hypnotists."

As for his personal life, Tessie said, he'd never talk about it. It was the women who did that, mostly to flatter themselves.

Kerstin was against Eula's going, aware by instinct, if not certain knowledge, of the danger in Miss Culmell. She mistrusted the woman's connection with the Paris dress. It fouled the whole meaning of the thing for the twins. Its main attributes had nothing to do with beauty, she argued, but excess and shame, and a whorish indulgence. And now the dress had spawn.

"Oh, go!" she said at last. To which Eula had no response, because the question of her going was past debate. She had not been waiting for permission, rather acquiescence, a blessing on her trip. Perhaps Kerstin was nervous about the influence the intellectual strumpet might have on her companion. If Eula had so little respect for Anaïs, why was she going? Kerstin didn't ask that. Eula asked it of herself, and without response.

She was received again in the Adams Hotel where Anaïs held her therapy sessions. The space was quite different this time, arranged awkwardly, with the chaise longue pulled away from the wall, and chairs on either side of it, making an inconvenient barrier across the room. She served Eula very hot tea, strong and bitter, and asked her to sit directly facing her across a small side table.

In the matter of trust, Anaïs said the two of them would have to start all over again, since their correspondence had degenerated into veiled spite before dwindling to nothing. She said again that she'd

been wounded by Eula's censure, brought lower among people she respected. This could only mean Otto, and Eula knew that wasn't so.

"A poor start for trust," she said. She asked if Eula would simply analyze and be analyzed in this hour, leaving moral judgments aside.

"I'm horrible, I know. Sick as the mirror-fanciers. But I put the mirror on the inside. I'm not interested in the mechanics. The mechanics always take care of themselves. Delightful. But I'm watching what's going on in my head. In his head, too. Whoever he happens to be."

"You're deceitful," Eula said. "Where do you stop?"

"Why is it," Anaïs asked, "that you would have me a liar, when Otto is content to say I make fictions in my life and then write about them?"

"Why do you care what I think?" Eula asked her. "It only shows you're ashamed of your behavior with him. Isn't he your real target? You've done your best to bring him down. And his work. To make him look a fool."

"Let me show you something," Anaïs said, "and you tell me which of us has a greater appreciation of Otto."

It was another passage from her diary, a tribute to Rank's egalitarian analytical technique, effusive and more perceptive than anything Eula had ever said about him. Anaïs had written that he was not practicing mental surgery as the Freudians pretended to do, as if each psychic organ was well known and in a familiar place. "He looks joyfully for someone neither he nor his patient knows. The therapy evolves as a poem of revelation, written by the two of them. He sees at once where the struggle is and releases one's power and will to deal with it."

Eula couldn't argue with any of that. It seemed a perfect fit. Just as Otto had done when she first met him, Anaïs was robbing her of an enemy. And besides, all Eula really wanted here was the ring.

The room brightened. They both turned to the window, where the sun was now streaming through the uncovered glass. The red stone set in gold was there on the sill, reflecting the new light.

"Oh," Anaïs said, "that," much too casually.

She was slighting her own interest in it, and Eula's as well, moving on to their mutual emotional states, their depressions and their cycles. Everyone knew, she said, that her own depression could only

be relieved by escape into the diary. Otto still called it her opium, though as she'd already explained, he'd decided her journals were not just a preparation for art, but the art itself.

Everyone? Eula had been over this with her before. Perhaps Anaïs remembered. There was a little fear in her glance. Maybe a fear that she was boring her guest, being judged again as a garrulous ego. She said she wanted to apologize for any ill will Eula had inferred from her criticisms. To get beyond their impasse, she said, she wanted them to speak only of "the others."

Her eyes were moist. Eula could believe at that moment that Anaïs was truly contrite, unaffected, and reaching honestly. She asked if Eula would mind discussing the case of the twins, and did Eula realize that Otto was wearing out his analytical mind, turning this way and that in his confusion with the double reflections of the beautiful "Gypsy sisters."

"They're not Gypsies," Eula told her.

"But they're wonderfully dark, aren't they?"

"If you think you're going to write about them . . . "

Anaïs raised her hand and swore, "I will never. But how are they?"

"They're doing very well."

"Yes, but I think they'll be leaving you soon. Yes?"

"Exactly what we've been waiting for."

"Aren't they really like your own children?"

It was Eula's turn to keep the moisture from swelling to a tear.

She was keeping her eyes off the ring, though not without a struggle.

Maybe to help her past the moment, Anaïs began to talk about men generally, and dismissively. She looked to heaven in exasperation with the whole universe of them.

Eula wanted to say, while you keep them in orbit all around you, but Anaïs was off, into the venereal underworld.

"So stupid! The way they think the top of their tongue is the softest thing in the world. Eugh! Sandpaper! So raspy! We don't need it."

Eula couldn't be shocked so easily. On the strength of a single unpleasant experience of her own, she had to agree with Anaïs, but the

woman would get nowhere in that direction. If she was provoking a sexual excitement, why didn't she say so, try some heated endearment, admit that what she most wanted was Eula naked on the chaise longue.

But no, she said, "The gown was mine first."

"You told me that."

"Did I? But you didn't want your Linda to copy it? Why such a fuss?"

She explained there was far too much money involved. It should have been out of the question.

"No," she said. "What I mean is, you told Otto you wouldn't let her fit the dress on the woman. Do you think that's where your difficulty really is? You couldn't imagine this twenty-one-year-old girl exploring the surface of another woman's body. The excitement of a mutual appreciation."

Eula turned in her chair and stared at the ring.

"Do you see where I've put it?" Anaïs said. "Out of your reach."

"My reach?"

"Beyond the *couch*," she whispered.

The rearrangement of the room came clear; a blockade in defense of the ring. To retrieve it, Eula would have to slide across the chaise longue, come under her yoke again. A submission to Anaïs or perhaps a surrender to her own inclination, with Anaïs as her guide.

"Sacrifice before the grail?" Eula asked.

"No. But perhaps desire into destiny," she said. "Take it if you want it."

It was a childish antic for a sophisticated woman, the transparent lure. Close to neurotic, Eula thought. She didn't fear her advance. She just wasn't going to put herself in that posture, she wasn't going to lower herself. She wouldn't climb around on her furniture, not even for the Greek brothers in the carnelian and all they meant to her.

She was angry, tired of Otto's woman, and she began to speak before she composed the words.

"You have no idea the pleasures I embrace. Your indulgence is strewn everywhere. Your own lies defeat you. You wander around in this sensual hell of yours."

Anaïs went to her bookshelf, ran her finger swiftly along the spines, and pulled down a journal from an earlier year. She riffled through its pages, and came quickly to the passage she wanted. Eula was struck by the ease of it. A single day in her past so easily recovered. Otto was right about this much: Anaïs was a phenomenal resource; a first-rate librarian of her own selfish life, with the selfishness admitted.

"Look! Look here!" she said. "Look what I repeat of Otto's. See what I honor?" and she read aloud to Eula:

> I fight the extremes; extremes in debauchery because they defeat their own quest for pleasure; extremes of love because they defeat love.

"Very well," Eula said. "Let's begin then. Where do you want to start?"

"Eula, please," she begged. "Don't challenge. Participate."

It was no use.

∞

Eula came home on the train without the ring. Let the woman keep it until she could part with it gracefully. It had been Otto's to give, and should have been Otto's to take back. He was no Freudian, no matter how he deferred to the master from time to time. He hadn't been for years, though he'd continued to wear the ring with some pride. He liked to quote one of the Irishmen he talked about: "Too much suffering makes a stone of the heart."

That's what happened to him with the Freud gang, Eula decided. They tried to destroy him over and over again. Why should he care anymore about their sacred stone, or loyalty? That would have been his way of looking at it though he'd never say so. To Eula it was something else, a bald symbol at the center of her own life, precious beyond any currency; it was her twins' talisman, and her own. In its handsome way it gave an ancient and comforting legitimacy to her own divided soul as a complacent double. Why wouldn't she want it for herself?

Wasn't she the guardian of her own Tripto and Lezzor? And let the brothers rage, or embrace, season by season. Silent in her parlor car, her eyes fixed on nothing, a hand under her head, this came to her: If they won't leave me, I'll leave them, my twin children and the trustees, all of them.

∞

Eula asked Becca more than once to accept her apology. And each time, Becca did, though not in a way Eula could believe. Even when she said, outright, "Miss Kieland, I forgive you."

Eula never tried to lay the blame on the various people she had relied on for her trust in the false Chinese-German Professor Wu. There were men in government who had trusted him, and instructors at two different colleges who had been fooled as well. Whatever had happened to Becca—maybe someday the girl would tell all of it to someone she trusted—Eula took responsibility for it, and would forever. She wanted to be the one to hear the worst of Becca's story, just as she'd been after Linny for the nastiest details of her house arrest in San Francisco. And Jennie Alexie was heavy on her conscience. She'd been working for months, through Tessie's "Eleanor in Washington," to get her brought back, too. Jennie's was a tougher case; it wasn't clear that she wanted to come home.

∞

Becca was still having troubled nights, the string of names, the Chinese singsong pestering her sleep. Sometimes she woke with her lips moving over the syllables she could not purge. Linny, lying next to her, had them by heart, too, an unwitting memorization, clear sounds and names, all of them a mystery, a secret that couldn't be kept forever. Becca was betraying those people over and over again.

∞

No ultimatum this time. It was a declaration.

"I'm going away for a year."

Eula gave them three months' notice. They didn't need more time than that, she said, because the one most suited to replace her, Ellen Reilly, was there and ready to take over.

"If you want me back . . . "

There was a consensus of regret. They said this should be a sabbatical, paid in full, and given full blessing. Even Roger Ney was saying this should not encourage her retirement. The thing was done without dissent, and a motion passed appointing Ellen to serve in the interim.

What would she do? They were all curious. They might have been pleased to hear she would study, write, think, improve herself in her profession. They had no doubt that even in her time away she'd feel an obligation to the institution.

Too bad.

Things had gone too dark in Europe for the grand tour. But away, she thought, as far as a dollar would send a postcard. Not just away from Drayton, but from social tinkering and tinkerers, from the duty-bound half of her own two-hearted life, a rebellion that would leave the French woman without an argument, speechless.

She imagined a black Ford automobile, herself at the wheel, the twins in back, charmed to a family rapture by the unfolding continent. An exchange of their three stories in detail to make the French adventuress blush. A regeneration, their own camp by a river, walking together into the water, proud of their three bodies, naked and glistening under the sun, observing the changing colors of their skins, not as nameable colors, but as their eyes knew them in the shifting light, changing moment by moment.

The dream of escape left Eula as quickly as it arrived. There was no one to hear the confession that she conceded defeat to her own double heart. No removal to a new region could change that.

∞

The twins had a different escape in mind. They understood Miss Kieland was still trying to be "Mummy," and that, after a fashion, she was. The second time they left her, it did feel like running away from home. In the back of their minds was the comforting knowledge that

they could walk back through the Drayton gate again, and Miss Kieland would feed them, and put them to bed with a kiss and a sigh. And get them busy again. A lot of people still couldn't get work.

Becca was sick of Nurse Jean telling her, "You're not yourself today."

Of course she wasn't. When had she ever been? She was finally pushed to rudeness:

"No," she said. "I'm not myself. I'm the other one."

Linny and Becca discovered they could be angry again without reproof, because the adults around them were so full of guilt themselves, and patient with their moods. While Miss Kieland was still in New York, they got Mr. Henry to move some of their things into Fifth Street using the Drayton station wagon. It wasn't fair to him, but they were only thinking of themselves. Becca could see his hand shaking as he drove them into the city. She didn't think of it as risking his job, but taking the right side in their argument with the world.

The twins heard the news from Miss Reilly before Eula told them herself. She was going to take a year away from Drayton, just for herself. The Director thought she was leaving *them*.

∞

Mr. Henry came into Eula's office in a fret.

"She's here," he said. Mrs. Carey with her creel, and all got up in a fancy dress.

"It's Friday," Eula reminded him. "Everyone's just been paid."

She always came on payday. There was nothing unusual in it.

"You better come now if you want to see them."

What he meant was, see them for the last time, but Eula didn't know that. He was too excited; there was something going on. He got her in the station wagon, and drove to the entrance. The twins were already there, greeting their grandmother. Before Eula was out of the car, they had Mrs. Carey between them, all three of them heading for the village by the time Eula reached the gate. Mr. Henry called to them, "You!"

They turned and waved, looking a little ashamed, but were on their way again.

"They're gone," Mr. Henry said.

"No," Eula was sure. "They don't have their bags. They're just taking her to the village."

"They got their things in the city."

Mr. Henry was ashamed. He knew all about what was happening, and this was his tardy way of confessing it. Eula stood with him there for a long time, watching their legs, their backs, their shoulders, and at last their heads fall away behind the crest of the Pike.

Mr. Henry put a hand on her shoulder. Not to steady himself, she knew, but to comfort her.

∞

Ever since they'd been giving her money, their Grandma Carey had rights to the two rooms on her floor, and the bathroom. When she heard how much Linny was putting in the bank, she was eager to have them come into the city with her. They couldn't do that to Miss Kieland, they said. Until Eula told Linny she couldn't keep the three hundred dollars, and said Linny wasn't worth that much. That changed everything. Becca said they were leaving, and soon.

They thought of it at first as simply moving in with kin. The closest kin they had. It wasn't the first time Becca had moved among dark-skinned people, while Linny was only pretending she wasn't frightened. There were men standing around in the street all the time. Most of them only stared, but there was one who made foul noises and ugly signs with his fingers. The others would have to push him off the curb and out of her way.

It was a rude transition. Mrs. Carey was grabby. Becca said the whole history of manners had passed her right by. At table she was a fright: me-first and food all over the place. Linny sewed bibs for her. If they scolded, Mrs. Carey made the suction noise and shot her lower teeth out in their faces. When she was most upset, she'd say, "Look at me girl! Look at my face!" and they'd be forced to give witness again to the freckling, all the dark islands on the pink sea.

When she called them by name she could only be right half the time. They gave up correcting; it didn't help and it wasn't kind. Just one

name for both would be all right they told her. She switched back and
forth without a favorite. One day they both became "Goldie," the way
she thought of their skin, and finally the two of them were "Precious."
They could flatter themselves into thinking they couldn't be any more
loved, or be resigned that any name was just a troublesome interference
between her and the next thing their grandmother wanted.

Becca was staying up nights, later and later. Sleep was no restora-
tive for her, but a daily looming threat. She tried sitting up in a chair.
Her head lolled, her neck stiffened, and Linny dragged her off to
bed, mindful herself of what lay ahead in the night. Singing foreign
rhyme in her sleep, Mrs. Carey said. And then the screaming and the
thrashing around in the covers.

"You were 'cross the water too long, girl," she said.

"You, too," she said, pointing at Linny. "Oh yes, saying your
prayers back and forth."

Sometimes it got so loud she had to get out of bed and bang her
cane on the floor, which didn't stop the recitations, only woke the
people down below.

"Both of you," she said. "One bad as the other. You get going so,
it sounds like Chinatown."

∞

Unkind as their leave-taking was, Eula came to accept it without bit-
terness. Mr. Henry said they were afraid she'd try to stop them,
afraid she might use the law and the police to take them back.

"I couldn't do that," she said. "The law's on their side."

If she thought that, he said, she was just fooling herself. The law
could change as it pleased. He was muttering, "It could turn a
polka-dot grandmother into a common, black, no-kin liar in a half a
minute."

∞

Otto asked Eula if she had stopped to consider that her family cross-
country reverie did not include Kerstin.

"Does that make tings clearer for you?"

"No." Contrary as ever. "Kerstin couldn't possibly have gone. Not with her schedule. That's unrealistic. Why are you laughing?"

"It was all unrealistic," he said. "All but the honesty of your desire."

Anaïs had been right about her, he said. Eula was a poor candidate for anyone's therapy. She wouldn't allow anyone near her emotional parts. She only displayed the alluring exterior.

"And you agree with her."

"I don't want to. Perhaps someday there'll be a willing yes to the *must*."

And besides, he told her, Anaïs's conclusions are based partly on her frustration: "She was denied either half of you, intellectual or emotional, whichever way you split yourself."

Anaïs, he agreed, spent too much of her time prospecting on the sensual surface, mad for the raw materials of her diary, degrading herself and everyone else; she forgot about her own physical pleasure.

"And that's generosity?"

"No." He thought it was neither given generously nor received in passion. It only happened in order to be watched. An observed game, whose every move could be plotted, and would be.

Eula wanted to know what else Anaïs had said about her.

He said she told him she had thought of giving Eula the ring, but that Eula didn't really deserve it, that she hadn't earned it.

Did he agree that she didn't need to see her anymore?

Yes, he did.

∽

Eula did take a cross-country journey that year in her own black Ford, squatting in each corner of the continent for several months. She had a dozen notebooks and several fine-nibbed pens. For the whole year she was as bad as the French woman indulging the scribbling habit, preoccupied with her recollections and careful composition.

From Puget Sound to the Keys; she summered in Machias and then left for a canyon house in the woods east of Los Angeles, provided by one of Otto's clients, complete with a houseboy and gardener. From all four corners she sent a postcard to the twins at their Fifth Street

address in Philadelphia. She had only one reply, a letter written by Linny, but signed by both of them. Or maybe she signed for both. You couldn't tell by the handwriting. She thought Eula would be pleased to know that Becca was visiting Mr. Henry at Drayton at that very moment. She was bored and had gone for a day in the gardens with him.

They'd heard Eula was on vacation for a whole year and wondered if she would get to San Francisco:

> Just now I have another order for a dress. I'll go to the lady's house. You can't expect her to come here. I hope you won't mind hearing that I have to fit it right on her skin as she won't have a tailor's form in her home.
>
> We know many of the people in our neighborhood. Do you believe that most of them are very kind to Mrs. Carey? Becca reads to our grandmother from the funny papers as she won't sit and behave just for the news. A nosy lady from the first floor brings her a piece of salty ham every afternoon, as if she was feeding a cat, as if we didn't give her all the food she needs.
>
> I guess you know our life at Drayton was pretty good. I'd say you are taking it easy by all the addresses you are mailing from. I have forgotten about the three hundred dollars, and I hope you can forget the day we left you. Becca still has the bad dreams and she has passed them on to me. If you heard me, you might call it a miracle, or maybe think I'm lying about all the Chinese names I know.
>
> Your children,
> Linda Rebecca

∞

It was a boast and an obvious lie when the sisters said they felt right at home. Mrs. Carey told them so: "Don't be getting above yourselves when you know you just come down a step." But hadn't she told them before that they'd never come back to where she was? They knew exactly what she meant this time. She didn't want them standing smug with the angels just because they'd given up their feather beds to stand with kin: "You got more to learn here than you ever dreamed at that orphanage."

There were no books here, and still they believed her. They'd already discovered that people might accost them in this new world at any moment, as soon as they ventured into the street, with insults, insincere romance, or a genuine goodwill. The sudden approach disarmed them. The two of them stood out as pilgrims in a native population, forced to discriminate at speed. They were starting all over again, just as they had at Drayton, not scheming, but calculating their chance of survival, living in their grandmother's building until it became their home.

When Linny asked, "Have we decided? I mean for good?" Becca told her, "We don't have to decide. All we have to do is keep walking down the street and see if we come to the right address."

"Why do you talk that way?" Linny complained. "You answer without answering. You're afraid to answer."

"You're afraid to ask."

"Did I ever tell you Miss Croft thinks I'm an artist, maybe a genius? That would make you one, too, and I can't believe that."

"Shut up, Linny. You're just scared."

"Who's that coming? Let's cross over."

By nightfall it was Becca who was fearful, though not of her neighbors. She was determined to do away with the naïve and traitorous voice in her head, which spoke only at night and only to torment her, still rehearsing the betrayal, winding through the rhymed names. Sometimes she listened to herself inside the dream, caught herself, and stopped, but there was a drum beyond her control and its rhythm was not satisfied without the names. Her stopping places were only syncopation in a song demanding completion.

"Don't," she told Linny, who dragged her from the chair, long after Mrs. Carey had gone to bed. But Linny, waking without her, had wanted Becca's company on the mattress beside her, and led her sister across the floor. Becca came half asleep beside her, to bed, grateful for Linny's nuzzling love.

"Whoever those people are," Linny said. "It's too late; they won't be coming tonight."

They lay down together, with Linny's hand moving gently back and forth across Becca's shoulders, and up and down her back, a

promise against the demons. As Becca began to drift away, maybe too close to the names, Linny was forced to a stronger defense, her hand drifting further down, and across her sister's softest skin, answering a mumbled satisfaction, fingers sliding slowly down the cleave, and at last, to the center. There could be no sleep, no dream, no names this way. Don't finish. No. Wait. No!

Climax for one was climax for both; they drifted away, as far from the yellow worm and its toxin as geography and their clarified devotion could take them. But still too far from dawn to keep the rhyming names from their sleeping lips. Not just Becca's lips but Linny's, too.

Becca, close to the end of her recitation, was aware of struggling against the drum's demand. She sat up, glassy-eyed, and watched her other self, right next to her, separated, a fair target, stupidly, ignorantly, confessing the rhymed list, singing for Professor Wu, who stood across the room, encouraging, painting names on a scroll with his busy brush.

Becca called, "Stop!" but the betrayal continued.

All right then, hold still, she was thinking. I'll put an end to you. She felt for the sewing scissors on the night table, opened them in half for a needle-sharp blade, and lunged at the warbling throat of her separated self. The point struck hard. There was a satisfying penetration, a ripping down through flesh. Gripping tight to the scissors, cutting her own finger to the bone, she slashed again at her other screaming self. Then a double scream and double moaning. Linny's cries and her own.

The table light came on. Linny sat beside her on the bed, watching the blood seep from her shoulder and arm, running into her nightshirt and the bedclothes.

"What are you doing?" they yelled at each other.

"I'm sorry," Linny said. "I'm so sorry," as if she'd been wielding the knife.

Becca had missed her target, the image of her double's mouth and throat. The point of the scissors had ripped down from Linny's shoulder, alongside the scar the dog Tonsils had made. She bled to faintness; they supposed she was dying.

Becca tore up a sheet and wrapped strip after strip around her sister's arm. The bleeding slowed. Her own hand was dripping blood

and she wrapped it, too. In her nightshirt, barefoot, she ran out of the building, into the street to find help. A man sitting on the pavement, nodding, promised to call an ambulance.

The ambulance never came. They undid the seeping wound, and poured in a bottle of iodine, and wrapped the arm again with more of the sheet. In the morning they walked out to look for a doctor who could put stitches in Linny. Someone put them in a car and took them to a hospital. The man did not use a continuous line of thread, Linny observed, or an overstitch as she might have done herself, but forty-seven short threads, each tied into a square knot. For all the doctors knew about sewing, Linny said, with an extra hand she could have done it herself.

A week later there was infection. Not in Linny's shoulder, but a dark line spreading from Becca's finger, across her hand, and all the way up her arm. It put her in the hospital, out of her mind in fever, and this time Linny was convinced she had lost her sister. The doctors would only whisper their news. A week later she was home and singing church music.

They healed. It was Mr. Rank who'd said the only thing that might ever be used to distinguish them could be scars. Not the emotional kind; the visible ones. Mr. Knows What's in Your Head had been right about that much. Mrs. Carey never said much about it, except the two of them would have to stop fussing at night or move out. They couldn't afford the bad dream anymore. They feared its return. It did come back, but from then on, the first Chinese name from either of them brought them both to life, sitting up, wide awake, nipping off the recital before it was under way.

"Cut before bloom," Becca remembered from Wu's classroom, "the thistle dies."

She wanted some religion again, mostly for the singing. The man who sat by the front door of their apartment building took her to his church at the corner of Fifth Street and Oregon. It was noisy, and she liked it, but they didn't welcome her. Not until they heard her sing, and pulled her forward from her rear pew, and put her in the choir.

"You crossed, Precious," Mrs. Carey told Linny. She thought she was talking to Becca. But Becca didn't believe it was possible, even as

it seemed to be happening to her. She coaxed her sister into going to the Bethel Tabernacle one Sunday. Linny didn't like the way everyone agreed with the pastor, out loud. Religion confused the household. Becca was saying grace for them all one evening when Grandma Carey reached across the table to snatch a roll early, and Becca slapped her hand. Not hard, but perhaps too hard for Mrs. Carey who didn't snap her teeth, but began to cry.

When Becca walked out in the street, she said hello to everyone. Linny was more timid. When she had to go out, she just put her head down and walked on. Those who hadn't seen the twins arrive wondered what had gone wrong with the speckled lady that she would take in a crazy white girl with a personality broken in half.

∞

Becca was going to be the one who did the outside work, the dressing up and making arrangements with the stores, and delivering the gowns. There weren't that many, after all. She cooked meals for all three of them, taking a bus out of the neighborhood to do the groceries. The doctors never asked them for any money. Becca said they probably thought it was a charity case.

When Linny was paid the rest from Trowbridge's, they had more than two years' rent in hand, and they took the floor under Granny Carey's to set up tables and the machines. It was much harder than they'd imagined. After the first three gowns, Trowbridge's would only ask for one at a time. They had to wait till that one sold before they'd take another. Pretty soon Linny was taking in whatever sewing jobs she could get, and Becca was going across town to clear the dishes and wipe tables in a lunchroom.

∞

Eula didn't see them the year she came back, or the year after that. The orphanage ran along on an even keel, still fixed on the progressive star, though losing wind. It still received and discharged the sweet and the surly, the sullen and the angry, and cast-asides of the adoption agencies, some who were grateful, others who couldn't wait to be gone.

A few more families in Flourtown were sending their children to Eula's new summer school, a modest victory in her grand plan to fold Drayton into the larger community. Eula and Kerstin, devoted, wrinkling into middle age, living at the same fingertip distance from each other in their cottage on the Pike, saw the change coming with clear eyes—the reward for Drayton's generosity of spirit and its loving staff—a slowly diminishing enrollment.

The beautiful campus of rolling country acres, settled so handsomely with the cottages of mica-glinting stone, all roofed with shades of red and blue clay tiles, decorated everywhere to charm the young, administered with every caution and care—all this drifting toward old news. Losing the social thinkers' support season by season. Another orphanage like the others across the country, no matter how benign its intention, until it finally found its place in the world as a halfway house to foster homes.

In mind of her twins, Eula thought most about the children who didn't want to be there, the ones who couldn't wait to put long distance between themselves and Drayton. Tessie liked to remind her that could happen in any home: "No child chooses its parents."

Several times Eula had Mr. Henry drive her in to Trowbridge and Ranier in the city, where she took the moving stairs up to the fashion area, a small section, with its own stiff mistress. This woman took Eula for a fraud from the start, the way she fingered through the racks, ignorant of the merchandise. Not there to buy anything. It was more like the behavior of a thief. The woman was disdainful, barely tolerant of her nervous customer.

Eula, looking for the name on a label, couldn't find it. The woman came along behind her, straightening everything she mussed, much too close on her heels, advertising her suspicion. And the second time Eula came to visit, it was the same thing. The third time, she spoke to the saleslady.

"Something made here in the city?"

"Oh," she said, "Carey Soeurs."

"Yes, let me see that."

"I don't think so."

The woman turned her back for a moment, picked up the store phone, and covered her conversation with her other hand.

"All right," she said, doubtfully, "follow me."

She led Eula through the narrow hallway behind her counter, into a small room, where every wall was a mirror. There was a short rack of six or seven slinky, hand-sewn gowns.

"We show these by appointment," she said. "They're really just models. Unless it fit perfectly, we wouldn't sell one. They're all from Europe, all but this one."

Eula understood little of what she was describing:

"It's quite like a Madame Gres, I think, but the girl has her own eye."

Eula let the lady go on without interrupting.

"Ten years ago it was all abstractions with the decorative element taking all the attention. So fussy and false. Now it's the woman her-self, the body's silhouette. Lovely."

It was lacquered satin, she said, with a combination of straight and bias cuts.

"Right to the skin, you see, no matter what the motion."

She saw Eula was looking for something else, not paying much at-tention, and she took the dress away from her.

"You won't find a label. This is all you need to see."

She flipped a shoulder inside out. Turned up between her thumbs was a small circle of white silk, embroidered with the gray silhouette of the Greek twins. Linny must have copied them from the wax im-print on Otto's letter to her.

"Carey Soeurs," Eula said softly.

"Not really sisters," the woman corrected her. "It's just in the name. The one who makes them is the same who brings them in."

She seemed proud of her little secret: "I know there's only one. I've seen her picture in the fashion news. It's the same girl. And something else you wouldn't know if you only saw the picture. She's not French at all; I'm not even sure she's white."

Granny Carey died early in 1941 on her way up the stairs. None of her missing children could have known about it, and none of them came to the funeral held at the colored burial ground in Chester County, and paid for by the twins. Just the twins and the minister at the graveside. Knowing nothing about her, the minister could only say the ashes to dust and many mansions business. The three of them did say the Lord's Prayer together. That didn't seem enough. Neither sister would cast the first clod of earth into the grave.

Linny, leaning over the coffin, offered the only thing she could think of: "She was a leopard . . . "

Becca finished: "And not just the spots."

Later that year they got two orders at once from the store, and for the twice-tenth time Becca said no more restaurant work for her. Someone in a ladies' shop in New York City saw a woman wearing one of Linny's designs, and came calling in Philadelphia, right to their floors on Fifth Street. The twins were in the paper again, the Sunday gravure, and you could see them side by side; there were two of them after all. The writing under the picture made more fuss about where they lived—the ghetto—than the remarkable achievement, the gowns.

From time to time Mr. Henry would tell Eula the girls were doing all right. She thought that meant poorly. It hurt that they wouldn't show their faces at Drayton, but how many of her other graduates did? Very few, to be honest, and she tried to take the absence and indifference as a healthy sign. She couldn't cultivate strawberries and then ask for celery. There were things to be proven before returning to the scene of such an overwhelming charity. She could think of it this way: The more they'd been given, the more natural, the more stubborn the exile.

The fashion work must have been a now-and-then thing, she told Tessie. She thought their lives must be very bleak in that dark section of the city. She was afraid their fortunes had soured.

What made her say that, Tessie asked. Didn't Eula know they had their own little corner at Trowbridge and Ranier now?

She went back to the store to see for herself, the sign in shiny black, plastic script on the wall, under a little spotlight, Carey Soeurs. They'd been brought forward, out of the little European sanctuary into a more American kind of fame. She assumed they must have others working for them.

Otto was pleased to think his gift had helped inspire a career. He said the Careys' pathology was now as fugitive from one moment to the next as their identities. To watch them too closely was to put oneself in a reflective maze that left the observer more confused than the observed. They could be one, then dozens, then one again, and what matter if they did no harm to one another, if they were living in harmony, and fulfilled?

Otto's retreat from prescription for the twins, or for Eula, was of a piece with his broader retirement. He said it wasn't that he had no more time to live, but that he had no more time for work. He was re-married; this time to his secretary and companion of the last four years. He was free now, he said, of the compulsion to change his life according to any prescribed frame.

Eula was at ease talking to him, at last unafraid of what he might think. He was no longer trying to push her at the French woman, just going on in the most euphoric way in his last letter to her, a trib-ute to all of them:

> The fights against stupidity are over. You and I and your twins come back onstage, not just in the usual drama of life, but after the curtain is down, unmasked, unpretentious, naked. Not defrocked by edict, just human, and with no one to pull the strings or interpret us for the audience.

A few months later he was dead from an infection and a poorly chosen remedy that had only encouraged the disease. At the funeral the French woman nodded in Eula's direction. Eula never saw her again.

The war put an end to the fashion business for the duration. Her Carey girls both went off to Allentown, Pennsylvania, to prepare as

nurses. They never knew Kerstin was the one who arranged for their training. Linda was sent to France, they heard, and Rebecca to Italy. Eula didn't really worry about the separation, or which had gone where. What were a few hundred miles, or two foreign tongues, to them?

The ring came to Eula by mail, in a home-fashioned bit of folded cardboard, with a cunning message enclosed: "You never earned it. I'd like your twins to have it. You'll know how to get it to them."

She was reminded of Otto's small, soft hands as she placed the gold ring with its carved carnelian of Tripto and Lezzor on her own ring finger, a loose fit. The size and setting were too masculine for a lady. She burned the hateful note. Anaïs would have known she'd never give it to the twins, and never wear it herself, that she would hoard its shine and history. Even if Eula had been willing to part with it, she couldn't give it to one of the sisters and not the other. Anaïs was forcing her to admit and live with this measure of her own selfish will.

Yes, Anaïs would have guessed all this, how Eula would spirit the ring away for safekeeping, and frequent inspection, each time with fresh reproach to herself for not giving it up to the twins. Kerstin, who never knew of Anaïs's request to pass it on, said the carnelian must be removed, set in a brooch, and worn by her companion at the top of her blouse, a little anchor to antiquity, the double mystery and Otto, an alternate to the tiny braid of her grandmother's hair.

For a while, it stayed in her bedroom bureau to be seen daily when she opened a drawer for fresh stockings. Eventually she put the ring on a short gold chain, and kept it hidden behind a panel in her writing desk. She used it as the imprint in sealing wax on her correspondence with closest friends. Sometimes she pressed her own finger into the hot wax, a stinging penance for the pleasure she took in keeping it.

Eula was always grateful to Mr. Henry for her last sight of the twins, a memory several years old by then and still making a shambles of Linny's last request: "I hope you can forget the day we left you."

Not likely. Her trouble with their bold flight from Drayton diminished her; that she couldn't accept it gracefully. Not what they were leaving, but what they were going toward. She believed there was a

tragedy ahead in their crossing to the dark heart of the city. They had no idea of the staying power of the hatreds they invited.

Why had they been on foot, anyway? Mr. Henry said it was because the drivers who worked this section of the Pike wouldn't allow Mrs. Carey on their buses anymore, not after she struck one of them with her cane. Eighty-some years old, by her own reckoning, more likely over ninety by then, she was going to walk the whole mile and a half into Flourtown. The three of them had been on their way to take the girls' money out of Mr. Sampson's bank and into Philadelphia.

Eula was horrified, thinking this ought not to be a children's crusade. It wasn't even an adult's.

"Don't mistake me," she told Tess.

She was suffering no guilt of hypocrisy. If they had been mixing fractions of color at Drayton, no one was advocating a full homogenization. Not even Eleanor in Washington.

The twins had put themselves on either side of Mrs. Carey, their arms under her elbows, lifting, so that she seemed to float along the road. Still bound to each other, shoulder and hip, their heads golden in the afternoon sun, and their proud flag, stippled dark and light, raised between them. They were carrying a banner of justice that Eula wouldn't hoist herself.

They'd been two, and one, and two with her. Even in their most bitter struggle, with their arms flailing at each other in a pattern of reproach and love, a flurry of stitches turned to knots, binding.

Author's Note

The Drayton Orphanage in *Double Stitch* is patterned after the Carson Valley College of Flourtown, Pennsylvania, but not an exact copy of the original. Nor is the Director of the fictional orphanage, Eula Kieland, though modeled after the actual Director, Elsa Euland, an exact likeness of her would-be double. Liberties taken with the life and character of Jessie Taft, Otto Rank's American champion and a Director of the University of Pennsylvania School of Social Work, led me to change her name to Tessie Croft. Otto Rank and Anaïs Nin keep their own names. Their part in the story is in keeping with their relationship and their philosophies, and I think no damage is done to the reputations they have already established for themselves.

I am indebted to the following authors and their works: David Contosta, *Philadelphia's Progressive Orphanage: The Carson Valley School;* Han Suyin, *A Mortal Flower;* I. James Lieberman, M.D., *Acts of Will: The Life and Work of Otto Rank;* Deirdre Bair, *Anaïs Nin: A Biography;* Phyllis Grosskurth, *The Secret Ring;* and Otto Rank, *The Double.*

With special thanks to Sarah McNally, Wendy Law-Yone, Phil Ehrenkranz, and my wife, Joan.